IMMORTAL JOURNEY:

SURRENDER OF EGO

VOLUME TWO

Ruth A. Souther

The original volume of Death of Innocence has been divided into two parts as the original book was very long. This is the second half rewritten with minor adjustments to allow for the story to continue without interruption.

Reprinted with permission by Crystal Heart Imprints.
Immortal Journey: Part Two - Death of Innocence (original)
Copyright © 2004 by Ruth A. Souther

Cover Design by Chad Adelhardt
Photo by Sabrina Trowbridge
Editing by Michaeleen McDonald

Copyright © 2015 Ruth A. Souther
All rights reserved.
ISBN-13: 978-0-9721003-3-5

First Edition: 2004 - The Death of Innocence
Second Edition: 2015 - Surrender of Ego

DEDICATION

To my Mom and Dad,
Margaret and Tom Tipsword

Thank you for always
being there for me.
I love you.

I miss you so very much

ACKNOWLEDGMENTS

I respectfully thank my family and friends who supported me in both the original writing and the conversion of this story into a new format. I could not have done it without them. I also want to thank both writer's groups for keeping me on point and invested in the outcome. Special thanks to Beverly Oberline for finding the title for this volume and Michaeleen McDonald for her amazing editing skills, patience and encouragement.

By popular demand, there is a listing of characters and locations at the back of the book. And no, there is no pronunciation key. For this, you are on your own.

SURRENDER
OF
EGO

VOLUME TWO
OF THE
IMMORTAL JOURNEY
SERIES

Ruth A. Souther

PROLOGUE

"Surrender to me - it is the only manner of survival left to the mortal world."

I am Ares the Destroyer and I am War - all acts of rebellion and violence are my rituals. You may fall under the delusion that you are immune to my ways. Look again: every moment of aggression is mine, whether real or imagined.

Upon discovering the small village called Najahmara, I had no interest in what befell this cache of human misery. Nor was it of any consequence to me that theirs was a peaceful existence. They were a band of simple farmers, naive to the ways beyond their fertile valley.

I was indifferent to the legion of soldiers' intent upon the conquest of Najahmara - there would be no battle, no clashing of blades, for those plain folk had no weapons. I am attracted to violence and this was not true to my creed.

And then I learned of a priestess who had lived far longer than any human could possibly survive: three hundred years.

Niala Aaminah appeared a tantalizing mystery, neither mortal nor immortal. She lived in quiet supplication, serving as a loyal priestess to the great mother goddess, Gaea, asking nothing in return. She spoke not of what she had been or why she had come to the valley. Rather, she spoke of what the present delivered to her people - a rich and satisfying life which included any wayward folk who stumbled upon their ground.

That my son, Deimos - he who reflects Terror to the mortal world - would do anything to protect Niala Aaminah caught my attention. His failure to do so was epic. The town invaded, the death toll was high and his beloved Niala Aaminah released a horrifying aspect of herself.

Niala Aaminah shape-shifted into the Blue Serpent, Kulika, and brought destruction upon the invaders. In her transformation, she destroyed her own people. It was then that I, Ares the Destroyer, captured her. She did not struggle, for there was no other choice. Once mine, always mine.

ONE

King Hattusilis watched dawn creep into the simple bedchamber by way of shadows on the ceiling. He managed little sleep during the night and as the patterns of murky gray crawled across the wooden beams, he was further reminded of the destruction outside the walls of his residence.

As if he needed prompting to recall how terribly wrong the invasion of Najahmara had gone. The once glorious campaign led in the name of Hattusilis' deceased wife, Azhar, ended in a bitter setback: in a blind panic, he went into the unlit caverns high upon the ridge and fell prey to an unseen enemy.

His legs were crushed beneath a stone urn, one foot nearly ripped off, the bones broken in both ankles, the flesh bruised and swollen. The pain was maddening and still, after seven months, he could scarce walk on his own.

The incursion to Najahmara was supposed to bring wealth and position after he and his legions of soldiers conquered the fabled Najahmara. Hattusilis snorted in derision. Benor the Trader had said the streets were paved with gold and the lush valley was ruled by a beautiful queen just waiting for her king to come along.

Lies, all of it.

What waited for them was a monster that spit fire, one who

killed everything in the path of its fierce flames without discretion. Soldiers and natives burned to death in tandem - those who were fortunate, for the others suffered a hideous demise - torn to bits by the same creature.

Hattusilis shifted in restless agitation as the guilt once again built inside his chest. The stories of the beast were just that, stories, for he had witnessed none of it. He had been caught up in what seemed to be a wondrous adventure, a ritual that brought him into the presence of the earth mother Gaea. He had been delirious with joy, unaware that his nephew, Telio, thought he had been stolen away.

Telio began the brutal attack on Najahmara to find him. Which, of course, suited Telio's bloodlust. No one need deny that was the underlying reason Telio took command.

Hattusilis shifted again and gasped as the pain in his left leg shot from his toes all the way to his hip.

Much to his frustration, he needed a crutch to support his dragging leg when he attempted to walk. The simplest tasks took great concentration. When Hattusilis coughed, dull pain pressed inside his chest and he could not yet take a full breath. Though his injuries were healing, it was too slow.

Gripping the blankets between his clammy fingers, he eased onto his back, eyes closed, taking care that he did not disturb his wife, Pallin, who lay next to him.

Did he deserve such punishment for the carnage of a peaceful valley and her people? For the souls of his own men who trusted him?

Before he knew it, Hattusilis dozed and the vilifying thoughts receded. When next he awoke, the morning had brightened to a rosy glow. The winged creatures outside launched into glorious song, invoking a brief smile on his sallow features.

He wished to rise out of bed as any normal man would do and sit alone in the gardens behind what was left of the temple. However, he could no more climb to his feet without help than Pallin could with her burgeoning pregnancy. More often than not, his temper got the best of him and he would curse Najahmara's goddess.

Pallin chastised him for his impatience, repeating over and over how fortunate he was to have survived the accident in the caverns. She did not understand why he was in the recess where the harvested grains were stored. She said it was Gaea who kept him alive, not his god, who would rather deal death than life.

Each time Pallin mentioned the mishap, Hattusilis shuddered. He dreamed often of that night in vivid detail. He remembered the mystery of slithering sounds and sibilant echoes of a voice that had no owner. It was the siren call from an invisible beast that led him from the entrance into the depths of Gaea's sacred chamber.

The fear increased even in the daylight as he recalled the way he followed the voice deeper into the darkness as if entranced and without wits. He felt as if something followed him, something large and dangerous. He recalled when the torch blew out, even though there was no wind, leaving him in pitch black, frantically groping along the cave walls. He stumbled along bathed in sweat as he crept deeper into the tunnels rather than out.

The most terrifying of all was a hissed warning, then the lash of coils that knocked him into the urn that rolled on top of him. A strong man alone could not have pushed it over and yet it fell, trapping him under it. Every night he relived the excruciating pain and the fear he would die alone in the darkness. He prayed it would be swift, all the while knowing it would not, and felt the panic rise all over again.

At times he heard the hiss of the invisible serpent while awake - a maddening whisper that said *let me in and I will heal your pain.*

Was he mad? He simply did not know.

Hattusilis laid for a moment longer, listening to the bird's sing and the chatter of small animals as daylight erased the pink wash of early morning. In the distance, he heard the muffled sounds of his household and knew soon his own morning meal would arrive.

To be treated as an invalid was worse than death.

If he believed an apparition such as the giant serpent could truly heal him, would he say yes, join me?

Feeling foolish, Hattusilis shook away his nightmares. He should call for help to get up but could not tolerate one more day of this pandering to his injuries. With a deep and determined breath, Hattusilis struggled to a sitting position. He made it to the bedside, threw off the linen sheet and put feet to the floor, in spite of the stabbing pain.

Though wobbling, he pushed himself upright. One leg cooperated, the other remained stiff and unbending. As he reached for the cane leaning against the foot of the bedstead, he lost his balance. Twisting to catch himself, his chest exploded as if a firebrand ignited within his body. He gasped, clutched at his side and fell with a loud thump. The woven rug covering the solid-packed dirt floor did nothing to break his fall and the jarring of his wounds left him sobbing in pain.

Pallin woke with a start, one hand extended to feel for her mate. She heard a noise, but could not tell if it came from outside or inside. When she discovered the space beside her was empty, she called anxiously, "Hattu? Where are you?"

"I am here." Suppressing the agony, Hattusilis lifted one hand above the side of the bed. "Go back to sleep."

"What is wrong?" Pallin floundered to sit up within her nest of covers. "Are you ill?"

"It is nothing."

"Why are you on the floor?" Scooting to the edge like a lake crab, Pallin peered at him. Seeing all color drained from his face save for a sickly ashen cast, she said in a low voice, "Did you dream again?"

Hattusilis gave an abrupt shake of his head to ward off the question, all the while biting his lip to keep from crying out. He could not muster the strength to tell his story to Pallin, though he adored her.

"I attempted to go about my duties as a man should." A sour taste was in his mouth as he finished, "I could not manage even that without help."

"My husband, are you hurt?" Pallin climbed from the box-like platform they slept on, one hand held against her bulging middle. As she stood up, she, too, groaned and rubbed her back. "I do not like this thing, Hattu. It is too hard. It is not good on our bones."

"I will have Zan add more padding."

"Do not think about that now." She crouched beside him and touched his face with cool fingers. "You are warm with a fever, let me get you a powder."

As she went to rise, he grabbed her wrist. "No. I do not need it."

"But you do, I can see it in your eyes. I will send for Jahmed while Zan helps you back to bed."

"No." Hattusilis tightened his grip. "I do not want it. I do not want anyone to see me this way. Leave me alone for a moment."

"Hattu, do not fret so. You will heal from these wounds, it just takes time."

"How much time? The winter season is gone, planting is upon us and still I cannot move about on my own."

"You walk, just slowly, and far sooner than either Jahmed or I expected. Hattu, you suffered grave injuries. We did not think we could save you and yet, here you are with two legs, two feet."

Pallin smoothed his hair back and kissed his forehead. "Now that you have thrown yourself to the floor and had a tantrum, we must get you up. Since I cannot alone lift you, I must get Zan."

Raising one hand in protest, Hattusilis let it drop and nodded. He knew she was right though it still rankled to know he was as helpless as a new babe.

He was rewarded with a loving smile as Pallin pulled on a gown before going to fetch Zan. When Zan arrived a few moments later, he gave Hattusilis a glower that spoke far more than words.

"Were you hovering outside our doorway?"

"I brought your breakfast," Zan responded with an injured tone. With ease, he picked Hattusilis up and set him on the edge of the bed before handing him the crutch that had been out of reach.

"I will not take my meal in bed."

"As you wish, though I should raise the question with Queen Pallin."

"Do not ask her. I have given an order." Hattusilis plucked at the covering, his features squeezed into a peevish frown.

"You have?" Blinking, Zan bit back a grin. "Of course. Where do you want to take your meal?"

"I do not know. Anywhere but here." Disgusted with the ordeal, Hattusilis shrugged. "The gardens."

"Perhaps you should rest before we take a walk."

"I am your king, it is time I behaved as such and did more than lie down or sit in that god-forsaken chamber."

Zan nodded with all earnestness. He understood Hattu's frustration, for he, too, was a man who was accustomed to a life out of doors, a man who preferred a canopy of stars to a roof and walls. It was cruel to keep Hattusilis locked inside, particularly when he must hold court in the round room where his nephew Telio had died.

Though the women scrubbed and scrubbed, they could not wash away all the bloodstains, nor could they erase the presence of evil that had invaded their temple. For Zan, it was the giant serpent that killed his men, but he knew for Queen Pallin it was the rape and murder of her sisters.

The degradation could never be entirely cleansed and thus the priestesses gave up the chamber without argument. They set their altar to their goddess somewhere else, somewhere hidden, for the atmosphere in Najahmara had changed with the second wave of invading soldiers. Those men who had fled in terror had now returned, along with the wave of soldiers on foot and the women who followed behind.

Najahmara had evolved into a diverse community at extreme odds with each other. Not a day went by without some odious deed committed in the name of a god or goddess.

Did either of those deities revel in the pain?

Zan wondered but said nothing.

"Where is my wife?" Leaning on Zan's arm, Hattusilis glanced in both directions of the corridor. Dressing had worn him out thought he would not admit it.

Zan flushed. "She had need to relieve herself and then she said she was getting a fever powder."

"I do not want a powder. I told her as much." Hattusilis' voice grew spiteful. "She does not listen to commands at all."

"She fears you knocked something loose and wants a cloth to bind your ribs. I beg you to be more careful, my King."

"Yes, careful. I grow weary of being careful." With a sigh, Hattusilis sank down in a chair shaded by an open-sided tent facing toward the lush growth of the gardens.

The path in front of him led to the sparkling pool in the center. It was a vision of blue and green, surrounded by a riot of blooming flowers and fully leafed trees that offered a perch to the melodious song of many birds.

There was no such oasis in the Steppelands. Water was scarce, too precious to do more than serve the people and the herds roaming the hills. Water could not be wasted on beauty.

"Not that our homeland does not have its own attraction," Hattusilis mused to himself. "Though the plateaus of the Steppelands are stark and rocky, the valleys are covered in a fine green blanket of grass."

He smiled as he recalled the heady scent of the tiny blue flowers that sprouted on the hillsides and the beauty of the bushes that bloomed fiery red in the spring. Trees with needle-like leaves lined the higher slopes as sentinels watching over the land and stayed dark green throughout the coldest months.

In Najahmara there was no true changing of the seasons for it remained warm most of the time.

"What is that?" Zan emerged with the meal tray and set it beside Hattusilis. "What do you mumble to yourself?"

"I was thinking of the Steppelands."

"Do you miss our native soil?"

Chewing absently on a piece of bread, Hattusilis paused before speaking. "Sometimes. Life was simple there. A king was king. There was no discussion around it. A king took a wife and she became queen. We did not debate on what it meant."

"You speak now of your bride." A twinkle lit Zan's eyes.

"She resembles Azhar, but she is nothing like her. Pallin behaves not like a queen but as a servant. As now, where is she? She leaves a warrior playing nursemaid." Hattusilis clicked his tongue. "As my wife, she should attend only to my needs. It is not fitting for her to work in the kitchens or care for the sick. It is not right."

"Hattu, you judge too harshly. Azhar was raised to be a queen, albeit not intended for the enemy's king, but as wife to a man of her own royal lineage. Still, she knew her place within her tribe." Zan chuckled. "Pallin also knows her place. It is just not where you expect her to be."

"She is pregnant with my son, my heir. I do not approve of these activities."

"You fear you will lose her and the babe the way you lost Azhar."

Hattusilis spit on the ground to show his annoyance, but did not respond. There was truth to Zan's comment.

He stared at the towering plateau behind the gardens. From his seat, he could see the cave entrance off to the right. He was struck by an instant chill and shivered in his thin, ankle-length tunic despite the fact the heat of the day was already bearing down on the land.

"Pallin is in no danger of wasting away." Zan continued on as if Hattusilis had responded with favor. "These are a different people, Hattu, unlike any we have encountered."

"That much I see for myself." Hattusilis winced as a drumbeat began, slow at first, but growing into a steady cadence.

For the past few days, from dawn until dusk, the constant

pounding of rhythms echoed across the broad landscape, bouncing from one side of the valley to the other. Hattusilis was reminded of the cave ritual, of the dazed state that took him before a goddess, and left him in a trance so profound he did not remember making his way back to the cave the next day.

He had awakened inside with torch in hand, gripped with fear, knowing he was not alone. He had heard a voice calling him, calling him to go further into the depths.

Eyes glassy, he heard the voice speaking into his ear, *Let me in, King, and I will restore your health.*

"Hattu, what is it?"

Wiping the sweat from his brow, Hattu sucked in a deep breath. "I hate the drums. Make them stop."

"Is that all? You look ill. Are you certain you did not hurt yourself when you fell?" Zan gave Hattusilis a lowered-brow, squinty-eyed gaze that penetrated beyond the visible. "It is not just the drums."

Licking dry lips, Hattusilis croaked, "Water, please." After drinking, he wiped his face with his sleeve. "Pallin tells me it signals another celebration."

"Yes, that is true. They prepare for their spring rites, though it is some weeks away. It is to be held up there." Zan pointed toward the rocky ridge.

"The cave?" Panic etched a shrill tone to Hattusilis' words. "I will not allow them to hold this ritual."

"Not the cave, but above it, on the plateau."

"Up, down, in, out, I do not care. I command they do not hold the rites." Rising on shaky legs, Hattusilis gripped his cane and held himself steady. He ignored the shooting pains from thigh to calf and the numbness of his reattached foot. His other leg was crippled at the knee, still swollen from the injury and painful to bend. Limping, he moved along the path between the flowers and the herbal plants.

"I wish you would wait for Queen Pallin to return with the medicine." Zan blocked his way.

"She has forgotten me, so eager is she to tend to others. Get out of my way."

Stepping aside, Zan followed Hattusilis' slow progress. "Hattu, we cannot take this away from the people."

"And why not? I am their king now. It is not our way."

"Our way is not always best."

"Do you speak treason?" Hattusilis paused in his hobble toward the shining pond of water.

"That is not what I meant, my King. I believe our way is not always best, that is all. I see nothing immoral with roasting meat and feasting though-out the night."

"And drinking barrels of beyaz until everyone falls down senseless only to wake the next morning, sick and puking with a head the size of a boulder."

"What is wrong with that?" Zan grimaced. "I have done my share of it, to be sure, as have you, and yet I tire of that game. These people offer us something new."

Hattusilis turned to stare at Zan, his lips puckered into a frown. "You have changed, Zan. I can scarce believe as much since you disdained any tradition brought from the sand dwellers. You called them barbaric, uncivilized."

"Yes, and you took offense because they were Azhar's people, though we slaughtered them like sheep."

"I did not want her to know of the killings for she suffered enough as it was." Regret was plain on Hattusilis' face.

"It was you or death. She chose you."

"In the end, she made it clear she would rather have died with her tribe. She never forgave herself. Or me."

"Neither have you. Still you do not learn your lesson."

"What lesson?" Sinking down on a backless bench near the water's edge, Hattusilis concealed a moan. "What gibberish are you spewing?"

Zan sat beside him, hands clasped between his knees as he stared at the reflection of the clear sky in the green water. "Have you ever seen the night sky reflected in this water?"

"No, nor do I wish to see it."

"It is as if their goddess rises from the earth in all her radiance and floats on the surface to bask in the silver light of the moon. The most peace I have had in my life has been beside this pool."

Zan bowed his head, staring at his interlaced fingers. "I grow weary of war, Hattu. I am no longer a young man and I have not the stamina to continue traveling. I have no wife, no children, no home. That disturbs me."

"Does that mean you have found a woman?"

At Hattusilis' sly glance, Zan turned red.

"No. But I search for one who could love me. These people have been grievously wounded and yet they hold no ill will. They do not smolder beneath the surface and plot their revenge."

"How do you know that? Perhaps they hide their planning well."

"I walk among them day by day. I witness their generosity. Over half of them were killed in the fires along with our men and, now after the foot soldiers arrived, along with the service women, we outnumber them."

"All the more reason they should accept our way."

Zan ignored the comment and went on. "Their homes were destroyed, but their will to survive is strong. They offer me whatever they have, food, water, shelter, a simple smile. I have wandered beyond the valley, to those who care for the orchards and fields of grain. It is the same there, they, too, hold no grudge."

"You have become soft," snorted Hattusilis. "It is best you do not engage in battle again for you would surely be killed."

"I always believed I would die in battle. I thought that was where I belonged and what I wanted." Zan shook his head. "I have found it is not."

"And what does that have to do with this lesson I have not learned?" Curiosity drove Hattusilis to ask, though there was no other whom he allowed to speak to him in such away.

"Control, Hattu. You seize power and then you wield it with unbending zeal."

"As any sovereign would do."

"You do not allow for change. Everyone must conform to our way."

"I do not see the problem."

"And so it is, my King, you suffer loss with no solace except to take more."

"What have they done to you? This does not sound like the Zan who set out on the journey to Najahmara."

"I am not the same man." Zan met Hattusilis' gaze and read the thought behind it. "Do not question my loyalty. I will forever stand beside you and serve your will. I am asking, though, that you reconsider your decision to stop the ritual."

"I do not understand this stubbornness," Hattusilis grated.

"It is important. They celebrate spring, when new life begins." Shifting uncomfortably, Zan added, "It is a mating ritual."

"A what?"

"A mating ritual." Zan coughed. "Many of our men are looking forward to it."

Hattusilis rubbed his naked chin, unaccustomed to his beardless state. "They need not wait for a ritual to take a mate."

"Do you hear yourself?" Zan rose, irritation strong in his voice. "Take. Always we take. It is time for us to give and this celebration is something they need. It will help heal the wounds and allow us to partner with them."

Hattusilis sat in silence for a long time, watching the face of the ridge. With a sigh, he held out one hand for Zan to help him up, while the other dug the cane into the soft earth.

Closing his eyes for a moment, he attempted to blot out the wretched cave. "Have your celebration. I hope you find a woman to lie with and it improves your disposition."

Smiling, Zan murmured, "Thank you, Sire."

"There is just one thing, though." Hattusilis paused on the return to the temple. "Do not hold it on the plateau."

"Where would it be, if not there?"

"Anywhere else." Cocking his head to one side, Hattusilis pursed his lips. "If it is to be a healing ritual, then let it be on the shores of the lake. It is suitable, is it not?"

"I do not know."

"That is where it is to be held. There, or nowhere."

"As you wish, my king." Zan gave a slight bow, grateful that he had won even a small skirmish with Hattusilis.

TWO

At best, Athos offered a crisp clear night exposing a heaven full of brilliant stars as the fresh scent and unmistakable sounds of the surf crashed over the rocky base. At worst, it was the battering of one element against another. Howling winds sought to rip the clothing off the backs of those who braved the mountain while snow and ice made the passage treacherous. Countless men had frozen to death before reaching Ares' fortress at the summit.

In the spring melt, rotting carcasses and bones of the dead were exposed along the winding pass. The oncoming warriors stepped over these remains, uncaring as to how their comrades died. By the end of the brief summer all signs of their untimely demise was erased by scavengers. When early fall brought torrential rains and mudslides sent boulders hurling down the mount, the men were not deterred.

They kept coming with offerings to their god, no matter what the seasons had in store. Niala Aaminah was the sole witness to this parade of doomed souls who celebrated Ares the Destroyer with blood sacrifice.

She was brought up that same path as a slave intended to die at Ares' feet, or so she was told. Niala had no recollection of such a journey - her memory was gone, erased for her own good as Ares had attested - leaving her with nothing more than his version of the story and the occasional flash of another life so frightening she refused to acknowledge it.

Niala clutched a brown woolen shawl around her shoulders, drawing it closer for warmth though the air was mild for Athos. She tread with care on the weathered boards of the walkway as she returned to the sea side of Ares' fortress where the crash of the surf was deafening. Clouds gathered on the horizon, promising a heavy storm, disheartening yet necessary to bring spring buds bursting forth on the sparse trees.

Trees that provided the only color to a cold drab mountain, that and the small purple flowers that appeared and disappeared all in the same week.

Absently, Niala moved her left hand to her belly.

Ares spoke of a child that should have been birthed from his seed yet did not happen. He voiced great anger over this exclusion, blamed her for not bringing this child to bear and swore there would be another between them. This child was their destiny, one who had waited an eternity for Niala to bring to fruition.

She understood nothing of what Ares intimated. He spoke of other lives and other times so far gone into the mists no one remembered.

Niala bit her lip and stifled a slight laugh. She could scarce recall yesterday let alone these things. With a shake to her head, she released the idea of a child for who would help when the time came now that Thaleia - her only friend - had vacated Athos?

Thaleia had been her only friend at Athos, an advocate who effectively countered Ares' demands with her own buoyant advice. She was present with her smiling countenance, lighting up the rooms when she entered. Niala looked forward to her company, and there was so little to look forward to at Athos.

And then Thaleia was gone. No explanation, no goodbye - just gone away. Ares brushed aside Niala's questions with a brusque grunt and a terse, "Thaleia does not belong here."

As fat raindrops began to dot the wooden walkway and the winds picked up, blowing the knitted wrap up like wings, Niala returned to her quarters. A fire burned in the great stone hearth, giving off welcome heat.

It was a curious thing, though the fire was never fed logs it continued to flame up when she was near and bank down when she was not. The same occurred with the bathing and bed chambers. What went on beyond those walls, Niala did not know for she never ventured past them, save for the veranda.

A youth named Eris brought her food and water but seldom spoke. Each time he entered the chambers, he gave a winsome smile and a polite nod and perhaps a word or two. That was all despite her best efforts to draw him out.

He, too, was an oddity. Eris' skin was tinged a pale green, his mop of unruly curls brown, like the bark of a tree, his teeth pointed and a bit scary, but his eyes were wide and brown, and held guarded sympathy. When she tried to engage him in conversation he always hesitated, as if he longed to stay with her, but instead, his gaze dropped to his bare feet and his naked shoulders lifted in a shrug before he hurried away.

It always ended that way.

Niala cried from the loneliness but no one heard her weep, no one at all. Until Deimos visited her. There was something familiar about him, something that instantly drew her.

Was it his resemblance to Ares? For Deimos was, indeed, a beautiful replica of his father, though leaner and more wary. He kept his black hair cut short and went without a beard, as if to defy his heritage. The air crackled with his energy, just as it did when Ares appeared, and tiny bumps rose upon Niala's skin when Deimos entered the chambers.

The thought of him, his scent, the feel of his hands, made Niala weak in the knees. Lowering herself to the backless couch, she pressed her fingers to her forehead. She wanted to erase the culmination of their time together, that moment of weakness after a shared meal, sweet laughter and too much wine. The moment she could not resist kissing Deimos, when she lifted her skirt and made love with him. It was brief yet intense and she immediately regretted her actions. If Ares were to discover their liaison, death would be imminent. For her, at least. She had no idea how an immortal being was punished for such transgressions.

She did not want to know.

Sending Deimos away was all that she could do. Allowing him to believe she cared nothing for him was a gift for she did not want him penalized for her desires. The last she saw of him was moments after sex when his face was soft and filled with devotion. He would do anything she asked, anything at all, no matter the consequences.

He would take her away from Athos, but she could not ask this of him knowing the price he would pay, so she let him go.

It was for the best.

*****

Deimos lay stretched out on his bed, too weary to expend the energy to disrobe or climb beneath the blankets. Propped on two thick pillows, he sought the peace of sleep but it refused to come to him. Instead, the events of the past few days turned over and over in his mind leaving him with a dull headache.

He could dismiss the sick feeling as a result of the wine and food he had shared with Niala Aaminah but neither mortal drink nor fare could explain the pain in his heart. Never before had he belonged so fully to his mother's realm as in the moment he realized Niala was his true beloved.

For eons, Aphrodite's talk of love had fallen on deaf ears. Deimos had never had the spiritual components connecting him to another. He could never understand the depth of such love. His parents felt that kind of devotion toward each other, though the passion was a broad mixture of passion and distrust, tenderness and loathing, worship and condemnation.

Ares and Aphrodite were forever bound together, united in their tale of love, for good or bad.

Deimos longed for the same with Niala, for he adored her more than he could express. Though they had lain together only once, it was a perfect union - a melding of two bodies into a single arc of pure pleasure so flawless that it pained him to know it would never happen again.

They laid in each other's arms afterward, content in the moment until Niala withdrew from him. Pulling away, she smoothed her gown, turned her back to him and did not speak again. After a long silence, Deimos left the chamber with the realization Niala was no longer the valiant priestess of Najahmara with whom he had fallen in love.

She was not the mortal woman who could host the spirit of the great mother goddess, Gaea, within her own body without harm. She was not the woman capable of destroying a legion of soldiers to protect her people. She was not the one who had the ability to shape-shift into Kulika, the Blue Serpent, Protector of Earth, and destroy all in her path.

No, the woman Deimos had consoled was a stranger to him. His gentle compassionate Niala Aaminah was now broken and without memory. Her love-making was not reciprocal of his devotion but an empty gesture made out of loneliness.

Worse yet, she accepted her role as a prisoner of Ares, God of War. The very thing Niala hated became her sole focus. Ares, who sired Deimos; Ares, who commanded Deimos' very essence, held Niala within his grip. It became clear that Niala belonged to Ares, body and soul. Regardless of whether or not she regained her memories, Ares was in control of her destiny.

It made no difference how much Deimos loved her for if, in fact, Niala was the lost goddess, there was no hope at all for him. With a slight groan, Deimos closed his eyes as the headache that plagued him deepened with a host of unanswered questions.

Could it be true? Could Niala Aaminah be an immortal who refused to embrace her real role in the human realm, and instead, chose to turn a blind eye to her destiny? If so, why was she abandoned on the mortal realm to be raised by humans? Who were her true parents? Immortal children were born with a purpose - if Niala was of the immortal race, what was her purpose?

There were no answers and moments later, his eyes flew open as Phobos stirred, crying out in his sleep.

Deimos glanced toward Phobos, his young charge, who was curled up on his side in the center of the blue and green rug. The weak light from a fire burned down to ember gave just enough illumination for Deimos to see Phobos' thin shoulders hunched against the cold air. Even the dimness did not hide the child's distress as he rolled toward Deimos. His face was pale, pinched, and smudged with streaks of dried blood and silvery tear tracks.

Phobos caused his own grief, though Deimos bore some guilt in the matter. A few days before, the boy had burst into tears when Deimos bid him get ready to go out into the snowy mountains for training. Phobos refused and tore down the staircase as fast as a streak of lightening. It so took Deimos by surprise that the boy was able to disappear into the depths of the fortress before Deimos could stop him.

Furious, Deimos gave chase until it occurred to him that it would be an effective punishment to allow Phobos to think himself lost within the massive castle. Even one accustomed to the many stairwells and levels could become disoriented without a lamp to find his way.

Deimos decided to leave the rescue of Phobos for later and visited Niala Aaminah instead, knowing Ares was away from Athos. He did not expect to linger so long with her, nor did he anticipate their sexual liaison or the depths to which he would sink in morose contemplation of love.

Somewhere after those hours of madness, Deimos was startled by Phobos' frantic shrieks, issuing from the lowest reaches of the fortress. By the time Deimos heard the commotion and located him, the damage was done. Phobos was huddled in a tight ball on the floor, trembling and weeping, unable to speak.

The boy had wandered into Ares' throne room and had come face to face with the horrific altar of blood, bones, and decaying flesh. His screams of panic brought the warriors spilling from the anteroom. Thereafter, Phobos became their amusement.

Deimos was shaken, for though Phobos suffered little more than a few scrapes, the specter of rape and blood sacrifice loomed within his mind. The men had no way of knowing the child they tormented was the son of their chosen god. It was clear their entertainment would have turned tragic had Deimos not interfered.

As it was, Deimos exercised great control not to kill all the warriors before snatching Phobos from their midst. They, in turn, believed him to be Ares and immediately fell to their knees in worship. Before they knew it, Deimos was gone and with him, Phobos.

Deimos dragged Phobos upward to their living quarters by the scruff of his neck. Ignoring the piteous cries and stumbling steps, he threw the boy to the floor where he still lay. Deimos then threatened to beat Phobos senseless if the boy stepped one foot off the rug until he was told he could do so. He was denied food and drink as part of his punishment.

Deimos had been so angry he could not even look at the boy. Instead, he reclined on his bed and thought of Niala Aaminah, wishing that Ares had never discovered her whereabouts.

"If ever I was like my father, it was in that moment of rage." Deimos sat up, hands on his knees, and stared at the shivering child.

In truth, it was terror that drove Deimos to his harsh reaction. Phobos had not yet stepped into his power. He could have been irrevocably wounded, if not killed by the savagery that went on in the warriors' chamber as they waited for Ares.

Sickened at the thought, Deimos rose from the bed.

Phobos was innocent; a boy accustomed to running naked on hot sand and flowering fields, then suddenly thrust into the frigid, brutal mountaintops and forced to learn the art of War. It would be enough to make anyone behave badly.

Except Deimos.

He had not shed a single tear, nor shown a solitary moment of weakness during his years of training. He would have died before giving Ares the satisfaction of knowing the abysmal pain in his heart as he awakened to himself as Terror. Yet he knew he was better for it, and Phobos would be the same once he completed his trial.

"But Phobos must first survive it." Deimos knelt on one knee next to him. "Phobos. Little Brother, wake up."

With eyes no more than slits, Phobos looked up at Deimos. New tears trickled from the swollen lids, but the boy did not have the strength to wipe them away.

"I...I...am...sorry." With a sobbing hiccup, he went on, "I am sorry."

"Yes, I know." Deimos brushed the thick black curls from his ashen face. "Are you hungry?"

"No, I am tired."

"Well, then, it is to bed you must go."

With a slight moan, lips trembling, Phobos turned his head away. From the beginning, he would not go to his cot in the adjoining chamber without a constant light to clear the shadows from the echoing corners.

Up to this point, Deimos had insisted his small charge be alone in the hope it would help Phobos gain courage, though it seemed to have no effect. The child continued to cry himself to sleep and thereafter suffer from nightmares which caused him to flail at unseen demons.

Thaleia, the second of Aphrodite's Graces, had been the

child's only comfort on the rare moments Deimos would allow her to intervene but Thaleia had been summoned back to her home on the Isle of Cos. Though Thaleia was reluctant to leave her little charge, she had no choice than to obey Aphrodite.

Deimos confessed he missed the smiling Grace. Her bravery in the face of Ares' wrath had been inspiring and the clever way she inserted herself into the care of both Phobos and Niala was every bit as devious as Ares himself.

Thaleia's presence brought a bit of relief but now there was no one to soften the pain of the child who did not understand what was expected of him. With a sigh, Deimos lifted the child in his arms, ever amazed at how little Phobos weighed, and carried him the few steps to Deimos' own bed.

"I think, tonight - only tonight - you may stay with me." Deimos spoke with a quiet tone, uncertain if the boy even listened.

As Deimos tucked Phobos under the thick blankets, Deimos murmured, "You will get through this, Little Brother, though right now it seems impossible."

But Phobos was already drifting off. Deimos lay down on top of the coverlet, his head propped by the pillows. Phobos settled closer, his back pressing against Deimos' side through the wall of blankets. The boy's contented exhale spoke loudly as he fell into a sound sleep.

There was a certain twisted humor in it all, thought Deimos. Terror chasing away Panic, yet he had no laughter to back it up. They both knew Deimos would have to take the boy out into the cold and damp weather to practice combat skills on the morrow, but for the moment, the child was peaceful. Thankfully, when Phobos next opened his eyes it would be daylight. It was small consolation, but all that Deimos could offer.

"And because of my own reckless nature, I chanced Ares' ire by going to Niala." Deimos spoke into the darkness. "What did I expect to come of it? That she would profess her love for me?

"Instead, she longs for Ares' caress." Deimos frowned at Niala's desire for Ares, loathing that she had expressed it to Deimos during one of their shared moments.

And yet, Deimos could not stop thinking of her, of Najahmara, of the army that had turned their lives around. He merely wanted to know Niala was safe, that was all he intended when he visited Ares' chambers.

How could Deimos have done anything less than what he did? He wanted to ease her pain, to help her remember, so she would remember him. It was a selfish thought that turned their conversation to Ilya, Anyal, and Elche, those ancient souls, parents to all humanity.

When he found her with no memory, alone and distressed, he longed to comfort her. They first begun talking of the immortals who abandoned their gifts, content with a life addicted to self-gratification.

And then their conversation turned to a deeper subject, one Deimos should not have indulged. He should have turned away at that moment, but he was too entranced, too caught up in the dream of taking Niala as his own mate.

Deimos shuddered as he recalled the story he had shared with Niala. A story that could possibly explain her origin and the reason Ares held her prisoner.

I must first tell you what happened before the mortal race was born, so you will better understand their role. First, there was Chaos - a vast pool of elemental energy that desired form. From this mire sprang Earth and Sky, Night and Day, Sun and Moon, Wind and Water and Fire and many others.

Many others, but we are concerned with Earth. Gaea is the ground beneath our feet, the soil; she is Fertility, the egg from which life springs. Kulika is the sky above us.

Kulika is Proliferation, the seed of life. At creation, the Blue Serpent coiled around the Abundant Green Earth. Together they brought forth the seas, the mountains and the vast plains, and all the creatures that abound there.

Kulika brought fecund growth to Earth, thus Gaea turned lush and green, and was pleased. They birthed Uranus, the Starry Sky, who was to surround Earth at night while Kulika and Gaea made love.

Uranus watched over Kulika and Gaea, but instead of remaining their protector, he became jealous of his father and amorous of his mother. Ultimately, Uranus usurped Kulika's place and became Gaea's lover, and from them came the first race of immortals, giants called the Titans. Of the Titans, Chronos and Rhea gave birth to my grandparents.

Those are stories for another time. Let us go back to Uranus and Gaea. Uranus was created to be truly magnificent and given great power, power that kept Kulika at bay. But this did not stop Gaea from longing for Kulika. Uranus, ever watchful, sought to block any attempt they made to be together.

Gaea saw the form the giants took. She watched as their bodies moved about on two legs and feet, with strong trunks, arms and shoulders, hands to touch and faces that shone with beauty.

She desired form very much, for though she is the Spirit of Earth, she is without body. She is everywhere and she is nowhere. She could not walk or speak or touch or smile. She could not make love in the way she saw her children and this she yearned for.

Gaea approached her children to ask them to share their bodies with her, so that she could be like them. Not at all times, mind you, for she was what she was, but sometimes, when the desire struck. She wanted to enter one of them, to feel, to smell, to touch, to make love with one of their bodies. She also wanted Kulika to enter form to be with her. With such an arrangement, Uranus would not suspect they were together.

The Titans were appalled at the suggestion and whispered amongst themselves that Gaea and Kulika planned to overtake them. The Titans feared they would wind up banished back into the Netherland of spirit without form.

As a whole, they refused. Gaea was furious but she could not force them to accept her request. Instead, she decided to create another race, one that would be made up of the elements and, in the end, would return to the elemental state.

She formed a body from mud, taken from her very bosom - one solid body with two heads, four arms, and four legs, already joined together, a being that Uranus could not tear asunder. The wind gave it breath, water gave it blood, and fire fused it into flesh. She and Kulika eagerly inhabited this body but at their first attempt to unite as a couple, it did not work as well as she had hoped.

The body was awkward and inanimate. They could not make love to each other. Frustrated, she searched the Netherlands for two spirits who would join together and descend into the body she had created. Gaea wanted them to bring life to the form, and once it breathed, accommodate herself and Kulika whenever they requested.

There were two who volunteered. Why would spirit do such a thing? There are many reasons offered, most likely it was curiosity. These two joined and descended into this one body, giving it life, but it was still awkward and not at all what Gaea wanted. In a fit of pique, she split them in half and they became male and female. Gaea called them Anyal and Ilya, First Man and First Woman.

Deimos remembered Niala's astonishment and disbelief that she could be this ancient spirit brought into form. He felt shame at having thrust this upon the gentle priestess during a moment when she was most vulnerable. And yet, he did not let it alone but continued the story.

He believes me to be Ilya, this First Woman? Niala stared at Deimos, eyes wide, jaw dropped with doubt.

Who you once were. And there is more to this tale. Another task was given to Anyal and Ilya, and that was to birth the mortal race. As the tale goes, there were no children born to Ilya, though they tried for a very long time.

In the end, a grief stricken Ilya fled into the wilderness leaving Anyal alone. Gaea refused defeat and brought forth another female from Anyal and called her Elche, Second Woman, and Elche became the mother that Ilya could not.

And then Ilya returned, out of love, out of guilt or desire, no one can be certain, but when she discovered that Elche had replaced her and that Elche had borne the children meant for Ilya to have, Ilya became very angry. She felt had been betrayed, not only by her mate but by her creator.

He recalled how Niala pressed fingers to her temples and spoke in a distant voice. *Even if I had been this Ilya, this ancient creature made of mud - and I do not accept this as truth - why does that concern Ares now?*

You were all spirits drawn from the chaotic darkness and thrust into physical form to satisfy Gaea's desires. Even so, it was a temporary state as those bodies made from the elements could only exist a short time. Short from an immortal standpoint, that is.

From a mortal view, it was hundreds of years before their bodies began to deteriorate, and when they did, death took each one. As a gift for servicing her needs, Gaea made it possible for these three spirits to incarnate once again, but this time, they could become one of the immortals and choose the role they would fulfill.

Gaea thought this an appropriate reward and was pleased that Elche and Anyal accepted. Elche is now Aphrodite, to bring balance and harmony in her role as Immortal Love. Anyal chose to become Eternal War - Ares, the Destroyer, he who causes upheaval and pain.

Cursing, Deimos ran his hand through unruly hair, picturing Niala as she digested this story, the hint of fear in her amber eyes. He remembered how frightened he had been when she lapsed into the throes of some strange spell and he could do nothing but watch.

A sheen of sweat dampened her skin as she went glassy-eyed and stared off into a distant place only she could see. Her lips moved but what she said was lost to Deimos even though he rose to stand beside her. When he touched her shoulder, she shrieked and struck out at him.

With a little gasp, she sagged into his arms, her lids fluttering as the whites of her eyes rolled upward. Deimos held her against his chest, feeling her heart beat next to his own. Longing once again settled across his shoulders and he placed a kiss on her forehead. He could not help the wish that she would stay in his arms with a willingness brought on by ignited passion.

A tremor shook her body. Deimos found a fur to wrap around her, and led her back to the cushions before the hearth. When he felt the coldness of her flesh, he folded her icy fingers into his own warm hands and pressed her palms to his lips. When she moaned, he put his arms around her and held her until she could regain focus. Then he kissed her and she returned it with passion.

Throwing caution to the mountain winds, Deimos made love to Niala. She was willing - frantic - to forget her circumstances even for a moment. For Deimos it was the soul connection that had been missing in his existence. Niala's touch ignited the other half of himself, the side that belonged to Love. He had never felt such joy. He fell into the chasm with no resistance, embracing the boundless expansion of his spirit though he knew should Ares discover this traitorous act, death would be preferred over his vile punishment.

He held no regrets over their liaison. The moment of divine pleasure when their bodies arched together in completion was perfection. He ached to hold Niala in his arms once again but she had turned away from him.

She did not love him.

He rolled to his side, pulled a spare blanket over his shoulders and sank deeper into the down padding, determined to sleep. He would not be like Ares, his father who lived with constant assault on his psyche since each and every act of aggression was drawn to War.

Closing his eyes, Deimos struggled to clear his mind and leave his concerns for another time. He exhaled slowly and forced his limbs into laxness. Sleep was but a moment away, a nice, drifting nothingness that would relieve both mind and body when a sudden thought thrust into his consciousness.

Thaleia.

In all the turmoil, Deimos forgot Thaleia knew about Ilya, Anyal, and Elche.

Upon Thaleia's discovery of Niala and her grave injuries, Ares had threatened the Grace to remain silent - she was not to pass on Niala's presence at Athos to her mistress. Thaleia agreed only to prevent yet another quarrel between Ares and Aphrodite. However, Thaleia had told Deimos, if it was true that Ares had discovered the whereabouts of Ilya, whatever form contained her, then Aphrodite must be told.

Deimos sat bolt upright, throwing off the blanket. He ignored Phobos' whimper of protest and stood up, uncertain of what he should do. Should he warn Ares? Should he protect Niala? Should he go to Cos and try to reason with Aphrodite?

Deimos rose and began to pace.

Why had there been no word from Aphrodite? When aroused, his mother was like a tidal wave, one gargantuan wall of water sailing across an otherwise passive sea to come crashing down on the unsuspecting. She did not temper her emotions, nor withhold them. They simply were what they were. Deimos hunched his shoulders, consumed by a sudden chill. He brought fire up in the hearth and brooded as he watched the twisting yellow and orange flames.

Such news as Niala's presence at Athos should have brought a storm into their midst. That it had not was frightening.

THREE

Thaleia stood before Aphrodite, working hard to appear her usual happy self, and yet doing her best to avoid direct eye contact. "Yes, Princess? You called for me?"

There was such a long pause that Thaleia glanced at Aphrodite through her lashes. As always, Aphrodite was lovely.

Her beautiful face was unblemished by a frown as she lounged on a woven-reed couch strewn with pillows beneath her favorite pavilion high on a grassy hill overlooking a sparkling azure cove. White pillars outlined against the crystal blue sky that swept up to support a rounded ceiling cast of fat cherubs, demure young maidens, flowing fountains and flowering foliage.

Three steps up led to a mosaic marble floor in the pattern of an underwater landscape. Turquoise water with shades of aqua and cobalt blue, exotic fish in bright colors of yellow, orange, green and red, with lush sea grass undulating at the edges. In the center was the open pink clamshell that brought Aphrodite to the surface as the fully formed goddess Eternal Love.

At the opposite end of the pavilion was a raised pool. Sweetly scented steam rose from within the marble sides of the spa, just waiting for Aphrodite to immerse herself in the luxury of her watery birthright. Small blue and green inlaid tiles swirled in a soothing pattern that mimicked the swell of waves on high tide.

The temple was Aphrodite's favorite place on Cos. It was a haven where the water afforded a most quiet setting, as opposed to the crashing surf on the other side of the island. At night, Aphrodite was soothed by the surf, for the noise brought her comfort. By day, she enjoyed the sounds of rippling tides in the inlet.

Aglaia and Euphrosyne were arranged on either side of Aphrodite, their hands folded in demure servitude. Their expressions were filled with sisterly concern though they, too, avoided direct eye contact. Thaleia cast a sharp glance at her sisters and saw a hint of guilt puckering the corners of their mouths.

"You have been avoiding me." Aphrodite stretched her arms over her head in a sensuous pose, knees to one side. "Your sisters tell me you behave in a strange manner. That you are rarely here. Pray, tell me why?"

"Well...I...I...." Thaleia skimmed over a variety of responses, rejecting them all at once, for one could not lie to Eternal Love and get away with it. Aphrodite responded only to truth. Anything less was a direct insult. "I have been very busy."

That was true. Thaleia had been deeply occupied while at Athos. She did her best to appear at Cos often - even for a few moments - to avoid suspicion as to her whereabouts but it seemed her ruse failed.

"I see. What have you been doing?"

"Ahh. Sewing?"

"Sister!" Euphrosyne raised one hand to her lips as she heard the lie emanate from Thaleia's mouth.

"You do not sew." Aglaia spoke with bluntness, eyes narrowed.

"I am learning." Thaleia crossed her arms over her chest and wondered how she could produce the proof she was about to announce. "You will see when I show you the gown I make for our Princess."

"I have seen no evidence of this gown." Aglaia directed a frown at her sister.

"Nor I," added Euphrosyne. "Though, she does tend to...."

"Enough." Aphrodite moved to a sitting position. "Thaleia, your nature is not such that you could sit in quiet to thread a needle, let alone sew a seam. I bid you tell me what is wrong."

"There is nothing amiss, Princess. I apologize for not being attentive but now that you have summoned me, how can I be of service?"

Aphrodite raised an eyebrow in question. "You have been at Athos and I wish to hear of Phobos well-being."

Thaleia's cheeks burned with shame. She should have realized Aphrodite would know of her travels - to keep silent had been a travesty. "Please forgive me, Princess, for not being honest. Yes, I have been to Athos. I could not imagine little Phobos trapped in that monstrosity with no comfort."

"How is my boy? I fear for him under Ares' tutelage. Phobos is tender in nature and I do not believe he will fare well upon that dismal mountain."

Praying her expression did not reveal the anguish gripping Phobos, Thaleia plucked at the skirt of her gown. "Phobos is stronger than expected and holds his own in the face of his challenges."

"Although I would rather you had advised me of your visit to Athos, I am relieved to hear my sweet son rises to his father's challenge."

"Yes, yes, everything is satisfactory. No worries."

Again Aphrodite arched a brow, sensing there was more to Thaleia's story. "You seem agitated. What bothers you?"

"Nothing." Thaleia shook her head. "I am rarely away from Cos and Athos is a dreadful place."

"Agreed, Athos is appalling. Would you mind very much if I bid you return there and care for Phobos - if Ares will allow it?"

"If that is your request, I willingly do your bidding, but I...." Thaleia's fingers knotted together as she fought the urge to tell her mistress of the mortal woman and Ares beliefs on Niala's origins. "It is difficult to describe the, um, circumstances at Athos."

Aphrodite held out her hand. "Come, Thaleia, tell me what has happened to cause such uneasiness."

Though her voice contained a lilt of good humor, Thaleia knew Aphrodite's iron will had been invoked. There would be no room to wiggle free of her questions.

"Yes, sister, tell us why you are in distress." Aglaia's lips pinched together in disapproval for she knew the extent of time Thaleia had spent away from Cos.

"Truly, Phobos is in good hands. Deimos...." Thaleia flushed again for she had been utterly tempted by the young god. Unlike Ares' rude dismissals, Deimos spoke with kindness and she found his smile enchanting. She knew her attraction was born of loneliness, but before she left, she had begun to imagine what was beneath his warrior clothing. "Deimos takes good care of him."

"Did something happen with Deimos?" Aphrodite tilted her head to one side, an appraising gaze on Thaleia.

"No," Thaleia said, her blush increasing. "Of course not."

"Are you certain? You twitch and jerk as if you have a secret." Aphrodite swung her legs over the side of the chaise and sat on the edge. Her white-gold hair flowed down her back in a river of ringlets, playing hide and seek with her milky skin.

Her gown was a diaphanous green material as soft as a cloud. It looped behind her neck, draping over full breasts to mid-thigh, but leaving the rest of her naked to the elements. A playful breeze blew up from the cove, stirred her curls, revealing more gleaming skin and the low cut back that rested at the curve of her hips.

"I would tell you if I had taken Deimos to my bed." Thaleia clamped her lips shut and glared at her giggling sisters.

"Yes, you would," Aphrodite murmured. "However, it is something lustful, for I can see it in your eyes. If not Deimos, then who?"

At the mere suggestion of sex, the wind tried to pluck the gown from her body. It swirled about her legs and lifted the skirt, letting it drop only as Aphrodite rose and smoothed it downward with one hand.

"Was it Ares?" Aphrodite's tone sharpened. "Did he assault you?"

"Ares? No, mercy, no!" Thaleia spat at the ground. "I would not have him, Princess, even if he offered. Which he did not."

"He is not above such behavior, Thaleia, and you are beautiful in your own right."

"No. No, his interest was elsewhere." Thaleia turned away and bit her thumbnail, afraid she said too much. She was right.

"What do you mean?" Though small, Aphrodite brought herself to her full height and, in her instant jealousy, she seemed to grow. "Has he taken yet another lover? Who is it this time?"

Slender fingers clutched Thaleia and forced her around. "Mistress, please, it is not what you think."

Aglaia and Euphrosyne fell silent as they watched Aphrodite's eyes blaze. "With him, it is always what I think. And worse. It is always worse. Tell me."

"I cannot. I am sworn to silence." Thaleia said, hiding her face in her hands, angry at herself for letting slip even a hint of the bigger story. "I am afraid."

"Of me?" Aphrodite shook her. "Why would you be afraid of me? I could never hurt you."

"Not of you, Princess." Thaleia brought her hands down to hold Aphrodite's. "For you. I am afraid for you."

"Why?" Aphrodite's tone sharpened. "What insult awaits me?"

"I do not know how to tell you what I have seen."

"Please, Thaleia, just speak the truth."

"It seems that he...that Ares...." Thaleia straightened her shoulders. Closing her eyes, she prayed she could explain Niala to her mistress. "There is no easy way to say this, Princess."

"Then do not hold me in suspense any longer."

Releasing a held breath, Thaleia gave up. "He keeps a woman at Athos."

"At Athos?" Aphrodite's breath came out in a low hiss. "I do not believe it. He does not allow women in that cursed place, other than myself, and even then...."

"She is there. I have seen her."

"It makes no sense." An ugly expression crossed Aphrodite's delicate features. "Is she an immortal?"

"I cannot say for certain, Princess. It seems Lord Ares thinks so, but she - Niala, for that is the name she goes by - is smitten with the loss of her memories. There was an accident, for this woman, Niala, fell from the uppermost floor."

"The walkway?"

"The courtyard." Thaleia grimaced. "Upon my first visit, to summon him to your side - I am sorry, Princess - she was there at that time. I should have told you but Ares forbid me to mention it. He said he did not want to upset you."

Thaleia held up her hand, palm outward. "He swore he would tell you himself. I knew there was something very important about this woman. I was curious, so I returned to Athos."

"So that is where you went," breathed Aglaia, a sharp glint in her eyes. "I knew you were not learning to sew."

Thaleia shot her sister an annoyed glance. "I wanted to find out more. My intention all along was to hear the truth and tell you. I swear it, Princess. Please forgive me." Thaleia hesitated, for the expression in Aphrodite's eyes was not of the forgiving nature.

"There was no easy way to know what happened, for though I cared for her wounds, Niala was dreadfully cut and bruised. It became clear she did not remember who she was. She did not know when or how she came to be at Athos. She did not remember where she hailed from. She was too ill to prompt, and then Phobos arrived and I turned my attention to him."

Thaleia rubbed her cheek. "Still, I could not clear my thoughts of her, for there was something about her that disturbed me. It was not just that Lord Ares behaved strangely. I was drawn to her in a way I cannot describe.

"As she healed, I found opportunities to visit her when Ares was absent. I hoped she would speak more to me so I might better understand why he kept her there. She was so very sad, Princess. I felt sorry for her. Adding to the grief of not knowing her origins, she was plagued by Ares' insistence she had been at Athos since she was a young girl."

"What? That is impossible. I would have known. I would have heard. He could not have kept this a secret." Aphrodite clenched her fists as she paced to and fro.

"He told her she was delivered to him as a blood sacrifice by his warriors, but he refused to have her killed and instead kept her at his side."

"Merely to bed her? I do not believe it." As Aphrodite's ire grew, the sea before them began to churn with whitecaps. "Though sex and blood are his due, there must be something else."

"I fear you are right, Princess. It seems there is much more to this story than lust." Thaleia twisted her fingers together. "Lord Ares insists she is an unawakened immortal."

Aphrodite inhaled with a hiss and stared at Thaleia as if she had sprouted a second head.

"He claims she is one of us and will force her to accept her role in the Greater Realm. That is why he keeps her there as a prisoner."

"He thinks her an immortal?" Aphrodite sank down on the foot of the chaise. "Does he keep her in the dungeons?"

There was a faint hopeful tone to Aphrodite's voice.

"No. He...he...." Stuttering, Thaleia could not meet Aphrodite's darkened gaze. "He keeps her in his own quarters."

"His quarters?" Aphrodite repeated. "His bed?"

Thaleia shot a look of panic at Aglaia and Euphrosyne. "She does sleep there. As to what else goes on in his private chambers, I cannot speak into."

Cursing, Aphrodite jumped to her feet. "I have begged him to agree to conceive the daughter that waits in spirit for us to bring her forth. I have waited patiently, for I know how he is and I may not rush him to conclusion, but he swore it would be soon. Instead, I hear he toys with another. I will not let him get away with this. Come, we will go to Athos."

"Hold, Princess," Thaleia begged. "There is more."

"How can there be more than this? Ares denies me while he beds another? That is enough."

"Please, I must tell you this, though I can scarce relay it, for I know it will upset you beyond anything so far." She took a deep breath. "He claims she is Ilya."

Aglaia and Euphrosyne inhaled in tandem, for they all knew the story behind Ilya and they knew how their mistress would react. Both hesitated, waiting for Aphrodite to speak.

"Ilya?" Aphrodite went very still.

Her lips were pale and stiff as she repeated, "Ilya?"

"Yes."

Aphrodite's face was an odd shade of blue, the palest blue, like the blood that beat in the fragile web of veins at her wrist.

"He is certain she is Ilya?"

"That is Ares' claim."

"When you look at her, do you believe it?"

"There is something hidden within her, Princess. I sense it yet I cannot guess what it is."

Aphrodite was silent so long that Thaleia grew afraid. "Perhaps she is none of these things. Perhaps she is no more than a mortal who has captured Lord Ares' imagination."

"Ares has imagined endlessly he has found Ilya." Aglaia waved one hand toward the ocean. "It is an obsession and every time, he is disappointed."

"Yes, Princess." Euphrosyne stroked Aphrodite's bare arm, her voice soft. "He will discover it is not her and grow weary of this one, like all the rest."

"I have always known that someday - someday - that wretched willful creature from a time beyond time would come back to him. It is as always in those days, she would take her pleasure with him - my husband, my mate - make love with him while I sat in the corner with my head covered, as if I were nothing."

Her voice rose. "And then she would run away, back into the wilderness where he could not find her. His grief would steal him from me again and again. He will always want her. Always."

"It is most likely not true." Aglaia shook her head at Thaleia, angry that she brought this distress upon Aphrodite. "Is it, Sister? Ares makes this up to suit his own wicked purpose."

"But you believe him or you would not tell me this. Is that not true?" Aphrodite clutched at Thaleia's hand.

"There is something about Niala that is different. I do not know if it is the spirit of Ilya, but I see the dawning of immortal energy."

"And that is what he seeks." Aphrodite bowed her head, swaying as if she would faint. "Not Ilya, who was the mortal woman, but Ilya who is the source, the spark that ignites. She turned away from Gaea and would not do her bidding. She refused to take on her role within the Greater Realm."

"Sister, you speak with a certainty you cannot have." Aglaia put a supportive arm around Aphrodite. "Princess, it is Ares' evil nature holding back from you. He uses this woman as an excuse to deny your request to bring forth a daughter. She is not Ilya for Ilya is lost. She has not appeared before and it is not her this time."

"I must find out for myself." Aphrodite smoothed her skirt. "If it is Ilya, I will know, for we were bitter rivals. Ares cannot see for the lust in his heart, but I will know."

"Be kind, I beg you." Thaleia took Aphrodite's hand in her own.

"You dare ask me to treat Ilya with sympathy?"

"No, Princess. I ask that you have compassion for Niala, for whether or not she is this lost one from your past, she is wounded in this life."

"You find her appealing?" There was wonder in Aphrodite's voice.

"Yes. I do not know who or what she may have once been, but she is sad and lonely, a gentle soul who treats everyone with respect."

"Well, then," Aphrodite sniffed. "She cannot be Ilya."

"There, you see." Euphrosyne clapped her hands together in relief. "It is all a big mistake, Princess. Princess?"

Aphrodite did not hear her, for she had already gone to Athos.

She wasted no time, entering Ares' private chambers without a warning in the hopes she would catch him abed with this female. He could not then deny her accusations as he so often would.

The greater part of her wanted to destroy Niala without question.

"Act now and do not think why." Aphrodite lifted one small fist, ready to strike.

Her gaze swept across a neatly made bedstead, empty of bodies. The grate was alive with glowing embers but a distinct chill was setting in even though the doors and windows were shuttered.

Aphrodite's thin gown was little protection against the frosty air, but her anger brought a flush that needed no help in warming her. Disgruntled, she dropped her hand to her side.

"This time, I do not find you in flagrant display, but still, I do not believe you sleep chastely."

Stalking across to the double doors, Aphrodite caused both to fly open at once and bang against the walls. She strode into the central chamber and stood with her hands on her hips, scanning the larger room. It, too, was empty, yet here was greater evidence of a woman's presence. The hearth held a great crackling fire with a table set before it filled with dishes and partially eaten food. Plump pillows showed the indentation of a body and a wool wrap lay crumpled next to them.

A quick glance above the mantel told her Amason was absent. That could only mean one thing - Ares was also absent.

With a smug smile, Aphrodite gave a tight nod. "All the better, my Love, for now I have ample time to smite the woman who would steal your attentions from me."

Where could she be? Somewhere in the vast corridors of the fortress? Or in the bathing chamber?

Aphrodite turned toward the last set of doors, vengeance in her heart. She moved in silence for her intent was to give no warning. She arrived on quiet feet and stood in the shadowed doorway, keeping herself invisible to the eye. It was a talent she held above all others, the ability to cloak herself from sight even unto another immortal.

Zeus forbade Aphrodite to hide herself in the Council's Great Hall. He was disconcerted he could not readily see her, which gave rise to his already pompous view of females. Aphrodite found it amusing. With eyes held wide and innocent, her response to the self-proclaimed King of the Immortals was always, "It is Love's way to move with stealth and strike when least expected."

She never failed to use this gift as it suited her.

After tearing through the cavernous chambers in anger, Aphrodite returned to calm for the moment. She now wanted to observe the woman without being seen herself.

Was she Ilya? Possible, but not probable. An unawakened immortal? Also possible and much more probable. Creatures who never became conscious of their roles in the world were neither human nor deity, but somewhere in between. Most were long-lived, but not immune to death.

That Ares sought to quicken this one was most suspicious.

The air in the bathing room was strong with the oil of the sandalwood tree, a scent Ares favored. Eyes closed, Aphrodite let the damp warmth curl about her like arms taking her into a caress. Light smoke from the burning wood layered over the scent bringing with it thoughts of the pleasure she had experienced in that same pool.

It was the only thing that pleased her about Athos.

With her back to the heavy-paned door, she felt solidness fold around her, as if Ares stood there to remind her of those delightful moments. However, if he sought to discourage her actions, she refused to comply.

Beloved, why do you do this to me? Aphrodite's lashes fluttered open. She knew the answer. Ares was a restless spirit who could not be contained. It was his way to wander. Still, this went beyond anything he had ever done. To keep a woman at Athos for a lifetime in the hopes she was Ilya?

That was madness, even for Ares.

He would expect Aphrodite to forgive him. A wicked smile curved her lips. Of course, she would forgive him, she always did. He knew it and she knew it but first she would make him suffer. Delicious, painful suffering - the kind that made him vibrate with exquisite need. Need she denied until he was crazed with desire, begging her to afford him relief.

Perhaps then he would not be so quick to deceive her.

With a small shrug of her shoulders, Aphrodite dismissed the thought. Ares punishment hovered on the horizon but for now, she turned her attention to the marble pool. The woman called Niala floated on her back, staring up at the carved figures dancing along the arches.

Her face was a smooth line from forehead to chin, her full lips slack and expressionless as if it was too much trouble to form a judgment. She lay without effort in the water, her body the color of tea brewed by leaf and the heat of the sun, a clear verdant brown that would surely taste as good as it looked.

Aphrodite, given a whiff of the fragrant tea laced with golden honey, could not help but lick her lips. The woman was lush in other ways as well, with rising mounds of breast, a soft swell of belly, and rounded hips playing hide and seek in the foamy water.

Every now and then a glimpse of strong thighs, a shapely calf or a sturdy foot would surface. Then a smooth shoulder would lift, or the woman would sink lower and all that could be seen was her face. Spread behind her was a veil of thick brown hair glinting with shades of red in the lamplight. It looked very much like a cloak that would wrap around her when she stood.

The woman called Niala was entrancing. Aphrodite could scarce tear her gaze from the wet skin and serene features. There was a quality about her that did indeed speak of the immortal realm - a certain energy rising up from her body, like waves of heat. It was subtle and hard to see, but no doubt the trait that drew Ares attention.

Was she once the ancient human, Ilya? Aphrodite could not say without drawing closer. Even then, would she recognize Ilya after the passage of so much time? She was not as certain now.

Creeping forward, her gaze riveted on the woman, Aphrodite caught her toe on a crack between stones and stumbled. Though she returned to balance, Niala brought her feet under her and stood up in the waist-high water.

"Who is there?" Niala's voice echoed against the domed ceiling.

Aphrodite froze, holding her breath.

"I know someone is here." As she spoke, Niala drew her long, curling hair over one shoulder and began to squeeze water from the strands. It was an absent gesture, done so often it went without thought. "Please, show yourself."

Aphrodite heard the slightest hint of anxiety in Niala's voice. Did she wonder who might have breached Ares' most private of places? Did she think it was Ares himself, playing a game? Or another who came to lay claim on her? Aphrodite smiled, for she rather enjoyed causing concern.

Niala turned in a tight circle, scanning the shadowy corners. As she faced the hearth at the far end, Aphrodite could not contain her gasp, though she brought a hand to cover her mouth. She stared at the tattooed image of broad wings and pointed tail feathers, the hooked beak and one black eye. She knew what it was and did not have to be close to hear the raspy whisper, *Corvidae.*

The Corvidae was an elemental creature of Air, a loyal servant of Gaea. When he was called forth, it was to give Gaea form, to let her soar over the peaks and valleys, the vast waterways and deserts, the forests and the plains of her body, the Earth. It was to give Gaea freedom, to let her caress the Sky.

Strong magic was attached to the image. To see it written upon mortal skin was unheard. The Corvidae did not lend himself to enchantment without purpose - ritual was the only way to bring him forth in such a manner. Whoever or whatever this woman Niala was, she was also servant to Gaea, Mother of All.

Niala's shoulders twitched as she turned toward the doorway, straining to see into the shadows. Her gaze flicked back and forth between the exit and the hearth.

"It is rude to watch without being seen. Show yourself. Please."

She waded to the water's edge and reached for a drying cloth, pulling it around her as she climbed out. Though it was a long piece of unbleached linen, it was not wide enough to cover her entire body.

Aphrodite caught a glimpse of the serpent winding around Niala's leg and of the dark patch of hair its tongue licked toward.

Aphrodite gasped again, for Niala carried both Air and Fire on her body. She could contain herself no longer and allowed herself to come into view. To her credit, Niala did not scream, but stood her ground, unblinking and silent, though her beautiful brown face paled to an ashy gray.

"You must be Eternal Love."

Niala spoke first, her voice calm, though she clutched the sheet to her chest as if it would protect her. She neither smiled nor bowed, as most were wont to do at first sight of Love, but instead remained expressionless except for the slightest hint of wariness in her eyes.

Aphrodite's brows drew together as her gaze moved from the now-covered body to Niala's face. Resentment descended in a hot flush. She wanted fear, not recognition. She wanted cowering instead of conversation. She wanted to strike out in rage, knowing this woman slept in her husband's bed night after night.

"How dare you." Aphrodite clenched her fists. "Do not speak to me or look at me, for I do not offer you any part of Love."

Instead of lowering her gaze to the floor, Niala continued to watch Aphrodite. Confusion flooded into those amber eyes even as the apprehension grew. This brought a tight smile to Aphrodite's lips, void of any warmth.

"I can destroy you if I so want. Give me good reason why I should not."

"That you hesitate to strike is reason enough." With a sigh, Niala's chin sank and she looked away. "Though I would not care if this was ended."

"It is just like you to take the easy way out. To let blame fall upon my shoulders."

"How could you understand what I am like? Do you speak from first-hand knowledge, or do you borrow from the same tale as Ares?"

Niala's tone was wretched, giving Aphrodite pause. The waves of anger receded, allowing her to center herself, to find solid ground rather than the sinking sands of jealousy. With a critical eye, she looked once more upon the woman and thought, *Could this truly be Ilya?*

Aphrodite was certain she would recognize Ilya, believed she would know the demon who sought to worm her way back into Anyal's affections. She thought if that creature did surface sometime in the eternity since it all happened, she would know it. She would stop Ilya from pursuing Ares, even if she must kill her, for Aphrodite was no longer the weak and helpless Elche.

Yet as she stared at Niala, she did not see Ilya. There was none of the chaotic energy that signaled the wild one's existence. No, this could not be Ilya. Not unless she was buried so deep this one did not know of her continuation. If that was so, what, then made Ares believe it? How could he know she was Ilya?

He could not. What he saw was the glow hailing immortality and prayed for it to be Ilya. Aphrodite was certain it was not. Every soul held the same potential; it was desire that made the difference. Aphrodite did not see that drive in Niala's eyes. Ares might try to force her into immortality, but it would not happen if she declined.

Aphrodite was clutched by a sudden fear for Phobos. What if he lacked the aspiration to receive his immortal spark? What if he did not want his godhood? Would he be destroyed if Ares forced him to accept it?

Distracted, Aphrodite glanced about the chamber as if her son was hiding in a corner. Guilt tweaked, for she was at Athos and had not given one thought to her child. In her own defense, she could not reclaim him. Come what would, Phobos now belonged to his father. She could seek the boy out but it would cause further harm, for then he would want to go home to Cos. Better she left him alone.

Aphrodite refocused on the woman before her. Niala was taller, broader of shoulder and hip than herself. With an angular face and high cheekbones, flaring nose and up-tilted gold-shot amber eyes, she was striking but not beautiful as in Aphrodite's own delicate splendor.

Niala's complexion was unblemished, a sun-kissed brown that made Aphrodite want to stroke her cheek. Under different circumstances, she would have caressed the silken skin for pleasure as she would with any mortal that struck her fancy.

It was the lustful tightening of her lower extremities that brought Aphrodite back to herself. The feeling frightened her, for it was always so with Ilya. Aphrodite hated Ilya with all her being yet also longed for her touch.

"What manner of creature are you that he keeps you here? Are you Ilya? Reveal yourself to me if that is so." Aphrodite tipped her chin up and gave a sharp shake of her head.

"Not you as well." Niala's shoulders slumped forward. "If I am this Ilya, I know it not."

"Then why do you call me by name?"

"Who would not recognize Eternal Love?"

"Too many." Aphrodite pressed her lips together for she did not want to spill her most heart-piercing emotions to this woman. She would not share the hurt of unrequited love or the pain of those who purposefully turned away. Those wounds were private, too painful for any to witness.

"Even though I scarce know my own name, I recognize you." Niala let drop the cloth as she turned and took a folded robe from the table.

Before she drew it on, Aphrodite caught another glimpse of the Corvidae etched on Niala's back. The single black eye sent a stern warning. Aphrodite's lips parted to argue that the woman was fair game but then the long-sleeved gown covered it and Niala once again faced her.

"You carry the mark of both Air and Fire upon your body. You did not gain those elemental beings at Athos."

"I know not how they came to be with me, or even what they mean." Niala smoothed the front of the robe and tied it with a belt.

"You are more than you seem, and yet I cannot tell what you are. If not Ilya, then what? What are you and why does Ares keep you here?"

"I do not know the answers you seek." There was despair in Niala's voice. "He says what he says and it is a story you seem well aware of. It has been repeated many times and yet it makes little sense. I know only that he…that he…."

"That he makes love with you?" Aphrodite's turquoise eyes flared with righteous anger.

"Not even that." Niala brushed past Aphrodite, as if to give ample opportunity to strike her.

Aphrodite would not take the dare, though Jealousy taunted her. She could hear Zelos laughing, her whispers prodding Aphrodite ever closer to the violence she abhorred.

How could she let this one steal Ares' affections? How could she, Eternal Love, allow another woman to steal her husband?

Pressing her palms to her ears, Aphrodite shut out the ugly whispers of Jealousy. She would listen no more to Zelos, but deal with the woman in her own way.

Aphrodite was not afraid to penalize one who would take Ares to her bed. She did not fear Ares' wrath for he knew better than to interfere once caught. No, she was not ready to mete out retribution. There was too much mystery surrounding her existence.

Aphrodite would first have answers.

Following Niala into the outer room, Aphrodite stalked across to the dying fire. The cold enveloped her slender body but Aphrodite would not bring forth a wrap to keep from freezing. She would not be seen as weak in front of this woman. Instead, she invoked fire and flames began to lick the top of the hearth, flames that would roll like the tide across the black floor if she allowed it.

"You sleep in his bed. I can smell your scent upon the coverings."

"It is not what it seems." Niala stood apart from the hearth, to one side of it, with her arms folded around herself.

"It is exactly what it appears."

"Is it?" Niala dipped her head in denial. "I know not what you see, but only how it is. I am left alone day after day without comfort."

"He gives you the seed that belongs to me."

"He gives me nothing but what is necessary. Food, drink, shelter, never any part of himself."

Grief was heavy in Niala's words, but Aphrodite would not hear it. "I do not believe you."

Aphrodite moved closer, deliberately causing her small stature to appear larger, to loom over Niala with a menacing shadow.

"Still, it is so. He has not touched me since...." With forehead creased, Niala's gaze wandered over Aphrodite's head to a far corner of the chamber. "Since - I do not know when. It is true, we have lain together, but I cannot say when last it was."

Her gaze returned to meet Aphrodite's and she smiled.

A sweet sad smile.

Nonetheless, a smile.

Aphrodite all but gaped for the woman must be mad to stand before Love and declare she bedded War. "Ares is my consort, my Beloved, my mate. You understand this, do you not?"

"I do. It is not to cause pain that I say this. I try only to find my way back to who I once was. It is not this Ilya that I seek to remember but something else." Niala touched fingertips to her chest. "Part of me is missing. Ares holds the key."

"He offers you no clue?" Aphrodite's anger began to seep away, though she tried to cling to it. She wanted to hate Niala, for hatred was her other side, the darkness that would consume her if she was not careful.

The balance was so fine, Aphrodite could scarce keep herself upright, yet now, when she wanted to embrace the loathing, she could not. Instead, there was a swell of compassion for a woman lost to herself, blinded further by Ares, willing to suffer at the hand of Love rather than float in a sea of despair.

"He says only that I belong here. That I have always been here. Yet what he says does not feel right."

"It is not." Aphrodite inhaled a breath of smoky air and resisted the urge to cough. "For you bear the marks of a Priestess. You did not get them here."

Their gazes met again, solid amber and liquid blue, each appraising the other, seeking more than words could describe. A current passed between them and although Aphrodite tried to reject this small bond, she further softened.

A rush of raw truth flooded over her.

Alas, Aphrodite thought. *This is what I wanted from Ilya. I did not want an enemy. I wanted a sister.*

Niala reached to brush her bare shoulder and tears came into Aphrodite's eyes as a shudder passed through her body. It was a light touch but it spoke legions and therein changed everything.

"I am sorry if you are hurt." Niala withdrew her fingers. "I would not willingly harm Love."

"You have not." Aphrodite's voice trembled. "It is as it has always been. Ares is the root of my pain."

Niala nodded once in acknowledgement. "He suffers as well for I have seen it even in his sleep."

"Do not defend him. He must be held accountable for these lies, and they are lies."

"Yes." Niala's voice was faint. "Yet I cannot protest for I have no weapon to defend my position."

"You do not, but I do." Whirling, Aphrodite shouted to the ceiling timbers, "Ares, I bid you come here now. Do not delay."

FOUR

A moment of silence fell as they waited. Like a breath held in expectation then released, the air around them stirred as Ares responded to her call. Niala stumbled back at the sight of him, but Aphrodite stood grim and accusing.

There was a faint glimmer of fire reflected in Amason's blade as Ares appeared. He was a ferocious sight, for he came from battle, Amason still raised with murderous intent. Blood dripped along the razor-sharp edge in a slow descent to the stone floor. His face was smeared with sweat and dirt; his hair matted with gore. The forearm and hand gripping Amason was covered in carnage as if he ran his entire arm through the bodies Amason claimed, and then withdrew taking entrails and bone as trophies.

Ares wore the fur and skin clothing of the savage lands to the west, though they were coated in filth and an unidentifiable stench. His legs were bared save for the rough calf-high boots laced with leather thongs and heavy with slog. His lips were drawn back in a snarl, his teeth clenched. He took one step toward Aphrodite with the madness of battle reflected in his black eyes as if to slice Amason through her flesh.

"You would not dare lay that wicked blade on me." Aphrodite withdrew a step though she spoke with boldness.

"If I took Amason to you, your soul would be cut away and set adrift. Do not threaten me unless you wish to die."

Aphrodite froze, both hands lifted, fingers splayed. Eyes wide, scarce breathing, she whispered, "You would kill me?"

Ares' gaze traveled from Aphrodite's drawn features to her slippered feet and then to the shimmering blade bathed in its latest butchery. Amason's eagerness quivered between them, as if it would gladly guide his hand forward and bury itself in the white breast of Love.

"No." Ares inhaled with great force, as if he had forgotten to breathe. "I would not."

"You want to slay me." Aphrodite's voice shook, for bloodlust was still written upon his face in deep lines about his mouth. "I see it in your eyes."

"Killing is what I do."

"I am your wife!"

"You dragged me from battle, what else would you expect?"

"Cursed battle." Pressing her hands to her chest, Aphrodite steadied herself. "Do you not discern the difference between friend and foe?"

With a slight shake of his head, Ares lowered Amason to his side. There was a sense of disappointment, a sigh as the sword slipped from battle ready to passive presence.

"There is no judgment, only bloodshed with no victor." Ares shifted Amason, grasping the hilt with a stronger hold. "When you make such flagrant demands, you see me as I truly am."

Aphrodite twitched with impatience. "Change now, then. I despise the look of you."

With slow consideration, Ares glanced down at his clothing. "No."

"You revel in your bestiality."

"There are times when Love need look upon the horror of War, to be reminded it is not such a pretty world we live in."

"You think I do not know the ugliness that lurks beneath the surface of every living thing? Therein is the biggest difference between us. I choose to see the beauty while you purposefully bring forth destruction."

"You surround yourself with false harmony."

"And you live amongst the dead and dying." Aphrodite stomped her small foot. "In a frigid monstrosity that nurtures rebellion."

"Better a revolt than annihilation." Flicking a glance toward Niala, Ares added, "Shall I guess what this is about or would you rather tell me?"

"Hades has nothing on you, when it comes to tormented souls. If it is true each creates his own hell, you are a master." Aphrodite gave a mocking smile. "Did you really think I would not find out about her?"

"She is none of your concern."

"Oh, but she is. Our marriage is still in effect - do you seek to break that now?"

Startled, Ares raised Amason as if to defend the union Aphrodite called into question. His breath whistled between his teeth as he hissed, "Do you?"

"Only guilt would throw that question back onto me. I have done nothing except wait to receive the daughter you promised me, while you...." Aphrodite flicked her fingers at Niala. "You lied to both of us."

"What lie?"

"Thaleia has told me of your tales."

"Thaleia is no longer welcome at Athos."

"To that, I have no doubt. She bears witness to your brutality and has told me all about it. She says you keep this woman here at Athos and have for many, many years. She sleeps in your bed and for all I know, bears your children. If that is not brazen enough, you claim her to be Ilya."

"I do not know if she is Ilya." Ares gritted his teeth.

"That you continue to search for her after all this time, that you would have her again at any cost."

A sob caught in Aphrodite's throat. She did not want him to see how much this hurt, to know that he wanted Ilya more than he wanted her.

"What cost? I want only to know where she is."

"You want her." Aphrodite beat at his chest with a clenched fist, ignoring the vestiges of War's slaughter. All thought of control left her as rage welled up. "That you would take her as your wife destroys our union."

Grabbing Aphrodite's wrist with his free hand, Ares held

her away. She gasped at the pinching hold.

"You have kept her here since she was a mere girl, is that not true?"

"What if I have? It is not your concern." Ares released Aphrodite with a small push.

She fell backwards a few steps before catching herself. She stared at the blood now smeared across her pale skin, blood in the shape of Ares' fingers. With effort, she slowed her breathing and smoothed her gown only to see the blood transfer to the silken material.

One small reddish-brown streak on an otherwise perfect chiton, and now that was all she could see. Not the beauty of material made to catch the sunrise in its weave, just the tiny smear of someone's life across the front.

"She is my concern." Aphrodite's voice was soft as she stared at the ripple of material marred by War's vengeance.

"Do not stand there and deny the trail of broken-hearted mortals that you dawdle with. Do not make me count them out for you." Ares clenched his fist and raised it in front of his chest.

"Mortals?" Her gaze rose to meet the harshness of his black eyes. "Short-lived and far fewer than you have taken. I do not speak of mere humans, but of one you believe to be immortal. That, Beloved, is forbidden." Her voice shook with the effort to stay calm.

"She came to me as a sacrifice. You should be happy I did not allow a female to be delivered onto my altar. Instead, I kept her. I admit it." Ares stared down at Amason, at the black crust thickening upon its blade. "But she is a mortal."

"Then prove it." With a sharp intake of air, Aphrodite's beautiful features transformed into an ugly mask. "Kill her."

"What?" Ares' gaze snapped up to Aphrodite's face.

Niala shrank further into the corner.

"She was to be a sacrifice then, let her be one now." Aphrodite's face lit with lust. "Let her blood renew our promise to each other and strengthen our alliance."

"You cannot be serious."

"Oh, but I am. Strike her head from her shoulders."

"You do not mean this."

"I do. Spill her blood upon this floor and I will forgive you."

"And if I will not?"

"Then I will do it myself." Aphrodite moved toward Niala, one hand outstretched. "Either way, I will have proof that she is mortal."

Ares blocked her path, shaking his head. "Neither of us will harm her."

"You put her before me?"

"You deliberately twist this about."

"Do I?" Aphrodite crossed her arms over her chest, her eyes reflecting the leaden sea before a storm. "All I want is a sacrifice on the altar of our love. Is that too much to ask of bloodthirsty War?"

For long moments, they stared at each other. Aphrodite appraising, kept still by rigid control; Ares smoldering, unable to hide his disbelief. He glowered at her, as if he tried to read her mind, to see what it was she really wanted from him, but there was no comprehension.

He opened his mouth to speak, then clamped his lips shut and turned to look at Niala. She crouched with her back against the wall, her robe clutched to her breast.

"Do not fight because of me." Niala's eyes were filled with sadness. "I have no place here, therefore, if I must die, so be it. I will be your sacrifice."

"Do you hear that, Beloved? She is a willing sacrifice. For you." Aphrodite spit the last words out as she went toward Niala.

Ares flung his arm out and stopped her. "Do not touch her."

"I will do as I please." Aphrodite slapped at his arm, furious that he blocked her path once more.

"Aphrodite, enough."

His tone was such that she stopped but her gaze remained fixed on Niala. She was down on her knees, head bowed, her damp hair clinging wetly to her robe. Reddish-brown hair, the color of drying blood. A blood offering to War, but a Priestess of Gaea? How did she come to be here? Aphrodite jerked away from Ares as he made a sudden move.

He raised Amason, rocking the great sword back and forth to catch more of the firelight. It lit up like a torch, glowing beneath his scrutiny. In seconds, the dank matter clinging to it burned away until its honed edge was clean. Ares opened his fingers, releasing the now shining Amason to balance upon his palm before it disappeared.

It reappeared above the mantel upon the large hooks made to hold its weight. At the same time, Ares erased any sign of the brutal battle from himself. He stood remote and stern, dressed in brown leggings and tunic.

"There will be no death here." His words were laced with weariness. "Neither by my hand, nor yours."

"Then you admit she is immortal?"

Aphrodite's triumphant tone brought a flush to Ares dusky complexion. "What is it you want, Beloved? Agreement?"

"After Eos, you swore you would not humiliate me again and lie down with one of my own ilk. If you have broken that trust, our marriage is over."

"Niala has lived the life of a mortal."

"She has *lived the life of a mortal*? Where, here at Athos? This one came here as a child and never left - is that the tale you spin? Thaleia repeats this with words out of Niala's own mouth."

"Thaleia carries tales with the intention of causing harm."

"How so? I am less harmed if I do not know our pact is broken?" Wringing her hands, Aphrodite turned away. She could no longer look upon him. "I now understand your reluctance to give me a daughter."

"You cloud the issue. Our arrangement was to bring forth a daughter - we have not committed to a time."

"Why have we not? Because of her." Aphrodite scowled at Niala. "I have done nothing but wait patiently for you to uphold your half of our agreement, only to find you give your seed away. Do you seek to make a child with her, such as you did with the Sylph?"

"Niala is not the cause."

"Then why?"

"Our liaison has not taken place because I am deeply troubled by your reluctance to name the child - which has nothing to do with Niala."

"Are you certain? For I know she is not some simple child brought here for sacrifice. She bears the marks of a priestess on her body." Aphrodite paused, her lips pressed together in a smirk as his eyebrows flew up at her announcement.

Gritty delight swelled her chest knowing he would not ask how she knew of the tattoos, though his fury was evident. Holding a finger to her lips to simulate secrecy, she added, "She did not get them here, not unless you have hidden away a gaggle of Gaea's women in the bowels of Athos."

With effort, Ares kept himself at bay.

"They were indeed Gaea's women, but they were not here. They were at dockside, at the foot of Athos. It was there they found Niala when she sought to run away from me. I have not lied to you. Niala came here as a girl just past her menses. I did see something in her, something I could not identify. Immortality? Possibly, but I could not prove her to be either Ilya or an immortal."

"So she has not been here all this time." Though Aphrodite would not have Ares know her relief, she could not contain the sigh that issued from her lips.

His head wagged from side to side as if to break free from the discussion. "These women took her away. They disguised her so thoroughly, I could not find her, though I tried."

"Because you thought her to be Ilya." Aphrodite's bitterness was evident.

"Because she was different. Would you not have done the same if faced with a mystery that would not reveal itself?"

"I am not obsessed with one who is long dead."

"Ilya, the mortal woman? Yes, she has been dead for countless millennia, but the one who sparked her life? Where is she? She cannot die, for her spirit is immortal. I will know what happened to her, whether you approve or not."

"Perhaps Ilya has never returned to life, not this one or any other. Perhaps she cannot stand the thought of you."

A stab of abject pain creased Ares' forehead and, for one moment, he appeared vulnerable, sad and defeated. Aphrodite was instantly contrite.

She was gripped by a sudden tenderness, for she knew Ares better than he knew himself - he was predictable even in his anger. Lurking beneath the brazen exterior, behind the shield of dark eyes that denied everything but rage and lust, was one who carried the shame of the mortal world upon his broad shoulders. No one else knew how personal that guilt was, nor what it was like to live an eternity without forgiveness.

She touched his cheek as hope lingered that he would give in and send the woman away, but he was unmoved by her caress. She could see the rebellion in those twin wells of midnight sky guarded by thick black lashes lowered halfway. She saw the tension in his jaw, the tightening of his mouth as he rejected her compassion. It hurt her to know he would risk everything for Ilya and yet, in a strange way, she understood.

"When did she come back to you?" Aphrodite's own guilt now rose to the surface as she caught another glimpse of Niala.

Aphrodite knew she betrayed that tiny spark of trust between them, and yet she had to know, had to feel the wounding of rejection in all its throbbing pain. It had come to this, a final showdown. Aphrodite must take courage in hand and hear the answers. Hugging herself, she moved closer to the hearth.

"Niala did not willingly return to my side, if that is any consolation." Ares cast a gloomy gaze toward Niala before fixing on Aphrodite. "Ahh, Beloved, forgive me this one last time for I cannot help this desire. It is too deep."

He touched Aphrodite's bared shoulders and felt the chill on her skin. He did not miss her flinch and thought he well deserved it. He drew forth a fur cape and draped it around her as he told the story of Layla and her cohorts, the sly witches who befriended Niala on the docks below his fortress and then stole her from Athos, how he finally found her on the shores between the great Maendre River and the Bayuk, in Najahmara.

"I would not have discovered her whereabouts if Deimos had not sought to invade Najahmara with his armies. When I heard Niala's name I knew it was the same female, yet it was three hundred years past. A mere mortal could not live so long."

"No." Aphrodite's gaze traveled back to the corner where Niala huddled. "Three hundred years. A dozen lifetimes to a mortal."

"At least that. Look at her - she reached maturity and aged no further. What was I to think when I saw her?"

He left out their quarrel on the plateau, describing only the massacre in the temple. "She shape-shifted into Kulika, Gaea's mate. She destroyed her enemy. No mortal could bear the monstrous energy of the Blue Serpent and survive if she did not have our blood."

"Agreed." Aphrodite let the fur cloak drop to the floor. "And that brings us back to where we began."

"I have not made love with her."

"I do not believe you."

"She sought to fight her enemy and, instead, slaughtered her own people. Her heart was broken and she has not been the same since."

"You would have taken her had she not thrown herself onto the rocks."

"But I did not and that was the condition of our agreement."

"Why have you kept her here as a prisoner? Why do you not return her to this Najahmara? She has told me she longs for home, though she cannot recall its name."

"The doors are not locked. She has the Corvidae upon her back and the Blue Serpent upon her thigh. If she can host Kulika, she can host the Corvidae and find her way home. Since she does not, I assume she wants to stay."

"She is weak and heartsick. You take advantage of her fragile state. Return her to her home and I will forgive this transgression."

Ares made a rude sound. "A moment ago you would have me take her head off and with that you would forgive me. Now, I must release her, though she scarce knows her own name. Then, only then, you will forgive me?"

"Yes, that is what you must do. Nothing less. If you will not kill her, then release her." Aphrodite tossed her froth of curls and faced Ares. "Take her back to Najahmara."

"Najahmara is not what it once was. She would be disappointed, distraught, if not in dire straits. The invading army has taken control in spite of her best efforts. It is best that she stay here." Ares shot his wife a grim smile. "We can be proud of our son and the army he commands for they overcame Kulika."

"I do not take pride in War's games. I loathe that any son of mine is part of it and I will hear no more excuses. Return her to Najahmara."

Ares' jaw twitched. "Do not dictate to me. I will not have it. I said she cannot go back and she will not go back."

Aphrodite's gaze became flat and dangerous. "Then let me take her to Cos where she can fully recover in an environment more conducive to healing."

"You want me to allow you take her to Cos?" Astonishment colored his words.

"If she is an emerging immortal, she has need of me more than you."

"So now you think she has immortality in her veins?" With

a short bark of mirthless laughter, Ares sank into his chair.

It was his way of dismissing her.

Aphrodite went still, her gaze sliding away to a spot beyond him. The inevitable was upon her - that dreaded moment when she must push forward for her own sake. She searched Ares' expression for some bit of hope that he would concede to her. She saw nothing.

"Then you forsake our marriage?" Her voice trembled.

His handsome face remained expressionless. "No, I do not."

"If you choose to bed her...."

"And I will." He answered without passion, though he spoke the truth. "You know I will, which has nothing to do with our union."

"You humiliate me. You shame me before the Council."

"You think sex drives our alliance? That our power revolves around our bed? Nay, making love is what we do. It is not who we are. Let the gossipmongers say what they will, but Love and War are forever united. One cannot exist without the other in the Mortal Realm." He inhaled deeply. "And it is so in our realm. Our alliance stands."

"No, Ares, it is over. I declare it is so."

"You cannot without my permission."

"I do not need your agreement." Aphrodite punched the air in savage disgust. "You always do as you please. This time, I will not allow it. Do you want to know the worst of it? The very worst?"

Choking, she held a hand to her throat. She never believed it would come to this. Never. But here it was, and her sorrow burst forth like a hurricane. "Do you want to know who it is I dream of? The one who calls to me to birth her into this world, the one who would have been our daughter?"

Ares sat in stony silence.

"You cannot even bring yourself to ask, can you? She who calls is Victory."

"Victory?" Stunned, Ares came to his feet.

"Yes. The world has long awaited her and now she hovers on the edge of existence, but in your stubbornness, you refuse her."

"I have not refused - you have deceived me. You dare accuse me of lies?"

"She would have been your daughter as well but no longer. I will birth her without your help, for that is what you have accomplished here this day."

"So that is your devious design. With all your pretty talk of a daughter who will better understand you than all the doltish men in your life. Now I find you seek to align Victory with Love? This is beneath you."

"What better place for her? What hope would the world have if Victory belonged to War? What bitterness would arise and tear apart the fragile fabric of humanity if mortals knew true victory was possible?

"Now, they merely overrun each other, one layer over the other, the weak succumbing to the strong, no different than the beasts of the human world. In the end, they are no better for it, in spite of the violence. But should they see the spark of victory - the possibilities - the destruction would be endless. War exists because the Mortal Realm demands it, but you do not have to abet it."

"I see that naivety has not left you." Ares paced back and forth as he raged. "You have convinced yourself that Victory would support Love in the most altruistic of ways? How do you not see that both Love and War spur the mortal world to its utmost pinnacle of destruction, whether we have the ultimate in victory, or not. Why do you think Victory has not yet been born? All are afraid to bring Victory to life. It would mean accepting responsibility, not mere existence."

"Do I hear you, the great and glorious War, admit fear?"

"I admit nothing. For I feel none, yet it is here…." He tapped his belly. "Waiting."

"You sire it for others, why would it not howl at your own door?"

At no response, Aphrodite went on. "As for myself, I do not merely exist, as you put it. I do not live on the fringes of the mortal coil and wait to be tossed about by their emotional frenzies. I am their desire in the flesh."

"You have decided Victory should belong to Love alone."

"Yes, she demands to be born. She has come to me in my dreams and spoken of her birth. It is time for her, whether or not we are ready, it is time. If we do not have her, she will find another way. Do you truly want Victory to align with another realm?"

"I do not doubt Victory's time has come, but I believe you pervert the message to fit your own desire."

"Of course." Aphrodite did not bother to disguise the

resentment. "I should have expected nothing less. And you wonder why I would not tell you of her?"

"That is where your ego overrides your sense."

Silence descended as they glared at each other.

"Then it is truly over if you will not let Niala go." Aphrodite's voice shook. "I forsake my vows to you and declare the alliance between Love and War ended."

"No!" Ares slammed his fist into the black marble mantel.

"Yes," Aphrodite shrieked. "And there is naught you can do to prevent it."

Niala locked her arms over her knees and buried her burning face in her robe. She tried to block out the argument raging around her, to pretend she was elsewhere - anywhere - but she could not escape it. The ugliness of their words penetrated like arrows as the very air became charged with lightning strikes of energy. She saw it as colors careening past her head, crashing into the walls, the furniture, and the floor, shattering into flickering shards that faded within a few moments.

She could stand no more of it, for with each brilliant flash she saw yet another piece of her missing life. That which she mourned for, begged to remember, cried to have restored, was returned to her in the same manner it was ripped away. The void that held her prisoner and siphoned off her memories now flung them back at her with unexpected cruelty.

Had she thought it would be a gentle stream of memories?

Niala gave a low moan and tried to shrink further into herself. She prayed only to know who she was and where she came from, giving no thought as to what violence might have brought her to Athos.

She listened to Ares' story of how she hurled herself over the parapet as if he spoke of a stranger, wondering only in a vague way why she would have done it. The tale of her childhood trek to Athos was the same - it held no meaning, therefore no more horror than a distant event in another's life.

With the furious exchange between Ares and Aphrodite came new images, visions that burst like an overfilled water skin. The memories were jumbled, as if the void kept them in no certain order and now shot them back one after the other in rapid succession. Holding her hands over her ears, she could scarce absorb one before the next was upon her.

Fire streaming through the streets, agonized squeals
A swarm of soldiers, too many to count
Panic
The darkest night studded with countless glittering stars
Blood spilled, bodies broken, a temple desecrated
A smoky cave, the scent of oil
Drums
Terror and pain, rape and murder
Dancing and laughter
Tthe voice of Earth in her ear
Gaea filling her body
Release
White hot fury, revenge clawing at her eyes
A serpent rising
Hideous desires
A windswept plateau kissed by the beauty of a full moon
Utter hatred
Blind love
Mindless killing
Beloved friends
Blood in her mouth
Frantic, desperate screams
Slow death
Lost family
Empty eyes
Gaea calling
Ares answering
Silence
Thick, heavy silence
Waiting silence

Niala held her breath until stark pain shot through her chest. What was next? What horror would rain down upon her next? Weakly, she lifted her head and listened. All she could hear was her own quivering breath.

It was dark and hot, but then she knew her eyes were closed and the heat was her own body churning in defense. Dazed, she leaned against the cool wall and tried to reorient herself.

With care, she cracked her eyes open and slid her gaze to one side. Everything was blurry. Where was she? Najahmara? The temple? And then she remembered; she was at Athos.

She was with Ares. Najahmara had been destroyed.

A whimper rose in her throat but before it could find its way out there came a deafening crack. The wall shook and the floor beneath her shimmied and creaked in protest. The sound of rock falling, great chunks crashing down followed by the rush of small chips.

Niala shuddered as someone screamed.

She found it was herself as Ares dragged her by the hair across the plateau and threw her onto Layla's grave.

Five white stones, four broken off into jagged stumps while she begged him to stop.

Your punishment, he roared.

She watched him destroy the ones she loved even though death had taken them first. He snatched Layla's bones from the ground and threw them over the side in a rage and then held her back as she scrambled to pick them up.

There. He pointed. Your end.

She saw the soldiers who came to crush Najahmara.

Sobbing, panting, Niala clawed at the wall as if it were Ares' leg. Stop, stop! Do not do this. Do not do this. I will give you anything, even myself. Do not destroy all that I love.

Too late.

Aphrodite stared at the mantel, now cleaved in half, the two sides hanging from the ends while the middle lay broken on the floor. Ares still clenched his fists, unfazed by any pain. He did not even glance at the crumbled stone but fixed an intimidating gaze upon her.

"You declare this alliance over?"

"Yes." Aphrodite could scarce get the word out. "Yes." She spoke louder, with boldness. "You have brought it upon yourself."

"And you are innocent?"

They both turned at the crazed moan that came from Niala. They watched her scrabble in the corner playing out some unseen story, all the while sobbing and begging for it to stop.

Aphrodite could feel the desperate fear oozing from Niala. "What is wrong with her?"

"She should not have been witness to this debacle." Ares left Aphrodite's side and went to Niala. He crouched beside her and placed one hand on hair still damp from her bath. The curling tendrils caught on his fingers as he tried to stroke down and pulled instead.

Niala cried out, hunching her shoulders. "I will give you

anything you ask. Please...please...stop this travesty."

"Niala." Ares grasped her chin and turned her head. "Look at me. You are lost in a dream."

Aphrodite's gaze narrowed, for here, indeed, was proof Ares did more than service a mortal. She could see the care he took with her, the instant concern creasing his forehead. He had already put aside their argument in favor of Niala, while she, his rightful mate, stood wounded by his callousness.

"Leave her. Let her suffer. Perhaps then she will think twice before she offends me."

"She has done nothing to you."

"She is a Priestess to Gaea, therefore one of my own followers. I am the essence of all Gaea's rituals, born to her by the sea to embody her love. Do not tell me this one has done nothing to me!"

"She has done my bidding. No more and no less. Her offense is through me." Ares glanced sideways at Aphrodite as she moved closer, her small fists clenched as if to strike.

"I do not disagree, however, I want her banished far, far away from here."

"You do not give me orders." Ares turned back to his charge. "Niala, look at me."

When her wandering gaze came to rest on his face, Niala whimpered, "Forgive me. Do not let this happen."

Ares realized Niala's memories were surfacing. The torment had returned to her eyes as if it had never left. "Niala, it is already done. Your people are dead and Najahmara is destroyed. I was too late to stop them. I was too late to stop you."

"You knew."

"No." He shook his head. "No, it was not my plan. Deimos brought the army."

"Deimos?" Niala whispered. "He swore he would not."

She trembled against Ares' hands, her head bobbing as more recollections poured in, things she could not give voice to, things even he did not know about. Her life beyond the walls of Athos, her loves, her losses.

"Deimos promised he would spare Najahmara." Niala sagged in defeat. "He lied."

Ares was not certain where Deimos fit, what part of Niala

Deimos had taken for himself. His disapproval was heightened by the images brought forth at Niala's grief. For the first time it occurred to him they might have been lovers.

Grasping Niala by the neck, he stood, lifting her to her feet. "What was Deimos to you?" He shook her.

"Not enough, if he could do this awful thing."

Though he did not want the answer, he could not help asking the question. "Did you bed him?"

"Why do you ask these things, for they have no meaning now?" Niala answered, tears flowing down her face.

"Did you?"

"Why did he send the armies against Najahmara?" Niala could not stand without his help. "If it was because of me, I will never forgive him."

"She places blame on our son as well?" Nose wrinkling, Aphrodite sniffed. "Do you see the treachery behind this one? A woman who beds both father and son is without honor. Be rid of her."

With a glance of pure malice, Ares silenced Aphrodite.

"I remember the invasion," Niala whispered. "They came under cover of night and entered the temple. They murdered Seire. Sweet innocent Seire." An animal wail was torn from her throat and rage burned in her streaming eyes.

"Yes." Ares kept her from falling to the floor. "The last of your line, dead at their hands. Yet you fought back. You opened to Kulika, you permitted him to take form. His nature is to kill without discrimination in protection of his beloved Gaea."

"Ahh, how do you live with it?" Great quaking breaths shook her shoulders. "How do you have the blood of thousands on your hands and still go forth? How do you know those you love are dead, never to be again? How?"

Ares touched Niala's cheek with the back of his hand and then stared at the sheen of wetness left by her grief. His gaze shifted to Aphrodite and back again before he licked the tears from his knuckles with the slowness of one who consumes pain for amusement.

"There is only one way for me to quiet the violence. One way. And you know it well."

"No," Niala leaned weakly against his arm. "It is wrong."

"It is War's escape."

"What kind of escape is it to take pleasure when so many suffer?"

"Mindless. Sex engages the body and does not allow for thought. I am lost within its grasp and when I emerge I am renewed."

"It is callous and cold to put yourself before all others."

"If I do not relieve my pain the world's suffering increases for then my only outlet is in battle."

"I am not like you. I cannot."

"Yes, you can." Ares cupped her chin in his broad palm and brought her gaze up to meet his.

The agony in her eyes spoke more than any word, even when she whispered, "My wound has not lessened, but instead spread this dread disease throughout. I am poisoned - I am dying. Will you not pity me and let me end it?"

"Niala." He caressed her face with his fingertips, feeling wet eyelashes and trembling lips before his touch moved to the pulse at her throat. "You do not have to suffer such torment. I can take it away for you, if you would but allow me."

"How? When you have not done as much so far? If you could, why did you not? To punish me? To see me ruined?"

"Never, though you try my patience - always rebelling against what I think is best, always disregarding what I tell you. Even then, I would not see you harmed."

"Then why?"

"Because I cannot force you to take what I offer. You must accept willingly. You must indeed sacrifice yourself to the better good, but not for me. For you."

Before Niala could answer, Aphrodite intervened. "Ares, what is it you are saying? Stop this foolishness now."

Ignoring her, Ares continued. "Niala, I offer you immortality, the power to heal your pain, to rise above your humanness."

"No!" Aphrodite snatched at his hands. "This is nonsense. Niala, he cannot do what he claims."

"I can. Niala let me show you how. Let me take away your grief." His lips brushed hers. He could feel the panic rising in her, the shallowness to her breath and the pounding of her heart as the fingers of her hand curled around his wrist. "I tried before, but you would not surrender your pain."

"It is a betrayal, to forget those I love."

"You will not forget. You will remember more than this lifetime, you will see beyond this physical moment. All you have ever been and ever will be, all those you have loved."

"I cannot bear those losses again."

"They will be part of your pleasure."

"It does not seem right."

"Give yourself fully to me. Hold back nothing and I will give you peace." He spoke into her ear, pulling her closer. "Relinquish yourself and I swear, you will be at peace."

"You swear?" Niala looked up at him with swollen eyes, her last bit of strength leaving, for what she saw was his face as she had seen it in the temple. It was as if she lay there once again with Seire next to her and Inni's broken body close by. "I will give myself to you if you swear I will not carry this horror with me the rest of my days."

"You will see with detachment."

Aphrodite charged at Ares, flailing her arms, smacking him anywhere she could. Ares swept her away with one arm, knocking her to the floor. Though she continued to beg him to cease his actions, her cries fell on deaf ears.

"It is not mine to erase, but to offer relief. It is your decision alone and I will abide by it, but if it is so, I bid you swear it is so and I will take you into your power." Ares kissed Niala's forehead. "It is your choice."

"Yes. Yes, I swear I want peace." Niala went limp in his arms, her legs giving out beneath her. Ares folded her against his chest, his arm locked about her shoulders.

"Beloved." Aphrodite raised a stricken gaze to his. She watched Niala's face, at the horror written upon those earthy features. She heard the tenderness with which Ares coaxed Niala. "If you love me, if you are mine, do not do this. It is wrong."

With arched brow, he fastened a wicked look upon her over Niala's head. "You wish our alliance to be undone? Then so be it. Now leave us. Seek your daughter wherever you will."

Aphrodite stared at him with hollow disbelieving eyes. Her lips parted to speak, but there were no words left. She gave one slow nod and a heavy sodden sigh. There was nothing more to say.

"You cannot let her go." Niala clutched at his tunic front. "She is Eternal Love. You cannot let her go."

Ares' gaze, fixed on the spot vacated by Aphrodite, now moved to Niala. "It was her choice."

"You did not have to let her go."

"She will regret her rashness and return to me." His lips curved in a tight smile. "Eventually."

"What if she does not?"

"Then War untempered by Love will be a most terrible thing."

"And the mortal world - who will champion them against this new tide of violence?"

Ares shrugged. "Perhaps because of them Love turns away from me. We are little more than a mirror of their weaknesses."

"If that is so, then I do not want your immortality. If I cannot make better earthly existence, there is no reason for it."

"Oh, there is reason." Ares bent over her, his lips next to hers. "And you will see it soon enough."

The kiss he laid upon Niala made her dizzy. It was not a kiss of passion but a promise of the power that lay waiting for her. His breath rolled over her tongue and down her throat, expanding her chest until it hurt, until she broke free of it.

"Do not turn away from me. This is what you want." His eagerness fell over them both like a shadow as his mouth closed on hers again.

He exhaled into her and a burst of color beat against her skin with the heat of white flame. She shuddered and tried to pull away, but he held fast, his kisses now inflexible, demanding she relinquish her soul to him. Body writhing, images whirled through her mind in a profusion of desires, lust laced with blood, first in pain and then with pleasure, defeat with agony, valiant and victorious.

Niala could not help herself. She returned his embrace with fervor, straining to merge with the fires of War. His call was a bright flame dancing before her eyes, inviting her to join its sensuous swirling energy with a promise of victory over torment. She tore at his clothes, for now she wanted to be next to his skin, to feel his vigor, to caress the hard contours of his body, to revel in the innate strength suffusing every part of him.

His strength would save her. She knew it, recognized it as the immortal spark wavering inside her. That spark responded to him, rose up with a desire of its own and attempted to push past her fear of lost humanity. Very real fears, for there were things she did not know, things she should ask but could not fathom the questions.

And still the fire burned and immortality beckoned. Was that not what she wanted? Yes, yes, she wanted her suffering to end, but at what price? Along with the horror that ended Najahmara was the joy of its creation. Along with the sadness and grief of death was the contentment and love of life.

This path, then, was not as simple as he made it out to be.

"Wait." Gasping Niala tried to pull away.

Cupping her face between his hands, Ares whispered, "I know you are frightened, as all of us have been when we stood on the brink of our greatest discovery. Each and every one of us must face our worst fears before we can take our power. It is that very fear that births our role in the Greater Realm."

He moved his hands to her shoulders, his fingers digging into her flesh. Niala flinched, not from his grip, but from the heat that drove down through her like a spike entering wood.

"Hear me." Ares went on, his voice filled with urgency. "Taking on immortality is much the same as passing through a doorway where all mysteries are revealed. You see this life and everything beyond it. All that you once were and what you are meant to be. But only if you accept it. Fully, absolutely surrender your will."

"I cannot."

"You can."

To relinquish the thread that bound her to her mortality on the grounds that she had not the courage to live with her actions? Niala quaked with doubt. Somehow, it was wrong. She had invoked Kulika and killed. Should she not then live with the remorse and guilt as her penance?

Though she struggled to back away Ares would not let her. His mouth was on hers again, forcing her lips apart, his tongue pushing between her teeth. This time there was no tentative offering of his energy. This time his energy engulfed her. She stood in the heart of his fire and was bathed in the red flame of War. Whatever doubt she had, whatever fear loomed within, it was burned away.

There was nothing left to hold back.

She accepted her power.

Ares saw an infusion of new awareness, a subtle shifting of energy that drew her skin tighter, smoother, no longer creased with fear but glowing with the surety of an immortal. He felt the human restrictions fall away, replaced by coiled tension born of undiluted, willful strength.

"Rebellion." His voice was unsteady as the truth dawned. "I should have known. You are Rebellion."

He kissed her once more before loosening her robe. Niala let him slide it from her shoulders and cast it aside. With eagerness, she went into his arms. He, too, was naked. She stretched with languid grace, arching her back, arms over her head. Her breasts rose up, full and inviting, the supple skin glistening with a reddish cast in the soft light.

She slid against him with a slight purring, left hand slipping along his shoulder to his chest and between them to his belly. In one silken movement, she touched the hardness that lay waiting, her fingers exploring to the root. A gasp was torn from his lips.

Eyes glittering in the firelight, she gripped his neck with her right hand and brought him to her. All the while she stroked his manhood, and laughed with wicked delight as he squirmed against her hot palm. With tongue and teeth, she kissed him until blood ran. Then, only then, did she pause to lick it from his lips with a sly smile.

With heightened strength, Niala rolled him onto his back and sat astride him. Her dark triangle of woman's mystery poised above his manhood but did yet allow entry. Ares could do naught but lie in slavery as she took her time. He watched with ragged breath and fevered body as Niala drew her heavy braid between her breasts and began to pull it free. She released the wiry, curling hair from its confinement and lifted it with both hands, letting it drape about her in untamed abandon.

Slowly, she ran her hands along her breasts and belly, touching nipples and navel in soft circles. When her hands dipped below, into the dark hair between her legs, he groaned and thrashed beneath her. Thighs tight, she held him in place until sweat glistened on his forehead.

Never did she take her eyes from his face, yet he could not keep his frantic gaze on anything but the slow and deliberate fingers that moved now to her thighs, to trace the serpent's head on her leg. One forefinger caressed the blunt nose and forked tongue with sensuous delight, pausing once to wet her finger, to draw a path from serpent to cave.

The serpent appeared to shimmy, as if he, too, felt the

overwhelming need to glide into that secret woman's place, so far denied to both. Ares grunted and reached to pull her down onto him, but Niala resisted. Instead, she bent and took him in her mouth, hot and wet and sharp with teeth.

"Sweet mercy. Niala...."

But it was not Niala that led him to the brink of lunacy. It was Rebellion. She had only to direct him where she wanted and he went without protest. He had no more thought than to thrust into her over and over until his mind was unfocused and even he, the great and powerful War, could no longer bear her relentless quest.

"Enough. Enough! Give me release or I shall go mad."

When the primitive wave of power burst over their heads, it rained down with unnatural force. The surge brought a new struggle between them - the child who waited to be born. The child who suffered the consequences of Love gone wrong, growing impatient with the boundaries that kept her from taking form.

This energy sparked between them and a babe quickened.

Niala knew the moment she conceived. She felt the burgeoning of her womb, the satiated fullness that began a pregnancy. She knew it was to be a secret. Inside her was an extraordinary child, one who chose War as her father and Rebellion as her mother. She was a gift, a new beginning, a liberator who rose from the rubble of anguish and pain.

Niala threw back her head and howled. She shrieked at the hilarity, the utter madness of the spiraling dance that led her back to her own beginnings. With fierce joy, she let loose a shrill rapid ululation to welcome Victory.

Ares stared up at Niala in a dazed panic, for he, too, felt the shift, but he could not see what it was. He could only hear Niala's mad screams of laughter as he went into the throes of his last release.

Afterward, when Niala slept, Ares saw a placid smile turn her lips upward. She seemed at peace, her face softened by the flicker of lamplight. The wild energy of Rebellion was gone. She had returned to her former self, that of a gentle and humble priestess.

He had invoked Niala's immortality only to see it seep away like so much sand pulled out by the tides. There was naught he could do to prevent the loss if Niala herself would not contain it.

FIVE

"Jahmed, please." Pallin met Jahmed's gaze and flushed at the hard brown anger reflected back. "All Hattu wants is to move our spring rites from the plateau. It is a simple thing, a small request."

"All? It seems of late he makes these 'small' requests far too often."

"He wants to attend our celebration, it will help him understand."

"It is we who adjust to his desires, but I see nothing in return for these favors." Jahmed ground a stone pestle with relentless zeal against a handful of dried berries until they were powder. Her many braids bounced with her efforts and would have fallen into her eyes save for the yellow scarf tied around her head.

"He directed his men to help us rebuild Najahmara." Pallin handed Jahmed a small bowl to store the mixture.

Snatching it from her hand, Jahmed slapped it down on the table with a bang. "Hattusilis - or 'King' as he would have us call him - brought those men to our doorstep. Save for that, we would not need rebuilding."

"It was not Hattusilis, it was his nephew. Hattu would have come in peace."

"They are soldiers, Pallin, all of them, including their king. There is no peaceful way to invade another's land, in particular when the intention is to conquer."

"That is not what he wants to do."

"It is what he has done. Everything he says, everything he does is opposite our ways. He commands, he does not request. He wishes to replace Gaea with worship to his bloody god and, do I need remind you, the same god who stole Niala from us?

"That is not true."

"Can you see nothing?"

"I see that the white stones are broken, Jahmed. They are destroyed and by whose hand? Not Gaea. How can we hold our spring rites there? It is a reminder of all we have lost. On the other hand, the lake - it would be a new start, like birth water."

Jahmed shook her head. "It is wrong. We have always held the spring rites on the plateau. To move it is a travesty."

"Gaea does not care where we honor her, all she needs is you to be her vessel."

Laying down her tools, Jahmed went to the doorway and stared in the direction of the lake, where the Bayuk and Maendre rivers met. She had heard rumors that Hattusilis wanted to build a port, to bring ships in from the sea, to begin a trade center.

She was appalled at this plan, however vague, for it would further alter Najahmara and bring an influx of more strangers into their midst. If Niala were here, she would stop such a disaster from coming to fruition.

But Niala was not here and there were more pressing matters than the possibility of such a port. Besides, when the heavy rains came, as they did once every few years, anything built along the shore would be destroyed.

Did not Hattusilis wonder why all construction was well away from the edge of the lake and rivers? The two bridges that connected Najahmara to the surrounding area had been washed out numerous times.

How long since the last flood? Jahmed could not recall, which meant the next rainy season would occur sooner rather than later. This thought made her chuckle in spiteful delight.

"Sad," she mumbled. "Sad that I would find joy in further

destruction just to punish the invaders.

"What are you going on about?"

"I said I am worried about Inni. I do not like to leave her alone for such long periods but there is so much work to be done, I have not been able to check on her today."

Once the temple was taken over by Hattusilis and his guard, Jahmed had moved Inni to the outlying area on the far side of the Maendre River. Inni was so afraid of men, of any stranger, Jahmed had no other choice than to take her away.

She found a small hut abandoned after the fire, its owner presumed dead, and prepared their new home. Each morning she made the trek into Najahmara, went back to Inni at midday and made the return trip to the medicine hut for more labor. In the evening, if no crisis occurred, Jahmed went home for the night.

All day she fretted. If someone were to stumble upon their dwelling, and if that someone was male, Inni would be terrorized.

Jahmed's greatest fear was that Inni would retreat from her once again, returning to the stupefied state where she sat and stared at nothing. Just as she had done for months after witnessing their eldest priestess, Seire, brutally murdered, after the soldiers abused the younger girls, after Inni, herself, was beaten and raped.

Jahmed could not lose her again.

"I do not want revelry anywhere near our hut. Inni will be frightened."

"Perhaps Inni will decide to attend. It would be good for her."

"You do not know what would be good for her." Dumping the ground herbs into an earthen jar, she turned to Pallin. "When have you visited her? When have you spoken to her? I will answer for you - not since your belly began to grow with the enemy's child."

"We are so busy since we are the only ones, there is no time." Pallin's eyes widened with guilt.

"I do not want to hear your excuses." Jahmed rubbed her face with her fists.

"You are not being fair. It is difficult for me to go that far with Hattu so ill." Pallin twisted her fingers together. "I am sorry, Jahmed. I know you are right. I love Inni and I miss her. I just cannot bear to see the changes in her."

"So your answer is to ignore her?" Jahmed's voice was filled with resentment. "After what was done to her by your husband's men, you should be the first in line to see her."

"Hattu did not cause this."

"He did. The blame is forever at his feet for he sought to invade Najahmara. And why? What had we done to him? Nothing. We merely exist. We harm no one. We live in peace, yet still, they cannot leave us alone."

Anger stained Jahmed's cheeks with red. "Why do they not leave alone? We have no gold. We have no treasure. We have nothing. What do they want?"

"They stay because of the waterway." Pallin's tone was soft.

"Yes, I see how they build on the river's bank regardless of the warning of floods. They want more of their kind to come here." Jahmed slammed the jar onto a shelf and reached for the next bundle of dried herbs.

The truth of Jahmed's words hit Pallin as if physically struck. Her belly tightened into a hard ball and she gasped with the jab of pain. It passed as she massaged both sides but she sat down on the stone bench to catch her breath. "I am certain you are right."

"I hoped they would leave once they saw we did not have streets of gold." Jahmed waved at Pallin's bulge. "But they will stay because their king stays."

"I cannot help that I love him." Pallin's gaze pleaded with Jahmed to understand, but Jahmed turned a cold shoulder to the distress in her voice.

"Is it truly love or something else?"

Pallin swallowed hard. "Love, of course."

"Then leave with him. Go back to his land and take his beasts with him."

"Jahmed, you do not mean that."

"Yes, I do."

"You want me to leave?"

"If it will take them out of our midst, then yes."

Pallin's breath caught in a quiver. "If Niala was here, you would not say such things."

"If Niala was here, they would be dead or gone."

"She would not have killed them."

"She already did, when she allowed Kulika to send fire throughout our village. She killed the invaders and she killed our people." Jahmed sank down on the bench beside Pallin, her face buried in her hands.

"She was protecting us. If she had not summoned Kulika, the Sky God, Inni would be dead. All of us would be dead. There would be nothing left but ashes." Pallin watched as Jahmed's shoulders began to shake but she made no sound other than a heavy sigh.

"Would you truly want me to leave?"

Blindly, Jahmed reached for Pallin's fingers and squeezed them. "No," she whispered. "Never."

Pallin put her arms around Jahmed even as Jahmed gripped her in a tight hug.

"What is to become of us? What are we to do without Niala?"

"We do as we always do."

"I cannot. Look at me, I cannot think straight. I fear I give out the wrong medicines. I am filled with hatred. How can I go into ritual and open myself to Gaea?"

"Niala passed the power to you for a reason. She trusts you."

Jahmed lifted her head, gaze hard. "Have the celebration at the lakeside, but I cannot do it."

"Jahmed, please."

"No, I cannot. It does not matter anymore. I could not have done it on the plateau either. I cannot."

"You are exhausted and despairing, you cannot see past this. Everything will sort out. I know it will. Go home, now, and rest. Be with Inni. I will stay here."

"You cannot be alone."

"I am not. Ajah is here and so is Tulane. Please, rest. We will work this out later."

Jahmed nodded and got up. She stood for a moment in the doorway, but did not glance backward before she left. Pallin felt again the cramp in her belly as sharp as the pain in her heart but she withstood them both and rose to do her duty.

Jahmed made her way along the path through the remains of Najahmara, taking note of the efforts to restore the village.

The worst of the debris had been cleared yet still there was the underlying scent of charred flesh.

Real or imagined?

The fire had been so intense that bodies were unidentifiable, would it be surprising if the surviving structures were forever imprinted with the odor? There were stories of people fused to the stone walls of their homes, leaving behind images too sickening to contemplate.

Here and there she saw one of the invading men working next to a native Najahmaran, but she averted her gaze and refused to greet any she did not know. A small voice spoke in Jahmed's head reminding her that this embittered behavior did not behoove a priestess.

What is done is done. Now we must make the best of it.

Niala's words over something far less difficult but no less true.

"We have relied strongly upon your gifts, Niala, so much that we scarce know what to do without you."

Jahmed spoke aloud as she traversed one of the surviving bridges across the Maendre, where the river was at its narrowest. The adjoining fields were dotted with sheep and goats, some of whom scattered up the side of a mesa at her approach. This ridge was the mirror of the one behind the temple save for the crest was not flat. It was rocky, steep and treacherous for a human to climb.

She took the path circling around the base and into a lightly wooded area. Nestled amongst the pine trees was the small cottage she had discovered when on a walk to find a medicine plant used to treat burns. She had not found the desperately needed Cumbungi, but had spotted the shelter.

It was untouched by the devastation as the river had created a natural fire break and the flames had not passed beyond the Maendre's shore. Where the original owners had gone, whether they died or simply left, Jahmed did not know. She accepted the little house as a gift from Gaea.

As soon as Inni was able to walk, they had taken up residence in the concealed hut. Jahmed still feared a passerby would notice it tucked under the great pines but could not ignore the temple work. Each time she left, she prayed Inni would be safe.

After that, Inni was in Gaea's hands.

"Hello, my Love." Jahmed announced herself before entering. Inni's fear of strangers, particularly men, could be aggravated by the slightest unfamiliar noise.

"Jahmed." A wan smile lit Inni's face as she looked up from stirring a pot that hung on a tripod in the large hearth.

The remnants of root vegetables that were cleaned and chopped lay on the simple table, along with a few leaves from fresh herbs used to spice the stew. There was no evidence of animal fat as an ingredient. Since the invasion, neither woman could bring themselves to eat meat for the smell reminded them too much of those killed or injured.

"You are early. Our evening meal is not yet ready." Inni tapped the long-handled wooden spoon on the side of the cauldron, laid it on a clean plate and rose with the stiffness of one much older.

Jahmed watched her with great sadness but did not offer to assist. Inni's staunch spirit dictated that she do these menial tasks herself even though the pain intensified with certain movements. She had trouble kneeling, standing and carrying items with much bulk or weight but her stubbornness led her to make many trips rather than ask for help.

The once straight-backed priestess now shuffled with curved shoulders pressing forward as if to propel her steps. Her lovely blonde hair had turned white from scalp to ends and her thin face had become creased with lines around her mouth, nose and stamped upon her forehead. Her pale skin was paler still, making the tiny freckles further stand out.

Even her eyes had changed. They had been a sparkling blue, like water with sunlight dancing on the surface, unlike any Jahmed had ever seen. Now Inni's eyes were faded, as if left out in that same sun for too long.

Yet her resolve was stronger than ever. Inni never offered a single word of complaint nor expressed any bitterness at the horror that had befallen her. Her sharp tongue had melted away, replaced with an uncomplicated cheery outlook, as if she had forgotten the serious person she once was.

Simple-minded.

That was the ugly words Jahmed had overheard more than once when folk saw Inni at the medicinal hut. Bad enough this sentiment was voiced by those crude women and uncouth soldiers who came with the second wave of invasion, but to hear it from the mouths of Najahmaran villagers was too much to bear.

It was the final blow that led Jahmed to relocate from the common sleeping quarters of the temple to this remote cottage. Away from those hurtful thoughts, away from those discouraging words, away from the backlash of collective pain.

Here Inni could take time to recover. She could dig in the tiny garden arrear of the hut, plant seeds, tend the plants and bring them to harvest. She could putter around in the woods, picking up pine cones, finding flowers and leaves to arrange, cooking plain food, watching birds feed and animals play.

A simple healing life.

That's all they wanted, to be left alone.

Jahmed sighed and began to clean up the vegetable leavenings.

"I hear the drums." Inni leaned against a chair for support, an excited smile bringing a glow to her pallid complexion. "There is to be a celebration soon?"

"The remaining drummers merely teach the rhythms to their new students."

We lost so many, it is a miracle any survived to sustain the cadence of Gaea's rituals. Jahmed thought but did not speak this truth to Inni. Best not to refer to the tragedy, for Inni scarce remembered the circumstances of her injuries.

"You cannot fool me, Dearest. I know a celebration is nigh and I want to go. I am well enough to be part of the celebration and it is long since I have seen everyone."

The leaves and stems went into a bucket for the chickens scratching for bugs in the yard. What they did not consume would become mulch for the garden. Jahmed worked with her head down, not wishing to respond.

Inni brought bowls to the table, along with spoons and a basket of flat bread. "I do not begrudge Niala her absence, after all, a pregnancy cannot be easy for her, yet I long to see her."

A tiny jolt went along Jahmed's spine. She froze with one hand raised, reaching for a cloth to wipe her fingers. Inni did not know Niala was gone, stolen from them in the midst of all the madness.

"Niala is not pregnant, Inni. She has been busy with…with many things."

"She *is* pregnant." Inni clapped her palms together in glee. "I know because I dreamed it. I saw her with a mate, someone I do not know but perhaps has recently come to our village, and she is most definitely with child. Though I cannot quite tell if she is happy about the babe, for her face is not clear."

Jahmed lowered herself to one of the chairs and stared at her beloved. Inni had been blurting out sentiments just like that for weeks, things she could not possibly know, yet many of those declarations were proven true.

"You dream of someone else, then."

"No, it is Niala. I would know her anywhere, on this plane or any other. Jahmed, we are to have a tiny one in our midst again!"

"You think of Pallin, for she carries the child of one of the…." Jahmed paused to rearrange her words. "She married one who has recently come to Najahmara and expects her firstborn this summer."

"Ah, yes, Pallin, too." Inni winked. "If I had not already known this, I would have been surprised when she brought a basket of fruit a few days ago."

"Pallin was here?" Shame suffused Jahmed's cheeks. She spoke harshly to Pallin about visiting. Why did Pallin not correct her?

"Have I become so impossible to speak with that our Sisters would rather remain silent?"

"What are you going on about, my Love?" Inni ladled stew into the bowls and sat across from Jahmed.

"Nothing. It is nothing. You think of Pallin and not Niala."

Inni smiled a secret smile. "Of course."

"I do not think it would be wise to attend a celebration at this time, Inni. You are so much better but still weak. It is a long trek in and there are many strangers."

With a deep inhale, Inni nodded. "Perhaps you are right."

She ate a spoonful of food before adding, "But will you ask Niala to come and see me? I miss her so very much."

To this, Jahmed could only return a smile and pat Inni's hand.

SIX

Weeping bitterly, Aphrodite lowered her face into her hands. Her hair slid around her shoulders in a golden curtain drawn to hide her grief from prying eyes. The Graces surrounded their mistress, her misery reflected in each of them. They cast glances over Aphrodite's head, nodding in agreement at the woe caused by one they all detested.

"Do not worry, sweet Princess, he will fly back to your side in good time." Aglaia began to comb Aphrodite's long locks, curling each strand about her fingers.

"He has done such things before with and always returns to your side." Euphrosyne held a cool cloth wet from a natural spring to her face, but Aphrodite pushed it way. A new round of wailing issued as she refused their ministrations.

"It does no good to weep after that one." Thaleia made a rude noise deep in her throat. "His heart is as cold and dead as his fortress."

Thaleia shuddered, thinking of the damp gray stone and the dismal darkness that no candlelight seemed to penetrate. When she looked at her sisters again, they both glowered at her. "What have I said that is wrong?"

"Hush, Thaleia, do not cause her more grief." Aglaia continued to comb Aphrodite's lush mane.

"Please, Sister, do not distress her further." Euphrosyne pinched her lips together in disapproval.

"Neither of you have been in his clutches," retorted Thaleia. "And you speak of misery. I will tell you of his hateful ways, and then you will agree with me that our Princess should not concern herself with his insolence."

"Let me sing to cheer her, rather than listen to your dreadful tales," chirped Euphrosyne. "It will lighten our hearts."

Aphrodite raised red and swollen eyes to the Graces, ignoring their little murmurs of distress. "Good Sisters, I know you have only my best interests in your hearts, but I have no one to blame for this save myself."

"How can it be your fault?" Aglaia snatched the compress from Euphrosyne and dabbed at Aphrodite's blotchy completion. "Pure and simple, it is the Master of Misery who has caused this harm with his treachery."

"I should not have gone to Athos." Aphrodite pushed away Aglaia's attempts to wipe her face. "I should not have issued an ultimatum. It does no good with him. This I know. There are better ways to deal with Ares, but, no, I chose the worst possible route."

Aphrodite returned to mourning, the sounds of her sobs echoing in the high eaves of her bedchamber. Since her return she had huddled within the cushions of her bed and wept with endless sorrow.

"I do not believe there was any other way." Thaleia stared up at the ceiling, her voice echoing in the chamber. "This woman is different. She is not a mortal he toys with, but neither is she from the Greater Realm. She falls somewhere between."

"He loves her." Aphrodite spoke in a tiny pinched voice. "He would not say it aloud, for rarely does he even say it to me. Yet I saw it in his eyes. I saw it in the manner he cared for her. It is not his way to show affection and yet he did. To her. In front of me."

"Done purposely, no doubt." Aglaia threw the cloth into a bowl of water, disgust written upon her rounded features.

"It is true, Princess." Euphrosyne stroked the blonde curls of her mistress. "He does these things to upset you. He wants you to be angry."

"He would not send her away, even when I asked. He would not do that for me. He would rather let me go than give her up."

Pressing her hands to her chest as if to staunch an open wound, Aphrodite wept harder. "I am inflamed with anger. I am tormented by his actions. How could he do this? He has no proof she once was Ilya. I saw no sign of Ilya, no recognition, no sense of one who was part of us then."

"But you did see the flicker of immortality?" Thaleia clutched Aphrodite's shoulder. She disliked this line of talk but what else could she do? They had yet to find out what transpired at Athos to send their mistress into such a terrible storm.

"Yes, I saw it, but she does not want to claim it. Ares forces it upon her."

"He cannot make her." Aglaia sought to restore reason. "Even he cannot compel one to accept a gift she does not want."

"I pray you are right." Aphrodite lifted one limp hand and allowed a cup of cold nectar to appear. "But last I heard, she was swaying his way and there was naught I could do to stop it."

"There, you see, Princess, you have spoken the only truth there is when it comes to Lord Ares. If you love him, you must accept him the way he is, or do not have him at all. He will never change."

"Everything changes." Aphrodite sipped the sweet drink and licked her lips. "Even War."

A cloud drifted in front of the brilliant midday sun, casting a shadow across the room. It was as if the sky sought to reflect Aphrodite's unhappiness and throw a pall over them. All three Graces shivered in response. Silence fell and only the wind singing through the eaves was heard over the distant roaring of the ocean.

"I have done something terrible." The tears were replaced by a hollow empty gaze as Aphrodite stared toward the tumbling seas outside her open doors. "And you are wrong, Aglaia."

Aphrodite exhaled with closed eyes before continuing. "It does not always have to be his way. Many times - most times - it is I who make the demands and, though he is loud and rude and behaves as if he will not consent, he always complies. Therefore, the rest of the Realm believes it is he who is in control, when in truth, it is I."

She swallowed another sip and choked a bit as it lodged in her throat. "I do not care what others think. If I did, the jealousy, the envy, the coarse words and conniving actions would drive me further than Cos from Olympus. It would drive me back to the sea."

Her face grew red and again tears threatened but she breathed in and held silence for a moment before she continued. "I went too far this time."

"Princess, what is too far with Lord Ares? He is known for his extremes. He has no middle ground. Whatever it is, he will welcome you back into his arms."

Having said as much, Aglaia exchanged a worried glance with Thaleia. Euphrosyne's gaze swept back and forth between them, frightened, but unwilling to ask for details.

"No." Aphrodite shook her head. "No, this time he will not. This time - I beg you to understand how angry and injured I was - I said something unforgiveable. When I saw that he would sacrifice me for one who might be Ilya - might be, for there is no proof - I ended our alliance. Our union no longer exists."

Her words twisted with renewed acrimony. Her chest rose up and down with small pants until she calmed herself again. As her breathing leveled, a sad expression creased her face. "Good Sisters. Why did I do this? For the sake of a story that is older than time? For the sake of a rivalry that no longer exists? Even if Ilya has returned, I am Eternal Love.

"I need not be afraid of her. And should I not trust my beloved better than I do? To that, I could speak volumes. Yes, he dallies here and there, but I have been his one true love for so long no one remembers any other."

Aphrodite lifted her hand as if to hold up this example, to show them what it meant to love and trust. Instead, she dropped her hand to her lap and stared at her fingers.

The Graces stood in stunned silence while the raucous cry of seabirds could be heard over the thundering of the incoming tide. The filmy white cloth draped at the doorways fluttered with a sudden breeze and the scent of saltwater and seaweed became prevalent. At long last, Thaleia spoke.

"Finally. I am glad that beast is gone and will not darken these halls again."

"Yes, indeed," echoed Euphrosyne. "He is gone at last."

"We have waited long for your freedom from his tyranny."

Thaleia spoke in support yet her lips set in a forlorn line.

"For you, perhaps, it is freedom." Aglaia frowned, fine creases marring the Grace's forehead. "But War will now go unchecked. Without Love to bring balance, War goes unbridled. What will happen to both realms if Ares has no one to call him to account?"

Aphrodite bowed her head. "We must pray Zeus, Hera and the Council of Ages are strong enough to keep War from destroying all the realms with violence."

"Oh, mercy." Euphrosyne held a hand to her forehead. "They could not control him within your alliance - they will not be able to without Love. This is a catastrophe."

She exhaled in a sharp gasp as Thaleia poked her in the ribs. "I mean, Father Zeus will have to curb his son, will he not?" Euphrosyne gave an uneasy giggle and looked away.

"Do not quiet her." Aphrodite tossed the empty cup to the floor. "Euphrosyne speaks the truth."

Aphrodite met the gazes of her Graces, her turquoise eyes filled with both grief and fear. "What is to become of Love? Without War to give me strength, I become mired in turmoil. Without Ares to abet my courage, I am lost in an emotional tide. Without him to lend me balance, I cannot walk across the waters. I will sink within the depths and flail until I drown."

Scalding tears began anew. "I am lost without him, and yet, it was by my own hand that I have cut loose the only anchor I have ever known."

"Princess." Euphrosyne reached for her. "We are here for you. We will not let you go into the dark depths."

"You are here for me." Aphrodite clutched at the hands of all three women, drawing them to her.

"Has this news reached the ears of the Council?" Aglaia stroked Aphrodite's back.

"No. No, nor has it been whispered anywhere in the Greater Realm save for Athos. It is between Ares and myself and no other." Aphrodite paused, her lips trembling. "Except for Niala, for she was witness to this ugliness."

"Oh, dear." Thaleia bit her fingertip.

Aphrodite raised her eyes to meet those of her trusted friend. "I had forgotten you like her."

"It is not that," Thaleia answered quickly. "I just wonder…."

"What Ares will do with her? I, too, wonder." There came the image of Ares holding Niala to him, murmuring into her ear, caressing her, offering tender kisses to her right before Aphrodite's very eyes. "He will make her his wife."

Aphrodite spoke with a monotone, for into the maelstrom of heartache and regret came brittle cold anger. It brought her up short, as if dashed by icy water, as if submerged in an underground spring that fed her with a fresh crisp infusion of insight.

She breathed deeply and pushed the women away to climb from her bedstead. Defeat was replaced by fury. The Graces drew back as a whole, staring at her, for the transformation was lightning fast and alarming. The red blotches and swollen lids smoothed away to the perfect pale shimmering beauty that sent both man and beast into a frenzy. Gone was pathos and self-recrimination.

Revenge was exposed.

Somewhere in Love's Realm, Nemesis responded to her mistress. The Graces could see Nemesis filling Aphrodite as the spring rains swell the riverbanks. Vengeance oozed from Aphrodite's chest as it flooded throughout her like a raw wound. Euphrosyne pressed her fists to her mouth to stifle her cry while Thaleia and Aglaia came to their feet, unsure of Aphrodite's next move.

Aglaia went to her mistress and touched her arm. "What are you thinking?"

Aphrodite's ocean eyes held a devious glint as she answered in a steady voice, "Ares would form a new alliance with one such as this priestess? One untried and powerless in our realm? She will burn alive if she dares step into the fiery hell that marks Ares' path. He will be alone with her blood on his hands. He will have nothing, while I...."

She paused and gave them a chilling smile. "I will have Victory."

"What do you mean?" Aglaia wrapped her fingers around Aphrodite's wrist. She could feel the pounding of Aphrodite's pulse, the exhilaration tensing her limbs. It was not a good sign for the future.

"If Ares is not to father Victory, then there is another who will."

"Do not be hasty," pleaded Thaleia. "Ares cannot intend to

form a union with Niala. He adores you. You are his beloved mate."

"This will pass, Mistress, like all other quarrels you and he have." Euphrosyne wrung her hands together. "He will forgive you."

"Forgive? It is not for him to forgive. It is I who should forgive him, and I will not." Aphrodite's tone was unrelenting. "He seeks to make her a goddess. Is that not proof enough that he wanted our union to end all along? He intended for me to discover his duplicity so I would be the one to forswear our alliance, allowing him to create a new one."

"No, Princess." Thaleia shook her head. "No, it did not seem that way to me. You must rest, for this strain has undone your mind."

"What is this? You accuse me of madness?"

"It is not my intention to accuse you of such a thing."

"Enough." Aphrodite brought her hand up, palm out, a gesture meant to bring them to silence. "I have made up my mind. I will seek another to father Victory, but I want no word of this spoken outside these walls."

"Anteros," began Euphrosyne. "I should summon Anteros. Right now."

"No. You will not tell him of this, or I will inflict a terrible punishment on all of you."

Aphrodite whirled upon them, her eyes blazing. Never had the Graces seen her behave in such a manner. Never had she made such dire threats to anyone in her household. Distraught, they stared at her as if she were possessed and knew not what to say to soothe her.

"Princess, please." Aglaia reached for Aphrodite. "If you do not wish Anteros to know of this, so be it."

"No one is to know until I am ready to birth Victory."

"Fine." Thaleia gave her sisters an arched look that said do not argue. "Whatever you want, Princess. We are your Graces, your servants. We do as you bid."

The storm abated as fast as it arose and Aphrodite smiled. It was as if a rainbow crowned the sky and relief was thick in the chamber.

"Let me prepare you a bath." Euphrosyne smiled with forced brightness. "For it will make you feel better."

"A bath." Aphrodite nodded. "Yes, a bath would be good."

"Yes, a bath," agreed Aglaia.

"And lay out my best gown, for tomorrow I will visit the Forge God."

"What?" All three Graces froze in place.

"Hephaestos. He loathes Ares and he will not refuse me."

"Aaack." Thaleia could not even speak to the folly, but only choke and turn away into a coughing fit.

"He will not refuse, Mistress," Aglaia murmured, trying to keep an even tone. "Hephaestos is deeply stricken by your beauty and would do anything to lie abed with you."

"Hephaestos will be overjoyed to accept my proposal." Calm had returned to Aphrodite and she smiled. "It is appropriate, is it not, that Ares' nemesis will father Victory?"

"It is ironic, to be certain." Thaleia stared at her mistress, fear leaping into her eyes. Ares would not take this well.

"Actually, it is true of all the immortals," giggled Euphrosyne. "They would all give their most precious possessions to bed you, including the females, if truth were told, which is rare. However much I detest Ares, he is the only one who speaks with absolute honesty."

"Honesty that draws blood with its sharp edge," said Aglaia. "Would you rather not have a honeyed tongue wagging at you than to be wounded within an inch of your life?"

"Sweet lies over brutal truth?" Euphrosyne frowned. "I would have lies to soften my bed, for what harm can it cause?"

"Ares can be brutal both in bed and out, yet there is no other who can hold me with as much tenderness and care. I would take his truth over anyone else's dishonesty." Aphrodite's face had further paled as her intention collided with her desires. "But I cannot rescind my declaration. Instead, I will go to Hephaestos to spin a tale of infatuation and invite him to taste Love's delights."

"I fear this is a perilous idea, Princess. The rivalry between Ares and Hephaestos is well known, an age old grudge that may serve to destroy what small amount of civility is kept in Council."

Aphrodite nodded, deep in thought. "It is true and I am at the root of that grudge, this I know well. But there is no other who would fly directly in Ares' face. It is not enough that I would choose one, but there must be motive behind it for him to agree. Hephaestos has long desired me and that, paired with his hatred for Ares, will propel him into this union."

"How can good come of this when it is a betrayal?" Aglaia gripped the foot of the bedstand. "Lord Hephaestos is decent and kind and does not deserve this treatment."

"There is no betrayal, Aglaia. My alliance with War is done and I shall be truthful with Hephaestos of my motive." She turned away and mumbled, "If he should ask."

"In any case, this will cause an uprising such as we have never seen."

"Nonsense. Hephaestos will have what he has always wanted and I will have Victory." Staring off to the horizon, where the azure blue of the ocean met the faded blue of the sky, Aphrodite smiled to herself. "Do not worry, good Sisters. Ares is preoccupied with Niala and will scarce notice my absence. His arrogance will dictate all is well in his realm and I shall not destroy that mirage."

SEVEN

"What is it you want?" Hephaestos glanced up from his workbench but continued to dig through a pile of scrap metals scattered across the surface. "Speak or get out. Preferably out."

Aphrodite took a steadying breath and gave the Forge god a brilliant smile. To him, she would appear unruffled by his rudeness. She would not let him see his careless response to her gentle greetings deeply cut. She expected something different from one who fought War for her love, perhaps a certain gladness of heart? At the least, civility.

How wrong could she have been? From the first sight of his island, she felt a dreadful chill down her back. She did not know where to find Hephaestos, therefore, she arrived at the front entrance like all other visitors. She stood transfixed by a towering mountainous inferno behind the castle, watching the crown of the mount belch forth rings of black smoke.

The ground shook from its rumblings and the air was thick with an acrid scent that sickened her. Beneath her feet, she could feel the grit of fine ash spewing from the volcano. Trailing down the sides from the raw edges at the top were dull black tracks, like exhausted tears dried on the sorrowing face of a woman.

She almost turned away.

As she now looked upon Hephaestos, she could see the resemblance between him and his volcanic island. His face was rugged, like the terrain, freckled from heat, and creased from frowning into the sparks of his anvil.

His nose was crooked, appearing as if the hammer he used had flown up and hit him. Bright blue eyes squinted from beneath shaggy brows that matched the sunset red of his hair, worn long, braided and tied with a leather thong. His untrimmed beard was the same shade of red with streaks of yellow.

He wore a sleeveless leather jerkin and apron, both heavily pitted and stained. His arms were thick and corded, freckled like his face. His hands were big and calloused. She could see the grime of the forge was ground into his fingers and beneath his nails. He always seemed indifferent about his grooming, even when joining the Council - a dismissal of their power, perhaps?

Aphrodite admired his courage in the collective face of Council's arrogance.

His height was well above hers, and yet, not towering. On the outside, he seemed like the mountain, a solid, immovable mass. Beneath the surface, he seethed with the same sort of molten liquid waiting to burst forth like the volcano outside his door.

Hephaestos had not the beauty of Ares, nevertheless, he was not loathsome to her. She could readily see the gifts he would pass to a child between them and it pleased her.

She forgave him his disrespect and said, "I have come to ask a favor."

"You?" Although his tone was incredulous, Hephaestos kept working. "What bauble do you seek to further muddle the minds of men?"

His inference brought a flush to her pale skin. It was not a mere suggestion that she seduced mankind with deliberate intention - he flatly accused her of it.

"It is not toys I am after, but something of deeper value."

He raised his head to meet her gaze, directing an unfriendly glare at her. "I have nothing here for you."

Aphrodite opened her mouth to retort. So unkind - he did even not know what she wanted. As she paused she saw a glimmer of pain behind the brittle edges. Exquisite pain, illustrated throughout the castle. If the isle seemed dirty and primitive, the inside revealed the true nature of its owner.

When she stepped beyond the dull sheen of the outer doors into the entryway, a collage of precious metals greeted her. The flooring and walls were lined with thin sheets of bronze delicately hammered into complicated designs.

The ceiling was a giant sun made of gold and silver, its rays reaching to the furthest corners of the room. Aphrodite stepped with care in her sandals for fear of damaging the soft metal, but felt no give in the floor. When she glanced back, it was perfect, unscuffed by her feet.

It was the only room spared from clutter. As she made her way through the many chambers searching for Hephaestos, she came across astonishing treasures left in heaps about the edges of the rooms. At times the piles encroached upon the walk space and all she could find was a path to take her from one place to the next.

Warm and sparkling gemstones lay amongst plain rock and bits of cloth. Statues of the finest marble were draped with strange trappings. Coins, bolts of cloth shot with gold and silver, spools of thin wires lay mixed with pots of rare pigments, and everywhere, chunks, pieces, piles and piles of metals.

Every inch of wall and ceiling was decorated in every room. There was no balance, nor even an appearance of harmony. Wild spirals of colored gems spread across one wall and over the ceiling, while another shone with iridescent flames created out of layers of shimmering metallic tiles. It was wondrous, yet maddening - no form, no order, no reason.

Aphrodite at last found Hephaestos in the bowels of the castle in his workshop, behind a table hewn from a gigantic tree. Across it was spread a similar chaos. Amidst the stacks were sketches on thin slices of parchment. In the hidden corners of the room were partially erected ideas, half built and then abandoned, illuminated by the white-hot fire of the forge centered in the room.

And so it is with the Forge god, himself, Aphrodite thought. Remote and forbidding on the outside, abundant and exotic on the inside. "Do I offend you with my presence, Lord Hephaestos? It is not my intention."

"You have never paid me a visit before." He spoke with abruptness, but his tone was not as sharp.

"I had no reason until now."

"So it would seem your mission is an important one. What is it you have to say?"

As she met his bright gaze, Aphrodite felt the heat of guilt pressing down on her just as surely as the fires of the forge. The hot pungent scent of melted ore burned the inside of her nose and mouth, just as turning away from Ares burned her heart. For a moment, she faltered, for Hephaestos did not deserve to be caught between them. While red flames danced with the high shadows, the hiss of the bellows carried on behind them, Aphrodite hardened her resolve.

She would not turn back.

"Could we find another place to talk, Lord Hephaestos? I am uncomfortable here and it is a delicate matter I wish to discuss."

Startled, Hephaestos laid aside a large chunk of shiny black rock and made his way from behind the table. "I should offer you a place to rest, and refreshment. Please forgive me."

With stumbling steps, Hephaestos led Aphrodite to a back staircase and upwards to emerge into a much cooler chamber. Narrow window casings allowed for a limited view of the volcano and bits of blue sky smudged with wisps of soot. Through the openings, she could hear birdsong, but it was unlike any she listened to before.

These birds were raucous and hoarse; there was no melody about them at all. The birds of her isle happily twittered and chirped. When song came from their throats, it burst forth with throbbing joy.

Aphrodite gazed about the room and was more than pleasantly surprised to find the amount of litter to be far less. There were low couches covered in glimmering fabrics and intricately carved wooden chairs with cushions. A thick rug woven of goat hair dyed with yellows and oranges spread beneath her feet.

Where flooring was exposed, it was of the same bronze tiling as in the rest of the castle. The walls were decorated with splashes of color, though not as gaudy as the outer chambers. Through an arched doorway, another chamber could be seen. It held more furniture and a bed made of gold at the center.

She could not take her eyes from it. It was a thing of exquisite beauty, a shining vessel that rose from the floor like a ship at sea, with gossamer golden sails that reached upward. That would be the setting in which Victory would be conceived. She was certain of it.

Her doubts dissolved; confidence revived her. She would bear Victory with Hephaestos as father - one honest and forthright, who deserved to have as his daughter the champion of the mortal world.

Hephaestos stood before her awkward and embarrassed now that they were within his private quarters. "May I offer you something cool to drink?"

"Yes, of course." Aphrodite cast a keen eye toward him as she daintily lowered herself to a couch

In the light, he appeared filthier than he had in the shadows, with streaks of dirt and sweat on his face. His shoulders, chest and arms were wide and strong from his work, but beneath his tunic were his scrawny crippled legs encased in soiled leather. The scarred knee boots appeared too big and the cause of his lurching gait.

She noticed he did not sit. Instead, he called out once in a guttural tone that brought a small brown being scurrying into the chamber. This new one said nothing. He looked about with sharp eyes, left quickly, and returned with a tray of fruit juices.

Accepting the drink with grace, Aphrodite set it on one of the tables without a sip. "Lord Hephaestos, I beg your indulgence as I explain my visit. It is not an easy tale to tell, and I…I…." She dabbed delicately at the corners of her eyes with a small square of embroidered linen. "I do not know how to begin."

"Do not rush." His tone was gruff. "I am in no hurry."

"Thank you." Aphrodite gave a slight sniff, the cloth pressed beneath her nose. "It is best, I think, to simply state it outright."

"Yes, I agree."

"I have had a dream, a vision of a child. A daughter whose name is Victory." Aphrodite paused at his sudden rasping inhale. Victory would come as a surprise to many, she thought. Many, indeed.

"It is her time to come into the world and I am to be her mother." She watched Hephaestos from beneath her lashes. His face remained impassive and his eyes suspicious. "You are to be her father."

His skin mottled with a deep red stain as he clenched and unclenched his fingers. His mouth opened but nothing came out. After what seemed an eternity, he turned away. With his back to her, he said, "I have already tasted the cruelty Love has to offer and I do not wish for it again. Leave me, Aphrodite, before I become angry."

"I do not jest." Aphrodite went to him. "I offer myself to you for Victory's sake."

"I do not accept."

Although Hephaestos protested, he did not ask again for her to leave. He also did not look at her. In this, Aphrodite saw hope, but deep in her heart, she was scornful. There was not a single one of the Ages, male or female, who would not indulge with Love if they could. She need only be persistent and Hephaestos would do as she bid.

"It is beyond us, Hephaestos. Victory is strong. She has commanded the Fates to allow her birth. We cannot refuse."

"You cannot, but I can."

"But why? I offer you Love's sweet haven and a daughter of such valor the world will never be the same. Yet you would refuse me out of hand?"

"I am not as stupid as the Council would have you believe, Ocean Princess." He completed a dragging circle of the room to face her once again, yet she had to turn to see him. "If it is true Victory is to be yours, then why not hold Ares the Destroyer as her father? You have taken him to husband and he is the rightful heir to your bed."

"So he is. And I have sworn to be honest with you, even though I would rather spin a sad tale than speak the truth." Aphrodite held the handkerchief to her lips and gave a small cough that could be mistaken for a sob. "Ares has refused me."

Hephaestos snorted. "He would not."

"He has - unless Victory rides with War and I cannot allow that. She yearns to give the mortal world a chance to overcome the bloodletting, to let Love conquer rather than Death. If winning in battle is possible, there will be no end to the suffering, for pure Victory will be an irresistible reward for bloodshed."

Hephaestos stared at Aphrodite, mouth slightly open, his eyes wide with naked yearning. When he spoke, it was with difficulty. "I do not believe Ares would refuse. He could tell you anything and do as he pleased."

"What he does not believe is that I would come to you."

"He knows you are here?" Sharpness returned to Hephaestos' voice.

With downcast gaze, Aphrodite examined her pink nails. "He

knows I will not have him as father to Victory." She rose from the couch and stood before him.

"But he does not know you have chosen me?"

"No, Lord Hephaestos. I thought it would be best for him to discover that after instead of before." Turquoise eyes wide, she smiled wantonly at him.

With deliberate hesitation, Aphrodite reached out to stroke the red-gold hairs along Hephaestos arm, then down to the back of his hand. He flinched at her touch.

"Why me?" His breath was choked as he tried to speak.

"I wish Victory to have the gift of creativity, of patience and focus. I wish her to look beyond the visible into the depths, to see the beauty that is buried beneath the surface. It is what you do Hephaestos and it is a gift you can give our daughter."

"Our daughter." The words filled him with longing.

"Yes, our daughter. Do this, Hephaestos, and you will forever be crowned with glory to have given the world such a creature as Victory."

"I feel Love's spell cast over me and I can scarce think. But I do not believe it is worth my life, even considering the respect you offer me from the world."

"What do you mean, your life? Your life will be uplifted. You will be Victory's father."

"I will surrender my breath to the great blade, Amason, should I make love with you."

"Amason? Ares would not raise Amason against you."

"No? He scarce restrains himself now. To have just cause would delight him beyond reason."

"Ares is not so reckless he would forfeit his standing in the Council to...to...." Aphrodite flushed. "To make a point."

"Over the beauteous Aphrodite? Ares would fight to the death. I think it is time for you to leave me."

"Hephaestos, please." Taking his hand, Aphrodite held him to her side. "Ares need not even know of this, if that is your condition."

"I want to continue living. Have ever you seen Amason in action? It can cleave a man in half with one stroke. A god, as well." Hephaestos extracted his fingers from her grasp.

"Amason cannot harm the immortal cast, for it is a mortal weapon. We live on, always - sometimes even to our regret."

"Fair Aphrodite, innocent even yet. Or should I say naïve to the way of the Ages. Who can blame you, for you did not have the same harsh upbringing as the rest of us." Hephaestos spoke with heavy sarcasm. "But you did have the benefit of War's education, did you not? In all manner of his ways."

His eyes sparked hatred. "It is very tempting to me to see what seduction you learned by his hand, and yet - do I wish to die? No."

"He cannot kill you. Hurt you, bloody you, but not destroy you."

"Now you are truly foolish, for still you do not listen. Have you asked him of Amason's origin? Why it exists? A one of a kind weapon that is lusted after by the Ages and Man alike. Why does he guard it as jealously as he guards you?"

"Does he? I pay little attention to what he does outside." Aphrodite's smile was coy. "When he is away from me."

"Have you never noticed how he threatens all of us with our very lives if we so much as glance after you? Or that he has the power to carry out his threats?" Hephaestos' limp was exaggerated as he crossed the room to point out toward the volcano.

"It was I - yes, I - who gave him this ability. Cursed Ares. He is a bully, a coward, and a menace to all of us, yet we have no way to protect ourselves should he go on a rampage."

"I do not understand." Aphrodite sat down on the edge of one low chaise, fingers toying with the satin brocade.

"It was long before your time, when giants and their beasts roamed Earth, fighting us for control. Mortals quaked with fear whenever their footsteps came near, for the giants showed no regard whatsoever for humans. The giants would as gladly snuffed them all out to claim more territory for themselves, destroying all of us as well, if they could.

"We represented the mortals and, therefore, we were worthless. They sought to imprison us forever in darkness and, if they had, this earth would be in shambles. To fight them, I went into the very depths of the volcano you see out there and retrieved its heart. With that, I created Amason."

Hephaestos stared at the ring of smoke around the crown of the mount and was silent for a moment. His expression was a study in conflict, a mixture of regret and triumph.

"There was only one of us strong enough to take Amason into battle against the giants. Only one who was willing to sacrifice himself for the pure lust of bloodletting. His arrogance was insurmountable, insufferable, but still he went forth. Ares the Destroyer killed many and imprisoned the worst in the bowels of the earth. Some joined us in peace. At least one you are familiar with."

Aphrodite shrugged a delicate shoulder, but in her heart, Aphrodite was certain of the name Hephaestos would say.

"Eos, the Morning Sun. She was Ares' reward. He was given Dawn, to mark the dawn of a new age."

Aphrodite nodded, but spoke through clenched teeth. "I have heard this story but I did not believe him."

"Therefore, you dismissed it because you were jealous of Eos?"

"Because it is told differently by others."

"Most have no idea where Amason sprang from or the true damage it can do. They only know Ares is dangerous."

Hephaestos sighed. "It was an embarrassment to Zeus to have Ares succeed where he failed. Have you not wondered at the bitterness Ares holds for the Ages? They let his courageous deeds sink into oblivion to soothe their own egos.

"Not even his own father will acknowledge his courage in battle. And, I must admit, I feel the same. I created the sword that allowed Ares to wreak havoc yet there is no mention of my craftsmanship. In that respect, we share a small piece of each other."

"Even so, this has nothing to do with my request. I do not care what took place then."

"You should care." Hephaestos plucked a bronze vase from a table and stared at the intricate design etched upon it. "You miss the implication. Amason, and therefore Ares, has the power to kill immortals."

"That seems impossible."

"Alas, it is true."

"But if he could kill an immortal, why does he not? He detests his father."

Hephaestos replaced the vase in its original position. "He despises all those at Council, but there are laws. To kill one of our own is to suffer a horrible penance. However, if I were to take his wife in lust, there would be nothing that could stop him. I would surely be dispatched into Hades' waiting arms."

"This is impossible." Aphrodite stared at Hephaestos, her

pale complexion tinged with pink. "Why did you let him keep Amason? Why did anyone let him keep it?"

"And who, do you suppose, would take it from him? He was to return it to the volcano, but he did not."

"It is like Ares to be stubborn."

"It is like my brother to want power over all."

"What shall we do now?" Rising, Aphrodite drifted around the room, feeling stifled and very warm. "If this tale is true and known by all, then who shall I find amongst the immortals brave enough to father Victory?"

Hephaestos watched her move through his possessions with such grace it brought an ache to his chest. Never would he have thought that the fair Aphrodite would choose him - the crippled and imperfect one, the butt of many cruel jokes, the least favored of all in the Council - above all to bring forth such a gift as Victory.

How many would suffer the torments of the damned to lie with the beauteous Aphrodite? How many would willingly die to bed Eternal Love?

Who would be coward enough to turn away? Hephaestos knew the answer and it caused pain deep in his heart.

"Do not chastise yourself over this." Aphrodite turned to him, her face drawn. "I understand. Ares is a terrible force and there is no one with courage enough to go against him. We have already witnessed that."

Hephaestos' features caved, as if he was suddenly stripped naked before her. It was almost more than Aphrodite could bear to see and when he spoke, it was in a voice filled with shame.

"Never has anyone loved me. Not even my mother, who detested me upon sight because I was not perfect. I was cast aside then and so it has always been."

He twisted his fingers together and stared at them. "Standing before me now is all I have ever longed for, all I have ever wanted. You offer me the greatest gift of my life, still I have not the courage to accept and sacrifice myself on Love's altar."

"Dear Hephaestos." Aphrodite came to his side in a rush and placed her hands over his. Her heart swelled with affection and all she thought to do was to ease the anguish in his gaze.

"There is one way Ares could not seek revenge, for I know what you say is true. He would kill you. He would kill anyone, even though he...." She caught herself with a deep breath. "Ares is jealous though he takes no care to remain faithful to me."

Hephaestos could only nod. A spark of hope rose with an intensity that left him speechless, for in Aphrodite's eyes there was desire, and it was for him.

"I will forsake Ares and take you to husband. He will not be able to lift a hand against our alliance. He will be forced to honor it."

Hephaestos sank down to the couch, Aphrodite still clutching at his fingers. He gaped up at her as the world swam before his eyes and his breath came with difficulty.

"You would do that for me?" he whispered.

"Yes." Aphrodite leaned down and kissed him.

It was as if a butterfly swept gossamer wings across his lips.

"Consider it done, if you accept." Aphrodite kissed him again.

Hephaestos did not want to know what was behind her declaration. He did not want to consider the consequences of this act. He wanted only to see what was before him at that exact moment, to revel in triumph.

"I accept." His eyes filled with tears. "I accept."

EIGHT

"Niala," A stern voice called to her. "Wake up." She was shaken while the voice went on. "You dream."

Niala knew she dreamed. She did not need to be told it was so. She was caught somewhere between dozing and wakefulness, aware of her body yet unable to move her limbs. Her eyelids would not open on command but stayed stubbornly shut, providing a dark background for the strange collage of images.

"I know." Her eyes were sealed shut. "Are you here or there?"

Here being the bleak world of Athos. There, a place of green growing things and long ribbons of shining water. She lived in both places, one foot in each world. Here. There. Which call was strongest? Where was she supposed to be?

"Here, as you are." The voice was gruffer, the touch more insistent. "Come awake, for you cry out."

"Not me. It is the child who cries. I hear, but I cannot see."

She held out her hand as if she would calm the child, but the babe was silent now. Niala's hand dropped to her belly and she smiled, for she had a secret. Should she keep her secret? Everything was quiet except for the crackling of firewood. It popped and snapped in a roaring bonfire as dancers circled it, caught up in the pounding of drums.

Drums. The beat was familiar, so familiar she wanted to be part of the dance. She ached to be with them, twisting and turning with the ecstasy of Earth's rhythm. It reverberated within her, feeding her own rhythms, joining her with Gaea.

Gaea.

Mother Earth.

Home.

Najahmara.

"Niala."

The beauty of the green Earth dissolved into mist and became thick with smoke and fire and the stench of burned flesh. Tortured screams echoed along once serene streets and terror reigned.

Empty eyes. A child.

Her child.

Crushed and bleeding.

"Niala."

She was shaken harder and her eyes flew open. A ghastly specter stood over her, its rear to the hearth, its face in shadows. Niala scrabbled backward to flee from the hand that clutched her. She could smell blood and filth upon the creature, could hear its wheezing breath, and feel the cold settle upon her as Death took form.

"No, no, do not - my children!" As her eyes focused, Niala saw the glint of metal beyond the specter's shoulder and drew in a shuddering breath. It was the icy form of Amason above the mantel.

It was no apparition that tormented her.

Ares had returned from his travels.

"You frightened me." She had fallen asleep on a low chaise positioned before the fire. As Niala sat up, feeling disheveled and out of sorts, her wrap slid to the floor. "I asked you to give me warning rather than just appear."

Ares bent to retrieve the shawl. "What more warning can I give when you do not hear me speak? I called to you but you were in the grips of a nightmare."

Niala frowned, trying to recall the details. "There was a child crying."

"It was nothing. A dream." Ares knew she had heard Phobos.

The boy shrieked upon the sight of his own father and wept, panicked at what next would befall him. That he was no better prepared disturbed Ares, particularly since it was clear Phobos' passage into his power was near. That Deimos shirked his duties with the boy was equally disturbing.

"Is it Deimos? What has happened?"

Ares appeared the same as always, indifferent and taciturn, answering with as few words as possible. As Niala peered up at him, she could see tension in his stance.

Ares looked with keen interest at her. Niala's eyes were still droopy from sleep, her face soft. He would kiss her that moment, make love to her and forget his aggravations, except for the filth that covered him.

That, and the way she asked after his son. Ares did not like the tone she used, for the breathless concern spoke far more than she intended.

"Why do you ask after Deimos?"

"You called him by name in such a way that I...." Niala touched her tongue to her lips. "I thought something had happened."

"And what would happen to him? He is immortal."

"He can still be wounded."

"So he can. In more ways than one."

He was bothered by Deimos' failure to instruct Phobos. Upon his arrival at Athos, Ares had observed the boy's progress and found it lacking. Deimos was too lenient, allowing the boy more freedom than he deserved. The boy was running wild. Perhaps it was time for Phobos to train with Priapos, the Centaur.

"Hmm." As Ares handed the shawl back to Niala, another thought occurred. He scowled at her. "It is you."

"Me?" Startled at his ferocity, Niala clutched the wrap to her chest. "Have I done something to anger you?"

"Yes." His voice was flat and ugly.

"What, then? I do as you ask, I try to be a good companion, better than...." She flicked her gaze beyond him. "Better than last time. What have I done wrong?"

"There is nothing simple in my world, Niala. No right or wrong. Everything just exists for its own purpose. Everything." Ares spoke slowly, drawing out the words. "Involves pain and disappointment, or worse."

"Is that it, then? Have I disappointed you?"

"Disappointed? No. Betrayed, Niala. It is always about betrayal." Ares straightened. "How often does Deimos visit you?"

"Deimos?" Niala frowned, for though weariness roughened the timber of his voice, there was now the added flavor of suspicion. "Why do you ask?"

"He has been here to see you?"

"He has visited once." Niala regretted the admission the moment the words were out of her mouth. Ares stared down at her, his lips in a tight line, his gaze narrowed.

"Do not look at me that way." Niala rose, so close to him he could surely hear her heart pound. She could smell the sourness of battle on his clothing and see the trails of dried blood and entrails, but she did not flinch. "I have done nothing wrong."

"And yet," Ares bent close to her, his tone low and dangerous. "Deimos behaves oddly. He is distracted, as if his heart is somewhere else. Perhaps even in my bed."

"Only you would think of such things."

"No, Deimos thinks them as well. Pray I do not discover you and he have consorted with each other."

"Stop." Outraged, Niala pushed past Ares to stare at the broken mantel. It brought to mind the four ruined stones marking the graves of those so long gone only she and Ares remembered them.

"You offer me no comfort, you do nothing to ease my sorrow. You force me into a place of such confusion I fear I will go mad. Without Deimos I would have been eaten alive by both past and future."

"He should not provide such relief to you."

"It was once. Only once that we shared...." Niala caught her breath. "A meal. We shared a meal. That is all. And there is no one else since Thaleia left save for you, and you choose to make me more miserable each day."

Gathering the wrap around her, Niala stood nearer the flames for his shadow cast a sudden chill. "Especially since you imprison me within these walls."

"You are not prisoner here."

"So you have stated before, yet I cannot unlock the doors. I cannot go outside and breathe the air or look upon the landscape. I cannot enter into the corridors of Athos for those doors are also bolted. If that is not imprisonment, then I do not know the meaning."

"My intention is only to keep you safe."

"You fear I would throw myself over the rail again?"

"It is my concern, yes."

"I was stricken with grief, filled with guilt, I lost my only kin and from my hand so many others died. Yes, then, I could scarce stand to live on."

"Listen to how you rant. How can I be certain you would not attempt to ruin yourself or something equally as spiteful?"

"Because I tell you so, but you do not hear me. There is no trust between us. Is it any wonder I fled these walls before?"

"Twice." Ares spoke with grief. "Both times you would sacrifice your life to leave me. I will not allow a third opportunity."

"You want me to stay with you and yet you will not let me ease your pain or even speak of it to me. You offer nothing of yourself."

"I give what I can."

"You give your body. You give sex as if it is a magical potion to heal all wounds, inside and out." Niala turned to face him. "I tell you, it is not the answer to every illness."

"It is all I have."

"No, it is all you are willing to part with." She pointed with an accusing finger. "You think it is the sum of all relationships. Deimos is your loyal servant. He would give his life for you, but do you see that? No, you think the worst of him."

Niala inhaled sharply. "And the worst of me."

"I cannot afford to trust anyone." Ares sank down onto the couch and stared into the flames.

"Not even your son?"

"Not even my son. You ask me to believe you will not harm yourself, but you refuse to embrace the power that fights for life." He held his breath for a moment before releasing it in a heavy sigh. "Nearly two full months have passed since the night your immortality surfaced. I have waited patiently for you to accept your role and yet you refuse."

"No, I do not."

"Niala." His tone calmed. "I do not speak of sex, though it is my way of healing. In that respect, you are generous and bring me what tranquility I am allowed, but there is something beyond that."

"Something you already have with Eternal Love." Niala twisted her fingers around the ends of the shawl, unhappy with the twinge of jealousy that flared within her.

"Had. It is no more."

"But you are gone so much, I thought you to be at her side."

"No. She has forsaken our alliance." A wretched expression crossed his face, quickly covered with a derisive snort.

"Her actions make it all the more important for you to embrace Rebellion. You are the spark, the wildness that rises from despair and triumphs over the profane. You must accept this. Without you...." He shook his head, his black gaze unblinking upon her.

"I try, but I do not feel it here." Niala pressed a palm to her breast. "I am empty."

"You must try harder." Ares gripped her elbow until she winced. "We will form our own union once you have accepted your place within the Greater Realm. Until then, I am more vulnerable than you know."

Niala jerked free of his hand. "I do not know how."

"I showed you the way."

"You showed me what you want me to be. You impose a task on me that is impossible. I am a simple priestess who longs for her people and nothing more, in spite of your desire. All I want is to go home."

Ignoring her plea, Ares slapped his palm against his thigh. "You hide behind that identity because you are afraid."

"I am not afraid." Niala clenched her jaw. "I just want to go home."

"No, I suppose you are not afraid, though you should be. When you are gripped by Rebellion - as you are right this moment - you are fearless."

"Take me back to Najahmara. It is where I belong."

"Do you feel the strength inside when you fight against me? You have always rebelled, even from the beginning."

"It was Kulika."

"Before that."

A strange glint came into his eyes and Niala shivered. The air grew colder in spite of the heat from the hearth. "When I was captured and brought to you for sacrifice."

"Before this life." Ares reached for her hand, unwinding

her fingers from the cloth until he could cradle them in his palm, his other hand covering hers. "When we were Anyal and Ilya. You rebelled even then. You fought me." His words trailed off as he stared at her. "You ran away. Again and again."

Niala met his gaze. "Why?"

She was afraid to ask, did not truly want to know, and yet she did, for she dreamed of dark things, of caves and pain and blood. Of loss and being lost. Of love so fierce it drew her back again and again only to leave once more. "Why did I run away?"

"Because you were Rebellion waiting to be born."

"That is not why." Niala squeezed his hand. "There is another reason."

"Yes - that reason is the wound that pierces my soul yet today."

His eyelashes flicked downward, as if he did not want her to see his thoughts. "It is my deepest shame, my worst regret." He released her hand and still avoided her gaze.

Niala was now frantic to understand. She could feel Ares withdrawing from her. He had already told far more than he was willing She could see that in the sadness in his face, in the lines etched upon his forehead and around his mouth. "But, why? Why did I run away?"

To that, he merely grunted as he sank into his own reverie.

A lull fell between them as smoke curled from the dying fire and the embers glowed red into the room. No torches or candles lit the corners and the chamber darkened as the silence lengthened. Ares leaned forward, elbows balanced on his knees, fingertips pressed to his forehead.

Niala lifted her gaze to the shining silver shaft of Amason and wished that swords could tell tales. Therein she might discover its master's secrets.

"Why is your sword unsheathed?" Niala's voice echoed into the recesses of the room. It was an idle thought that leaped to mind in the void and was spoken before she could stop herself.

Ares lifted his head to stare up at the sword.

"Why do you have your weapon unsheathed? It has only occurred to me that always, warriors keep their swords encased in leather so the edges do not dull." She waved toward the great sword. "This one is without cover."

"Amason is like no other. She has a soul of her own and does not like to be hidden from my eyes."

"She?"

"Yes. The Phallus of War." Ares' chuckle was grim. "The Fallacy of War. I am defended not by male-driven metal but by feminine spirit. Amason is my protector and to her I owe every defeat. I could never place her under wraps."

Rising, Ares moved past Niala to stroke the razor tip of the sword. Though he was filthy from battle, Amason was not, for she was wiped clean upon first arrival at Athos. "There, I have revealed something to you that no one else knows. Does your heart sing with my secret?"

The hint of sarcasm was not lost.

"Perhaps it does not sing, but at least it hums somewhat." Niala hesitated at Ares' slight smile, unwilling to break the small bond between them. If she would say no more, if she would kiss him instead, if she could look past the scars of battle and the stench of death, if she would go forward instead of backward, perhaps there was a future for her here at Athos.

"I am called to Najahmara." Her voice was just above a whisper. "I need to go home."

"Niala," Ares spoke with bone-depth weariness. "Let us not argue again."

She persisted in spite of the tightening of his mouth. "Since that night when Rebellion rose, my memories have returned. I realize now that I have not mourned my losses."

"Why can you not do that here? They are gone into spirit. You can commune with spirit from here as well as from there."

"I am tied to Earth. Yet I have not felt her beneath my feet for many months. All I have here is cold stone. I need to feel the soil, to touch the grasses, to breathe the scent of flowering bushes. I need to lie upon the ground where my loved ones are and then...."

Tears came to her eyes as she rose to her feet. "Only then can I truly let them go. Please."

"No."

"I will come back, I swear it. Please."

"No." He moved away from her, toward the bathing chamber doors.

"I will not stay here," Niala shouted after him. "You can try, but you cannot keep me. You have never been able to keep me."

Ares came to a halt at the entry, his voice floating back to her. "So, that little bit of cruelty is by design. I always knew it."

"You speak to me of cruelty? How dare you!" The image of four broken white stones haunted her and the bones of her beloved Layla as they scattered over the side of the ridge. "What you did on the plateau was beyond cruel - it was malicious. You intended to crush me."

"I was angry." He did not use his violence as an excuse. It was an explanation.

"Angry because I left or angry because I would not accept what you wanted me to be?"

"Both, and still, you do not accept what I say as truth."

"How can I when you use force to get what you want?"

"I have attempted to convince you in many ways but your stubbornness gets in the way."

"Then let me go home."

"Najahmara is not what it once was. To see it would only cause you more grief."

"It is not possible to cause more grief than I already feel. I have lost so much."

"Yes." Ares turned to face her. "There has been so much pain, but going back will not resolve it. The only thing that will ease your soul is to embrace Rebellion and become the goddess you were meant to be."

"If you let me go back, even for a little while, I will forgive you." Niala bit her lips, weighing her next words with care. "If you let me return to Najahmara - then, and only then - will I fully embrace the immortal side of myself." Her gaze did not waver. "Only then will I become what you want."

"I do not make bargains."

"Then you are more fool than not, for I swear, I will remain as I am for as long as you hold me."

"You would stay between the worlds to punish me?"

"Yes."

As Ares looked into Niala's determined eyes, his mouth twitched. She prickled with energy, raising the hairs along his arms and at the back of his neck, but she seemed unaware of the sparks she created. The glow that came upon them all as they cast outward with their power was on her face. He could fair hear the roar of the masses as they fought against their enemies, rebelling over the injustices of life.

He smiled.

"Do not gloat." Niala raised her fists as if to strike him. Rebellion lived.

Ares had to bite down to keep from laughing outright. "If you wish to return to Najahmara, I will not stop you."

"You lie to me, Ares?"

"No, I am sincere."

The sound of bolts being thrown, locks chucking, and wood creaking came from behind Niala, to each side, in the distance and from the bedchamber, until finally the sweep of cool, crisp spring air washed over her. Riding the wind was a fine mist of rain, the scent of salt laden with flowering mountain bushes and the musty corridors of Athos.

Niala whirled around to see every entry flung wide.

"There, you see?" Ares spoke behind her. "I no longer bar your way."

"Then you will take me home?" She completed her circle to face him.

"Oh, no." Wagging his finger at her, Ares smiled with wicked pleasure. "No. You must find your own way back to Najahmara."

"It is months by sea and years by land," Niala's voice caught.

"So it is." Ares nodded in solemn agreement. "So it is."

Without another word, he went into the bathing chamber.

Ares floated in the hot water, enjoying the flow over and under him, while steam rose in wispy curls to gather at the ceiling. Through half-closed eyes, he stared up at the naked and wanton ones who lay in shameless pleasure with each other.

Robust men and carnal women, orgasmic and sensual, all wound together so that it was a delightful puzzle to figure out who was making love to whom. Man to woman, woman to woman, or was it man to man? It was always curious the way it seemed to change, as if the art had life of its own.

Perhaps it did. Perhaps it was he that never changed. The frieze danced across the ceiling, mocking him. "Niala is right, I am more fool than not," he mumbled. He was too tired to care any longer.

Wearily, he climbed from the pool and dried himself with a linen cloth. If he was fortunate, sleep would visit him this night.

The blood was no more than a black shadow seeping from the broken head in the twilight. He held in his hand the rock that smashed open the tiny skull, the rock that was now marked with the same black blood. Unheeded, it ran down his fingers and arm and dripped onto his knee as he crouched next to it.

Feeling nothing, he could only stare with blind eyes at the small body at his feet. It had no face. A gash where the mouth should be, two holes for a nose, and misshapen eyes sloping to the sides of the head, that was all. No face. The body was twisted, the hairline low, the jaw sunken, the tiny fingers and toes webbed.

It was not human.

He did what he had to do.

The harsh sounds of his breathing rent the silent night, for no other creature stirred. There was no witness to his act, or to his hesitation as he listened to its thin cries. With one blow, he stopped the mewling, and now he watched its blood slow to a trickle and finally end.

Wearily, he turned away from it but could not go back into the cave, for there he could hear the frantic shrieks of his mate as she pleaded with him to give her back the babe.

Please, please, please, she howled, a keening wail that went on and on and on. He covered his ears, smearing the blood onto his face.

Stop, he roared. What is done is done. We will try again.

She crawled from the cave to the crumpled body of the babe and scooped it into her arms; her wailing grew louder still. No more...ahh...no more.

Yes, we must. We will try again.

I will not do this again.

He slapped her, leaving a handprint upon her cheek in the blood of her own child.

You will. I say you will.

She fell sobbing onto the ground, the babe beneath her, as if to protect it, but it was too late.

Ares woke with a jerk, eyes wide, staring into the darkness. Ilya's screams still echoed in his ears as she clutched the demon child to her breast.

Poor pathetic creature. Dead by his hand.

He could neither calm his pounding heart, nor stop the hot tears as they trickled from the corners of his eyes down into his hair. Niala murmured in her sleep, shifting restlessly, and brought one hand up to lie with palm cupped against his face.

He held it there for a moment, his fingers curled around hers, and thought how wicked - how very, very wicked - the Fates could be. Then he rose from bed and went to stand on the walkway and stare out at a thundering merciless sea.

NINE

Before the week was out, Aphrodite called the Graces to Hephaestos' palace and instructed them to prepare a wedding feast. Though they begged Aphrodite to return to her own isle to be bathed and dressed, their pleas fell on deaf ears.

Aphrodite knew if she left this strange bronze palace for her own sunny home, she would never return. She would lose all courage and Victory would be left waiting in the darkness for another who would birth her into the world.

Euphrosyne wept as the last cord of Aphrodite's golden girdle was tied around her pink chiton. "Princess, I beg you, do not do this. It is not right."

"I do what I must to bring forth Victory."

Though Aphrodite spoke with conviction, her complexion was paler than usual and without spark. Her gaze avoided meeting any of the three women who attended to her as the Graces exchanged worried glances over Aphrodite's bowed head.

"Truly, Princess, if you would only give Ares time to reconsider."

Thaleia felt most at fault over this turn of events for it was she who delivered the news of Niala into her mistress' hands. She paused to tuck a curl into the elaborate headdress, complete with a veil that would be attached at the crown. "He will abandon her like all the others and return to your side."

"He may wish to return to me but I will not have him," Aphrodite touched her fingers to the crown to steady it. "He has gone too far with his obsession. No, he will not give her up and to do any less is an insult to my honor."

"Even so." Aglaia frowned. "You need not rush into this with Hephaestos. Why must you have a union? Why not just take him to your bed?"

With difficulty, Aphrodite raised dulled eyes to her women. "Because he will not have me any other way."

"He cannot make those kind of demands on Eternal Love." Thaleia's tone was sharp.

"Dear Sister, he did not. He merely refused."

"Refused? He refused you?"

"Yes." Aphrodite paused to wet her lips. She could not tell them of Amason's power in the Greater Realm for she had sworn to Hephaestos she would not speak of it to anyone. "Hephaestos would not lie beside me without benefit of marriage between us."

"What? But that is madness. Ares will not stand for it."

"Ares has no say in this." Aphrodite's voice was cold. "He forfeited that right when he chose her over me."

"It was colossal stupidity on Ares' part, Princess, but he will change his mind. He will seek you out again and then what? You will refuse him because you are wed to another? Oh, disaster!" Thaleia held her palm to her forehead.

"I am quite pleased with this match. Hephaestos is honest and good and his love springs from a far deeper place than between his legs." With each affirmation, Aphrodite felt stronger, more certain she had made the correct decision.

"But you do not love him," cried Euphrosyne. "Love without love - no, this cannot happen."

"She is right." Thaleia folded her hands together in a prayerful clasp. "Eternal Love must feel the same to bring balance and harmony to the mortal world."

"There you are both wrong," Aphrodite answered. "I feel

great affection for Hephaestos. He has shown already that he will
cherish me in ways Ares is not capable. He is a brilliant craftsman,
kind and generous to a fault. His gifts will bring added dimension to
Victory. She will not seek bloodletting as a sport but will remain on
the side of faithful creative love."

"You do not need another alliance." Thaleia stamped her foot.
"Once you were new to the world, naïve and unsure, but no more,
Princess. Now you are every bit as strong as anyone in Council,
including Ares. You need not put yourself in this place merely to
strengthen your position."

"Love cannot be alone." Aphrodite's response was swift.
"Eternal Love must have a partner, for sharing is my nature."

"But you must love the one who shares your life, your bed.
Affection is not enough."

Squaring her shoulders, Aphrodite cut Thaleia off. "Let there be
no mistake, it is my choice and I have made it. It is done and I will
hear no more about it. I must go now to meet Hephaestos."

Like a pall, silence fell as the Graces finished arranging
Aphrodite's hair and apparel. All that could be heard was an
occasional sniffle and that fast disguised. Aphrodite bore their
wordless protest as long as she could and then took their hands in
hers.

She offered them a sad smile. "It is fitting, is it not, that this
union take place before the sun sets rather than under cover of the
night? It is a revelation that I go to Hephaestos in light rather than
Ares in clandestine darkness."

As they began their trek from the guest quarters along a corridor
to Hephaestos' chambers, a rumble shook the castle walls. Thaleia
shuddered. "I dislike this place even more than the cold and dismal
mountain at Athos. There you would only freeze to death. Here,
molten rock could rain down upon us at any moment."

Aglaia shrugged. "I find it rather captivating, for there are things
here I have never seen."

"Many things," whispered Euphrosyne as they entered a big
echoing chamber with a vaulted ceiling of gold.

She nodded toward a small brown being with pointed ears and
many silver hoops lining the edges. He had long ropey hair and was
naked save for a short fur skirt and sandals. His hooked nose rose
above thin lips and pointed teeth, which were bared in a grimace
meant to be a smile. He stood guard with spear in hand before the

wide bronze doors to Hephaestos' chamber.

"Do not be frightened, it is only Cedalion, Hephaestos' servant. He appears fierce, but I have found him to be accommodating."

Cedalion stared at them with shiny black eyes, but said nothing. His gaze traveled across them, stopping at Aphrodite. To her, he gestured at the doors. "This is where I leave you, my Loves, but stay close, for I will have need of you later." Aphrodite kissed each one, clinging to Thaleia before she took her leave of them.

"We shall stay here," Thaleia said firmly. "You have only to call us and we will be at your side."

"Here?" Euphrosyne shivered. "I do not like the way he looks at me."

Cedalion's curious gaze had settled on Euphrosyne and followed her with each step.

"I think he likes you," mused Aglaia. "But come, let us make ourselves comfortable, for we shall be here all night."

They settled on the couches and ate their own feast while sipping rich red wine that soon made them drowse. There was no sound other than the grumbling mount to disturb their peace. No sound at all from the inner chambers.

Cedalion stood silent vigil at the bronze entrance, his spear ready should they decide to storm the doors. He was the last they saw as their heavy lids closed and the first they saw when sharp voices brought them awake.

It was not Cedalion who made a ruckus, but another visitor.

A youthful male cloaked in a short tunic edged in gold, with a golden winged helmet upon his dark locks, stood scowling at the dwarf. Cedalion held his spear at the ready, its sharp point pressed mid-belly against the white cloth.

"I do not wish for a skirmish, Cedalion, I have come only to see Lord Hephaestos. He is not in the caves, therefore must be resting in his chambers and I must speak with him."

There was no change in Cedalion. He glared at Hermes and jabbed his spear a bit deeper, forcing Hermes to take a step back.

"Why do you greet me so? Hephaestos will not be pleased, especially when it is Zeus who sends me to speak with him. Now step aside."

Hermes moved forward only to have Cedalion crack him

on the shoulder with the spear. He did not draw blood, but it was clear the next time Hermes would not be so fortunate.

"That was uncalled for." Hermes rubbed the sore spot. "I bid you move aside so that I may carry out my task, or I shall be forced to call Zeus himself to set you straight."

Cedalion growled deep in his throat and bared his teeth. Hermes opened his mouth to speak again and heard the giggling behind him. He whirled about, disregarding, for the moment, the spear tip and its owner. Advancing further into the dim room, he saw the three women clutching each other in laughter.

"My, my, what do we have here? The Graces? At Lord Hephaestos' palace? What could possibly bring you three, and at this late hour besides?" Hermes sly gaze slid from Thaleia, Aglaia, and Euphrosyne and back at the guarded private chambers of Hephaestos.

The Graces stopped laughing and grew serious. "It is none of your concern, Hermes. You would be wise to do as our friend Cedalion bids and leave now."

"It is because he works so hard that I will not leave until I have delivered my message."

"Then pass your wretched message to me." Thaleia stood up and smoothed her gown. "I will see that Lord Hephaestos receives it."

"So kind of you, but no. I reveal the words of Zeus only to those ears decreed to hear it."

"Then you will have to return, for Hephaestos is asleep and cannot be disturbed.

"Is that so? Do I need to advise Zeus that his favorite craftsman has fallen ill and cannot do his work?"

"You need not advise Zeus, but return on the morrow to see Hephaestos."

"And let the mystery go unanswered as to why the Graces - the loyal servants of our fair Aphrodite - are gathered outside the bedchamber of Lord Hephaestos?" Hermes gave a mock bow in their direction. "Oh, I think not."

A cunning expression settled on his youthful face as he advanced toward them in a menacing way. "I think I shall make you tell me what goes on behind those illustrious doors." As he reached for them, they broke apart and Euphrosyne screamed.

Immediately, Cedalion abandoned his post and ran to her aid. As he did, clever Hermes swung about and was at the entrance before any could stop him. He flung wide the heavy doors and strode into the chamber beyond, with Cedalion and the Graces tumbling after him. There he paused in shocked delight, for he had in certainty uncovered a tantalizing scene.

Although both Hephaestos and Aphrodite were fully clothed, it was the finery that caught his eye. Hephaestos, bathed and trimmed, with hair loose down his back except for a topknot, struggled up from a richly appointed couch before the hearth.

He was dressed in a fine white linen robe edged in bronze thread, a thick belt of the same about his waist and upon his twisted feet he wore matching soft slippers instead of his usual scarred boots.

Aphrodite appeared astonishing in her beauty. As Hermes gazed upon her, all else vanished. He could think of nothing but Love's passionate embrace and himself lying in her arms. He could not take his eyes from her in a seashell pink chiton girdled in gold, for it was so thin as to see every inch of her pale skin through it.

"Be gone, Hermes, you are not welcome here," thundered Hephaestos.

Hermes blinked, and was brought back into the time and place. He grinned as he took a lengthy look about the chamber.

Remnants of a feast of exotic foods and fine wines, honey cakes and cream lay on a trestle table. The fire burned low and seductively. The air was strong with the perfumed scent of oils and incense.

And beyond this pretty picture, Hermes could see the inner chamber, alight with the soft glow of candles. The shining bed was draped with shimmering gold netting, as if a carefully wrapped present.

There was no doubt he had stumbled into something enormous. The evidence before his eyes spoke of old alliances broken and new ones formed. Hermes did not need to be told twice to leave. He could not wait to return to the palace of Zeus to spread the word of this discovery.

With a grin, Hermes said, "As you wish, Lord Hephaestos." He nodded to Aphrodite. "Ocean Princess."

In a blink, Hermes was gone from the wedding chamber.

With slumped shoulders, Hephaestos dropped his chin to

his chest. "It is over. Ares will hear of this and storm the castle. I will have lost you before I could love you."

"I am sorry, Master." Cedalion spoke for the first time within their hearing, and all the Graces peered at him, for his voice was melodic and lovely. Their first steps were toward Aphrodite, but stopped at her sudden gesture.

"It is not your fault, Cedalion." Aphrodite spoke with kindness. "Hermes takes undue liberties when on a mission from Zeus."

"Princess," began Thaleia.

"I have no need of your services, dear Sisters. Take your leave now, for the night still awaits us."

A protest died upon Aglaia's lips when Thaleia touched her arm. There was naught they could do if Aphrodite had decided her course of action. Privately, it was Thaleia's opinion that Hermes was a message from the Fates.

She believed this union should not be conjugated, but there was no moment to voice her case. Instead, they left with bowed heads. Cedalion followed behind them, once more drawing the doors closed.

As soon as they were gone, Aphrodite rose from the couch and held out one slender hand. "Come, Hephaestos, we have delayed long enough."

She knew Hermes would not hesitate to seek out Ares and cause further mischief. Hermes would delight in watching War's reaction to this bit of gossip. Should Ares arrive in a fit of jealous rage, all would be lost. With a forced smile, Aphrodite went on. "Let us retire and consummate this agreement before there is further interruption."

"You would still have me, knowing that before our lovemaking is done the entire Greater Realm will know of our alliance?"

"It is well and good they know, for once we have had our private celebration, my intention is to announce our union." She gripped his fingers in her own. "Our bed awaits us and I long to take your mind from this aggravation."

In truth, Aphrodite wished for Ares to know what she had done. She wished to inflict upon him every bit of the humiliation she felt at the sight of Niala in his arms. She wanted him to know so she could savor the taste of his defeat on her lips even as she kissed Hephaestos and swore allegiance to him.

*****

It is your choice.
The words haunted Aphrodite throughout the long night.
It is your choice.
She heard them in her dreams. She heard them now.
It is your choice.
Spoken with such finality.
She had chosen and now reaped the harvest of her decision. Lying naked in the huge bed shaped like a ship with gold netting for sails, Aphrodite reaped her bitter harvest. Her breasts would not swell, nor her belly quicken. There was no sense of victory. There was no Victory.

There was no child.

There was nothing but the ache in her heart.

The voice of Victory that had whispered in her ear was gone. The energy that begged to be brought from spirit to body was no longer about her. Not even the faintest shadow hovered nearby in the hopes next time there would be success. Victory had disappeared without a trace.

But why?

Aphrodite's gaze wandered from the highest peak of the bed where the fine curtain draped over the mast-like crossbeam and followed the flowing lines to her side of the bed. She reached out with muted curiosity and touched the filmy material only to discover it was the tiniest links of chain woven together.

Over and over, she let it glide across her fingertips, feeling the weight of it and marveling how much it appeared like cloth, though made of metal. She was not alone in the bed, for Hephaestos snored on the other side.

One freckled arm lay outside the coverings and, in the first rays of dawn, the red-gold hairs lit like fire along the brawny line down to his wrist. Blunt fingers lay relaxed against the white sheet, a reminder of how he touched her during the night. The thick mane of red hair was tangled upon the pillow - she could not see his face for it. Not that she wished to.

She felt no eagerness to look upon his face or to kiss his lips again. That said, she could find no fault in his sex. There was awkwardness at first when he groped at her like a goat herder milking a nanny. It nearly made her laugh aloud and turn him aside, for that was no way to make love to Love. Then she discovered the shyness beneath the zealous uprising of his body when Hephaestos snuffed all the lamps before he would disrobe.

He did not want her to see his twisted legs and ruined feet. Honoring him, she conceded to the darkness after realizing his fears. Even then she had to slow his clumsy touch and demonstrate the finer skills he lacked. He learned quickly and with great eagerness.

She was well pleased by the end when he spilled his seed into her and not upon the bedside. He wept when they were done and clung to her whispering sweet words of idolatry. Once he recovered his wits, he turned away from her and fell into a deep sleep.

And it still was her choice. She was neither stolen away, nor coerced. She was not bedazzled nor besotted. She chose to leave Ares for another so Victory could be born.

But there was no child. Victory abandoned her. Now Aphrodite lay beside her new husband in a golden room on a golden bed with the finest of all the jewels in the world at her feet. True loyalty and absolute devotion, a husband who would never neglect her for others.

But she did not love him. Where was the victory in that?

Aphrodite could not even shed a tear for the loss, for Victory was never hers to begin with. She could see that now.

TEN

Zeus took the news of Aphrodite's alliance with Hephaestos with grim visage. His lips pressed into a thin disapproving line as he stroked his beard and stared wordlessly at a point beyond Hermes. Hermes was surprised by the reaction, for the contention between father and son was well known. He expected, at the very least, that Zeus would sanction the alliance, and thereby assign Hephaestos a more powerful place within the Council. In turn, Ares' eruption into a blind rage causing commotion of colossal proportions in the Greater Realm was guaranteed.

It would have been lovely to behold, an amusement worthy of the gods to feast their eyes upon.

Disappointed that Zeus was displeased, yet refused to take action, Hermes turned to Hera and found she was delighted by the news. Hera had promised Aphrodite to Hephaestos long ago, when Aphrodite was new to the world, but Ares had stolen her away before Hephaestos could claim his reward. Hera had been very, very long in forgiving her wayward son for such a trick and now thought Aphrodite's desertion was due justice.

However, it was clear nothing would soon come of this disclosure for the only thing they agreed upon was that the union should be kept quiet. The ramifications had to be thoroughly explored before the Greater Council would accept or deny the alliance. Until then, Zeus forbade Hermes to speak of it.

Hera commanded Hermes to leave well enough alone. She threatened him that if he dared to share this information with anyone, she would punish him in a most vicious manner. Hera spoke with the same sternness to her own messenger, Iris of the Rainbows, advising her to keep this news bound in silence. Iris needed no further admonishment. Unlike the unruly Hermes, Iris was a sweet-natured and obedient servant to Hera.

In spite of the cloak of secrecy over this juicy bit of gossip, they all knew sooner rather than later Ares would discover his mate's betrayal. It would be a terrifyingly terrible moment.

Hera spoke with a smile on her face, yet her voice held the tiniest bit of regret, for she did love Ares well in spite of his violent ways. She was caught between her two sons along with an age-old promise to one of them.

Zeus was not as kind. With ominous granite eyes, he told both messengers, "Do not interfere or you will find yourself serving severe penance."

Though the words echoed in his mind, Hermes could not deny his own nature. When he left Olympus, his promise under solemn oath rang in his ears but the desire to impart such information won out over any threat.

Hermes found Ares in the northern reaches, where the savage lands begot a fair-skinned breed of bestial men who would rather die to the last than surrender a single blade of grass.

Hermes hovered in the air, unseen to mortal eyes below, and looked upon the blood-soaked moor where Ares and his minions did their awful duty. Hordes of fur-clad men slashed away at each other, oblivious to those who fell as they trod upon and over muddied bodies. Even from his vantage point, Hermes could not distinguish which side was which, for they all appeared the same: hideous hairy brutes with wild eyes wielding crude weapons.

The flash of Ares' sword was like lightening against a black sky, both stunning and frightening. To the mortals struck down by it, it could seem no more than a specter, for the likes of it was nowhere else in their midst. With a thrill of dread, Hermes watched Amason slash through flesh and bone, to rise again and again in a rain of blows that took a horrifying toll.

He knew if he got too close, he could be its next victim. For a moment, he weighed the entertainment of telling Ares of Aphrodite and Hephaestos against certain death if that cold sword should turn toward him. There was always the possibility Ares broke the alliance - perhaps he was already aware of this arrangement and cared not.

As Hermes looked upon the fierce countenance of War, streaked with sludge and gore, murderous glint in his eyes, he knew Ares would never relinquish Aphrodite.

Hermes grinned.

Coming to ground in the shadow of Death, Hermes whispered of Aphrodite in Hephaestos' arms, of a golden bed lit for lovemaking and a celebration feast half-eaten. He detailed the wedding clothes, Hephaestos in a white tunic edged in bronze as a promise of purity and faithfulness. Aphrodite in transparent pink, a symbol of both love and lust.

Hermes told of Cedalion steadfastly guarding the doors into their secret marriage chamber. How the Graces waited outside for their mistress. There could be no mistake what it was about - a new alliance was formed, an old one discarded.

Ares froze. Amason held high, a red stream dripping from its razor edge, he stared at Hermes. The slaughter continued around them as the screeching throngs swept past, with stench stirring the air and jostling against them. Suddenly panicked, Hermes cowered under the flat venomous gaze and offered quick words of solace.

"It pains me to bring you such impossible news, Lord Ares, but I could not bear for you to hear of this depraved turn of events from any other than myself."

Hermes found he could not stop his babbling. "I traveled to Lemnos to pass a message to Hephaestos, never expecting to discover the ugly truth. It is unforgivable that Aphrodite betrays you."

Hermes was struck once across the face, a hard backhanded blow that sent him whirling to the ground. Bits of light burst before his eyes as he collapsed into the muck. Mud caked his nose and mouth and he could not breathe as a starburst whirled in his head.

As he lay there in the bloody slime moaning, Ares grasped his hair and jerked Hermes' head back. His spine bowed under the pressure of Ares' foot. Through watering and swollen eyes, he saw Ares lift Amason high and, with a choking roar, start the downward swing to separate Hermes' head from his body.

"No, Father!" Eris leaped up to hang from Ares' massive forearm, his feet braced against Ares' chest. "Stop."

Strong enough to deflect the downward blow, Eris kept Ares from inflicting death. Hermes received no more than a glancing wound on his shoulder from Amason's tip. Ares released Hermes and reached for Eris as he lifted Amason for another strike. Weak with relief, Hermes lay helpless and bleeding into the mire beneath him.

Eris continued to cling to Ares and shriek, "Do not do this. He is not a worthy victim for Amason. He is only the messenger. There are other, more deserving of Amason's blade. Stop, I beg you."

Frantic, Eris looked into the stark madness that gripped his father and knew he could not prevent Ares from following through on this crusade. Eris could not let Amason's blade harm another of the immortal caste, for it would doom the House of War. It would doom them all.

He changed his tack and began to scream at Hermes to take his leave, for Eris knew he could only delay the forbidden blow.

"Go," he shouted. "Go now - leave, quickly, lest you die."

Ares shook Eris loose, tossing him under the cruel feet of the hordes as he made a wild swing toward Hermes. It was a cut that would have severed the top half of his body from the lower half had Hermes not taken heed and vacated the battlefield. Even so, he felt the sting of the blade slice across his ribs before he was beyond Ares' reach.

Sobbing, Hermes fled to the safety of Olympus.

Ares threw back his head and howled with animal rage before launching full force into the midst of the ongoing skirmish. He fought without discernment, wantonly killing whoever stepped in front of him, regardless of which side he decimated. He fought until no one was left and all around him were sodden corpses, headless, limbless, filthy, beaten bodies that once were human beings, now food for scavengers.

He stood in the midst of carnage, bloody Amason before him.

Aphrodite had betrayed him.

With Hephaestos.

As the sunlight played across the blade, Ares the Destroyer knew he was not done killing.

From the peak of the volcano, Ares could see the entire isle of Lemnos. From its far-reaching peninsula to the clear green waters of its broad bay, to the large land area lying to the east. A white, sandy shore outlined the island, with low foliage that grew thicker as it marched closer to the center. High-plumed trees and vining fruits began midway and rose up toward the mountainous area in a great tangle.

He stood upon a thick slab of lava rock slick with steam from the fires within the mount. Every now and then vapor belched forth with nauseating fumes followed by a rumble.

Thick trails of slag burned through the forests and underlying growth in black lines going all the way to the shining sea, where it became blurred as the sand blew across it. There were no signs of human inhabitation, though the jungle was alive with a raucous noise. Birds and animals of all type joined together in the boisterous song of Lemnos.

From Ares' vantage point, the bronze rooftop of the Forge god's palace was highly visible. Though the foundation was concealed by flowering bushes and broad-leafed trees, the top reflected the sun with a wide aura of colors. It was all angles, curves, dips, and jutting edges, which caught the light and sent it back toward the heavens in a brilliant wave.

Ares brooded with the darkest of thoughts, crouching on the mount, fresh from the battleground. Amason lay next to him eager for more blood, for she could feel the yearning of her master to rend flesh and bone. While Eris lay dazed and Enyo was occupied with the dead, while the rest of the hordes feasted on flesh, Ares sought out Hephaestos and Aphrodite with the intention of destroying them both.

They deserved nothing less.

He pictured Hephaestos beneath Amason's wicked blade, savoring the agony he would suffer just before his death. Ares held in his mind the image of Aphrodite begging, pleading with him to spare first Hephaestos, and then her own life. And he saw, felt, tasted, and heard the raw wet plunge of Amason into her breast.

She deserved nothing less.

And yet, as he hesitated to enter the castle, the bloodlust began to fade. Why did he waver?

They deserved to die.

Breaking off a chunk of slag, Ares hurled it down the mountainside. It landed in a thick crop of trees and a flock of bright birds flew up with alarmed cries. Ares' lips thinned in a cold smile as he threw another large piece into an adjoining grove. This time he heard the chatter of tree-born animals and saw the branches shake as they scurried to safety. Another nearly smoldering lump of black rock went skittering down the mount.

He wanted them punished.

Horribly punished.

Suffering tormented punishment.

With a string of curses, Ares sat cross-legged in the only patch of grass to be found and stared out toward the calm ocean.

Aphrodite's birthplace.

He would never forget the first time he saw her, for it was then he truly felt the stirrings of love. The first time his heart ached with desire rather than his body driving him to lust. She was the most wondrous thing he had ever seen, the most amazing presence any of them had ever beheld.

Her birth was a phenomenon like no other in either Realm and was heralded by Poseidon as the greatest gift the sea could offer. Ares remembered how they all gathered on the shores of Cos, those many eons ago, to witness the birth of a goddess.

Who was she to be? No one knew until Aphrodite rose from the sea enclosed in a giant clamshell. It opened with maddening slowness, all breaths held, waiting to see the treasure within. The hinged shell formed a lustrous backdrop in pale iridescent pink, and at its center was the jewel for which they waited. They stared in astonishment at the fragile, resplendently beautiful creature birthed by the sea.

Conceived in the depths of the ocean, Aphrodite's mother was the vast emotional waters of life, her father the dismembered virility of an ancient god thrown into the fertile sea. Cherished by Poseidon and his wife Amphitrite until the moment the young sea goddess was destined to rise to the surface, she was innocent and unscathed by indignity.

Oh, yes, it had been a much-heralded event. Like another star born into the night sky. Once mature, this perfect pearl was brought to the surface as a gift to both the mortal and immortal worlds.

She was glorious to look upon, her frothy pale hair to her ankles and skin as smooth and luminescent as the inside of the shell. Even the little triangle where her legs joined was like the delicate lace of sea foam, hiding from view her virgin turf.

As she raised shy turquoise eyes to look upon them, there came the tides of emotion like none had ever felt. Love poured over them, engulfed them, bathed, nurtured and held them in her arms with such extraordinary tenderness. One and all wept with joy.

Eternal Love was born.

Zeus immediately proclaimed her name as Aphrodite - pearl of the sea - and took her under his protection. He forbid any to approach the timid maiden for they frightened her. The immortals clustered all around with awe in their eyes and instant lust in their hearts. Their vying had already begun, for there was not a single being who did not want Love for his or her very own.

It was well and good that Zeus took Aphrodite under his protection, for if he had not, Love's trials would have begun on a very early basis. Though Ares held hatred in his heart for his father, he approved of Zeus' action. Holding Aphrodite in his private residence created an obstacle, but not an impossible task, for one such as Ares.

He was no older than Deimos and far less experienced. There had been no one to guide him, as Ares did Deimos. It was bitter lesson after bitter lesson - what Ares learned, he learned by himself, alone and at the mercy of the treacherous Fates.

An impetuous youth who threw caution to the four winds, he fell madly wildly in love with Eternal Love. For the first time in his life as War, something other than brutality touched his heart.

Ares would never forget how he gazed into those wide innocent eyes the color of a sparkling underwater reef. She was like a newborn babe, guileless and trusting. Yet beneath the surface, just as in her oceanic birthright, was a tremendous power waiting to be released. And something else, something that called to a deeper part of him. Ares did not know what it meant for it defied the obvious and spoke of things beyond his comprehension.

He knew he had to have her.

As for Aphrodite, she did not seem surprised when Ares stole into her chambers in the dark night. It seemed she waited for him, dressed in filmy white, with silver moonlight spilling over her hair and shoulders. She did not reach out to him but stood with hands folded upon her breast as if to hold her heart steady. They stared at each other for a very long time, not touching, but exploring with hot gazes and a tangible yearning.

The only refinement Ares ever learned was to dance, to anticipate from a warrior's standpoint the next move of the enemy. The bloody dance of war did not equate to his desire for Aphrodite. He did not know how to show this divine being how he felt, and there came over him an awful awkwardness. Terror shook him by the throat and he could not breathe for the pain of desire in his heart.

He knew no other way, so he kissed her. Tenderly, his lips barely brushing hers, one sweet kiss in exchange for a thousand words. Drawing back, Ares hovered in agony until Aphrodite let him know the truth of her heart.

The message came in the form of a long sigh and the slightest leaning into him. That was all he needed. He lifted her into his arms and carried her away to a private place where they would be alone, where no one could find them.

Ares did not regret what he had done, though he was punished for his audacity. He had not known that his mother, Hera, planned to give Aphrodite to her crippled son, Hephaestos, as a reward for his service to her.

Why had Hera promised such a thing and without Zeus' knowledge? Ares supposed Hera's promise was born of envy, for Zeus made much ado over the new goddess. What more appropriate place for such beauty than in the arms of imperfection?

And now, an eternity later, that was exactly where she resided. Aphrodite, the only thing Ares ever truly loved in this life, in the beastly arms of imperfection.

He simply could not endure it. Not now, not ever.

"Ahh, there you are."

A voice startled Ares. He turned to see who interrupted his contemplation, gaze narrowed with suspicion as he saw Zelos hovering next to him.

"Be gone, foul creature - I have no time for you."

"Yet, you called me to your side." She plucked at his hair, a mischievous smile curving her mouth upward. "I felt your stirrings."

Seduction glimmered in Zelos' eyes and her lips parted as the tip of her tongue followed the plump lines. "Deep stirrings, my Lord. I felt them. Here."

She placed one hand on her belly, just below a thick, gold chain riding low on her hips. The chain was all she wore. It was all she needed, for Zelos was Jealousy, and the chain was her weapon, her tool. She was a slender creature with long limber legs and arms, golden in color, with bright red hair that fell to her feet. Her eyes were liquid green, a moving current in which anyone could be ensnared.

Zelos took great delight in her gifts, embracing all aspects of possible enchantment but the chain remained her favorite way of binding one to her. She touched it now, stroking it as if it were a living thing, and smiled at him with her red, red lips.

"Go away." Ares' voice faltered.

"Look at you." Zelos made a soft clucking sound. "Ares the Destroyer, pathetic soul, the stain of battle is still on you and yet your lust has not been quenched."

She trailed her fingers through the stiffening blood in his hair and then stared at the gore on her hand. "And why not?" She slowly licked her fingertips. "Because Jealousy cannot be quenched by blood sacrifice. Death is too easy."

Ares shuddered and shook his head. "Go away."

"Why?" Zelos whispered. "I know you think about her." One slim hand went past his cheek to point at the bronze dome rising up from the green trees. Ares inhaled her intoxicating scent as the arm slid back, her fingers brushing his face. His beard tingled where she touched. Words failed him as Jealousy settled closer.

"You think of Love, do you not? Our glorious Aphrodite and how she sleeps next to the hideous Hephaestos." Zelos knelt, her naked breasts brushing Ares' arm as she snaked up to gently bite his earlobe.

"They lay together from dusk to dawn. They sweat and strain against each other every single night. He thinks it is his due."

Her breath hot on his face, Ares' head began to swim with images he fought to keep out: Aphrodite in the throes of passion, Hephaestos pawing at her. Hephaestos heaving on top of the pale and fragile Aphrodite. She arching to take him further inside her.

"Arrgh." Ares dug his fingers into burning eyes. "I must think clearly. I do not have time for games."

Yet he listened to Jealousy, knowing he should not. After all, what did she tell him that he did not already know? Aphrodite had forsaken him. She went straight to Hephaestos in his littered and gaudy castle without delay.

"Why should you deny yourself? Give yourself to me and forget how she opens her legs to him."

"I do not care what she does." Ares pushed Zelos aside.

She clung to his hands and pulled herself back, hooking her legs around him to sit in his lap. "Oh, I think you do. Why else would you linger here watching and waiting, knowing she cast you aside in favor of Hephaestos?"

Ugly images of Aphrodite and Hephaestos flaunting their union rose up before Ares though he sought to erase such thoughts.

Zelos ripped his leather tunic aside and pressed her hot moist mouth against the pulse beating madly at his throat. She nipped his neck as she pulled at the front of his trousers, releasing him into her hands.

Ares gasped. "Stop."

But he did not stop her.

"I answered your call, my Lord. I do only your bidding." Zelos ran her tongue across his parted lips. "But I can see you worry about your little ocean princess, how she has gotten away from you."

"She will not leave me." Ares' breath was labored. "Not for good."

"Are you certain? What if she chooses him?"

"She will not."

"She already has."

"She did it to spite me. It is not real."

"No?" Zelos leaned closer and whispered, "They make a babe."

Ares gripped her shoulders. "You lie."

"Never to you, my Lord. Never. Aphrodite carries Hephaestos' seed even now."

Though Ares fought against her, a monstrous storm overtook

him. He allowed Zelos to fasten her ripe red mouth to his in a smothering kiss. Laughing, Zelos lifted his hand to cup her breast.

"Think about it, Ares the Destroyer. He does this to her." Zelos threw her head back and moaned. "How do you stand knowing what he does to her?" She wiggled her hips, drawing him inside her.

Zelos kissed him again, open-mouthed and hungry. Sweating, Ares clenched his fists, seeing nothing but Aphrodite and Hephaestos, naked, locked together in lust.

"Take me," she taunted. "Like he takes her."

Enraged, Ares threw Zelos face down to the ground and rolled on top of her. He pinned her arms beneath her, his heart filled with a malevolent desire. Following the curve of her spine to her slender waist, he found the heated links of her chain straining against her flesh. It strove to bind him with its magic, luring him with whispered promises of revenge.

He knelt, naked and ready. Zelos tried to crawl away but he dragged her back, ripping tender skin wherever the jagged rocks caught her body. Hooking his thumbs under the thick gold links, he dug cruel fingers into her hips and brought her to her knees, face pushed into the dirt.

"You want me to take you? Then I shall, but not like he would. Oh no, Zelos, you are to have War. I am not a crippled pathetic creature who must hide behind closed doors to take pleasure."

Forcing her legs apart, he held her thighs so she could not slink away and sank his fingers into the moist opening.

"Forgive me," Zelos begged, clawing at the tufts of grass.

"Forgive? It is too late. You have deceived me with your lies, laid waste to my trust, and left our alliance in ashes. Now you will feel the full potency of War, as you have never felt it before. As Amason slices through flesh, so do I."

"No, it is Aphrodite you speak of, I have only tempted you. Aaiee." Zelos screamed as he thrust into her.

The beast that surfaced was no longer simple jealousy. It was a ravening madness that consumed Ares as he pounded against her, forgetting who took the brunt of his rage. He became lost in the spiteful pain he inflicted, enjoyed her wails, and took pleasure in the agony of torn flesh.

"No," she moaned. "No more."

"You pander to me. You thought to trick me. And now I give you all of what you deserve."

Zelos' shrieks echoed down the mountainside.

Deimos entered the altar chamber with apprehension. Ares had abruptly called him to appear and demanded he bring Phobos, yet he did not do as he was told. He could not, for Phobos went into hysteria whenever they approached the lower area of the fortress. Deimos found he could not even exit from that location without an outburst of magnificent proportions, so frightened was Phobos of the warriors.

Standing before Ares, Deimos was somewhat mystified as he watched his father swing a thick gold chain back and forth in idle bemusement. The chain glinted with a sinister brightness in the torchlight as Ares twirled it around his index finger, first wrapping it one way, then reversing until it was wound the opposite. He did this repeatedly, his gaze fixed on a far corner of the chamber where nothing lurked save shadows.

Deimos could not take his eyes from the golden links whirling through the air. The chain was mesmerizing as it flowed like water through Ares' fingers, the slight clink as the chain hit against itself growing louder with each loop. Frowning, Deimos was gripped by a sudden flush of resentment.

He served his father well, did he not? Always by his side. Always loyal. Why then was he never rewarded? Why was it Ares took all the glory for each and every endeavor made by the House of War? Why was it Ares took what he wanted but Deimos was denied his desires?

All Deimos wanted was Niala.

Why should he be denied the one he loved?

Why?

His lips parted to speak his indignation when the gold chain dropped out of sight into Ares' palm. Deimos blinked, staring at the fist holding the chain. Just as it came on him, the tension retreated. He shook his head, confused.

"Where is the boy?" Ares' voice held an unusual hoarseness.

"What?" Deimos continued to stare at Ares' hand until he lowered his arm to his side and the chain disappeared into the depths of a pocket.

"Where is the boy?"

"Phobos is resting." Deimos wiped his hand across his face and onto his shirtfront. "He is asleep."

"Asleep?"

Ares made it sound like a vile act.

"Yes, Father, sleeping. Some still require rest even if you do not."

"It is early."

"It is past nightfall and we work very hard during daylight hours. Phobos grows weary soon after his evening meal."

Ares leaned back, his legs stretched out before him. "My order was to bring him here. I do not care what hour it is or whether he sleeps. I want him here. Now."

"Why? To what purpose do I raise a child from his rest when he so badly needs it?"

"Because I command it. You need no other reason."

Ares' expression was impassive, his voice neutral, but as Deimos looked closer, he saw the stain of battle was still upon him. Ares face was streaked with dried blood and grime, his leather tunic and trousers soiled with the same.

The creases from nose to mouth were deep, his eyes drooped as though exhaustion was scarce kept at bay. Ares would never admit that he, too, was weary, but there it was, etched upon his body. He slumped rather than sat, his shoulders sagged, his chin was low and his hair matted to his head and neck in a dismal helmet of black strands. Amason rested beside the throne.

Even so, danger lurked beneath the surface and Deimos knew he must be careful. "Of course, Father. If you wish his presence, I will fetch him. However, he may be a bit groggy."

Ares gestured with one hand, the hand that had held the chain. It was empty now as he waved with impatience. "Still, you argue. Bring the boy to me. He is to be here while I am paid homage."

"I do not believe he should be here for those tributes."

"Do not defy me, Deimos. I am in no mood to argue." Ares' black brows drew together in a fierce frown. "I want him to witness the mortal warriors and the favors they call upon me to grant."

"No." Deimos straightened his shoulders. "No. Phobos is

too tender."

"Too tender for what? Do you think he has never seen an animal slaughtered in sacrifice?"

"I am quite certain he has not. He would most likely embarrass himself."

"Embarrass?" Ares stopped, for he remembered well how the child had wet himself with little provocation. "He continues to wet himself when frightened? Though you work with him, he shows little improvement?"

"Phobos has limits, Father. He does the best he can, it will just take time to mold him into a warrior."

"Phobos' behavior is unacceptable." Ares tone was sharp with reproach.

"He is learning."

"Not fast enough. Bring him here."

"It would not be good for little Phobos to be in these chambers." Deimos exhaled, pulled up his courage and confessed the problem. "One day he came here by mistake and saw the altar. He was so frightened he cried out, which brought warriors into this chamber thinking you granted audience. Needless to say, the child was terrified."

"You chose not to tell me of this?"

"There did not seem to be a need."

"Where were you when all this happened?"

Deimos flushed and glanced away from the hard stare directed at him. He could not say he had been with Niala. "I had lost track of him."

"What does that mean?"

"Only that I was not as vigilant as I should have been. It was entirely my fault."

"I see."

An uncomfortable silence fell with only the strident laughter from the warrior's quarters heard in the background. Deimos shifted from foot to foot hoping Ares would leave well enough alone. That hope died a fast death when next Ares spoke.

"He must go to Priapos."

"He is too young for the Centaur's way."

"He is older than you when you were sent to Priapos."

"I was different." Stubbornness propelled Deimos forward on a suicide mission. "Phobos is still tender."

"He will go to Priapos at dawn."

"Please, Father, do not send him there. He is not ready."

"He must become ready, for that is where he goes. At dawn. And you will take him."

"I cannot."

"You refuse me?"

Deimos tried to picture Phobos in the caves of the Centaur, sleeping on bare ground, eating only the game he himself could catch, and worst, being taken into the wood and left to find his way out. The child would not survive.

"I must. Phobos is not strong enough for such endeavors."

Ares pursed his lips in thought, as though he considered what Deimos requested. His response was not what Deimos wanted.

"So there is the truth of this matter. You have put yourself in his place. You relive your own transition."

"Not true," Deimos protested. "I simply understand how daunting Priapos is to a mere child. His ways are rough."

"As they should be."

"I will not take him there."

Again silence fell until Ares nodded. "So be it."

Before Deimos could breathe a sigh of relief, Ares continued. "I will take him. Tonight." He held up one hand, palm out. "Do not protest, for already you have annoyed me."

"But...."

"Enough. And because you have refused, I will give you another task. Perhaps this will be more to your liking."

Deimos squirmed at the obnoxious expression in Ares' gaze. Ares rose from the throne and stepped off the dais, pointing to the right side of the seat. "Stand there, Deimos."

With reluctance, Deimos moved next to the throne and waited for Ares to speak, though he already knew what was in store.

"You will play host to the warriors who wait."

"They come seeking you, not me."

"And they will believe you and I are the same. They have never seen my face. One is as good as another. You will stand there."

Ares pointed again. "You will not sit. Stand there while these men pray to their god and you will answer them as that god, in whatever manner need be. You will accept their offerings, witness their sacrifices, and bid them well in their journeys."

With jaw set, Deimos closed his eyes. "How long?"

"How long?" Ares' smile was cold. He waved toward the back of the chamber and torches lining the walls sprang to life. "Until everyone has had his due. Every last one."

In a bold voice, Ares intoned. "Come forth warriors and pay homage to your god."

A wave of men and animals poured through the arched entrance. Wave upon wave until the yawning chamber was crammed, until no more could squeeze in and still, more waited. Deimos groaned as the prayers began and the first in line came forward to fall on his knees.

ELEVEN

Thaleia stood with hands on hips, frowning at Aphrodite. Euphrosyne and Aglaia bathed her in a gilded tub large enough for all of them, if they had been of a mind to join her. Instead, Euphrosyne and Aglaia stood beside it, dipping sponges into hot water that held the same spicy scent found everywhere on the island.

It was separate from the acrid brume coming from the volcano and different from the anvils striking hot metal in the forges beneath the castle. Those smells came to rest on Thaleia's tongue with disfavor, leaving a bitter taste behind, but this one was different. It was sweet and light, a flavor similar to the round green fruit that grew in abundance on the trees around them, fruit that was orange when sliced and fruit that appeared in bowls in every room.

As delightful as the scent and fruit were, they did nothing to lift Aphrodite's spirits. She lay back in the tub, head resting on a folded towel, eyes closed. Her glorious face was pinched and more pale than usual. She breathed with a sigh on each exhale. All worried, for all three Graces could feel Love crumbling, and the world was shifting because of it.

Unlike the rest of the Ages, Aphrodite was not born of

blood. She was preconceived in the depths of the greatest ocean. A child made of water, a child who lived the emotions of the human race.

From her emanated both the greatest hopes and the darkest despairs of mortals. She was the sparkling spring and raging waterfall. She was the murky deep and the clear pools. She was calm seas and killing typhoons. She was the flood and the drought that preyed upon both worlds.

No one could resist the Tides of Love. No one could go unaffected by Aphrodite's infinite unhappiness as an underlying sadness hung over everything and everybody. The Ages had noticed. All knew the mortal realm was in decline yet Aphrodite would not confess her actions were a mistake. She persisted with the myth that in Hephaestos she had found the perfect match, and would not listen to prayers of deliverance from either world.

"Princess, I think we should return home today." Thaleia disguised her concerns with a smile, for to point out Aphrodite's errors was not the way to win her over.

"I think not today, dear Thaleia," Aphrodite murmured without so much as a flutter of eyelashes.

"But, Princess." Thaleia cast about for reasons other than the obvious. "I long to see the white sands of our shore and the…the…."

"Our home, Princess," chimed in Euphrosyne. "I miss our home. I find that I cannot rest well here. I want my own sweet bed."

Euphrosyne did not tell an untruth with this sentiment. Since her arrival, it seemed Cedalion lingered too long by her side, unless ordered elsewhere by Lord Hephaestos. He stared at her with adoration from his huge brown eyes.

If she dropped something, like a flash, he was there to pick it up. If she wanted anything, she no more than thought it and Cedalion held it out to her. She was not accustomed to such behavior and found it quite unsettling.

Hephaestos saw, nevertheless, and chuckled mightily over it. Her sisters saw and giggled at her expense. Cedalion steadfastly ignored all but her.

"I really want to go home." Euphrosyne poured water over Aphrodite's hair.

"It is not time." Aphrodite reached up to stroke the youngest Grace.

"But, Princess," began Euphrosyne.

"If she is not ready to return, then leave her be." Aglaia spoke with a hint of sharpness.

Thaleia raised one appraising eyebrow at her sister. Aglaia's face reddened as she kept her gaze leveled at the suds rising from Aphrodite's hair.

"Aphrodite, your sons have need of you."

This brought Aphrodite's eyes open, though they held a certain bleariness, as if she no longer slept but was not truly awake. "My sons can care for themselves."

"Perhaps that is true of Anteros, but Eros is no more than a child and requires his mother still."

"Not according to their father."

"Their father is wrong and I pray little Phobos does not pay too heavy a price for his father's recklessness." Thaleia took care not to say Ares' name, for Aphrodite had forbidden it.

"There is naught I can do, no matter what the outcome."

"I fear that is true as far as Phobos is concerned, but Eros is yours to mold. He cries for you and you need to be with him."

Thaleia waited for the outrage, but there was none. Instead, Aphrodite dropped her hand to the water with a little splash. "He will be fine."

"But what if he should begin his rites of passage?"

"He is too young to take his power."

"How can you be certain?"

"His body must mature before he can delve into the mysteries of Erotic Love. I have no fear that will happen soon."

"But if it does, his passage could well be disastrous without you to guide him."

"Anteros - my darling son, my golden light, Love's Response - will see him through."

Gritting her teeth, Thaleia retorted, "Anteros has burden enough without this upon his shoulders."

Abruptly, Aphrodite sat up. "Eros is not a burden."

Thaleia's smile was grim for she had found the chink in Aphrodite's armor. Her sisters tried to stop the slide of soap bubbles into their mistress' wide eyes, pressing her back to rinse her hair and then wrap her head in a soft towel.

"Perhaps Eros should come here." Aglaia spoke softly with gaze averted from the quick eyes of her sisters.

Both Thaleia and Euphrosyne glared at her.

She shrugged and went on. "A change might be good. And if we could find a way to return Phobos to your side, we could bring him here, also. His dreadful sire would never approach the isle of Lord Hephaestos."

"Do not be so certain of that." Thaleia looked upon her sisters with disdain. "Make no mistake, Ares is not afraid to come here. He does not because Aphrodite has scorned him, but woe to any who would steal his son."

Her sisters gasped as Aphrodite moaned and Thaleia clapped her hands to her mouth in horror. What had she said? Worse, it sounded as if she favored Ares over Hephaestos.

Aglaia stormed to Thaleia, finger pointing into her face. "Lord Hephaestos does not fear him. He would defend Aphrodite's honor to his death and you should be ashamed of yourself."

Bursting into tears, Aglaia ran from the room as her puzzled sisters watched her retreat. Behavior such as she exhibited was quite abnormal for the quiet Grace.

Aphrodite ignored the outburst and sank down into the water until her chin touched, eyes closed, tiny lines of exhaustion highlighting her lids. Euphrosyne shrieked and pulled at one pale arm, as though she feared Aphrodite meant to drown herself.

As if she could, thought Thaleia, sourness wrinkling her nose. *Aphrodite is made of water, she was born of water, she cannot die of water. She can only be more water.*

"Mistress, do you see how distressed we all are? It is time to go home." Thaleia raised a stern eyebrow at Aphrodite.

"Ahh, Dear One, you have every right to scold me, yet I do not have the strength to go."

Thaleia drew a small stool up and sat beside the tub. "Euphrosyne, leave us. I would have a private word with our Princess."

Euphrosyne hesitated. With bowed head, she followed after Aglaia.

"What is wrong, Princess?" Thaleia massaged Aphrodite's shoulders beneath the surface of water, leaning her head against Aphrodite's.

With one quivering breath, a single tear fell from Aphrodite's eye upon the surface of the bath. It lay there like a precious jewel, distilled sorrow glowing in the flickering candlelight.

"I have failed," she whispered. "I have not conceived."

As if her body pained her, Aphrodite took Thaleia's hand and placed it against her belly. "My womb is empty. Victory has fled. I have sacrificed all I hold dear for naught."

Pressing her palm to the softly rounded white flesh, Thaleia prayed to feel the spark of life within. There was nothing. She bit back her own tears to hold her mistress while she sobbed out her grief.

When Aphrodite grew silent, Thaleia said, "Why, then, do we not return home and leave this humiliation behind?"

"I cannot. I gave my sacred promise to Hephaestos."

"I do not ask you to break off your alliance, only return to Cos. Even the Master of Misery does not insist you stay with him."

"That was not the promise."

"Then what do you speak of?"

"I must give Hephaestos a daughter."

"But it did not happen, Princess. What more can you do? Let us forget this and return home."

"I am honor-bound. I have not held up my end of the bargain."

"Neither has he." Rinsing Aphrodite's hair, Thaleia could not keep the brittle tone from her voice. "For it is the rare one who can be both dame and sire. Even you came from seed tossed into the womb of the ocean."

"Then why is this daughter denied me?" Aphrodite beat the water with her fists, stirring up bubbling foam.

"Princess, therein is the heart of the matter. It is not about Lord Hephaestos. It is about you."

"Yes, I have failed."

"The only failure was in renouncing your one true love."

"Do not speak of him, for if I must count on that love, I am lost."

"Not if you return to him."

"I cannot, you know this. He has taken up with another."

"But Princess, you did not even fight for his affections."

"He scorns me."

Thaleia found it most odd that she was put in the position to defend Ares the Destroyer. "Though he strays from your side, he always returns. There is no one else who holds his affections the way you do."

"There is one other." Aphrodite's delicate brows drew together in a frown. "One he would trade the world to have. Even so, it should not matter."

"Perhaps Victory wants War as her father."

"It was my womb that was chosen."

"And his seed. Ares has been unfaithful since time began, to your cause and many others. It was foolish to abandon him."

"This one is different. I will not reward his infidelity."

"Jealousy has created a nasty cycle, Princess, and made it impossible for Victory to enter the world."

"Your words are harsh and wound me." Aphrodite's gaze wandered to a far point.

"I speak the truth. You lie here bemoaning your fate - that is beneath you. The mortal world suffers because of it. "

"Do not speak so to me." Aphrodite blinked and met Thaleia's eyes.

Something changed in that brief moment. Thaleia could see the dawning of anger. It served to erase apathy, but was not a good exchange. Thaleia kept on talking.

"If I do not, who will? This arrangement is wrong." Thaleia could not keep the disdain from her tone. "Your pride stands in the way, but you refuse to see it."

"I have made a promise."

"This pledge means nothing. It was based on nothing. It deserves nothing."

"Thaleia, you have gone too far. I will not allow this disrespect."

"And what would you have me do, Princess? I beg this for your own good, for the good of your children, and for the world. Leave off this silly pride. Reject this ridiculous oath."

Aphrodite rose from the water naked and glistening, a true creature of the sea. Her fury swept over Thaleia like a storm breaking upon a hapless ship, making her skin crawl. Thaleia refused to cringe under her mistress' wild-eyed glare and instead lifted her chin with righteous obstinance.

"Leave me!" Aphrodite's voice rose higher. Gone was the whimpering self-pity, but in its place was something worse: determination.

Thaleia froze, "Princess, I did not mean to offend you."

"I will hear no more. I bid you take leave for I do not want to see your face. Return to Cos and become nursemaid to Eros so

Anteros is free to do as he pleases."

Aphrodite's tone was one of hard disappointment. "I would not have believed Anteros would abandon me." She lifted her chin. "Go and care for Eros. Do not return here unless I call you."

Euphrosyne and Aglaia ran back into the room, dismay written upon their faces. They had heard every word and now fussed over their mistress.

"Go, now, Thaleia. All will be fine. Let us care for her." Aglaia swallowed hard as she waved Thaleia away, for she saw madness in Aphrodite's eyes and was afraid. "Let us calm her. Go and see about little Eros. Just go."

Euphrosyne mouthed from behind one hand, "Send Anteros. Send Anteros here."

Thaleia cast one last mutinous glance at them, then did as her mistress bid and left Lemnos. Aphrodite clasped trembling fingers together as she stared at the vacated spot, her breath whistling in and out with little gasps. Red blotches stained her face and neck and her breasts heaved as she fought to speak.

"Why, why?" It was more a wail than a question.

"Perhaps you do not put your heart into it." Euphrosyne blushed as she offered her opinion.

Aglaia immediately hooted in derision. "Sister, you have never experienced love. Do not make rash judgments when you have nothing on which to base it."

"I may still be virgin," Euphrosyne replied. "But I know passion and it lacks in their embrace. He is lustful while she is tepid. He does not see because he does not want to see. She lies beneath him with no effort."

Euphrosyne fell into a startled hush, her mouth still open. Aphrodite and Aglaia stared at her with wide eyes, frozen in the moment. Horrified, Euphrosyne dropped to her knees, her head bowed.

"Forgive me, Princess, forgive me. I speak rashly and out of place. I apologize."

"No, you are right." Aphrodite took Aglaia's hand and stepped from the tub into a linen wrap. "Hephaestos is a good kind lover but my heart has not been in it."

She stroked Euphrosyne's hair and bid her get up.

Crimson-faced, Euphrosyne rose but kept her eyes averted.

"I will return to Cos with Thaleia."

"Again, no." There was humility in Aphrodite's tone. "I was too harsh with Thaleia. You are my sisters and I love you. If you cannot speak your thoughts to me, then I have no one whom I can trust. I must ponder on the wisdom of your words and decide what next."

Hephaestos was not accustomed to women in his palace. Even over the rumblings of the forge, he could hear them screaming at each other. Despite the fact he could never distinguish their words, he cringed at the sharpness of their tones. They seemed to fly from docile quiet, to chirping good humor, to fussing with everything in their path, to squabbling. He was mightily confused by the feminine nature and did his best to stay out of its way.

He was most comfortable within the confines of his forge workshop anyway. Hunching over an anvil, he tapped on a small bit of gold only to see it disintegrate beneath his mallet. Cursing, he brushed the pieces to the floor and threw down the hammer.

What had started out to be a bracelet for his new wife, now was useless crumbs. With disgust, he limped to the long table and began to sort through the piles for a suitable replacement. He was lost in the possibilities when he heard footfall upon the staircase and it was not the scurrying steps of his underground helpers.

Through narrowed eyes he watched the doorway, prepared for nothing less than War to appear, though it would not be like Ares to enter with politeness. Cedalion merged into his shadow, dagger drawn, alert to any danger that might threaten his master. Hephaestos held up one finger in a motion to wait, for it was unlikely an enemy would announce his presence with such noise.

The two of them stood side-by-side, ready for whatever might come. Visitors were rare beneath the walls of Lemnos and they could not be too careful. Cedalion grunted and Hephaestos' mouth dropped when it was Aphrodite who rounded the corner. She had been there only once before, when she first set foot upon the isle. Since she remained above.

She was dressed in a filmy blue gown that left nothing to his imagination, other than what he could do upon that pale playground. Her glorious hair was in perfect curls atop her head, her face was artfully made up and enhanced by the coy downward sweep of long lashes.

Speechless, he stared at her. "What are you doing down here? If you have need of something, you have only to ring the silver bell I gave you and Cedalion would be at your side."

"Though Cedalion is most gracious." Aphrodite spoke with an unusual huskiness. "It is your services that I require."

Knees already weakened by her fragile and resplendent beauty, Hephaestos flushed as she gazed at him most meaningfully.

"Now?" he stuttered.

"Now." She cast a sly glance over the dark and gritty cavern. "Here, in your workroom."

"This is not a suitable place for you to be, let alone for pleasure." Hephaestos licked his lips. "There are more appropriate places for our lovemaking."

"Is this not where you do your best work?" Tracing a finger down the stained leather front of his apron, she paused just under his belt. "Is this not where you create wondrous offerings for the Ages?"

"Yes, it is true, however…."

"And that is what you will do for me. You will create a gift that no other has."

"Aphrodite, I would do anything you ask." He stepped backward. "But I would not have you here, in the grime."

She grabbed the strings of his tunic, yanking him forward. "If this is where your most fantastic work is done, this is where we shall lie."

Her lips pressed over his slack mouth and her sweet breath filled him. Her fingers were deft and he could not deny his arousal, though he continued to mumble his objections.

"Not here. There is no privacy."

"Cedalion and his friends have fled."

Indeed, they had faded into the dark corridors, leaving them alone. Hephaestos flailed in helpless lust as Aphrodite tugged at his clothing, her body hot against his. He could feel her breasts taut through the thin material of her gown, feel the straining of her hips and the strength of her parted thighs.

"I cannot," he gasped, trying to push her away.

"Oh, but you can." she whispered. She held Hephaestos' hardened member in her hand, her strokes bringing breathless moans from him. "And you will."

With one swift sweep, Aphrodite cleared his worktable and

climbed on hands and knees to its top, glorious in her nakedness. Somewhere, she had discarded her clothing, but he could not say when, for never had he seen such a wanton display.

"Give me Victory, Hephaestos. Now."

As if he were a puppet on a string, Hephaestos scrambled onto the table and tried awkwardly to mount her. His breath came in pained gasps, his vision was clouded and his palms sweated so that he could scarce hold her. Though he slid into her once, twice, he missed more often until Aphrodite cried out with frustration and pushed him to his back.

He lay half off the table, unable to pull himself to a more stable position for Aphrodite was astride him in a fierce attack. She rode him until her eyes glazed while her spine arched and a high-pitched keening sound tore from her lips.

Warm and wet, Aphrodite's juices flowed down onto Hephaestos and he was finally allowed release. He came with such intensity that it felt as if his heart was torn from his chest, his insides ripped asunder.

Appropriate, was his last thought before he collapsed. He sacrificed everything he had on the altar of Love. He prayed it was enough.

TWELVE

Gaea vibrated beneath Jahmed's feet as the drums began pounding out the rhythm signaling the start of the Spring ritual. It had been long months since the great Earth mother was called to join her human children in celebration of her cycles.

Jahmed felt the eagerness with which Gaea awaited the moment she would be invoked, and could not help but wonder if Gaea was aware Niala Aaminah was not present. The one who had held the spirit of Earth within her body during ritual for hundreds of years was not among them. Did Gaea miss her? Did she care that her favored daughter had been stolen away?

Or was Gaea so immersed in her own vision that she could see only what was before her - the opportunity to inhabit flesh and blood - a body to move with and feel and see. It was the only way Gaea could experience physical pleasure and she was at the mercy of her children for such rituals. Alone, she could not take over a mortal body. Such mutinous acts were forbidden.

Gaea had no choice save wait until she was called forth.

Jahmed was reluctant to invoke the great goddess. She believed Gaea abandoned Najahmara during their greatest need. For this, Jahmed harbored anger and resentment, feeling that Gaea did not deserve to move about on two legs, to feel joy, to dance and love.

Spring was about fertility and growth, always offering Gaea the opportunity to make love with her mate, Kulika. But Gaea must call him into a male body of her choosing to enable their coupling, and that did not please Jahmed.

"I am not Niala Aaminah," Jahmed whispered into the breeze that lifted her skirt and ruffled her hair. "I will open myself to your spirit, Great Mother, but I refuse to open my body to a man for your enjoyment, especially one infused with Kulika, for he has not been kind to us."

Earth shimmied as if in agreement. Gaea longed to be free to move about under any condition. To this, Jahmed had to smile.

"And so it will be just you and I, Great Mother. I pray there is healing offered this night, for your people are sorely wounded."

"Who do you speak to?" Ajah hurried along the trail to catch up to Jahmed's longer stride. "And why did you not wait for me?"

"I needed a moment alone, before the ritual begins." Jahmed was halfway between the plateau and the temple gardens, as if the celebration would be held at the top instead of the lake shore.

"Therefore, you speak to yourself?"

"I speak to Gaea. We must come to an understanding if I am to host her spirit within myself this night."

"Hmmm." Ajah nodded, though not fully understanding. She also did not grasp why she and Jahmed must take the route all the way up, along the front of the caves and back down again to the shore when they could have walked a short distance, following the water's edge, and arrived at the same location.

However, it was not Ajah's place to question Jahmed's decision. She assisted with the ritual bathing and combed out Jahmed's braids into a tightly curled mass that lay midway on her back. She tied the braided leather band embellished with beads around Jahmed's forehead to indicate her role as Priestess.

And now, Ajah was to honor Gaea by standing at her right side during the ritual, seeing to the Great Mother's needs. She was to tend Jahmed afterwards, to see she was cared for with food, water and rest.

It was terrifying.

Ajah did not want Jahmed to know just how frightened she was, for there was no alternative. Pallin had decided to sit as queen to her king during the celebration, explaining that it was necessary to bridge between the old and the new. Inni was too ill, and the rest of the girls were too young.

There was no one else who could assist.

"After this night, we must carry out your initiation, Ajah." Jahmed reached for the girl's fingers and gave them a squeeze.

"Yes, Zahava." Ajah lowered her gaze to the ground so that Jahmed would not see her reluctance.

"Everything will go well. You must trust this moment and the Great Mother. No harm will come to either of us." With a smile, Jahmed released Ajah's hand.

As if in reply to the drums, the torches lining the perimeter flared against the night sky. Jahmed and Ajah stood halfway up the path, watching the folk who gathered for the celebration. Zan was at the bottom, ready to escort them into the center of the circle where a head-high pile of wood waited to be lit.

There was a tremendous amount of people Jahmed could not identify. The gathering was already ten deep, with more arriving from the outskirts of Najahmara where the valley opened into an enormous field.

The meadow was once a place of virtuous green beauty. Now it appeared as a stinking muddy bowl where the majority of the invaders camped. Just like the rest of the village, the innocence had been destroyed and replaced with an ugliness that defied description.

Jahmed was grateful the darkness covered the offending sight, helping her to come to grips with her role. To lead her own people in the ritual welcoming of Spring, to encourage the pleasures within the fertile season, to offer gratitude for their continuing presence upon the Earth - yes, that Jahmed could, and would, do with joy.

To offer the same to the trespassers - those who had raped, murdered and now sought to rule the land - that was a painful travesty.

Jahmed felt the resistance build within her breast and fought to contain the emotion. It would serve no one if she melted into an angry bitter woman who wished them all to disappear into the Shadowland.

No, she would not succumb to such base behavior. She would do her duty as a priestess to Gaea, and as a sister to Niala Aaminah. With an abrupt nod, Jahmed exhaled with acceptance, letting her own presence seep to the edges of her awareness.

As soon as Jahmed released her breath the energy began to rise through the soles of her bare feet. She embraced Gaea with a small prayer and the two women began their journey to the bottom of the path. There, Jahmed took Zan's proffered elbow and stepped into the ritual circle. Her gown billowed out and cast a disproportionate shadow. Her dark hair lifted with same invisible wind. Her face smoothed as her chin lifted and the gaze that swept over the crowd was not her own.

Those who recognized the presence of the Great Mother, Gaea, pushed forward and rejoiced. Those who did not still felt the change in the air and retreated with defensive arms crossed upon their chests. The drums paused and stillness settled across the valley.

When Gaea spoke through Jahmed's lips, her voice rippled across their heads. Ajah's grip tightened as Jahmed shook with the effort. Zan's startled gaze traveled along the priestess in awe as he, too, felt the power flow through Jahmed's hand upon his arm.

"Your...journey...brief. Waste...not with...suffering. Put aside difference. Join in love. What has been...is done. What is to come, is beginning."

The longer Gaea spoke through Jahmed, the less awkward the words. Jahmed felt her center straining to sustain the intensity of the goddess and the tiny bit of herself still conscious wondered how Niala could carry the force with such grace.

"I beg you accept each other without rancor or judgment, for there are many further woes that await. Find strength together. Find forgiveness."

A collective sigh swept through the people as Gaea pushed her vitality through the ground and pulsed it up into the gathered bodies. Tingling skin, raised hair and an overwhelming sense of peace held the crowd in sway for mere seconds before the drums once again pounded out rhythm.

This time the call was of a different nature. Not just to gather, but to join with each other. To choose a mate. To make love. To conceive and birth. Not just children but inspired thoughts, commitment to reconciliation and prosperity, to a new beginning for Najahmara.

Hands grasped hands, gazes locked and bodies came closer and closer together, ever on a mission to heal the wounds that nearly destroyed them. A swaying dance took precedent over suspicion as people saw each other for the first time: not as invader versus conquered or hunter and prey, but as human beings in search of love and kinship.

Jahmed and Ajah stood rocking back and forth in the center of the throng as Zan, caught up in Gaea's thrall, drifted away from them. Slowly, slowly, Jahmed pulled from Ajah's grip and began to dance, a soft hum trailing behind her.

With a sigh, Ajah followed, uncertain if all was well or if she should snatch onto Jahmed's gown and hold her back. In that moment, Jahmed began to dance faster, weaving in and out amongst the swarm. Ajah picked up her pace, pushing past people who did not appear to see or feel her shoving against them.

Panic rose in her throat when Jahmed disappeared amid the vibrating bodies. Ajah stood stock still, unable to breath. What was she to do? How would she find Jahmed together with so many folk? Ajah feared she would faint and fall down to be trampled to death in dishonor for not doing her duty.

"Ahh, Gaea, I am sorry," Ajah sobbed.

A touch on her back brought her whirling about with relief. Jahmed had returned. All was well. Her joy faded as she faced a man with a silly grin lighting his long features. She recognized him as one of the king's guard but she did not know his name.

"Partner with me," he whispered into her ear.

Before Ajah could protest, the man swept her into his arms, pushing his body against hers in a way that sent a shudder down her spine.

"No. No, I cannot," Ajah gasped, trying to break free from his grip.

His response was to press closer. Ajah felt his excitement, and though she was still virgin, she understood the carnal pleasure he offered. Her lower region first tingled in response and then desire such as she had never known existed burst forth in her belly. She clung to the nameless man as Gaea's will suffused her senses and all other responsibilities were forgotten.

As the throng moved nearly as one in a sensual winding dance, glazed eyes looking past their differences, King Hattusilis squirmed in his chair.

"I do not understand what occurs." His voice quivered with his own suppressed desires, and something more. Something that nudged against his thoughts, daring him to relent and open to his worst fears. "What are they doing? Stop them."

Pallin's lips curved in a wanton smile as she reached between her husband's legs. "It is Gaea calling us to make love, to be fertile, just as she."

Appalled, Hattusilis swatted her hand away. "You are already with child, we need not indulge in that behavior here in front of everyone."

"They pay no attention, my Love. They follow the Great Mother's will."

"Stop them. I will not have this. You swore there would be no concerns if I allowed this ritual to occur."

"There are no concerns." Pallin rose from her seat, moving awkwardly to the drum rhythm but with unmistakable intention. "There is only us. Come, be with me."

"Do not disgrace yourself, Wife. I will not be subject to your goddess."

Though he protested, the foreign power that prodded at his mind with relentless craving for sexual engagement took over. Pallin yanked him to his feet and suddenly the pain that gripped his every step was gone. The serpentine force coursed through Hattusilis' body bringing vitality and unleashed lust.

Alarm set off a warning deep in his heart as control faded. Hattusilis became the puppet of the creature from the cave and he could not control it. He was aware, as if watching from a distance, yet he was helpless to prevent himself from snatching Pallin's arm in a cruel grip, forcing her to her knees.

She cried out in pain, one hand held protectively against her large belly.

"Hattu, stop, you are hurting me."

Pallin's voice could scarce be heard over the sounds around them, and it mattered not that she protested. He would have his way with her. Was it not what she requested?

He threw her skirt onto her back and, already hard, loosened his trousers. Pallin sobbed, bringing added hunger as Hattusilis bent over her. Before he could impale his pregnant wife, a fist struck the side of his temple, knocking him to the ground.

Fury brought him quickly to his feet, a deed he could not have accomplished without the added strength of the serpent. He faced the priestess who stood before him, not as Jahmed, but as Gaea, Kulika's mate.

"How dare you?" A shriek burst from Gaea's throat, her face twisted with contempt. "I have not called you."

"I do not need you," Kulika taunted. "I have found the means to occupy this body without you."

"You are not strong enough."

"I am. Witness this." Kulika ran his hand over the king's chest, down to his still engorged member. "Play with me, Beloved. Let me show you what this human can do."

"I did not call you," Gaea insisted.

"Never again will I be at your service. I have suffered eons watching as you indulge, allowed only when you deem it. No more. I am staying."

Enraged, Gaea leaped upon her mate, both fists pounding at his head and chest. Kulika caught her as they fell and began rolling about in the crushed grass. The sway Gaea held over the massive crowd broke free as if an egg cracked and the insides poured out. At the same moment, lightening flew across the dark heavens in protest of such manners.

With the spell dispersed, people shook their heads, rubbed their faces and stared in dismay at those they held close. Najahmaran folk laid with invaders, husbands and wives with new partners, young with old, many in the full act of lovemaking. Screams rang out, fights began and what was once a field of passion became ground once more soaked in blood, seething with the bitterness, pain and distrust of the past.

The night sky - she who is called Nut - summoned the storm clouds and drenched Najahmara with torrents of cold rain. The lake became a tumultuous pattern of waves crashing on the shore from the winds that arose as a veil of fog settled over the land.

The fighting ceased and folk ran for cover, back to the separation of lives Gaea was desperate to heal. That which had just taken place was encased in a shroud of confusion and would scarce be remembered upon the dawn.

Gaea fled, as did Kulika, when both Zan and Con came to their senses and pulled the brawling immortals apart. Other guards returned to help, though dazed and squinting with disbelief. Hattusilis lay on his back in the now-muddy field, rain splashing in his face, eyes unable to focus or bruised mouth to speak.

Every bit of his body ached with a tremendous throbbing. He could not stand without assistance and had to be carried back to his quarters, groaning, in tears with each jolt.

A shaken Pallin stared at Jahmed, held upright by Zan in a gentle grip.

"Why did this happen?"

Jahmed bowed her head in shame. "I could not hold Gaea. She did as she pleased. We are in ruin."

Pallin had no response, for it was truth Jahmed spoke. Defeated, knowing there would be no recourse but for Hattusilis to strike out at Jahmed and all those who supported the temple, Pallin accepted the outstretched hand of a soldier. Hattusilis would force her to choose between him and the women. With a saddened heart, she began the journey back along the shoreline to their quarters.

Jahmed began to keen, her face buried in her palms. She would have gone to her knees if Zan had not held her in place. There was naught the big man could say, for the entire evening had been a disaster. He, too, knew that the ire of his king would bring much more misery to all the people.

With a sigh, he turned Jahmed, held her against his wet tunic, and allowed her to sob out her grief while the rain continued to fall.

THIRTEEN

With great distaste, Anteros scanned the living quarters of the Forge God. Gaudy, overdone and badly cluttered, just like the rest of Hephaestos' palace. Anteros was amazed anyone could tolerate the disarray, let alone his mother. The only welcome sight was Aphrodite, and the two Graces who remained on Lemnos.

Aglaia and Euphrosyne were lovely, as always, but Aphrodite's splendor was like a clean sea breeze sweeping through the Forge god's muddled possessions. If his mother was the warm misty breeze, he was the glistening shore. Tall and bronze, long legs and arms bare beneath a short white tunic, simple sandals on his feet, he was the calm within a storm of colors.

His waist-length hair lay straight, shimmering like sand with full sun reflecting from it. He was aware of his beauty, just as he was aware the sky was blue or the grasses were green. He cared nothing for this other than he was in deep contrast to his mother's vulgar surroundings.

He was gratified to hear Euphrosyne's joyful cry of greeting when she saw him. Clamping a hand over her lips, she glanced away as her sister lifted an eyebrow at her outburst.

Aphrodite appeared sullen and bored, extending a limp hand in welcome. Anteros found the situation appalling, worse even than Thaleia's description.

Taking Aphrodite's hand, he kissed her fingers as he knelt beside the chaise. She was cool to his touch. Around her lips and under her eyes, a blue stain marred her complexion.

"Mother, are you ill?"

"No." Aphrodite's voice was thin and high. "I am merely tired. What brings you here, Anteros? I would think you would have much to occupy your time."

Anteros flicked a concerned glance at the two Graces and back to his mother's taut face. "My allegiance is to you, Mother. Whatever you want, I gladly do."

"Oh, if that were but true." Aphrodite touched a square of fine linen cloth to her nose.

"Why would you think it different? When have I not been present at your request?"

"Ask? Always, I must ask. Can you not simply do?"

Withholding a deep sigh, Anteros remained patient. "I will try to do better at guessing what it is you want."

"Are you being snide?"

"Never." Anteros smiled a smile he knew was enchanting, for deep dimples creased his cheeks. His eyes, as green as a tranquil sea, lifted at the corners. Rare was the being that would not respond to this calculated offering.

Euphrosyne cooed like a contented bird until Aglaia jabbed her in the ribs. Aphrodite ignored them all. She laid a hand along her forehead and closed her eyes.

"This is highly unlike you. I have come to request your return to Cos."

"Thaleia sent you." It was an accusation.

"There is only one to whom I answer and that is you, Mother." Anteros switched to her name with the hope it would get her attention. "There is much discord in your temples, Aphrodite. You have been away far too long. You must return. Your worshippers yearn for your attention."

"My worshippers." She spoke the word as if it brought a bad taste to her mouth "They believe they know Love, yet they do not. They clamor for my gifts, yet it is not a fair exchange."

"They are mortals and give as they can."

"No, I give and I give and they take and take. I can do no more."

Her words flowed over him in a chilling ripple. Anteros shifted with unease, casting a glance over his shoulder. He had the feeling they were discussing an entirely different subject, yet what, he was at a loss.

"Aphrodite. Mother." Anteros' tone grew gentle. "The world suffers because you suffer."

"It is not so. I am at their mercy. When love's sweet scent is not in the air, they turn on each other. I become their target." Aphrodite sat up, eyes blazing in her gaunt face. "If I do not ride herd, they turn to Jealousy, Revenge, Pain and Misery."

"All those whom you have named belong to the House of Love." Anteros laid a firm hand upon Aphrodite's arm. "And they run amuck in both realms with no one to maintain discipline."

"The mortals also turn to Greed and Bitterness. They turn to War. So quickly, they forget Love."

"You claim then, that Ares takes all? You hold no fault in this?" He met the gazes of the Graces above his mother's head and saw the truth in their sad expressions.

"No, it is not his fault. It is me. I am not like the others." Aphrodite rubbed her face and blinked, staring into a past that none could see. "I was not born of a mother and father. I was not nurtured at the breast, nor held by strong arms. I was created from the sea and I have no choice but to roll with the tides. I am tossed about like so much driftwood, at the mercy of all emotion."

Standing, Anteros held up his hands in a gesture of confusion. "It is true your tie to the mortal world is much stronger than most, but this behavior is maudlin. It is beneath you."

With a swift intake of air, Aphrodite rose to a sitting position. The Graces drew back, preparing for an eruption. Anteros would be glad for an angry retort, anything but this pathetic speech. Though he was dully warned by Thaleia that Aphrodite was not herself, she did not speak the half of it.

Aphrodite poised on the edge of some thought for long moments, and then lay back with a sigh. "Go home, Anteros. My allegiance is here."

"Here?" He was genuinely startled. "Why?"

"Have you not heard? I have forsaken Ares and formed a new alliance with Lord Hephaestos."

"And what of it? Even though you spent eons in partnership with Ares, you did not take up residence with him, nor he with you."

"That was different." Aphrodite yawned, as if bored by the conversation.

"How so?"

"I do not have to explain myself to you."

"You have responsibilities that are not best served by this disorder." Anteros cleared his throat as he took another look about the chambers. "If you are not in an environment suited to your nature, you will surely wither. Then what of the world, Mother? If Love becomes an empty shell then War will most certainly win."

"He has already won." Aphrodite closed her eyes, feigned sleep and refused to speak again.

Anteros beckoned to the good sisters to step aside and tell him what had happened. Aglaia would not leave Aphrodite's side, but Euphrosyne was all too eager to move into the outer chamber with him.

"I have missed you." Euphrosyne cast a brilliant smile at him.

"And I, you." A twitch of uneasiness slithered along Anteros' spine. "Why is it you have not returned home? What has happened here that would cause my mother to behave in such a way?"

"Our Princess takes no interest in anything and, worse, no pleasure." Euphrosyne took up the ribbon tied about her waist and began to twist it back and forth. "She lies recumbent and listless, just as you have seen her."

"What of Hephaestos? Does he not question this?"

"Why should he? He has what he has always wanted, the most beauteous of all in his bed. What care does he have if she is unhappy?"

"He will not let her out of this alliance?"

"She chooses not. In truth, who could stand in her way, should she decide on another path?"

"Truth." Anteros nodded. "Though I am deeply puzzled by this reluctance to go home."

"It is because...." Euphrosyne stopped again, chastising herself for speaking out of turn. It was not her place to tell Anteros.

"Please, I need to know what beleaguers my mother so I may

help her."

"You can do nothing." Dropping the ends of the belt, Euphrosyne said, "You are a good son and you may try, but in the end there is only one who can make things right."

"You speak of Ares."

"It is so. I know you bear ill will toward Lord Ares, but I fear these doldrums will continue until they are together again."

"He is poison to her."

"Not really. They make it seem that way, but they need each other. They create a balance, not only for themselves, but for the mortal world."

"And you view the world through misty eyes." Anteros put his hands on her rounded shoulders. "Though I am Response to the call of Love, I know it is often a painful and misunderstood path. Ironic, is it not, that my mother yearns for one whose response is far less than she expects." He gave Euphrosyne a gentle shake. "Each and every time, she is deeply disappointed."

"You do not see this as your fault?" Euphrosyne put her arms around him. "Do not, Anteros, for what we make of our lives is up to us."

"Spoken like a true Grace."

"You ridicule me." She pulled back from him.

"Maybe a bit." Touching the tip of his finger to her chin, Anteros bent and kissed her lips. He did not miss the yearning in her eyes for more yet did not pull her into an embrace, but held her hands in his.

"You work hard to cloud my mind. You have not told me why Aphrodite is so distressed."

"I have. Because she misses Lord Ares." Euphrosyne's gaze was shy.

"I accept they have a peculiar relationship that feeds them, but that is not the source of the malady my mother has developed. Euphrosyne, you must tell me what it really is."

"I cannot, Anteros. Please, do not ask me to betray a confidence."

"I must." He spoke close to her ear, his breath warm on her neck. "Tell me."

"No." Her voice vibrated with the need to be close to him.

"You must."

"I cannot."

"Please, Euphrosyne, and I will give you anything you desire."

"That is not fair, Anteros, for you know what it is I want." She paused, her breath coming fast.

"All is fair in matters of Love." His voice was low, deliberately wrapping around her like a soft cloak. "Tell me what you desire most."

"I want you."

Anteros stroked her hair, letting the fine strands comb through his fingers. "I am yours, if you tell me what is wrong with my mother."

"That is heartless." Euphrosyne trembled at his touch.

"I am my mother's son, after all. Tell me." Anteros let his power to invoke response pour over her.

All the love she felt for him burst forth and loosened her tongue for, in that moment, she would do anything for him. "She cannot conceive a child with Lord Hephaestos, though she tries and tries. It does not happen."

"A child?" Anteros released her with a suddenness that left her sagging against the wall. "Why?"

"I have already said too much." Tears glistened in her eyes. "Aphrodite will be angry with me."

"Anything is better than this apathy that leaves her lusterless." Shaking his head, Anteros paced two steps then returned. "A child? This makes no sense to me."

"It was to be a special child. Though she gives herself to Lord Hephaestos, nothing comes of it. Now she has fallen into this blackness of spirit. We are at a loss to bring her back."

"This place, with its noise and stinking of fumes from that volcano, with all this…this…." Anteros waved at the clutter and bright conglomeration of textures and patterns.

It was as far from the clean, open and flowing seascape that was Aphrodite's choice of living quarters as was the cold mountain of Athos where his father resided. "This place will never soothe her spirit, nor her mind. She must go home."

"She will not leave. She beds Hephaestos at every opportunity and waits for the moment when her womb will quicken. It is all she cares about."

"Does he withhold from her?"

"I do not know what you mean." Her face and neck stained the color of ripe fruit.

"I mean, though they make love, does he withhold his seed from her, for without it, there will be no child."

"It is possible, for once Aphrodite gets with child she will have no further use for Lord Hephaestos."

Euphrosyne's brows drew together in a frown. "And yet, it seems he would be happy to accommodate her. It would surely be a source of pride to father a child upon Eternal Love."

"Indeed." Anteros turned with a quick move that sent his long locks sweeping outward. "However, it does not matter either way, for she does not conceive, and it is this obsession that holds her here. Something must be done."

"What? What can we do that has not already been done?"

"Though it makes me ill to consider it, there is only one thing I know to do." Pausing, he inhaled and then blew the air out. With steady gaze upon Euphrosyne, he finished, "Ask Ares to intercede."

"Oh, oh, I cannot. Please do not say I should go to him, for I fear him."

"He would not harm you."

"I do not like the way he looks at me."

"What? Does he try to seduce you?"

"No! No, it is just that his eyes are so black you cannot see beyond the surface. I do not know what he thinks when he looks upon me and my sisters." She hugged herself at the very idea of facing Ares alone.

"When we are present, he stares with a severity that is frightening." Her hands fluttered aimlessly. "Make Thaleia go. She has been to his fortress before."

"Contacting Ares does bear contemplating, for I do not know what else I can do. I know only that I will not leave my mother in this dungeon." Anteros rubbed his forehead in anticipation of the headache only Ares could provide.

As he turned to go, Euphrosyne stopped him. "And what of your promise, Anteros? I have been indiscrete and, for that, I may well be punished when all is said and done."

"I do not believe Aphrodite's brand of punishment could be more than a reprimand, if even that. She may well thank us both."

"You do not intend to...." she paused, distress written on her sweet face. "Follow through?" Euphrosyne lowered her gaze, as if it was what she expected.

With a sudden show of affection, Anteros took her in his arms, lifting her chin to meet his gaze. "I will keep my promise, Euphrosyne. When all is restored to its rightful place, you shall have what you asked for."

A surprised 'O' formed on her lips and her body tensed against his. Anteros knew she was still virgin and, yet, she boldly invited him to her bed as if she were not. It was a contradiction that was puzzling.

There were none who could remain innocent for long in the temples of Aphrodite, for though Love in its highest form was pure, at its base was raw need. Euphrosyne was the youngest of the Graces, perhaps the most inexperienced, but he could not see her as untouched. If that were so, then there was a reason why.

As this awareness dawned, along with the possible consequences, Anteros loosened his grip. Euphrosyne threw her arms about his neck and clung to him, crying out, "You cannot go back on your word."

"I will not, but answer this, why are you so eager for me?"

"I love you and have from the first moment I saw you." She drew him down into a kiss filled with eager passion. When their lips parted, she whispered, "Do you doubt me?"

"I hope you do not deceive me, Euphrosyne."

"There is no lie, Anteros, only my love for you. I swear."

Echoing across the hall came another voice, "Euphrosyne. You have been gone long enough. Aphrodite has need of you."

Aglaia's reprimand acted as a lever between them. They stepped apart as if guilt was written above their heads, each turning away from the other without a sound. As Euphrosyne started back into the private chambers, Anteros took his leave, his mind filled with doubt, though his heart glowed.

FOURTEEN

As in every other day, Niala stood at the railing of the courtyard and stared out to the farthest reach of the sea. The glory of fresh air mixed with the sight of serene turquoise water bumping into the blue of sky on the horizon cheered her. It was a mild day, unusual for Athos, with the sun peeking out from scattered clouds drifting across the heavens. A hint of rain was in the air, promised for later in the evening.

Spring had finally come to Athos, waiting until the summer season was mere weeks away, at least by Niala's count. She often lost track of time with the days and nights a blur as the winter months dragged on and on, overcast, cold and disheartening.

On the other side of the fortress, the arduous mountain path was slick with mud and the grounds a soggy swamp. Warriors continued to slog through the mess, unmindful of the inconvenience, driving their animals onward and upward. Thawed waste gave off an unbearable stench, drowning out the scent of the tiny purple flowers growing wild on the side of the mountain..

Opposites, Niala thought. One side of Athos was ugly and scarred, fed by constant streams of savagery - the other, stark and beautiful, swept clear by the ocean winds.

Much like Ares, himself.

Niala sighed and leaned her elbows on the stone rail. Her longing for Najahmara grew every day, so much so she could scarce think of anything else. Her dreams were a jumble of beloved faces at their day-to-day work.

They had shared laughter over meals and taught the young eager girls who would someday be priestesses. The quiet, peaceful streets of Najahmara before the violence, when it was a happy and productive valley filled with lush bounty.

Niala felt she was there with them. She could hear their voices and those of the people they served, for she knew every one of them with an intimacy brought by Gaea herself.

She had served them for nearly three centuries, attended every birth, held vigil at every death. She saw the valley go from a wild, untouched place to a home for the people who preserved the sanctity of Gaea's land. She helped a handful of people swell into a community happy in their isolation. Those who wandered in were absorbed into the population. The traders that passed through kept their secrets.

Except for one.

And there, Niala's dreams turned to nightmares filled with endless torture, pain-filled shrieks and burning fog. She was unable to stop the desecration. She could hear the roaring of flames, see the dead eyes of her beloved daughter, Seire, and feel the weight of Kulika as he pressed from within, eager to taste the flesh of the destroyers. She would awaken with heart thudding, soaked in sweat and tears, to find herself alone in the cool hushed quarters at Athos.

Ares was angry, vindictive and restless. He spent far less time with her than before and when present, kept to himself. Once the doors were thrown open, he seemed to take malicious pleasure in her dilemma. His offer to return to Najahmara - if she could - a mean and spiteful gift. She was relieved when he left her for other entertainment.

When he chose to lie beside her, the nightmares of Najahmara became something different, something equally as disturbing but less coherent. They became the distant cry of a grieving woman who held a babe in her arms, rocking back and forth while a desperate man attempted to take the child from her.

For hours on end, Niala dwelled upon the meaning of it and

could only fathom a single conclusion: Najahmara was her child and Ares sought to keep her from it. She loathed him for this act of vengeance.

And yet, she discovered tenderness toward him. When he was near, she could not help reaching out to that vulnerable piece Ares kept well hidden. He mourned the loss of his mate, Aphrodite, but did it in the most private place within himself. He would not allow consolation, believing he deserved to suffer. He would not concede any responsibility over the split, though Niala tried to make him see it through a woman's eyes.

"Opposition." Niala watched the soaring form of a predator bird. "It is the same for me. He refuses to see the pain he causes."

"It is difficult for any to see their flaws the way others do." A familiar voice spoke behind her.

"Mortals, perhaps, but a god?"

"Especially a god."

Niala turned to see Deimos, his hands clasped behind his back, his long legs apart in a contemplative stance. Tired lines creased his handsome face.

"How long have you been here?"

"Long enough to hear you muttering to yourself as if you were an old woman bent over a bubbling cauldron."

"Indeed, I have spent too much time doing exactly that."

"A lovely sight, I am certain."

"It has been long since you visited, not since…." Niala inhaled and held her breath, recalling the moment they went too far. A flush stained her face.

"Ares has kept me well occupied these past months, although now he has forbidden me from the very place he demanded I stay."

A slight smile touched Niala's lips. "I have experienced this convoluted side of Ares myself. It is not pleasant."

"He bid me stand and greet warriors who pray for his generosity in battle. Little do they know he has no goodwill. Now, Ares sits on his throne in the blackest temper I have ever witnessed."

Niala gave a short nod, acknowledging she, too, had observed this disposition. Their eyes met and held as the passion that drew them together in their ill-favored affair stirred once more. It was as if no time had lapsed, as if their tender love had just begun and the fires of ardor had never been dismissed.

Deimos started forward, unable to deny the love burning within his heart. He had banked the embers that now fanned to life at the sight of his beloved.

Niala held up a palm, warding him off. Her amber gaze was stricken with grief. "No, we cannot. You know we cannot."

Deimos halted but when he spoke, his voice was filled with bitter reproof. "I care not whether Ares discovers the truth. His punishment is naught compared to the anguish I suffer without you by my side. Do not turn me away."

"I must, for here, we cannot risk the consequences."

"Then I shall take you away from this desolate mount, somewhere he cannot find us."

"How I wish that was possible." Niala let her hand fall to her side. Deimos came to her, then, and took her into his arms.

"It is possible."

"If that is true." Her throat closed making it near impossible for her to speak. "I want to go home, Deimos, to Najahmara. Will you take me there?"

"Ahh, Niala, anywhere but there. In good faith, I cannot return you to the grief that exists in Najahmara. I wish to take you somewhere happy, where we can be content together."

She ignored his plea. "Ares says there is nothing left. If that is so, they need me more than ever. I can help heal the wounds."

"They do not need you, Niala. They survive. Take comfort in that." His tone pleaded with her to forget Najahmara. "Let us flee from Athos but not there. There is only heartache in Najahmara."

"That is true, but must I run from such anguish? Or should I embrace it? Much of it is my fault."

Inni's broken and torn body haunted Niala. With a heavy sigh, Niala went on. "And the others, Jahmed, Pallin, Ajah, Tulane, Deniz? What befell them at the hands of these soldiers? I could not see for the smothering haze."

She shook her head. "And what of the good people of Najahmara? How many of them lived through the night?"

"Those you name survived, as well as some of the younger ones." Deimos spoke with kindness. He wanted Niala to know her people were as well as they could yet wished to discourage her return.

"Seire, my daughter." Niala's voice caught. "I did not see her into the arms of our Mother."

"I carried her to her grave, Niala. She was returned to Gaea with proper respect. Pallin and Jahmed were there with her."

"But I was not."

"There is nothing you can do to change that."

"You sound nearly as heartless as he." Niala waved her hand at the doorway. "Look how he taunts me, but offers no passage. *Find your own way*, he says. *Go if you must, but go alone*, he says. As if I can."

Turning back to the sea, Niala gripped the stone rail. "It is the height of cruelty. And you. You offer me a means of escape but refuse the only place I wish to go."

"To return does not serve a purpose." Deimos touched between her shoulders. "They must go on without you."

"Why? Ares has given permission to return to my homeland." She lifted her chin, her head tilted toward the incoming breeze, for there seemed a voice in the shifting winds. "I hear Gaea calling me."

Niala whirled to face Deimos and pressed her hands against his chest. She could feel the heat of his body and the thumping of his heart beneath her fingers.

"Please, Deimos, take me home."

"It is the first place Ares would look." He gripped her wrists, his eyes unblinking.

"He no longer cares where I go, so consumed is he by Love's abandonment."

"I will defy Ares for you," Deimos exhaled until there was no air left. "I will do anything for you." Deimos freed himself and paced alongside the railing. "But do not ask me to take you to Najahmara."

"I must. I have no other way." Niala followed him the length of the courtyard. "Gaea calls me home, Deimos. I hear her voice everywhere. She is in the wind, in the groaning of the rocks, in the crash of the surf. She wants me to return."

He did an abrupt about face and Niala bumped into him. He held her there, a few inches apart from him. When he spoke, his voice was heavy with emotion.

"I confess I have never carried a mortal through a portal of sheer will. I am afraid you would be hurt. I could not bear it if something happened to you. My intention was to escape much the way you arrived the first time, by horseback. He would not suspect such action from either of us."

"Ares claims I am of the immortal caste. If that is so, there is no danger."

"If that is so. There have been other long-lived humans."

"Ares does not base it solely on that, but on many things. He says he can see the imprint of immortality." Niala's fingers tightened on Deimos' tunic. "You have said as much yourself."

"Still, there are many dangers in this land you call home. Let me take you somewhere else, somewhere safe, where we can be together. That is all I ask. To be with you. It is not possible in Najahmara."

Niala stroked his cheek and then placed a tender kiss on his jaw. Deimos closed his eyes and leaned into her touch. He gave no response other than a slight lift of his shoulders.

"Deimos, I am pregnant." Niala watched his eyes widen, his mouth tighten. She could feel him withdraw from her. She let him go. "I cannot bear a child here. I must go home."

"And this child, it is his?"

At Niala's nod, his hope sank and his heart contracted in misery. "He will never let you go. Not now."

"Ares is not aware of the child."

"How can he not?" Deimos' voice was edged with rancor. "He plants his seed with intention, it is never without design."

"He says nothing about it."

"Perhaps he thinks you are not yet aware of the babe."

"A woman always knows, from the moment of conception."

With a questioning expression, Deimos studied her face. "How?"

"It is a feeling like no other, a vibration of sorts. It brings a wash of joy. Sometimes fear." Niala paused for a moment, unblinking as she stared past Deimos. "Then our bodies begin to change. In the beginning, there is almost always illness. Even those who have many children often get sick. It is so we will know to take care, that a little one is waiting."

Niala placed her palms on her midsection. With her gown pulled tight, Deimos could see the outline of a swelling belly. "And then we grow bigger. Ares has not taken notice."

"Are you certain?" Deimos cleared his throat. "If he lies with you, he would be sure to take note."

"His desire for me has waned. No matter how he blusters, he can scarce bear his life without Love's gentle touch. He needs your mother."

"It is his own stubbornness that has brought this on. This babe swift retribution for Aphrodite's desertion."

"Perhaps, but as it is, he pays no attention to anything save his own misery. He did not see that I was sickly, nor does he see that my belly grows. Equally, he does not hear my discontent until I force it upon him and then he offers a hollow victory. This opportunity to leave is empty because he knows I, alone, cannot find my way."

She nodded toward the open sky. "Deimos, I beg you trust yourself as I trust you, for I would do nothing to harm this child. I did not think it was possible to bear more children. My blood ceased a very long time ago, even before I was of an age to have it so. The gift of my sweet Seire was through the manifestation of Gaea and now, she is gone. All I have left is this babe."

Niala placed one hand on her belly. "I treasure this one, no matter who is the father. I want her to birth at Najahmara."

"Her?" Startled, Deimos shook his head. "Ares has no daughters. It was the source of contention between my mother and he."

"Yes and if there is to be a reconciliation, I should not be here."

"I fear there will not be, especially if she discovers this."

"Another reason for my return to Najahmara. Please, Deimos." Niala came to him and put her arms around him, standing on tiptoe so her mouth reached his ear. "Please. Take me home."

With a groan, Deimos encircled her with his arms and held her tight against him. Love dictated sacrifice and it was his to release Niala to her destiny, however much he wanted to keep her. He was not Ares. He would not hold prisoner the woman he most loved.

"Pray, Niala, pray I do not destroy either you or the babe."

She felt him tense and then darkness swirled around her in an icy silent void. Tiny spots of bright light danced before her eyes, her body grew weak, went limp as her heart fluttered. If not for the strength in Deimos' arms, she would have fallen away into that void and never returned.

Next she knew she lay on the ground with grass all around her, and a bright blue cloudless sky overhead. The wind danced across her in a warm joyous song and the voice of Gaea sighed, *Welcome.*

Deimos bent over her, terror pulling the skin taut against his bones. "Niala?"

"Yes, I am here. Home." Tears streamed from Niala's eyes as she brought Deimos down to meet her lips.

"Thank you." She kissed him once, twice, tasted honey, felt his longing. Love overwhelmed her. She wanted him, now and forever. He belonged to her. She opened to him and took him into her body in a rush of all-consuming desire. He could do no more than sail on the current of passion until they were liberated in gasping unison.

Releasing him, Niala lay back upon the sweet earth, a satiated smile upon her lips. The wind tugged at her gown as if to pull it back into place.

Deimos rose to his feet, breath coming in harsh wheezes as he repeatedly ran his tongue over his mouth. He turned away so she would not see his confusion as he straightened his clothes. Did she want him or did she not? His fingers balled into tight fists as he fought the rage building inside him.

What did she want? Everything. Nothing. Ares. Himself.

As Deimos' sweeping gaze landed upon what was left of the monument, he froze. All thoughts ceased as he moved toward the stones.

"What happened here?" Deimos began a circle around the entire area. The grass grew wild, nearly covering the broken pieces, the worn path was no longer evident. It was clear the fire circle had gone unused as vines crept over the remnants of a long past celebration.

Niala stood up on, staring with blind eyes at the destruction. The jolt upon seeing it again made her ill. Somewhere, along the face of the ridge, Layla's bones were scattered, never to be recovered.

Layla was truly gone and Niala had no more than an empty grave to sit beside. And Seire? Where had they put her? Deimos said he carried her to her grave but where? Where was it? Was anyone left who knew where the burial grounds were?

"Perhaps Ares was right. Perhaps I should not have come back."

Deimos rubbed his forehead, taking care not to touch Niala. If he so much as laid a hand on her, he would become his father and steal her away, hiding her for his pleasure. He would not be as Ares.

"No, he is wrong. You could never put the destruction to rest if you do not face it once again."

"And you?" Niala heard the distance in his voice, the coldness as it settled into his voice.

"I must leave you. It would be best if Ares did not find me absent." He did not finish but the implication was clear.

"Will you tell him?"

"Sooner or later, I must. He will suspect I brought you here."

"I hope," Niala made a small sound in her throat. "I hope you do not suffer because of my selfishness. I should not have asked you to do this."

"You should not have made love to me again." Deimos turned to her with anger glinting in his dark eyes. "I made peace with our separation." His jaw set as he clenched his teeth. "Now all the torments rain down upon me once again."

"I am sorry." Niala reached for him and he jerked back. "I did not wish to hurt you. I simply had need of you." She laced her fingers together and watched the marks her nails did as they dug into her skin. "I love you."

"And I, you." Deimos steeled himself against the flood of emotion that demanded he take her in his arms. "I must go now."

"Thank you."

She reached for him again and this time he did not pull away. He held her next to his heart and returned her kiss with a tenderness that brought tears to Niala's eyes. She felt the sacrifice he offered in her name and was grateful.

In a blink, Deimos was gone and Niala was alone.

Torn with guilt, consumed by dark desires, enraged that he had let down his guard once again, Deimos returned to Athos. He paced the marble slabs in his quarters, counting each square as if the answers were held within its shiny black surface.

Dare he confess to Ares that he had taken Niala to Najahmara? Or that he had once again satisfied his carnal desires with her? Or that he loved Niala Aaminah more than life itself and cared not if Amason took his head from his shoulders?

Would Ares discover any of these truths if Deimos did not confess? Pacing, he counted and thought of every possibility.

Ares would be furious. He would go to Najahmara in a rage.

Or he would not be surprised Niala was gone and do nothing. Or he would see the betrayal from a different perspective, one of stolen love and inflict a punishment upon Deimos that would go beyond any he had ever imposed.

Or death.

Deimos snorted in derision. Death - Thanatos - was his cousin, son of Hades, always a phantom in the mortal realm. Thanatos begrudged those who lived in light and would be happy to take Deimos into the hallowed halls of the Shadowland.

"And I care not what happens to me from this day forth."

Deimos made his way into the depths of the fortress, his steps dragging, his mind racing. With each staircase came a pause, a reconsideration of his decision, but he knew it would be a lesson in futility to try to outwit his father. And he held no regret for what he had done.

No, it was best he pled guilty and accept the penalty. If death was the end result, so be it.

Deimos was no more than a few steps beyond the last staircase that would take him into the old council hall when a voice called to him from the darkened sideline. "Halt, Deimos, for I wish a word with you."

Deimos froze, tense at the sound of his twin's voice.

"I did not believe you would ever put foot into these halls." Deimos turned to stare at the silhouette of his brother.

"Dire times, Brother." Anteros stepped into the circle of torchlight.

"What crisis would bring you to War's fortress, Anteros, when you have sworn you would never cross into such a bloody place?"

"I seek Ares."

It was a simple statement and whatever threat had been present was withdrawn. Deimos inhaled and released his guard, however reluctant, and continued on into the great hall with Anteros following close behind.

The ring of Deimos' boot heels echoed throughout the cavernous chamber and, in the background, Anteros could hear the muted voices of warriors ever raised in libation to their god. Somewhere nearby the men gathered to wait for Ares. A faint trace of smoke from their fires crawled across the room and the underlying scent of manure followed close behind.

Though most of the hall was veiled in darkness, he could see the ghostly outlines of man-sized statues interspersed with thick pillars and low couches. A raised dais was at the end nearest them, backed by dusty draperies of a dark red color. The floor was black-veined marble; the walls gilded in gold. Murals painted on the ceilings were so cloaked in dusk he could not make out what they depicted.

"Why do you look for Ares? What do you want from him?"

Anteros did not answer with any haste. Instead, his gaze swept over the majestic hall with an expression of amusement.

"What is this place? I am surprised Athos would hold such grandeur."

"It is the hall that once entertained the Council of Ages."

At Anteros' puzzled expression, Deimos added, "They do not meet here any longer."

"I was unaware the Council ever met on Athos, but then, since I am not privy to their gatherings, I know little of their dealings. Only that which Aphrodite shares with me."

"Nor I." Deimos answered in a tone that made it clear he did not want to be invited to a Council meeting. "When Zeus held Athos as his own, the Council met here. Now this fortress belongs to Ares. They would not choose to convene within the hallowed halls of War."

"Zeus, resided here?" Nose wrinkling at the thick layer of dust, Anteros said. "A very long time ago, it would seem."

"It is a story hinted at, but never told outright." Deimos released his own concerns in favor of his brother. "Our grandfather once lived here. It has been said it was during a time when our grandmother was very displeased with him and would not let him inhabit the same palace as she."

"I did not know there was ever a split between Zeus and Hera."

"It was well before our time that the King of Immortals was thrown from his bed by his wife after one too many indiscretions. So the tale goes, he sought a distant mountaintop to hide from her rage. In due time, Zeus attempted to shift the balance of power and brought the others here, but did not invite Hera.

"Ares, who, as you know, loves nothing more than to stir the cauldron of trouble, sided with Grandmother. There was a great ruckus and when it was over, Ares wrested Athos from

Zeus and Zeus returned to Olympus to beg forgiveness from Hera. Ares has been here ever since, and the Council returned to Olympus."

"An interesting story. I have not heard it before."

"There are many stories you do not hear." Deimos' tone implied Anteros lived a sheltered life on Cos.

"My existence is different from yours, Brother, but no less adverse."

"Yes, I suppose that is true. Life with all those women must be difficult."

Anteros raised one hand, palm out. "Life without women would be equally dismal, but I do not come here to discuss our differences."

"You said you seek Ares. Why?"

"It is our mother. She greatly suffers." With an expression of distaste, Anteros added, "I must ask Ares to intercede."

A bark of harsh laughter echoed through the dusty chamber as Deimos answered, "Surely you jest."

"I would rather face the worst of Hades than go before Ares." Anteros cast a glance around the darkened corners of the great hall and a slight tremor passed over his face. "But I cannot ignore the state that Love has fallen into. She is not happy with her choice yet refuses to acknowledge it.

"She withers before our eyes and will not hear our pleas to leave Hephaestos and return to Cos. The blanket of despair that lies upon the shoulders of the mortal world causes great confusion."

Sudden understanding struck Deimos. All the anguish he had been feeling was a result of the imbalance between the immortal and mortal worlds. As hated as War was, should he abruptly take leave of them, all chaos would reign. He nodded and Anteros went on.

"She has fallen ill and now she fades."

"Fades? That is impossible."

"Impossible, yet true. You see my dilemma? This is not about my pride, nor my feelings toward our father. It is about the greater good. It is a call I cannot ignore." Anteros ran fingers through his long hair, pushing it away from his forehead, lifting it and letting it flow down his back. As it fell into place, it caught the light like a shimmering jeweled curtain.

Perfection, thought Deimos. He absently touched his own rough curls. He had no use for long hair for it would only get in his way, but as he looked at his twin, he could not help feel a bit of envy.

They were once inseparable, never suspecting the rift that now stood between them.

And how could it be different, for as he is Response and I am Terror, we are nothing but an endless reflecting circle.

"I must find Ares and beg him to intercede. I only ask that...." Anteros lifted his hands in a gesture of peace.

"Deimos? Deimos?" A nearly naked boy with pale green skin and brown curls tumbled into the lighted circle upon the platform and immediately went into a crouch.

Shading his eyes, he peered into the chamber. With animal grace, he leapt from the dais and reached them with lightning speed. Peering up at Anteros, he said, "Why is Anteros here? He is not one of Ares' warriors. He is far too pretty for War."

"Be still," Deimos snapped. "What do you want?"

In a slightly miffed tone, Eris said, "How can I be silent and also speak?"

"Do not be foolish." There dangerous irritation in Deimos' eyes.

Anteros felt a wave of dread ripple over him. It came and went so fast he wondered if he had imagined it.

"Eris." Anteros spoke with humor, hoping to diffuse the moment. "You annoy Thaleia to no end."

"And you, Anteros, annoy me, just by your presence."

Eris stared at Anteros, his pointed ears twitching. With gaze traveling back and forth between the two, he frowned, for though one was as golden as the sun, the other as if kissed by dusk, they were identical. A twinge of jealousy hit him.

Squaring his shoulders, Eris retorted, "I, too, am brother to Deimos."

"Then that would make you my brother as well," Anteros answered with a smile.

Confused, Eris turned to Deimos.

"I suppose it would. However, we will suffer a family reunion later. What is it you want, Eris?"

With a sly glance toward Anteros, Eris grinned. "The Centaur has sent a message saying he needs assistance."

"Priapos?" Startled, Deimos leaned forward. "What assistance?"

"I do not know."

"This is very strange." He stopped, unwilling to put voice

to his fear for Phobos. "He said no more?"

"He did not say why, but he specifically asked for you."

"Not Ares?"

"You." Eris grunted, bored with the game. He was more interested in Anteros, having never had the opportunity for so close an examination. He began to circle him, relishing the expression of alarm on the shining one's face.

"Eris, behave yourself. I bid you go to Priapos and tell him I will be there momentarily."

"He will wait." Eris fingered the dagger tucked into his loincloth. "I do not like to go to the Centaur's cave."

"You will go now." Deimos' stern tone bore no argument. "There is no reason to delay. Go."

"His cave is filthy and stinks. It is not fit for anyone to dwell." Eris spoke to Anteros, ignoring Deimos. "The Centaur does not understand my people, he expects me to sleep on dirt and rocks. Who can endure such a thing? Stone suffocates me."

"Eris' mother is a Sylph. He cannot seem to leave his past behind him." Deimos offered an explanation to Anteros.

"And why should I? You do not."

"I do not? What part of Love do you see here?"

Eris and Deimos locked gazes until Eris shrugged and said, "I do not want to go. I do not like him."

"You are afraid he will call you to task, for he remembers well your disobedience."

"He is a crude beast and I do not see the purpose in his training."

"He is a warrior of the finest quality and you did not pay attention."

"I still do not see why I should go."

"Nevertheless, you will do as I command and visit the Centaur with my message."

An unpleasant wave of foreboding swelled around them. Anteros shivered and crossed his arms over his chest as if to ward off evil.

Eris bared his sharp teeth, but his answer came in a sulky sigh, "As you wish, Brother."

As Eris left them, Deimos met Anteros' gaze. Therein he saw neither terror nor contempt, but the love a brother feels for his twin. It was the piece that had survived the many years of animosity calling to him to rise above their disagreements.

Slowly, Deimos reached out and put his hand on Anteros' arm. Anteros clasped his in return.

"I must go to the Centaur, for this concerns Phobos."

"Phobos? What has happened? Why is he at the Centaur's cave?" Fear spiked Anteros' voice.

"Ares sent him for training. I do not know what causes this unusual request but if the Centaur has need of me, I fear it means trouble."

"I agree." Anteros released Deimos and paced back a few steps, looking off into the darkness. "Where is Ares?"

"Last I knew, he was toying with the warriors who wait for him in the temple annex. I do not need to tell you the wickedness he achieves in their torment."

"No, I have but to imagine those in his thrall. What sort must they be? I say they deserve whatever he gives them."

Deimos did not answer for there were times he would agree but other moments when he would not. Some were courageous warriors, pure of heart, who came to Ares' temple with valor in mind and not bloodlust.

"I would wish to speak with him in some other place."

"It would be best, yes, but sometimes he stays there for days. Of late, he has been in a foul mood. One that is best left in the bowels of this fortress." Deimos hesitated and then added, "I would stand by your side before Ares if it were not for the summons to the Centaur."

Anteros grew silent. Bowing his head, his hair slid forward, hiding his face, hiding his thoughts. When next he spoke, it was with a firm tone. "No, dear Brother, I will not pull you away from your duty to Phobos. This is my bane and I will face him alone."

"Do not fail, Brother, for we cannot lose touch with Love."

"I will not fail. Ares is also my father and he owes me some due." Anteros turned to Deimos and embraced him. "I will not show him the face of fear. Now, go and see to Phobos."

Deimos nodded once and was gone, leaving Anteros alone in the shadows. Anteros could hear the commotion of men waiting to see Ares. He could smell the fires, the charring meat and the stale drink. The sickening scent of unwashed bodies stuck in his nose and throat and, overall, hung the stench of animal droppings. He could smell and he could hear, but he could not see them.

From the echoing chamber of the old Council hall, it sounded as though the temple and adjacent rooms were next door, yet they were not. Those rooms were dark and dusty, empty and unused. All along the corridor, door after door, there was nothing to be found. As he paced the arched stone corridor, the noise became muffled and, at some point, disappeared. It was only when he was in the great hall that he knew they were close by.

He stood very still, head cocked to one side while he listened. It was then he noticed the draft, a steady flow of warm air that ruffled the draperies along the backside of the raised platform. Everywhere else, a damp chill penetrated clothing and skin alike but, at the rear of the dais, the polished floor was slick with a layer of moisture. He could see it now, a darker circle around the split in the draperies.

As he drew back the curtains, he saw a narrow staircase and from that hole came a loud burst of laughter. The reek of burning meat was greater than before.

"There must be an easier way," he muttered but, having never been there, he could not place himself into their midst. Nor did he want to just appear. Even if the rough and ready men could not see him, Ares could. Though Anteros was no coward, the thought of dropping in on his father was too much to consider.

Instead, he crept down the steps, pausing frequently to listen to the raucous colliding tones rushing up to greet him. The quality and quantity of tongues spoken added to the general sense of chaos.

Drunkenness is a great leveler, Anteros thought. *Little does it seem to matter what language is used, the end result is the same.*

Another outburst roared up the stairs - this one with voices raised in anger. There was the clash of metal and a great deal of shouting and thumping, and then the swell of a murderous brawl. It went on for some time before all that was left was groaning and the sizzle of meat on a smoky fire.

Anteros emerged into the cavernous dining hall to find Ares' mark upon the floor: spilled blood and dead men. Only a few from the hundreds who waited were in attendance, but many of the men were wounded and lie dazed on a filthy cobbled floor. Those who were not injured paid no attention to the moans, continuing to eat and drink as if nothing had happened.

Upon Anteros' entry, there was a collective intake of breath and a calming sensation. Of course, Love's Response would bring a prevailing sense of peace, even to hardened warriors.

Though he was not visible to the warriors, for he purposefully kept himself unseen, his presence resulted in the formation of new thoughts and new responses to old actions. There might even be discussion rather than brute force amongst the men who thought only of bloodletting.

Anteros smiled in the hopes Ares might well have an altered set of warriors at his feet with these men. The dawning of tranquility within the ranks would be unexpected by Ares, the Destroyer.

Such is the influence of Love's Response, yet Anteros still skirted the edges of the chamber. He could not be certain his influence would offset the violence within the throng of men. His fear being that these men might turn their murderous intentions upon him instead of each other.

His sandal touched a pool of blood and from there he left greasy red footprints until he reached the opposite doorway. The entrance to Ares' throne room was wide and littered with the droppings from sacrificial animals which Anteros carefully stepped over. But he could not keep from coughing in disgust. His first view of the altar caused his gut to clench with a sickening jolt.

It was not the flower-bedecked laurel that hosted the worshippers of Aphrodite, but an evil rotting pile of flesh and bones that held court in Ares' temple. Anteros turned away from it to see Ares, dark and dangerous, sitting upon a monstrous throne with towering bull's horns rising from the top. There was not another living creature in the chamber but the two of them, and it was precisely at Anteros that Ares' flat expressionless stare was directed.

Anteros wanted more than anything to run away, but it was too late. He had been seen and he could do nothing less than approach and speak to the most feared god in both worlds.

His father.

If Ares was surprised to see him, it did not register. He sat straight up in the unadorned throne, his fingers curled around the ends of its arms. There was no padding, no gilded hangings, no crest, no jewels, just the upright, stark throne. Strange designs were etched into the back and sides, but not as decorations. Anteros recognized the symbols as an incantation to Spirits of Destruction.

He paled at the intention behind it.

When his lips parted, no word would issue. He stood like a ghost in his white clothing and golden hair in that cold bleak place and fell into the grip of despair. What use was love when this was the dominating force? How could any respond to such ugliness and call it right? He groaned and then turned his head aside.

Ares spoke in a harsh voice that cracked and rumbled against the rough walls. "What do you want?"

There was no glad greeting. Anteros knew there would not be, not from either side. Then why was there a tiny quiver at the abrupt and dismissing way his father spoke to him? Anteros shrugged away the sensation, for it held no meaning and he cared not to discover where it came from.

"Is there no answer from one whose life is all about reply? If you are here for Phobos, he is gone." Ares drummed his fingers with impatience on the chair arm.

"I know." Anteros forced himself to meet Ares' gaze without a shudder.

"You know? And how is it that you know?" Ares leaned forward. "Ahh, let me guess. You have spoken to Deimos."

Pushing a lock of hair out of his face, Anteros kept his eyes on his father. "Yes."

"And did he tell you where to find Phobos, if that is who you look for?"

"That is not my purpose, though my heart aches for my little brother." Anteros spoke with as much strength as he could muster.

"Your heart has the courage of a worm. Were you fit to be here, you would seek out Phobos, would you not?"

"You call me a coward?"

Ares snorted. "Yes. Among other things."

Standing tall, with feet planted apart, Anteros glared back at his father. "You think your world is the only painful place? Your scars are visible, your wounds shed blood, but in Love's realm those injuries are hidden from sight, still and all, no less crippling. You allow hatred to dominate, but that is the easy way out. To stay the course of Love takes great valor, more than I would ever find in War's house."

"So you would do battle here in Love's name?"

"I do battle for Love anywhere I must."

Ares stared through half-closed eyes, the beginnings of a smirk on his lips. "Then do tell me what this is about. Why would you, the Shining Son of Eternal Love, come calling on me?"

"Must you ridicule everything?" Anteros' upper lip curled. "And I am your son as well."

Lifting his shoulders in a gesture of dismissal, Ares reclined against the back of his throne. "What do you want? Speak, or leave."

"I have come to ask you to intercede on my mother's behalf." Anteros watched Ares with great intent and witnessed a mere flicker of his black lashes and a tightening of his lips to signal his disgruntlement.

"The answer is no." Ares turned his head away, toward the warrior's entrance. "Now leave me."

"Just like that? You dismiss Aphrodite without question?"

"What is there to say? She broke her ties with me. Therefore, she no longer has my protection."

"It is not about your protection."

"I do not care what she wants. There is no alliance between us."

"But there was, and a very long one. Does that not count for something?"

Ares hesitated in answering, but in the end, it was the same. "No."

"But she is in dire straits. I fear for her well-being."

"Aphrodite's repute is well known. She does not invite interference."

"Have you not the least consideration for what troubles her?"

"It is none of my concern."

"She is ill and fading." Anteros saw a flicker of interest before Ares could lock it away. "She needs you."

Springing to his feet, Ares came down the stairs, brushed past Anteros and stopped in front of the horrendous altar. "She has selected a new mate. It is now his chore to see to her needs."

"You speak as if we discuss the care and feeding of animals." Without thought, Anteros gripped Ares' arm.

Through the sleeve, he could feel the coiled power along his forearm and the instant strain of one who holds back from violence. Anteros let go as quickly as he grabbed and stepped back. It was well he did for Ares turned on him as if to strike him to the floor.

"She is no more to me than that." Ares pointed to the severed head of a bull crowning the altar. Its tongue hung out in grotesque mockery; its dead eyes stared in defiance. "A waste of good flesh."

"Do not speak so of Aphrodite. She is my mother."

"You do not have to hear it. You have only to leave me alone."

"I have seen her, Father." Anteros near choked on the word, but the memory of Aphrodite's weakness haunted his every moment.

"She lies wasting away in the castle of the Forge god and will not return to her beloved isle. There is no one who has been able to bring her about, for she ignores us all. As Love crumbles, so does the structure of the mortal world. We cannot stand idly by. Please."

Ares stared at him in silence. If he considered Anteros' words, it was not visible, for his expression remained stern and unbending.

"I beg you, justly go to her, see if you can stop this spiral into oblivion. For the greater good, if not for Aphrodite herself."

"You beg?" Ares spoke with alarming softness.

"I plead. Yes, I beg. She has not sent me. She does not know I am here."

"And what are *you* willing to sacrifice to save Love?"

Fear clutched at Anteros, for he could see in his father's eyes there would have to be an offering. Aphrodite could make no atonement for her misdeeds, nor would she, even if she could. Therein was only one thing Anteros could do. There was only one thing he could offer.

"I give myself."

A slow smile spread across Ares' lips. A sly smile that did not reach the depths of his black eyes. "And what would I do with the likes of you?"

"If you will go to Aphrodite, I offer my loyalty to you in whatever way you wish."

"Hmm. Then you will garb yourself in armor and ride into battle with me?" At Anteros' faint nod, Ares continued. "You will take weapon in hand and raise it with intention to kill?"

Again, Anteros nodded, swallowing hard. He could not keep his gaze from the bones upon the altar, the bones of those who had gone before him.

"You will live here and obey me without question?"

Anteros bowed his head and exhaled a shaking breath. "Yes, Father. I will do all that, if you will save Love."

"What if she does not want to be saved? What if I try, but she sends me away? What then, Anteros? Will you still belong to War?"

"If you will but make a true and real attempt to bring her back to herself, I will walk on the side of War."

Lifting his head, Anteros met his father's gaze. He did not like what he saw, for there was cruel purpose written across Ares' face. Anteros knew then Ares would use his power to further punish Aphrodite, but there was naught else he could do.

"Then speak it."

"I swear my allegiance to War and rescind all connection to Love, regardless of the outcome."

"So be it." Ares spoke next to Anteros' ear, his voice hard. "You now belong to me."

Anteros nodded, wordless, but Ares was already gone.

"Mother, please forgive me," Anteros whispered.

FIFTEEN

Night fell and still Niala sat at the base of the lone white stone finger pointing skyward. She leaned against its side to watch the valley below as Najahmara went about daily life. Her heart raced to see the beauty once again and her tears fell nonstop. They came in a continuous trickle, dripping down her cheeks to her chin and then to her breast. The front of her gown was damp with her joy, yet she was reluctant to start down the path.

She was full and content but fear was beneath the surface waiting to capture her in a tangle of what ifs. There were changes. Some she could see from her view: the clearing away of rubble and the construction of buildings. They had worked hard in the months she was gone, yet the underlying scent of charred brick lingered even though the land was a patchwork blanket of new color.

Some changes were etched upon the face of spirit. She could feel the pain had not dissipated during her imprisonment. The agony had grown and anguish was in full bloom within her beloved village.

The spring season was more than half over, as witnessed by blossoming plants along with those that had finished flowering. The last Niala saw of Najahmara was harvest, when the fields were cut, the vegetables and grains stored, and the remnants of summer herbs hung to dry. Though their winters were not harsh, the chill drew plant life within the bosom of the earth, save for a few hardier bushes.

Here, it was easy to see the seasons march by. At Athos, Niala lost all track of time. There the cold went on and on with snow falling all year long on the peaks of the mountain. Spring was very late and summer scarce more than a blink of the eye before the fall storms set in. Until she felt the warmth of the sun's rays and saw the few struggling flowers on Athos' rocky side, she did not know how long she had been gone.

Eight months. Ares claimed Najahmara was no longer the place she knew, with her priestesses dead and a new regime in control. He said she would be devastated for nothing was left of the peaceful valley where she and Layla found a retreat. Was he right? Just looking down at Najahmara, life seemed so much the same.

The streets were not teeming with soldiers.

There was no visible sign of abuse or force.

Everything was quiet. People went about their duties. Earlier, the scent of food cooked for the evening meals drifted upward to tempt her. Now the sounds of a town settling for the night were all she heard. There were no screams, no panic, no chaos. Najahmara was very much the way it was before the invasion.

Ares lied to her.

Or did he?

Something was different. Niala could feel a subtle shift of energy, the movement away from Earth and the vague infusion of Sky. It was as if once the door was opened to Kulika, he did not fully retract from dominion. The balance was off. Things were no longer equal between Earth and Sky, Sky took more than he should.

Yes, that was it.

Though Gaea greeted Niala upon her arrival, there lacked the same profusion of delight in Earth's caress. Gaea was wounded. She retreated, which Niala felt but did not immediately recognize. This rising awareness brought a swell of sorrow into Niala's heart.

"I will do what I can, Great Mother, to stem the tide." Niala caressed the ground beside her, running her fingers through the wild growth of plants.

The grasses whispered a reply, *Yes.* A breeze stroked her hair with a gentle hand before it died down, leaving the air as still and silent as the stone behind her. The single lonely stone that marked her future burial mound.

The tears continued, as if something besides the four white stones was broken, something inside her. The tears leaked of their own accord, and she could not descend into Najahmara until they ceased.

Niala awoke with the heavy dew of early morn dampening her clothes and hair. She lay nose-deep in the grass behind the markers, her pregnant belly creating an awkward crumpled position. When she tried to roll to her back, all parts screamed at the exertion. Groaning, she sat up and breathed into the soreness of her body. Her braid was partially undone, leaving her hair wild, matted and clinging to her like wet leaves. Her head ached and her eyes burned, yet there was nothing so beautiful to squint at as dawn rising over Najahmara.

The horizon burst with pinks and yellows on a vivid background of deep blue as the first rays of the sun stretched upward. Niala struggled to her feet and stood looking over the edge at the sleeping town.

No one stirred, yet, at any moment, they would awaken and she would see the day begin to take shape. Across the broad valley, she could hear the bleating of sheep in the distance. The bowl-shaped bottom was still cloaked in darkness as the fingers of the sun had not yet warmed the far-lying edges.

A lump formed in her throat at the sights and sounds of home. She swallowed the inclination to cry as there had been enough of that. The idea of descending into Najahmara disguised by darkness evaporated with the rising sun. She had nothing left to do but face the changes in full daylight.

On unsteady feet, Niala began the climb down.

The path was overgrown and slippery, another sign of abandonment. Treading with care, Niala reached the split, one way led into the gardens behind the temple and the other to the entrance of the cave. She hesitated, feeling a draw to the sacred cavern. Its pull was more in her own mind than real, for here too, Gaea's strength was diminished.

Disturbed, Niala took the path to the gardens. When she reached the oval pool, she sank down beside it and scooped a handful of water to rub over her face. Her legs were shaking, her head was fuzzy and her throat suddenly parched. As she reached for more water, this time to drink, she froze.

Above her, reflected in the clear pool, was the figure of a large man. He stood behind her without a word, waiting for her to finish. Her heart hammered, for she thought it to be Ares.

Not yet, she prayed. *Not yet.*

Her lips moved but no sound emerged. When she rose to her feet, she stumbled and he caught her elbow. It was not Ares but also not anyone she recognized.

"Who are you?" He spoke in the trade language, his voice gruff.

"Niala Aaminah."

"What are you doing here?"

"I am a priestess."

"You do not look like one of our priestesses."

Our priestesses.

Niala shot a questioning glance at the big man but did not speak her thoughts. Instead, she peered down at her bedraggled clothing, heavy woolens suitable for a cold climate and not for the heat of Najahmara.

He was dressed in the loose linen trousers and short tunic most of the Najahmaran men wore. Even so, Niala could see he was first a warrior just by his wide-legged stance.

Smoothing strands of hair away from her face, she smiled. "I have traveled a long distance."

"How did you get past the guards into the garden?"

She pointed to the plateau.

"Over the mountain?" He was incredulous.

"No."

"How, then?"

"It is not a simple tale." The more Niala talked, the better she felt. The dizziness left her and she was able to straighten her shoulders and meet his gaze with a directness that caused him to take a step back.

"I would first like to change clothes and eat, if I may. It has been awhile since my last meal and I am hungry."

As she said it, her gut rumbled and the big man nodded. "It would seem you are no risk to my king, yet, somehow you seem familiar."

"I was here the night of the fire, when your army invaded us."

"The fire." Zan's eyes clouded, the dark before dawn. When he met her gaze next it was with new wariness. "Niala, you said? The missing one."

"The same."

"No longer missing."

"And not the serpent."

"It was you," Zan cursed, reaching for the dagger at his belt.

"Please." Niala raised both hands in a weary gesture. "I am no threat, either to you or your king. I beg you let me speak with him, and with those of my sisters who still live. I will tell you my tale so you may see there is no cause for alarm."

"Why are you here?" His fingers lay on the hilt of the dagger, but Zan left it sheathed.

"I want only to come home."

"Why now? Why not before? Where have you been all this time, if not in the lair of the serpent who attacked us? The serpent who...." The big man flushed and clamped his lips together.

"Lost. Wandering." Niala spoke with honesty, though it was only limited truth. "I could not remember who I was or where I came from."

Zan's eyes narrowed. "Now your claim is recollection?"

"Yes. Most things, yet I am uncertain of who survived."

Deimos had told her which ones lived but to have confirmation, to know it was truth and not another story made up to ease her grief.

Zan's features softened. "Pallin. Jahmed. Ajah."

"That is all?" Niala could not contain a sob.

"No, many of the young ones." His answer was hurried. "I think it best if you come inside, as you wished, clean up a bit, eat, whatever are your needs. I will then arrange an audience with King Hattusilis."

"Where are Pallin and Jahmed?"

"Queen Pallin is, of course, with her king." Zan shrugged. "I do not know where Jahmed sleeps, but I find her most often in the medicinal quarters."

"Queen." Niala's voice was faint. "I should speak with Jahmed first."

Zan neither agreed nor disagreed, merely waved her toward the temple.

Niala's reunion with Jahmed was most joyous. They wept in each other's arms until they laughed. When they broke apart, Jahmed lovingly traced Niala's brow to her chin, and grinned through her tears.

"It is by the grace of Gaea that you have returned to us. I knew you would." Jahmed hugged Niala again. "I always knew you would come back."

Niala bowed her head, smiling. Pallin might be queen, but at the temple, Jahmed would always be in charge. Savoring the warmth of her homecoming, Niala surveyed the hospice area.

Once it was a pristine place, kept for those in need of overnight care. Now the room bore vague resemblance to that purpose, as it had become the women's refuge.

A deep bowl served as a fire circle, for warmth, for offerings to Gaea. The walls were lined with the drying herbs of the healer's trade. To the back, eight hammocks swung from low frames and, next to each, the meager possessions of eight girls.

"Eight?" Niala voice caught in grief. "Only eight are left?"

Jahmed scrubbed at her face with the hem of her apron. "Some died. Some went back to their families."

She bit her lip. "After the fire, there was so much destruction, so many dead. The girls needed to help their own families. Those who remain work endlessly to keep up with the chores."

Face set in harsh lines, Jahmed added, "We now care for the new king, and his people who have taken over the bulk of the temple. As well as see to the needs of the ill and injured."

Jahmed's bitterness was bleak homage to the transformation of Najahmara. Niala heaved a great sigh and felt a jab in her belly. The little one kicked already, though it seemed too soon. Niala put her hand to the growing mound and took a deep breath.

"You are with child!" Jahmed's dark skin suffused with red. "It is his?" She could not bring herself to speak Ares' name.

"Yes."

"He brought you back, knowing of this impending birth?"

With a shake of her head, Niala silenced Jahmed and began to tell the story. Jahmed did not interrupt, instead stared with slack mouth and wide eyes.

When Niala was finished, Jahmed whispered, "Mercy. He will look for you."

"Perhaps, but in a fit of bad temper he said I was free to go, if I could find my way. He has no cause to be angry and he has no need to search, for he knows where I am."

"But he will take you away from us again, especially when he discovers this." She gestured toward the unborn babe.

"We shall see. For now, I am with you. Let us be happy in that." Taking Jahmed's hand, Niala said, "Tell me about those who are gone. Seire." Her voice caught. "Inni."

"Not Inni." Jahmed squeezed Niala's fingers. "Inni is alive."

"I can scarce believe it. When last I saw her, I thought her surely dead."

"As did I, when we found her. She lives though she is unlike her old self. Her body has healed but her mind is not the same." Jahmed stared dry-eyed at a hanging bunch of lemon grass.

"She is frightened of everything and scarce takes a step outside our door. If she does, it is only to sit on the bench in front of our hut and then only in daylight hours. At the first sign of darkness, she scurries inside in a panic. I have managed a small garden, thinking she would work the soil. You know how she loved the gardens."

"But she does not?"

"She holds some interest but I have hope she will be more drawn to the earth during the summer months."

"I must see her."

"Yes, I think it will be good for her. Later, though. First you must eat and bathe. I will find you clean clothes."

Jahmed did not have to add the clothing would be cooler. "I have no doubt our new king will want your company." Her words twisted with anger. "He will be most curious."

"And Pallin?" Niala was anxious for the younger priestess. "What has happened with Pallin? I am to understand she is his queen?"

It was Jahmed's turn to describe what took place. Niala listened, growing sicker with each revelation.

"The funeral pyres flamed night and day with the bodies. We managed to return some to Earth, as it should be, as it should have been for all our people, but there were too many." Jahmed paused to touch Niala's cheek. "Seire was committed to Gaea's arms. We did not let her burn."

Niala nodded, speechless with a throat that closed on her.

"It was not enough there was one invasion, there came a second wave. We were in shambles, confused, injured and grieving. They marched in and took over. There was no bloodshed, not even a small skirmish."

Tears welled in Jahmed's eyes. "Nothing. We were weak and defenseless. I am ashamed to say we gave up without a fight."

"There was nothing else you could do." Niala hugged Jahmed close. "Nothing you could do."

Pallin fainted at first sight of Niala. Color flew into her cheeks before her pale skin grew paler and her eyes rolled back as she collapsed. Were it not for Zan's quick action, Pallin would have dropped to the floor with full force.

Zan laid her down with unusual gentleness and knelt beside her to offer a cup of water. Hattusilis made an alarmed gurgling noise and struggled to rise from his seat to help her, but could not hoist himself from his chair.

Guards on each side leapt to assist, but he waved them away as sweat beaded on his forehead and his mouth tightened into a thin line. His breath swept out in relief as Pallin opened her eyes. His gaze lingered on her largely rounded belly before flicking towards Niala, who also knelt next to Pallin.

There was deep suspicion in his gaze, as if Niala had caused his bride to fall. Perhaps with a hex of some kind, some ill twist of fortune that would steal the child from him.

Niala hid a smile at the superstitious nature of the man. She remembered him well from the cave ritual that seemed so long ago but was only eight moons past. She remembered his reluctance to give up the wound of losing his family but rather kept the pain of his poor Azhar's decline clutched to his soul as penance. She could see in his eyes he kept the shame of taking Azhar and killing her people and now embodied the same in Pallin.

In truth, it was similar circumstances. An invasion. Taking what did not belong to him. Niala's mouth tightened but she kept her focus on Pallin.

"Are you honestly here?" Sobbing, Pallin reached for Niala from her prone position. "Or do I dream?"

"I am here." Niala planted a kiss on her forehead. "Truly."

They clutched each other until their strength gave out and Zan lifted them both to their feet as if they weighed no more than a feather. Pallin's legs trembled so that she sought a stool at the base of the fur-covered chair serving as the king's throne. She leaned against Hattusilis' knee while he stroked her hair with an absent gesture.

An offer was not made to Niala to sit. She was left standing before Hattusilis and his guards, her transgressions to be reviewed as if she were a common thief. The air prickled between them as Niala met Hattusilis' gaze in an unwavering answer to his unspoken question.

Niala would not bow to him. She would not consent to be his subject, though Pallin's gaze pleaded for respect, if nothing else.

Niala gave a slight nod in his direction. "King Hattusilis."

"Priestess." He held his body straight with rigid determination.

An awkward silence descended. The soldiers shifted from foot to foot while Hattusilis shot a swift unreadable message to Zan. Pallin started up only to be urged to stay in place by a slight pressure of Hattusilis' fingers. Only Niala moved, turning in a circle to view the chamber where the Sky god, Kulika, had claimed his power.

There was nothing left for her to feel. Her grief had poured out with such completeness, there were no more tears to shed. Though the room was achingly familiar in its structure, with its rounded sides and domed ceiling, in the five corridors that fed outward to the rest of the temple, it was not the same.

The chamber could never be the same. Beneath her feet, she saw the faded patterns of blood spilled and the spray of drops across one wall. The faint echo of screams seemed to hover above her, ghosts of those who could not pass into the Shadowland with the terror fixed in their hearts.

So much needless destruction.

It was here Kulika began the challenge, and it was here Niala would end it.

SIXTEEN

The Council could not grasp why Aphrodite deserted Ares, yet the topic was too enticing for the gossipmongers to ignore. Ares knew he was always a favorite target, for they hated his arrogance. Aphrodite was next with her beauty superior to all.

But Hephaestos, Hephaestos was a laughingstock. He played servant to the Ages and was always rewarded with further humiliation. Even so, Hephaestos continued to accommodate the Council. He served every whim, answered every call to earn the little bit of grudging respect that was offered.

And, very soon, Hephaestos would be commanded to appear in the lofty chambers of the Ages. Ares saw to it that his mother heard the Forge god worked on a resplendent gift for his new bride. This gift was something so exquisite it defied anything Hera, Queen of the Immortals, had in her possession.

Ares was told she took the news with a gracious smile, but he knew she would brood over the indignity and, before long, Hephaestos would be summoned to Olympus.

Iris would arrive with a message for Hephaestos to go straightaway to Hera for a thinly disguised discussion of this sumptuous gift. Smiling with grim glee, Ares imagined

Hephaestos' surprise when Hera demanded something of equal or higher value.

Ares had only to sit atop the volcano and wait for Hephaestos to leave. Then he would have a few words with Aphrodite.

He did not believe she faded. He did not believe she willingly gave up control of her realm. Yet for Anteros to ask for his help was curious.

Ares rubbed his bearded chin as he stared down at the bronze-domed castle. Was there a crisis of devastating magnitude or was it a trick direct from Aphrodite's cheating heart?

Notwithstanding, Anteros now owed allegiance to War. Ares could not fathom how that could be part of any plan hatched by Aphrodite. Ares could make no sense of it all and that was the final draw to Lemnos. This time he would not linger on the outskirts like some callow youth who waited for an invitation.

He paused in his discourse as he felt the bowing of energy. Ares had to commend his mother - she wasted no time in sending Iris. And just as Ares knew he would, Hephaestos, obedient son that he was, went to answer his mother's request.

As soon as he knew they were both gone, Ares entered the palace. With unswerving instinct, he appeared in the private chambers of the Forge god and there, lying with the pallor of death upon her cheeks, he found Aphrodite. She lay on a bed of gold shaped like a giant sailing ship, as if she prepared for consignment to her cherished sea.

Like a queen upon a bier, she was propped on pillows, her hair combed, curled, and spread over the silken coverlet. Her small slender hands, bare of any jewels, lay on her midriff. Her face was a sculpture in ice, with the faintest of blue upon her lids and lips. Her breast scarce rose and fell with her breath. As he looked upon her, his anger faded.

It mattered not what she had done.

Ares made no sound, yet the two Graces accompanying her looked up in unison. Aglaia rose quickly, tipping over her stool. At the thud against the floor, Aphrodite's lashes fluttered. Euphrosyne slid from her place on the bed beside Aphrodite, grabbed her sister's hand and pulled her away.

There was a strange glint in Euphrosyne's eyes as she glanced at him before she whispered in Aglaia's ear. A slow expression of irritation mixed with relief spread across Aglaia's face and the two of them hurried from the chamber.

This added fuel to his consternation, for never in their existence had any of the Graces volunteered to leave him alone with their mistress. Now, on silent feet, they withdrew.

If this was a trap, then it was very good one. He turned his attention back to Aphrodite and crawled onto the bed, reclining next to her. He could feel the indentation of Euphrosyne's body and the warmth she left behind.

The smell of moonflowers clung to everything. Breathing in Aphrodite's scent, he kissed her lips.

Aphrodite woke with a start and opened eyes clouded by confusion. "Ares?" Her voice was a scant whisper of her usual melodious tones.

"Yes, I am here."

"Why are you here?"

"The Ages discuss your new partnership and cluck over your absence. They think Hephaestos has hidden you away deep in his foundry and will not let you see light of day."

"Poor Hephaestos, he draws their arrows no matter what he does."

"I see he does not lock you away."

"No, I choose to stay." With a sigh, her eyes closed, as if she did not have the strength to keep them open.

"Why?"

"Why?" She echoed, as if she did not understand his question.

"As you languish, so does your realm. The mortal world feels your loss. As do I."

"Do you?"

"Yes, Beloved." Ares kissed her cheek, his fingers stroking along her jaw to the slender column that joined with her shoulder. "Return to Cos. You have what you came for and I have been punished. Let it be over now."

Aphrodite covered her face with her hands. "What if I am with his child?"

"It is what I warrant. I cannot fault you for seeking another."

"Ahh, but I am not." Aphrodite wept into her palms. "I have been denied Victory. My womb is empty, for she has found me undeserving."

"How can that be?" Ares smoothed pale hair from a face flushed with anguish. "Victory could do no better than you, for you merit only the most true of heart. There is nothing more true than Victory."

"She has abandoned me. I can feel her no more."

"Perhaps it is not Victory's time after all."

"No. She wanted you as her father, but I turned you away."

"I drove you away."

"I let Jealousy rule my heart and for this, I have dearly paid. I do not deserve the Mantle of Love."

"How so? For love of me? Is that what you mean?" Ares pulled her fingers free from her eyes. "I fear I have brought you nothing but pain, from one life to another."

"Love should not be bound by conditions." Aphrodite touched his face, as if still she could not believe he was real. "Though I have allowed it to be so."

"Stupidity is not a condition, it is an action."

"No matter. I can no longer carry this weight, so I seek to fade from this earth and let Anteros take my realm."

"It will not happen that way."

"You cannot know that."

"I do know it. You will fade and so will Love's influence. Anteros will not come to relieve you and all hope of harmony will be gone from the mortal world. Is that what you really want?"

"I am so very tired, Ares. I can no longer face the trials that come with Love."

"Because you lie to yourself. Pleasure, yes. And why not? Have whomever you will if it gives you pleasure, but do not try to force a bond that is not there to suit a purpose that is less than honorable."

At this, indignation blazed from her eyes. She gave him a slight push, knocking him from his elbow and rolling him to his back.

"You speak of honor?"

"I did not say those qualities held true for War."

"Though they should. War should not be about the petty side of life, but only to protect those you love."

Ares stared up at the fine gold strands overhead. "I wish that were so, Beloved, but War is more about greed and lust and power."

"It is not necessary for it to be that way. You choose to have it so."

"There is much you do not understand." Ares met her oceanic gaze once more. "But if you cannot survive, then how will I?

Between us, you have always been the stronger."

"You tell tales simply to provoke me. I know who I am and I know I am a mere substitute for the one you truly love. Even as Elche, second woman, a simple-minded creature at best, I was a replacement for Ilya."

Aphrodite paused, her voice shaking, and took a deep breath. "I stood at your side, not above you and not below you. We were equal, as we are equal now."

"We were all simple creatures then, all three of us. We did only as we were driven to do. That was then." Ares touched her brow with gentleness. "Now, you are the only one who can stand against me and the only one who can stand with me. Do not abandon me, Aphrodite. I love you beyond reason. My presence here is proof of that."

"What of her?"

"She is what she is."

"A prisoner. If she does not love you, you cannot bind her to you, no matter how hard you try."

"She does love me."

"Let her go, Ares. Let her find her own way."

"I have thrown open the doors and bid her go if she must, but she has not left me."

"Not yet." Aphrodite spoke without rancor, knowing how Ilya's rejection pained Ares, even eons later. "But she will. She always does. And then you turn to me."

"I have never turned away from you." Ares' voice was hoarse with quickening lust. "I cannot be without you."

Aphrodite stroked his cheek, then moved her fingertips to his lips. Her gaze turned liquid, shifting as with the currents of the sea. Her desire swelled up from the depths, a breathless seeking of the spark that united them since the beginning of time.

Too long had they lain apart and now each sought the other with unspoken questions. Their bodies pressed together and their heat soon brought a flush to the paleness of Aphrodite's skin. She could feel him through their clothing and strained to be closer, aching to have him.

"Ares, my Dearest." Aphrodite wrapped her arms around his neck. "Make love to me, for I need you more than all else."

Ares ran his lips down her throat to the pulse that beat at

the base. One hand held her breast through the gown. The other cradled her hips, fingers wrapped around the thin material, ready to rip it from her. He could think of nothing else but the delights of her body.

"And I have great need for you."

The cloth gave way. He threw it to the floor with scarce a glance. He thrust his mouth against an already hard nipple and sucked at it, feeling her back arch towards him. Aphrodite hooked one leg over his and ran her foot over the leather of his leggings. Her fingers combed through his black curls to reach his shoulders where she began to tug at his shirt.

Though Ares could have blinked them away, he released her breast and took his time peeling off the leather jerkin and tunic, for he knew Aphrodite liked to watch. It gave her sensuous pleasure to see flesh bare as clothing fell away.

No more than his shirt was gone and she stroked his chest and belly, caressing up and down his sides, leaning up to run her tongue along his skin until she reached his trouser line.

Through disheveled hair, she looked up at him. "You tease me. Do not wait or I will no longer have need of you."

Ares paused, seeing the mirth in her eyes, the way her skin glowed as she smiled. He realized what sickened her was denial. She was fully in her power when she enjoyed a tryst, but without delight, it became a weight that dragged her down.

Ares groaned, for he felt he drowned in turquoise eyes now turned to him with reckless longing. It was not just sex. She wanted more. And he could give it to her.

Only he.

There came the invocation of harmony between them. The once old, now renewed promise of fidelity and kinship. An alliance resealed. He had no power to deny his beloved whatever she wanted.

When Aphrodite saw he was naked and willing, holding forth the gift she so desired, she took him into her body. She wrapped arms and legs around him, drawing him deep into herself, drawing out the seed that would bring her a daughter.

They drove against each other until exhaustion was imminent and then, as always, they came together, for long years of practice served them well. Drowsy and complacent, they lay in each other's arms, forgetful of where they were. They did not notice the sharp eyes of Cedalion watching from a hidden doorway leading to the tunnels below the palace.

Hephaestos stared without comprehension at Cedalion. Cedalion did not flinch under his master's unblinking dumbfounded gaze. It was not his nature to apologize or make amends, nor did he try to soften the announcement of his discovery. To him, it mattered not what might have been, what was, or even what could be. To him, time only existed in the moment.

Aphrodite and Ares lay together in Hephaestos' bed. That was all. He could not make it less hurtful, even if he knew how. He knew Hephaestos should be told, and there was no other who would speak of it.

The women who accompanied Aphrodite would stay silent. They kept all manner of secrets. He could not fault their loyalty to their mistress, just as they should not grudge his loyalty to Hephaestos.

The youngest one, the prettiest one, the one called Euphrosyne, pleaded with him not to tell. It was she who had seen him watching. He had not meant to spy on Aphrodite and Ares. His purpose was to see the one called Euphrosyne. Before Ares appeared, Cedalion watched only Euphrosyne as she lay drowsing beside her mistress.

He had never known love before and did not recognize it as such. It was just that she was so pretty and she was kind to him. She always offered him sweets, even though at times she looked as if he frightened her. She always smiled at him. He saw her with the tall male with long yellow hair, saw how her eyes lit up and her face grew softer. He imagined himself in place of the young god.

He knew he could not change what existed, but he could dream. How Hephaestos would scoff if he learned of this. These women were not for Cedalion, and now it was certain that Aphrodite was not for Hephaestos. Cedalion was not without sympathy, but there was naught he could do, for what he had seen was what it was.

Ares had stolen Aphrodite again.

Hephaestos buried his face in his hands, elbows resting on his worktable. He sagged onto a stool, unable to support his weight on trembling knees.

"How could this be," he whispered. "She promised fidelity."

Cedalion did not answer; he could not, for there was nothing else to say. He watched Hephaestos with his unreadable bright, black eyes, waiting for an order to action. He was certain there would be penance to be paid. Certain both Aphrodite and Ares would suffer for their deed.

"Has she gone?" Hephaestos wiped away the tears that leaked from his eyes.

Cedalion shook his head. No, Aphrodite did not go away with Ares. She settled in Hephaestos bed as if she bore no guilt.

"Why has she not gone? If she has betrayed me and returned to bloody War, then why has she not gone?"

Again, Cedalion shook his head. He did not know. Ares lay in Aphrodite's arms for some time after their lovemaking. Then he took himself away. Aphrodite stayed. Cedalion did not know why.

"Is it possible she loves me still and that despicable beast forced her to this awful deed?" Hephaestos spoke now to himself.

"Did that hateful barbaric creature come into my castle and demand husbandly rights when he no longer has that privilege?"

Hephaestos rose from the stool and lumbered about the cavernous workshop, talking to himself.

"Sweet Aphrodite could scarce fend him off for she is as delicate as a flower, and he like the whoring hound that is his animal. What could she do, but give in to his beastly demands? I bear no grudge against her. It could not be her fault. That craven blood-monger took her against her will."

Cedalion spoke not, however, he saw their acts of love and there was no force involved. It was by invitation that Ares laid with Aphrodite. She embraced him with a fervency nothing like the manner in which she held Hephaestos.

Yes, Cedalion had seen them. Once, when Hephaestos and Aphrodite lay together in the workroom. They paid no attention to Cedalion who toiled in one corner, near the forge. So he watched them, as well. And he noticed the difference.

Hephaestos tore at his hair, shouting to the beams above them, "He must be punished - Ares cannot wantonly take what does not belong to him. I will not allow it. He must be punished."

Pacing with a speed belied by his limp, Hephaestos crossed the cavern to the fires of the forge. "There is none who will call him to task, for they fear him, but I do not. He will not take Aphrodite from me again."

"He will." Cedalion's voice was steady.

"What? What say you?" Turning, Hephaestos glowered at his servant. "He would not dare."

"He will if she does not go back to Cos."

Hephaestos curled his fingers into huge fists. "I will not let her leave me, this I swear. I will kill him, if he returns."

"You must catch him first."

"Yes." Nodding, Hephaestos slid his gaze about his workroom tables, at the piles waiting in the corners, at his latest work. Somewhere in his massive collection was the one thing that could trap Ares. Somehow, he would find a way to kill War.

"Do not leave me, Aphrodite, I beg you." Hephaestos met with her in the vaulted chamber filled with low couches.

Aphrodite, as was her wont, lounged upon a backless divan filled with gilded cushions, while her ladies gathered at her side. The Graces averted their eyes during his impassioned plea. Hephaestos was certain they secretly laughed at him.

This brought him more aggravation, causing his voice too quaver, which in turn, made him seem a pitiful example. In his opinion, that is, for not one of the pretty faces before him bore any suggestion of this belief.

"I do not abandon you, Hephaestos. I merely return to Cos, to the realm of Love. There are matters I must attend that cannot be handled here."

"It is he, is it not?" Hephaestos stumped away from her, fiddling with a small piece of metal hooked to another. "He calls you. Therefore, you go."

"It is not Ares who has need of me."

"Can you say you have had no contact with him since you arrived?" He watched her with care, over his shoulder, for he knew the truth.

"I have not called Ares to my side."

Shameless one! Hephaestos thought. *Liar. He was here and in my bed, which I never again will share with you because of it.*

Aloud, he said, "Do not leave here, just yet, Aphrodite, for I do not feel confident in our allegiance."

"I have lingered here, my dear, ignoring all other concerns

just to soothe your fears, but soon I must see to other things. Thaleia has just returned from Cos and little Eros has need of me."

"Eros? I had forgotten about your son. By all means, bring the child to Lemnos. There is much I could show him."

Thaleia frowned and exchanged a quick glance with her mistress. Hephaestos detected the slightest headshake on the part of the Grace and immediately received a brilliant smile from his wife. That alone fed into his fears, for of late, Aphrodite had been wan and unresponsive to his advances.

Hephaestos admitted, with grudging reluctance, that there was little of Love he understood. One moment, she was seducing him in all manner of inappropriate places and he, the weak-willed being that he was, gave into her whims. The next moment, she rebuffed his advances without cause. He was embarrassed by the intensity of his desire for her and when she turned him away, he was confused and wounded.

To discover that she gave her favors to the War god instead was despicable. Hephaestos shook his head, trying to dislodge the images of Ares and Aphrodite engaged in adultery in his bed. The thought of their capricious love-making pierced his heart as Hephaestos was forced to beg for the smallest crumb of her affection.

It sickened him.

"Hephaestos. What is bothering you?" Aphrodite rose from the couch with the help of her ladies. "Your sweat and your face flushes. Are you ill?"

He avoided her gaze. "I am concerned for your well-being. You have told me you are newly with child." The flush upon his skin grew deeper. "I worry that you are safe to travel."

"There is no reason to fret. I have carried children before." Her laughter was like the rush of water falling over rock, musical and engaging.

"It took so long for this event to…to occur…perhaps there is danger in losing it. I have heard that such a thing could happen."

"Why, Hephaestos, I believe you are blushing." Aphrodite gave a delicate shrug of pale shoulders. "There is no need to concern yourself with such things. This child has a firm grasp upon my womb and will not emerge until it is time."

His child. Hephaestos was both thrilled and terrified. A child to be born between himself and Aphrodite, would that not set his tormentors on their ears? In the Hall of Ages, he was ridiculed, thought unworthy and odious to one as flawless as Aphrodite. But she lay with him and now together they would have a child. Proof he was not abhorrent to Love. Proof he could love and be loved in spite of his disfigurement.

He would show them all his worthiness.

And he would then show them all that Aphrodite's heart was tainted. He would show them her beauty existed only on the surface. Beneath it, she was as crippled as he. Once the Ages saw her true face, she would be forced to remain with him for all time, for their trust would be broken. No one else would have her. The war god would be dead, a just reward for his evil and, at long last, Aphrodite would be his alone.

But first, he must keep her at Lemnos until wicked Ares came to visit again. "I wish for you to stay with me awhile longer, for I cannot bear to part with you."

Aphrodite looked upon Hephaestos' face and saw naught but sincerity. Her heart was torn, for Hephaestos was a good and kind man and his love was true. She hesitated and offered a sweet smile.

"As you wish, Hephaestos. I will remain here for a bit longer."

Hephaestos touched his lips to her brow. His heart was gladdened by this decision and, for the moment, he let himself believe that Aphrodite's slip with Ares was no more than that, a slip, and it should never again happen.

"I must go to my forge, for I create a gift for you."

Aphrodite lifted one hand for him to kiss. "What is it your cleverness creates?"

"It is a surprise, my Dear."

"I do so love a mystery."

As Hephaestos limped toward the arched doorway, Aphrodite called after him. "You will visit me tonight?"

He did not readily answer, for he wanted her more than anything else, but could not bring himself to that hateful bed where Ares had lain. "We shall see."

As his figure receded into the corridor shadows, Euphrosyne crossed her arms over her chest. "He is a strange one, Princess."

"Indeed." Aphrodite's nose wrinkled. "I do not grasp his reluctance."

"And I do not grasp your resistance in returning to Cos." Euphrosyne spoke shyly but with fervor for she wanted to go home. "Neither makes sense."

"Cos will be there when this is ended."

"As it should be. There is no further reason to be here. You are now with child. Is that not what this entire nonsense was about?" Thaleia appeared in the doorway.

Aglaia and Euphrosyne cast coy glances at Aphrodite, waiting for her response. She sent Thaleia away in anger but now welcomed her with open arms. Both Graces were a bit disappointed.

"It is so, Thaleia, and it is well you have come to stand with me. I acknowledge I failed to read my own heart, for I find I care for Hephaestos and do not want to hurt him. He took me to wife in good faith."

Aphrodite paused at Euphrosyne's muffled giggle. She glared at the girl who dropped her chin to hide the grin that still curled about her lips. Though Thaleia looked askance at her sister, her attention was drawn back when Aphrodite continued.

"He took me to wife in good faith and I intend to keep my promise to him."

"What?" All three women chorused.

"I have deeply considered this and I see no good reason to forgo my arrangement with Hephaestos."

"That is madness." Thaleia glanced over her shoulder with unease, in fear they would be overheard.

Aphrodite raised a hand to silence her. "Our alliance will continue."

"But what of Lord Ares?"

"What of Ares?" Aglaia stared at her sister, uncertain as to why she defended him.

"Lord Ares will not stand for it." Euphrosyne, too, took Ares' side.

"Shush." Aphrodite flicked her fingers at the women. "Do not speak his name."

"Why do we not speak his name?" Thaleia, adding with suspicion, "What have you done, Princess?"

"Nothing, good Sister. Euphrosyne speaks of Ares' anger at learning of this arrangement."

"He was angry, was he?" Satisfaction colored Thaleia's voice.

"Furious." Aphrodite offered a coy smile.

"Outraged." Aglaia could not stifle the snort of laughter.

"More than that." Euphrosyne remained straight-faced. "Very much more than that. I would even say that he grew very hard toward our mistress."

"Yes, he was incredibly hard and gave her no mercy. Did he, Sister?" Aglaia turned away, biting her lips.

"No mercy at all," giggled Euphrosyne.

"Lord Ares was here?" Thaleia squinted with suspicious indignity at her sisters. "Did he fight with Hephaestos?"

"No, Sister. His anger was directed at our Princess." Aglaia slapped a hand over her mouth.

"It was not so much in what he said," began Euphrosyne.

"Stop." Aphrodite commanded. "Let us just say that Lord Ares and I have come to an understanding."

Aglaia and Euphrosyne laughing uncontrollably.

Thaleia placed her hands on her hips and glared at her sisters. "I should not have left the two of you alone with her, for neither of you sport good manners."

"Rather rude, are they not?" Aphrodite laughed as she spoke.

Thaleia sighed. "Even if you honor this relationship between you and Hephaestos, I see no reason to reside here."

"Nor do I. Soon I will return to Cos and take up the reins of my realm, but for now, I will respect Hephaestos' request to reside at Lemnos."

"It is against my better judgment," warned Thaleia, "for I do not believe that Ares will give up so readily as you say."

"Oh, he will not, Sister, that I will promise," coughed Aglaia.

"He will be on her again soon, I am certain," added Euphrosyne.

"That is enough." Though Aphrodite spoke with sternness, she too snickered. "I have other matters to consider."

"Yes." Thaleia's tone was thick with irritation. "We have yet to discuss Eros. He misses you very much - another reason to return to Cos."

"He is not alone. Anteros is with him."

Thaleia frowned. "Anteros is not with him. Anteros was called away." She shot Euphrosyne a scowl. "He has not yet returned from his errand."

"Not returned?" Aphrodite and Euphrosyne spoke at once. "Where is he?"

"That I do not know. I have left Eros with Lyda, where he is safe, but only temporarily."

"I do not understand where Anteros has gone." Aphrodite glanced about the chamber as if the answer was hidden somewhere within its depths. "It is not like him to disappear without a word. I am deeply concerned."

She swiveled to look at Aglaia, and in particular, Euphrosyne. "Have either of you heard from him?"

"Princess." Euphrosyne glanced up at the domed ceiling in an attempt to avoid eye contact with her mistress. "Not since he was here to visit you. He told me he intended to see Deimos at Athos. That is all I know."

"At Athos? He would never go there."

"He had something he wanted to discuss with Deimos."

"He keeps no secrets from me."

"You were not feeling well, if you recall. Perhaps he mentioned his intentions and you no longer remember."

Aphrodite nodded. "Perhaps. I will call to him and I am certain he will respond. It is his duty." A thoughtful expression came over her lovely brow. "And Deimos. I would like to speak with my other son."

She took a deep breath, nodding again. Deimos would tell her what went on at Athos and if, indeed, Ares had released Niala.

"On second thought, rather than I demand their presence, I wish for you, Thaleia, to find them both and send them here. It may be best if others did not hear my command to my sons."

Sighing in resignation, Thaleia answered, "As you wish, Princess."

"Wait." Euphrosyne touched Aphrodite's hand. "Mistress, please, let me fetch them to your side."

Startled, Aphrodite chuckled. "You would not want to go to Athos, for it is a harsh place and not suitable for one with such a sweet temperament as you."

Drawing to her full height, Euphrosyne lifted her chin. "I may have the air of innocence yet beneath it I am quite capable. I am not afraid of Lord Ares, or of anyone else at Athos. Please, send me. My sister is weary and well deserves a rest."

Cocking her head to one side, Aphrodite took a long look at

Thaleia. "You are a bit drawn. Perhaps Euphrosyne is right, perhaps it is time she went about in the world. What say you?"

She directed her last remark to Thaleia and Aglaia.

"I do not know," Thaleia began. "Though I am weary, I would return to Athos after a rest. I cannot say if Athos is a suitable place to send Euphrosyne."

"Why would you say that? I am perfectly capable of delivering messages."

"You frighten easily and there is much at Athos that is fearsome. What if you do not readily locate Deimos and find yourself in the clutches of one of the other creatures that reside there? What then will you do?"

"What other creatures?" Euphrosyne's eyes widened.

"There, you see? I have scared you and you have not even left this room."

Sniffing, Thaleia turned aside. "I will go."

"No!" Euphrosyne stamped her small foot and clenched her fists at her side. Her face flushed a pretty shade of rose. "I will, Princess, I swear to you, I will find them and bring them back for you. Please let me go."

With an appraising gaze, Aphrodite considered Euphrosyne's request. "Why is it so important to you?"

Hesitating, Euphrosyne searched the faces of her sisters, hoping to find the correct words that would send her on this mission. She could not admit it was Anteros she sought, for that would keep her from this task as surely as if she said it was Lord Ares she wanted.

Thaleia had already made it sound as if she were still a child. All the while, Aglaia remained mute, afraid she would be made to go. There was no help from either and that was plain for Euphrosyne to see. Aphrodite, too, kept her expression bland, waiting for Euphrosyne's answer.

"It would be my pleasure to please you, Princess. I am quick and discreet, none but those who need know will be aware that I have been there. Your words are for Anteros and Deimos only, and not to be shared with any other."

"In truth." Aphrodite considered this new plan. "I do need Thaleia to return to Cos, for the sake of Eros, and I have need of Aglaia here at Lemnos." A slight smile played about Aphrodite's lips. "Therefore, Euphrosyne, I bid you go and find my sons and bring them to me."

Delighted, Euphrosyne clapped her hands. "I will not disappoint you, Princess."

"I am certain you will not." With a wry lift of her brows, Aphrodite waved at the young Grace. "Go now and set your dainty feet out into the world."

SEVENTEEN

"It is well you have come," said Priapos to Deimos as they clasped hand to arm in greeting.

Priapos, the Centaur, was much taller than Deimos. Though age was showing in silver strands within his beard and hair, he remained a fierce sight. His chest and arms were thick, balancing the strength of his lower body. The width of the human torso matched the width of the animal torso, tapering down into the graceful body and racing legs of a stallion.

Priapos wore only a string of bones around his neck and a fur loincloth about his waist to cover one set of male genitalia. The animal body was on full display.

"I arrived as quickly as I could." Deimos searched beyond the Centaur for signs of Phobos. "Is Phobos disobedient? I found him somewhat unruly. It would be understandable if you thought it best to send him back to Athos."

There was a faint note of hope in his tone, which faded as Priapos shook his head, in clear distress.

"I fear it is not as simple as that."

The Centaur was never anything less than composed and focused on his work. For Deimos to see him shift back and forth on his front feet, clenching and unclenching his fingers, did not bode well for Phobos. Deimos cast a glance at Eris and they both raised their brows in concern. Eris kept his distance from Priapos, but was ready to charge in, if necessary.

"What has happened?" Deimos cast another uneasy glance around the campsite. There was no sign of Phobos. "Where is he?"

Priapos jerked his head toward the entrance to his cave. Deimos started forward, only to have Priapos extend one brown hairy arm to stop him.

"Before you go in, you need to know more." The Centaur's face was grim. "It was not explained to me what Phobos' contribution would be to the world." Priapos began with near accusing tone.

"Ares brought him to me in the night and asked that I do what I could. There was no intention for full scale training as the child was scarce weaned from his mother's tit and needed time to adjust."

"Ares meant only that Phobos was still very much a child of Cos." Deimos' mouth thinned with irritation. "Phobos should not have been subjected to these harsh conditions."

"Agreed, though I understood Ares' direction. I, too, saw Phobos was less than warrior quality. He did not seem to have the same mettle as you, Deimos, or even the green one with all his antics." Priapos turned to glower at Eris, never forgetting the Sylph's misbehavior.

Eris curled his lip in a warning growl at the Centaur.

"Phobos is timid and frightens easily and, as I said, Ares did not tell me the purpose he brings to the world. Only that the boy must learn to put aside his own fears in favor of his work."

"It is true." Deimos flicked his fingers with impatience. "The boy is not yet ready for his awakening."

Priapos nodded. "And yet, I fear that it has already happened."

Deimos stared at the Centaur. "Just speak it."

Eris choked then spit upon the ground.

"You will see for yourself. It was not my plan to throw him into discovery, nor would I without Ares' direct command. I assume Ares prefers to handle that aspect himself."

"Yes, so he does." Staring off towards the black hole of the cavern, Deimos' mouth settled into a tight line. He had a very bad feeling and did not want to know what lay beyond the entrance. Eris, however, began to creep toward the cave, a flinty expression on his face.

"The boy did pay attention." Priapos continued his story. "But he does not understand the concept of battle and questions everything. He is very quick, yet has not the capacity to grasp the instinct to fight."

"That is because his instinct would be to run away." Deimos frowned. "And so, he ran?"

Priapos nodded with grave concern. "Yes. You have learned well to read others, Deimos." There was affection and an underlying pride in the Centaur's voice. "We were out in the forest for a lesson in tracking when we were attacked."

"Attacked? By whom?"

Hanging his head with a shame unbecoming to a great warrior such as he, Priapos again clenched his fists. "I fear I am too old to train mortal or immortal. Regardless, I did not hear them coming. I did not sense either their closeness or their intentions. When I saw them, I mistook them for a hunting party."

Grief welled up in his voice and he stopped, unable to meet Deimos' gaze. For the first time, Deimos noticed the wounds upon the animal body, the deep punctures and slashes covered over with mud crusted pink by the seeping blood. Amidst the hair on his upper human body were also patches of the same poultice and Deimos now saw that Priapos moved slowly from the pain.

"Tell me."

"They were here to take Phobos." Wearily, Priapos shook his head. "There was a time when no one would have dared touch a son of Ares, but the world has changed, Deimos. They thought to gain power by having War's son in their hands. They intended to murder me and steal away Phobos."

"For which they will endure unbearable torment." Deimos' eyes belied his calm tone. "They will pay endlessly for this."

"They have already, my Son, for they all are dead." Priapos managed a slight smile. "Though I may be old, I am not without the strength to destroy."

"And what of my brother? Was he injured?"

"Not in the fight. He did as you said, he ran from the cutthroats. Ran with blind panic back to this cave, for it was the only place he thought he might be safe."

Sorrow was in the Centaur's eyes. "While I fought the throng, two escaped me and followed Phobos here."

As Eris listened, his ears and nose twitched. He turned with a jerk and stared at a pile of brush, causing Deimos to also turn. There, buried within the leaves and branches was visible a hand.

"It cannot be," Eris whispered.

"No." Priapos raised his arms. "It is not Phobos. The hand is of his attacker. I caught up to them, slew them both and there they lay. I feared as you do, since Phobos is most vulnerable at his age. He is an immortal child and could not suffer true death yet I almost wish it would be so for him, for what has happened is far worse."

"Where is he?" Deimos spoke harshly. "Take me to him, now."

Instead of leading the way, Priapos talked on, as if he forgot the brothers were present. "I could not find him. Once the offenders were dead, I called and called to him and searched everywhere, in every crack and crevice of the cavern.

"I even went back into the woods, thinking he might have hidden in the trees. Still I could not find him." He raised his gaze to meet Deimos, searching between he and Eris with panic in his eyes, repeating, "I could not find him."

"Take me to Phobos." Deimos spoke with a gentleness he did not feel. "Whatever has happened is not your fault."

Nodding once, Priapos started toward the cave. "I was to safeguard him."

"You were to teach him."

"It is all the same to me," he replied with sadness.

The trek into the depths of the cave was done in silence. Priapos led them further and further along narrow corridors until they came to a sheer wall of stone. There was neither left path nor right. It was a dead end. The only way out would be the way they came in. There was no sign of Phobos.

"I do not understand. Where is he?"

Rubbing a hand over his face, Priapos groaned, as if with more pain than he could bear, and then pointed to the wall. "Inside."

Deimos stared at the wall in disbelief. "You cannot mean...."

"I do. He went into the stone."

"He could not have."

"He did, somehow, he did. He merged with the very heart of the cavern. How did he do this? I cannot explain for I do not know."

"That is impossible."

The Centaur laid one heavy hand upon his student's shoulder and turned Deimos to face him. "When there was no place else to look, I sat and listened. I could hear him crying. Faintly, yet I could hear him."

"In there." Deimos stared at the wall.

Eris pressed his ear to the uneven surface and closed his eyes. Within a moment, he shouted, "I hear him. It is true, Deimos, our brother lies within the cave wall. Perhaps - perhaps there is a chamber on the other side. He may well be safe."

"There is no other chamber." Priapos' voice bounced from the low ceiling. "I have lived in this cavern for many thousand years and know every step of it. It ends here."

With his cheek pressed to the rough surface, Eris lay against the wall, his arms spread wide. "He weeps. He is so frightened. He does not know what has happened to him.

"He cannot move. He cannot breathe. He cannot...." Eris' voice rose into a shriek and he fell to his knees, his hands over his ears. "Deimos, Deimos, get him out!"

"I can hear nothing but his pleas." Tears leaked from Priapos' faded eyes. "I will never rest until he is released from this prison. Deimos, you must help him."

"Yes, Brother. You must." Eris rolled to his side, arms wrapped around his midsection.

Numbed, Deimos could not move his gaze from the damp moss-covered stone that rose in a solid wave to the ceiling and wrapped around all sides. It was cold and unforgiving. It mocked him as he stood before it envisioning the flesh of his little brother imbedded within its heart. He knew the stone did not want to release the only warmth it had ever felt - this tiny bit of blood and bone that had forced its way inside it.

When Ares taught the art of Arbitri - the ability to move from place to place by merely willing it - he gave serious caution to the many dangers of other realms. How each was different. How some were extremely difficult, if not impossible, to extract from.

Stone was one of those dimensions. He heard again his father's warning: *There are those who were careless, who stepped into another sphere without knowing how to return. Those folk have been forever lost.*

Before them stood a sheer wall of solid rock with Phobos locked inside. The boy had not been trained in Arbitri. How he had gotten inside was a mystery. How could he possibly get out?

Deimos did not realize he held his breath until the air forced its way out through his teeth in a whoosh. "I do not know if I can release him. I do not know if anyone can."

*****

Utter darkness. Absolute silence.

Not a glimmer of light or an indrawn breath. Nothing but screams, heard not in sound, only in thought. Phobos knew not what had happened or why, yet he understood he could not move, could not force even the faintest whisper from his throat. Could not see anything. Could not hear anything.

He remembered being frightened of the men who attacked the Centaur. They meant to kill Priapos - he could see it in their eyes. Empty brutal eyes and gnashing teeth was all he remembered. That and Priapos' bravery, his fighting, bleeding, shouting at him to run.

Run.

For a moment, Phobos had been frozen to the spot. He was fascinated, in a terrible way, at the sight of wicked sharp blades diving in and out of flesh. He had seen blood spurting and heard the gurgle of death as two of the enemy dropped with their throats slashed open.

He was mesmerized by the violence.

This was now to be his life. It was the purpose to which he was born. It was the reason he had been sent to Priapos: to learn how to fight. To be part of his father's world. To attend to War. It was so far removed from his beginnings he could not help but stare, wide-eyed and filled with dread. Then some of the men turned toward him.

Priapos shouted, "Run!"

So Phobos ran. He ran as fast as he could, blindly, madly ran until he hit something so hard he blacked out. When he woke, he could not feel his breath nor his body.

He could not feel his heart beating.

He presumed himself dead. Yet somewhere in the darkness there was an awareness. He could not touch with his hands, but he could reach out with something much deeper - an inner spark that that defied definition in his limited realm of knowledge.

And he knew he was not alone. Something else was there. Not those men. Not Priapos. Something inhuman. Something very, very old. Something ancient. Something alive. Something pressing all around him. He could feel it wanting.

Desperately wanting. Desperately yearning.

And still, he did not know where he was.

Was this truly death and he did not know it?

Phobos felt so very cold. Even worse than the cold on Athos - the kind of cold that took away life. And there was the relentless sense of another whose hunger was unbearable. The other, who wanted him, who waited for just the right moment before swallowing him all up until nothing was remained.

In that moment, Phobos knew the mindless screaming was his own.

*****

"Come away," begged Eris, his face dirty and streaked with tears. "We cannot help him."

He yanked at Deimos' arm to get him on his feet. Though he was strong, Deimos was stronger and would not withdraw.

"Do not lose yourself in this monster, Deimos, for that is what it wants. I know it will feed on all of us until there is nothing left but dried bones. We must come away."

Deimos sat in the ages-old dust of the cave floor with his head buried in his arms, elbows balanced on his knees. He was exhausted and his head ached horrifically, but he would not give up. He would not leave Phobos behind. He wanted only to rest a bit and then again risk all to reach his little brother. If necessary, he would sacrifice himself to the Monolith to free the child.

He shoved Eris away. "Stop. We do not leave without him."

"We have tried everything. What else is left to do?" Eris met Deimos' eyes and saw there the determination. "No! No, you cannot go in there, it will have you, too."

"I must agree." Priapos spoke in a rumbling harsh voice that showed his strain. "If you are lost, it would be death to all of us. And even then there would be no releasing the boy."

"I will make a trade. I will go in and Phobos will come out."

"You cannot reason with it. It neither feels nor thinks. It only takes."

"Why has it never taken you, or anything else?"

"Because it never had the chance. This…this thing…"

Priapos smacked the rock wall with his fist. "It has waited an eternity for one such as Phobos. Now it sits smugly in its hole, wanting more."

In a frenzy, Priapos began to pound on the face of the rock, shouting with profane fury until his knuckles bled. Deimos and Eris did not intervene, for their hopelessness was the very blood that smeared the shards of stone.

"Release him! Release him. Release him." Priapos dropped his arms to his side and knelt in the dirt beside them, folding his animal legs beneath his cumbersome body. He breathed with heavy gasps and appeared as if he would collapse.

"You have had neither food nor drink since we have been here." Deimos grasped Priapos' forearm. "Do not do us the disservice of dying."

The Centaur shook his mane of hair and tried to smile. "That would be too simple. I have never done anything the easy way."

"Nor have I."

"Then do not make a trade. Rescue the boy."

With a heavy sigh, Deimos dropped his hand to his side. "I will rest a bit and try again to reach him, however, each time I come close I feel Phobos' panic like a black pit with no bottom. He falls and falls and still I cannot grab him."

"It is the Monolith," hissed Eris. "It squats there, laughing at us."

"When I search, in there, I no longer recognize which is rock and which is flesh." Deimos wiped a sweating palm across his grimy tunic. "It is as if the Monolith is Phobos, and he is the Monolith. The images I see are not those of a child. I do not know if the two can be separated, but I must strive to make it so."

Eris and Priapos nodded in agreement, blank-eyed and weary.

*****

Phobos cried for his mother, though his mouth did not work and words did not come. He felt himself wailing for her, screaming for her, with the relentless, repeating howl of a child in need.

"Mama, Help me. Mama, Mama. Help me. Help me."

She did not answer and eventually his cries fell back into wordless shrieks of desperation. As much as he struggled and fought, he could not move. He could not see. He could hear nothing but himself.

And the Unidentified Thing was right there pressing down.

Then he heard the voice of his brother calling him. His name echoed through the darkness, wavering as if the distance was almost too great. For one moment he was uplifted, almost calm, certain he would be rescued. He knew Deimos would free him.

With all his might, Phobos did his best to answer. Deimos kept calling yet he did not hear Phobos' shouts. He shrieked and howled to no avail. Deimos did not hear him.

Phobos was scared his brother would give up. He was horrified at the thought he would be abandoned here with that Thing.

Unceasingly, Phobos tried to make himself known.

Deimos heard nothing.

And the Thing pressed closer. It whispered in Phobos mind that he no longer existed, that he now belonged to It. It swore Deimos would never find the flesh of the boy who once lived.

Phobos felt utterly and forever lost in the vast world of darkness. Frozen and alone, except for It.

Wave after wave of terror splashed over him, like burning flames feeding on him, swallowing his screams. Feral, savage terror tore into him with a thousand blades, ripping him to shreds, silencing him for good.

Disabling paralyzing terror as It spoke to him.

Do you know my name? It whispered. *My name is Panic.*

*****

Shuddering, Deimos hunched close to the fire, his forehead resting on his clenched fists. Every time he undertook to penetrate the thick wall of stone, he was repelled. The response was not the sensation of being slapped or even pushed, as when he entered the mind of another being, but of hitting a rigid unforgiving surface.

Seldom did Deimos pursue the thoughts of others, for it was a treacherous game. Most often, he did not want to know what went on in the deepest part of another soul, even one so basic as an animal, but he could see no other way. He had not believed the rock to have cognition.

To him, stone was like the bones of something dead, protruding, bare and exposed, having no thought or reason. What purpose it held was long gone, decayed into dust and forgotten. He did not expect the stone to be alive and holding memories within its abysmal heart. It was not like touching something alive with seething seeking energy. It was frozen and relentlessly silent, yet it was alive. It was unlike anything he ever felt in his existence.

And it would not let him in.

The ancient Monolith understood what he attempted, and it resisted. It would not trade flesh for flesh. It would not allow Deimos to enter nor would it release Phobos.

"What is it? What is happening? Deimos, tell me." Eris danced about the fire circle, taking care to stay away from Priapos. The huge Centaur had already knocked him senseless once and seemed more than ready to do so again.

"You are like a gnat to a torch," growled Priapos. "Can you not see Deimos is doing what he can?" Though he spoke to Eris in a forceful voice, alarm colored every word. "Truly, Deimos, you do everything possible?"

Groaning, Deimos lowered his hands and stared at the flames through bloodshot eyes. "Yes, but it fights me."

"What fights you?"

"The stone itself rejects me. I cannot begin to reach Phobos, for it blocks me from him."

"That is madness." The hair stood up on Priapos' neck. "It is rock, a cave wall that supports the ground above it, it neither breathes nor feels."

"So, too, I thought, but we are wrong."

"It does not move, it does not change."

"Yet it exists. We can touch it, and it knows we are there."

"It is inanimate. There is no vibrancy." Agitated, Priapos began to pace, tail switching. "It is stone."

"Yes." Eris ran to the other side of the circle to avoid the Centaur. "It does not cry out, it cannot feel. My mind is boggled that Phobos could be inside. Though I see many things that mystify me, this, by far, is queerest of all. He should be able to walk out as he walked in."

"He should," agreed Deimos.

"Why, then, does he not?"

"Because he does not realize he can. More, he has panicked. He has lost control. I seek to reach him, to calm him, but I cannot get through. The monolith will not let me."

"Force your way past its guard. It would not be the first time you have done the impossible." Priapos flexed his battered hands as if he would tear open the rock wall.

"It does not respond other than to deflect. I can scarce describe what it seems to me other than to say it is a massive sealed wall that I can neither go over, around, nor under."

"Go through it," shouted Eris. "Smash it to pieces! You must get to Phobos, or he will not survive."

"But he will." Grief was thick in Deimos' voice. "He will."

"Then we must get Ares." Eris danced about both men.

"Yes." Priapos sighed long and hard. "Though I did not want to call him, there is no other choice."

Deimos bowed his head and stared at his hands, at the broad palms and long fingers, at the squared off tips. These hands could pull down the wall. They could drive through solid rock and tear it apart. They could bring the entire cave down, but he knew that would not free Phobos.

In his heart of hearts, he knew Phobos was no longer whole, locked inside a bubble. He knew Phobos had been absorbed into the stone. His blood, his flesh, his warmth had become part of the ancient rock.

Was it even possible to extract the child from such a place? Deimos harkened back to the days of his own training and of the many lectures he received from Ares.

Yes, it was possible to return. There was only one who could do it, and that was Phobos. He must retain enough of his own sensibility to retreat, and if he could not, there was no hope.

"No." Deimos finally spoke. "Do not call Ares."

"But, why, Brother?" Eris jerked, checking behind him and to each side, as if Ares might be listening. "This is far beyond all of us. If he hears of this some other way, we will all be punished."

Priapos shifted from foot to foot with this statement. "Perhaps it is time, Deimos."

"No." Standing, Deimos took a few steps toward the cave and then returned. "Should Ares discover Phobos' misfortune, he will make certain no help is afforded him."

"What do you mean?" Eris paused his incessant movement.

"He will consider this Phobos' rites of passage into his power. Whether it was meant to happen or not, it has. Therefore, he will let it stand."

"He will not get him out?"

"No. Ares will leave him until such time Phobos can release himself."

"But what if he does not?" Swallowing hard, Eris stared wide-eyed.

"Then he will never be free."

"Mercy." Priapos lifted his arms to the heavens. "Even Ares would not leave a child terrified and alone with a monster."

He, too, stopped, for he knew Ares could and would leave Phobos buried in the cave wall for all eternity if he thought it would serve as a lesson.

"What shall we do?" Eris spoke in a hoarse whisper. His gaze darted beyond Deimos, to the forests he loved so much. He found it unbearable to think of never roaming free, never to climb into the treetops again, or to see the bright blue skies, or even to feel the rain as it beat down, feeding the ground.

Unbearable.

"What can we do?"

"I do not know." Deimos hesitated for a moment before he strode into the cave, retracing the path Phobos took. He stood once more in front of the jagged wall. The other two trailed behind him, until they all stared at the barrier between them and Phobos.

The layers of its birth were clearly defined on the face of the stone. Dark streaks amongst lighter patches here and there, and all with clumps of dirty green lichen growing in the cracks. Moisture seeped through and ran down the sides to be absorbed into the hard-packed dirt floor. Wet lines highlighted the layers of growth. How many more levels were beneath the ground? How far down did the rock wall extend?

Deimos shook his head, for hope was beyond him at that moment.

"Why do we not just break it apart?" Eris touched the damp film, running his finger along a trickle of water.

"Because Phobos is no longer whole. He is part of the stone and if we shatter the wall, we will destroy him as well."

Eris blanched. "This is worse than anything Ares could have dreamed up."

"And we do not want this trial to become part of his arsenal."

Unable to speak, Eris nodded, showing sharp teeth with a grimace.

Priapos stomped his hooves, leaving marks on the ground. "This is my fault. I should not have taken him into the woods, for I suspected he was not ready."

"Noble one, do not take this as your trial, for in truth, Phobos should still be with his mother. He was not ready for this. If there is blame to be laid, it is at the feet of Ares for taking him too young." Deimos stared at the ancient Monolith.

Old wounds swelled as he spoke and memories of his rites of passage brought a bitter taste to his own mouth. He had been far younger than Phobos yet so much sturdier in nature. Still, Deimos should have been in his mother's lap, not immersed in his father's brutal world.

There had been no comfort, no celebration, no care. He had been tossed into the pit of war either to survive or perish. And when Terror rose up for the first time, he thought he would go mad. He had been a mere child sent to face his worst fears alone and afraid, while Ares watched and waited to see if he failed.

Like Phobos, who was now in the grips of his worst nightmare, Deimos, too, had been alone and afraid. Deimos was not going to leave his brother there.

Deimos laid his hands on the face of the Monolith. Quiet fell around them like a soft rain and all to be heard was the sound of breathing. He pressed close to the rock wall, feeling its jagged edges cut into him. He ran his hands along the protrusions, touching each indentation, each chip, each aberration in the face of the Monolith. He called to it.

To it, not to Phobos, but to the ancient one who imprisoned him. Deimos waited for the Monolith to answer.

It was long in coming. For one who had stood since the world was created, there was no hurry. There was curiosity. And there was desire. There was hatred. And there was yearning. There was arrogance. And there was grief.

Deimos felt the raw envy of the Monolith splash over him - that he had legs and could walk, that he had eyes to see, hands to explore, and blood to warm. That he did not stand alone and silent, locked in a cavern without light.

Forever and ever alone.

The ancient stone's energy spilled over Deimos in a torrent of silent screams. Deimos felt himself being drawn into the heart of the stone as it opened up its ravenous maw seeking more blood, more heat.

Darkness closed in, whirling like a tidal pool that sucked him down into its depths with no hope of survival. He felt panic rising and knew Phobos was close. He felt his own terror returning with a vengeance that could strike him senseless if he allowed himself. He, too, would be swallowed whole by the Monolith.

Without knowing, he shrieked. The wretched sensation was suddenly torn away and Deimos found himself on the dirt floor, panting and sobbing. Eris gripped his hands, having pulled him back from the face of the abyss. The last thing Deimos saw before passing out was the Sylph crouched over him, with tears on his cheeks.

EIGHTEEN

"It has come to this." Niala traced the indistinct features of the statue once displayed in the temple.

The face of the Mother Goddess was deliberately blurred to illustrate that she appeared in the eyes of every living thing. Earth is her body: the rising plateaus, her breasts; the meadows, her belly. the unadorned valley of Najahmara, the mystery within the ancient deity. Gaea is the fertile fields and the clear waters running through the village. She is the beauty that surrounded them, nurtured them, held them with tenderness and joy.

And now, rather than in a place of honor in the temple dedicated to her, Gaea was hidden away in one of the many recesses of her own cave. Niala touched the statue's chipped edges with regret, knowing the damage was done during Kulika's rampage.

"I am afraid so." Jahmed, too, caressed the image of Gaea. "You see our temple is taken over by the invaders. One has claimed himself king and demands we bow to him."

Her mouth puckered as if she tasted something bad. "How we could ever feel at peace in that room again is beyond me."

"In time."

"No. Not in my life. I gave it to them, did Pallin tell you? I could not bear the sight of it, nor the sight of him."

Jahmed did not say his name but Niala knew she meant Hattusilis. Jahmed's voice was tinged with defiance. She avoided Niala's gaze, staring instead at the faded rug spread across the dirt floor. It was not the one that had been in the temple. It was ruined by spilled blood and had to be burned. There were other pieces missing from the altar, but Niala did not have the heart to ask what happened to them.

"The sight of any of those who raid our village disturbs me." Jahmed fingered her long braids, straightening the cloth she wore tied around her head.

"Once their leader was found and brought in to be cared for, we no longer mattered. Those of his legion surrounded him and we were pushed into the streets. The only thing we kept is the medicine quarters and that only because none of them are gods. They have ills just like us. They want our remedies but that is all."

With a quivering sigh, Jahmed lifted her eyes to the roof of the cavern. "This is our only sanctuary. He forbids us to use the cave, so we brought our altar here to hide it. He has gone so far as to demand that we move the stores out from the cave recesses."

"Why? What reason does he give?"

"He pronounced the sacred entrance to Gaea evil." Jahmed's nose flared as her lips tightened. "He might as well call all women the same. By casting slurs upon our goddess, he shows he has no respect for any of us. Not even his wife."

"He does not treat Pallin well?" Niala spoke with calm but her chest constricted.

Pallin was an innocent, born in Najahmara, never seeing beyond the edges of the outlying fields. She had no concept of the things that could happen as Jahmed or Inni did, no perspective of the differences that chafed between peoples. Niala had seen the brutality first hand, the utter insignificance of women in a man's world. Such a life would destroy Pallin. It would destroy all of the women.

"If you ask him, he will say he loves and protects her from harm but it is a disguised attempt to keep her from us. If you ask her, she will laugh and say he simply does not understand, and she goes about her tasks in spite of his demands."

Jahmed paused for a deep breath. "I say he will wear her down until she does what he commands, especially after their child is born.

She will be a dutiful mother and wife molded after his desires."

"That is a rather harsh view, Jahmed. Do you not give Pallin any credit for what she has learned from us? She has, after all, gone through the rites of a priestess. Would she forsake her promise to Gaea?"

Even as Niala spoke, she knew Jahmed spoke the truth. Though Niala had conversed with Pallin about the changes in the village and the lack of trust in her husband and his men, Pallin resisted. She did, indeed, love the man. For this, Niala was grateful yet concerned.

Hattusilis was strong-willed and stubborn. He would follow his own path regardless of the pain he inflicted on others. Niala had witnessed such inflexible behavior within the harvest ritual when he went before Gaea. He was frightened rather than uplifted. He chose to run away rather than embrace the opportunity.

"This child," Niala said. "When should it birth?"

Jahmed sat down cross-legged, her skirt tucked around her thighs. Niala followed, watching the shadows cast by the light of a single candle.

They could not have a fire for fear the remnants would be seen drifting from the cave. Jahmed said Hattusilis was not aware of the hidden entrance on the far end of the path from the gardens. She lived in fear it, too, would be discovered so the women disguised the opening and a different path was created to the top of the plateau to divert any who passed by from their secret.

"Pallin says she is not due until the end of the summer season, but I say she is far more advanced and will birth before summer begins." Jahmed lifted one hand. "You have only to look at her to see the babe is settling. She carries low. I think it will be a boy, born much sooner than she believes."

In a hushed voice, Jahmed continued, "I do not think her king is the father, but she refuses to speak of any such possibility."

Niala had an instant image of Pallin and Deimos left to together at the lake after the Autumn celebration. "Perhaps the child she carries has been fathered by Deimos."

As the words left her mouth, she felt a twinge of regret for pairing the two the night of the harvest ritual. It seemed the right choice at the time but now that she understood so much more of the immortal realm, now that she felt love for Deimos herself, she was uncertain.

Niala gave a slight shake of her head to clear her thoughts. Her hand had been guided by Gaea that night and Niala would not question the wisdom of the Mother Goddess.

"Would Deimos care? There have long been tales of gods who spread their seed amongst the human world without concern." Jahmed glanced at Niala's pregnant belly beneath the layer of material but made no further comment.

With fingers splayed across the bulge, Niala felt the babe kick, as if in protest. "My little one takes offense," Niala chuckled. "This is no ordinary child."

"I suspect Pallin's is not either. What misery will her king create when he discovers the truth?"

"And Deimos." Niala met Jahmed's concerned gaze. "The House of War will make claim to their own."

Jahmed nodded but chose to say no more about Pallin's child. "Will you visit Inni again today?"

"Inni." Sadness lingered between the two women at the mention of the injured priestess.

There was a flicker of recognition in the depths of Inni's blue eyes and a ghost of a smile when Niala first sat beside her. Both were quickly gone as Inni retreated back into the blank stare of a wounded soul. "Yes, I will go to see her today and every day after."

"I hoped you could do something for her. I so hoped." Jahmed trailed off.

"Do not give up on her yet, Sister, for there is life somewhere in that deep well where she resides."

"Never." Jahmed spoke with fierce loyalty. "I will never give Inni up to the horrors she suffered. I pray she returns to me, but if she does not, I will be with her until the end."

They reached to hold hands for some small measure of consolation and sat in comfortable silence until a cramp caused Niala to rise on unsteady feet.

"Niala, I have wondered about something." Hesitating, Jahmed also stood and stretched. "Do you know what happened to the stones on the plateau? There has been much fear over the damage. So much so, we did not hold Spring rites there. Our people feel as if their ruin is a warning from Gaea. She warns us not to abandon her for Teshub, the god the soldiers worship."

"Gaea had nothing to do with the broken stones. In a fit of temper, Ares destroyed them."

"But why would he do such a thing?" Jahmed snorted. "As if there is any rhyme or reason to War."

"To punish me." Niala paused to collect her thoughts before telling Jahmed of the women buried beneath the markers. Once started, she could not stop the flow of words. She recounted how Ares tossed Layla's bones about like kindling. How it was not ended between them when she saw the invasion begin. How she ran down the mount, frantic to warn Najahmara, and found it was too late.

"Mercy," Jahmed whispered. "Yet he left one marker standing."

"Mine." Niala saw the jolt in Jahmed's widened eyes. "And Ares knew it was mine. He left it intact to torment me."

"You just said it was the graves of the five women who founded Najahmara."

"It is."

"I do not understand."

"Four are dead and one is not. One waits endlessly to join the others." Niala pressed her fingertips to her forehead.

"I do not grasp what you are saying." Jahmed searched Niala's face and then took in a whoosh of air as she stumbled backward. "Are you...are you one of them?"

"Ahh, Jahmed, I fear it is true. Many things came to light while I was gone, things I cannot readily explain." Heat arose bringing sweat to Niala's forehead at the memory of the dark passion that consumed her as Ares invoked an unidentifiable source into her body. Their fierce lovemaking that resulted in the conception of the babe within her.

"Is that why he wants you? Because you are an immortal just as Ares? Mercy, I have seen you shape-shift with my own eyes. Niala, what are you? Who are you?"

"I am as I have always been regardless of my descent."

"You said you hailed from a nomadic tribe."

"Ares claims my origin is of the immortal caste and I was abandoned to mortal parents. It remains a mystery to both of us. Still and all, I cannot deny I am different. True death does not seem to come to me."

"Nor illness, nor age." Jahmed reeled with Niala's revelation. "Your cuts and bruises heal quickly, too quick. You never fall ill." She wagged her head from side to side as her breath wheezed.

"Sit, Jahmed, before you fall." With an abrupt shake of her head, Niala began to pace about the cavern.

The air was cool and felt good on her damp skin. It filtered through rock and gave off the clean scent of soil and stone. In the background, water trickled from a crack at the entry to the tunnel. With it came a whiff of rich, damp earth.

"You are the catalyst that brings Gaea to us. Without you, she retreats." Jahmed leaned against the cave wall. "If you leave us again, we are lost."

"It is true, I feel her ebbing. It is not because of me or the presence of these soldiers and their strange god." Niala did not add that Teshub was no other than Ares. "It is because her mate seeks power and she gives him free reign."

"Kulika takes what he wants." Jahmed's dark skin flushed and she broke her gaze with Niala.

"Kulika and Gaea do not have the freedom to move about like other immortals. They exist in spirit, they exist as two halves to make a whole." Niala made a circle gesture, earth and sky.

"Gaea found she could inhabit a mortal body and take pleasure in it as she is the stronger of the two. Over time, she began to long for her mate and caused him to take form in another mortal. This has gone on since the beginning of time. But Kulika could not do this by himself.

"He first needed Gaea's strength to be drawn down into a body. Until." Niala paused, eyes closed. She recalled the roaring flame that had coursed through her and the heat that expelled outward into a column of fire that incinerated half a town.

"Until Kulika fed on my rage, my hatred. He pressed endlessly at me until I allowed him entrance to my body. I knew all along he would destroy everything. He rode the wave of my fury, unleashing all his frustration and bitterness at having no control.

"Always, Gaea dominated. His resentment should have come as no surprise. Now Kulika lingers and feeds this king and his men. Indeed, I have noticed our own men seem affected as well."

"I have seen this shift you speak of. I thought it a mere ruse to fool the newcomers. I did not believe our own would turn on us, but, truly, Niala, so many men died. The women, too. They take up with the soldiers." Jahmed wiped a tear from her face with her skirt. "And it is my fault.

"The Spring rites were a travesty, a horror to behold. I led - no, I must be honest - I could not lead. I did not have the strength. Pallin's king would not allow us to hold the celebration on the plateau. He insisted it be at the lakeshore, near the mouth of the field they inhabit. A filthy place.

"And yet, I did my best, I swear. I called Gaea in the hopes we could heal some of the pain. Instead, it was no more than an opportunity for soldiers to mate with our women. Gaea saw to that."

Jahmed gave a bark of mirthless laughter. "Our goddess created an ugly random mating - mindless fools groping at whomever was near. I, myself, was under her thrall and could do nothing to stop it."

"Do not blame yourself, Jahmed." Niala gripped the grieving priestess' shoulder. "Gaea's will is hard to hold, even for me. That she saw a greater story to play out is not unusual."

"You do not understand what took place. It was far worse than my losing control. Kulika was here but she did not call him."

"How can you be certain? Gaea longs for her mate. She always wants to call him."

"She swore she would not." Jahmed's tortured gaze rose to meet Niala's. "Yet he was here, and she was furious."

Licking her lips, Jahmed sought to recall the exact circumstances but the event leading up to it was unclear. "Kulika took hold of Hattusilis and pressed him to violence."

She closed her eyes to the near-rape of a pregnant Pallin, unwilling to give voice to the horror. "Gaea saw him, recognized him and they began to fight. I know now that Kulika feared she would banish him back to his realm. And Gaea, she is furious with his behavior.

"Kulika would not leave this realm. He continues to haunt Hattusilis, though the man scarce knows it. Kulika is selfish. He chooses not to call his mate. She is wounded and refuses to help rid him from our midst."

Niala nodded. "Since my return, I have heard her disapproval on the wind and in the grasses. The rivers moan, the lake sighs, and Kulika ignores it all. He inflames all those he can. We are out of balance, Sister." Niala stopped in front of Gaea's image. "Far out of balance."

"What are we to do?"

Niala turned to look at Jahmed and Jahmed shivered, for the spark in her eyes went beyond earthly knowledge. "We will send Kulika back to the heavens, and it will be a long while before I ask him to return."

Hattusilis waited under the canopy for Niala Aaminah to make the trek down the mountainside. He watched her slow descent as she paused to scan across the valley with a certain air of ownership that set his hackles on the rise. He would not be ignored this time, for she must pass through the gardens to get inside. Zan waited to block her path should she try to avoid him.

"Good morning, Hattusilis, Zan." Niala greeted them both with cheer as she approached.

Hattusilis tried in vain to take no offense but could not help frowning. At every turn, Niala Aaminah tested him with word, or gesture, or worse, silence. Of late, absence.

"King Hattusilis." Zan's reminder was mild.

"King Hattusilis." Niala smiled and nodded. "Good morning."

There it was again, the patronizing smile that spoke volumes more than any utterance she could make. Hattusilis grunted with irritation and opened his mouth to retort.

Zan placed a hard hand on his shoulder. It was a clear message that a good leader did not let slip his thoughts while in negotiations with the enemy.

It had become clear that Niala Aaminah was, indeed, the enemy. She sought to influence Pallin, drawing her attention and affections away. Niala attempted to take control of the former temple by manipulating his men. She garnered support from those of Najahmara who survived.

The list of Niala's violations went on. In the Steppelands, each item would be viewed as treason. She would be executed without further argument if he were in his homeland But he was not in the Steppelands, and it was not as simple as issuing an order with unquestioned compliance.

"I have no doubt I would be assassinated by my own wife if I were to attempt to destroy the priestess." Hattusilis had complained to Zan earlier that very morning. "I cannot even have the woman beaten for fear of an uprising."

Zan watched him through a half-shuttered gaze and murmured, "It would be wise to have a word with her, do you think, rather than resort to violence?"

This from his captain at arms. Sometimes Hattusilis missed Deimos, for surely he would dispatch the woman without question. Yet again, he had forgotten Deimos was not what he seemed either. It would not come as a surprise if Niala Aaminah and Deimos were in league together.

Weary, Hattusilis closed his eyes and leaned his head back. Was there no one he could trust?

"Sire?"

Zan's rumbling voice came from a distance and Hattusilis realized he had begun to drift off to sleep. His eyes flew open to meet the level gaze of Niala Aaminah as she waited in patience for him to speak.

Hattusilis had the fleeting thought that perhaps she had placed him under a spell. To doze at that most inopportune moment was quite unlike him.

"Are you feeling ill? Perhaps I should...." Niala raised a hand to touch his forehead.

Blocking her, Hattusilis snapped, "No, I am not ill. I tire easily. I do not sleep well." He could have bitten off his tongue for confessing this to the priestess.

"I can have a sleeping potion brought to you this evening."

"No." Hattusilis thought she would no doubt poison him. "It is not every night. I have no need."

"Of course. If you will excuse me." She turned to go.

"Halt, for I would like to speak with you on another subject."

"And what would that be?"

Hattusilis did not like the way her eyes twinkled. "You go up that path every morning before dawn. Do you go to the cave? I have forbidden the cavern to your followers."

"So I have heard." Niala acknowledged Hattusilis with a slight bow of her head. "I go to the plateau each morning to watch the sunrise."

"It is now well past that, why do you linger so long?"

There was a brief moment of silence as she swept an appraising glance over him. Hattusilis shifted with impatience.

"The plateau has fallen into disrepair and I work to restore it."

"Teshub tore down that altar in his anger at Gaea. You cannot repair it."

"Teshub?" Niala outright grinned. "You are closer to the truth than you know. And you are right, I cannot put the stones back together."

"The one remaining should be knocked down for it appears like some apparition under moonlight. I do not like it."

"Odd that you speak of phantoms."

"Why? What do you know?" Hattusilis raised part way out of his seat before his arms weakened and he plunked down with a grimace.

Niala met his gaze with her amber eyes and said, "They are all around us. Everywhere. The dead walk because they cannot rest."

"Here?" Swiveling his head back and forth, Hattusilis sent a panicked message to Zan. "Now?"

"I think she jests," Zan responded. "They do not stroll along the garden paths as if sniffing flowers."

Niala turned to Zan. "You are a sensitive man. Can you not feel their presence? Sudden death begets phantoms for they do not know they should lie in their graves like decent corpses."

Hattusilis snorted. Zan sensitive? How far this one reached to flatter. Still, his flesh prickled and he saw Zan glance over his shoulder with a slight edge of concern.

"We burn our dead." Zan shifted with an uneasy twitch.

"All the more reason for your people to become lost between worlds. They have nothing to connect with, not even their remains."

"That never occurred to me."

"Then you must realize that you have left many of your legion behind, drifting around under the illusion they still live. How sad."

Shaking his head, Hattusilis demanded, "What does this have to do with the plateau?"

"I am glad you asked." Niala lowered her voice as if to impart a secret. "I had thought to bring this to you some time soon, but it is better for you to know now."

"Know what?"

"That we must lay these poor souls to rest. I work to restore the plateau so we might hold a cleansing ceremony there on the shortest night of the year."

"Is that not the Solstice?"

"Yes." Niala seemed pleased. "I chose that night because it would hold the least threat as fleeting as it is. If we are to share space with the dead, let it be for the smallest amount of time. Would you not agree?"

"Well, it would seem the right thing to do." Hattusilis frowned.

"Yes, my thoughts exactly. I am happy you concur. I will plan the ceremony and we will rid ourselves of this menace." Niala gave him a slight curtsy. "Good day, King Hattusilis. And to you, Zan."

"What?" Hattusilis lifted his hands palm up. "What just happened?"

"I am not certain." Zan stared at the retreating back of the priestess. "But it seems you have agreed to a ritual on the on the longest day."

"To lay our ghosts to rest?"

"Or something."

Niala smiled to herself as she entered the defiled temple, bypassing the chambers occupied by Hattusilis. She turned to the right and walked along a smoke-stained corridor that would take her to the dining hall-turned sleeping quarters of the women. Her thoughts were upon the Summer Solstice and the dire need to heal the rift that possessed Najahmara.

Between Jahmed's story and bits and pieces garnered from those who attended, Niala was able to understand what had taken place. Gaea attempted to force healing through sexual connection. Though it might have helped in the long run, the celebration ended in disaster.

Niala spent a great deal of time in search of the errant Kulika but he hid himself well. That he had not returned to his own realm, that of the Blue Sky, was certain, for Niala could feel trickles of his energy here and there. Each time she focused, with the help of a still hurt and furious Gaea, upon the hint of Kulika's force, the wisp disappeared.

Kulika knew she stalked him. He knew that Gaea wanted to send him back to the Blue Sky and he refused to show himself.

"We shall see, Sky God, who wins this round," Niala murmured as she entered the women's share of the temple.

"Zahava, may I have a word?" Ajah stood with hands clasped, head lowered.

Her voice was soft and when Niala touched Ajah's arm, she felt a tremor pass over the girl.

"Of course, Ajah. Do you wish to sit?"

"No, Zahava. I must confess my disgrace. Jahmed says I am not to worry, that what went wrong at the Spring celebration was not my fault but lies upon her head. I do not agree."

"It is upon no one's head, Dearest. Those unseen who walk upon this earth do not direct their energies the same way mere mortals do. There is no shame to anyone for what befell the gathering."

"But I left her. I left Jahmed alone." Distraught, Ajah tugged at her braid. "Jahmed says I must go through with the initiation but I am not worthy of such an honor. I feel I must leave the sisterhood and return to my family."

"It was not your fault." Niala smoothed Ajah's damp hair away from her face, her tone filled with kindness. "Such a thing could have happened to any of us under the circumstances. You are not to carry blame. I will not have it."

"I abandoned my post and worse." Ajah felt vomit rise in her throat and she began to cough. When she was able to form words once again, she continued.

"I became enthralled with a man - one of them, one of the guards. I am so ashamed. I lay down with him and I did not know Kulika was present. That Gaea and he fought, that Jahmed was injured. I did not do my duty and now, Pallin is not allowed at the temple. I fear their king will finally destroy us."

Niala brought Ajah into an embrace, holding the shorter girl to her breast in consolation.

"My dearest child. The only ones who should hold shame over this is Gaea and Kulika, though it is not their way to feel such contriteness. Their existence is much different from ours. You will learn the mysteries of the immortals when you take your initiation rites."

"I cannot. I have embarrassed Jahmed enough."

"Pffft." Niala kissed Ajah's forehead. "Jahmed and I could tell tales of such proportion your skin would prickle and your hair would turn gray. You will not leave us. You will finish your training and become a full priestess. I will have it no other way. Now steady yourself and let us go to our duties."

Ajah inhaled a deep breath and straightened up. "But what of the…what of the soldier that I…." Her face reddened. "We indulged together and I do not even know his name, though he appeared to have sought me out with purpose."

"If his purpose is love, then he will find you again."

"Love? No, that is not what I meant. I do not ever want to see him again."

"Hmmm." Niala linked arms with Ajah and urged her toward the medicinal chamber with a hidden yet knowing smile.

NINETEEN

"Athos is a very big place with many dark corners, a few of which I advise you to keep your distance." Thaleia winked at her sister. "The first is Ares' chambers. Do not intrude on his privacy, for you well know his foul moods."

"Do not concern yourself with that." Euphrosyne smoothed the wrinkles from her bodice. "I will seek only Deimos."

"Yes, and sometimes Deimos is in Ares' quarters, especially since Niala - this female - has come to stay. He resides at the top of the fortress, overlooking the sea. Stay away from there, if at all possible..

"First seek Deimos in his own lodgings. When you arrive, give little Phobos a kiss from me, for that is where he, too, resides, if he is allowed to rest, which seems to be seldom, these days. I swear, Ares is a beast."

"Yes, yes, Sister, I know."

"They are often gone, so you may not find anyone there. However, since Phobos arrived, Deimos stays closer to Athos than usual." Thaleia twisted her skirt in her fingers. "I fear you will find more trouble than anything else."

"I will be fine."

"But if they are not there, then you will have to continue your search. Wait. If they have gone, then call to me and I will help you locate them."

"I will not need help."

There was only one thought in Euphrosyne's head, as she prepared to travel to Athos, and it was not about who was in residence. She knew Deimos would go to Aphrodite's side as bidden.

No, she did not worry about carrying out her duty. She worried about Anteros. He was as predictable as his twin, yet he had failed to return to Cos.

Anteros had indeed visited his father and convinced him of the urgency, just as he swore, as it appeared Aphrodite and Ares had reconciled. Where, then was Anteros? He promised he would come to her when all things were resolved. He said if she told him about Aphrodite and Hephaestos, he would give her anything she wanted.

Anteros pledged, when it was done, they would be together.

An instant deep flush started at her neck and traveled first to her face, then down through her body to settle in the lower regions. The feeling both excited and frightened her. She had seen arousal and knew what happened next.

She had seen lovemaking of all kinds, for Aphrodite turned no mortal away. Sex was not a mystery, but this, this involved Anteros.

Love is for everyone. I care not which way you have it. All acts of pleasure are my temple.

Aphrodite's declaration at the advent of each festival on Cos and words to remember. Euphrosyne smiled, for she intended to have great pleasure with Anteros. Yet now she feared he did not want her.

She would pass the message to Deimos, then seek out Anteros, wherever he was. She had to know if he avoided her, if his promise was in vain.

"What is the matter?" With brows arched, Thaleia looked askance at Euphrosyne. "Have you a fever? Perhaps you should not go to Athos." She raised a hand to touch her sister's forehead.

"No." Backing away, Euphrosyne felt the flush intensify. "I am happy to have such a mission."

"Well, do not be too pleased with yourself, for there are

dangers at Athos that I cannot describe. Do not linger there any longer than you must."

"Is it time for me to go?"

"Almost. Nightfall is best to find Deimos, for he settles in with Phobos at an early hour."

"But it is daylight for many more hours."

"Here, Sister, here it is daylight. It is twilight at Athos." Shaking her head, Thaleia muttered, "So much to learn, but she thinks she can skip about with no more than a smile."

Euphrosyne withheld a sigh. "All the more reason for me to tend to this matter. I must learn these things sooner or later."

With a sharp nod, Thaleia shook her finger at her sister. "Go first to Ares' temple in the lower area of the fortress. Do not let the mortals see you, for they are loutish vulgar men who follow the bloody ways of War without question. See if either Ares or Deimos holds court. If not, make your way upward.

"Carefully," Thaleia admonished. "Take the staircase."

"Why would I climb stairs when I can merely go there?"

"Caution, little Sister. Always move with caution at Athos. To suddenly appear can be a misjudgment."

"No one would see me."

"Arrgh." Thaleia slapped her forehead. "Do you think Ares would not know you were there? The moment you appear in his realm, he knows. It is where you step that is important. Heed my words for I do not want to see you injured."

"I will, Thaleia." Euphrosyne assured Thaleia just before she left for Athos. "I will take care."

Euphrosyne bit her thumbnail and peered about with trepidation. She was not in the lower reaches of the fortress. It seemed she had made a small error and was, quite possibly, in the master quarters of Ares the Destroyer.

Holding her breath, she tiptoed across the darkened room, praying she did not make a noise. Of course, if Lord Ares were there it would not matter either way. Her heart pounded at a slight scraping sound and she froze in her steps.

Looking behind her, she saw nothing in the thick gloom. Swiveling, she scanned the rest of the chamber and near fainted, for in the shadows near the huge hearth there was an indistinct outline of a figure. It stood in ominous silence until she gasped, and then it turned. She saw a flash of gold reflecting the embers of the fire.

Shrieking, Euphrosyne ran to the door and tugged with frantic haste at the iron bolt. She could think of nothing else but to escape and that on her two feet instead of by willing herself into another place. Abruptly, a hand clamped down on her shoulder. She collapsed to her knees, pulling her skirt over her face.

"Forgive me, forgive me, Lord Ares, I did not mean to intrude, I swear it! Please forgive me."

The cloth was pulled away, not with unkindness, and a familiar voice spoke. "Euphrosyne, what are you doing here?"

The soft light of an oil lamp sprang to life as she gazed through her fingers to see the surprised smile of Anteros. Such relief flooded through her that she well-nigh passed out and swayed toward the floor. Before she could catch herself, Anteros brought her to her feet.

"What are you doing here?"

"What are you?" Breathless, she stared at Anteros with adoration in her eyes.

He glanced toward the hearth where Amason hung crookedly above the mantel. "I wanted to practice wielding a weapon and there is no finer blade than this."

"In the dark?"

"The battle I found to join was in daylight, but it was an odd thing, for the warriors did not seem to want to fight. They merely wandered about on the meadow as if lost."

"Why would you search for a battle? That is not your place." Euphrosyne straightened her gown, shivering in the thin material.

"And what is that you are wearing on your head? And beneath your cloak? Anteros, what is it you are doing? Why did you not return to Cos as you promised?"

Anteros smiled as he transferred the heavy woolen garment to her shoulders. Grateful, she gathered the edges and hugged herself within its warmth, unable to take her astonished gaze from his garb.

He was resplendent in a golden armored breastplate and red-feathered helmet, his hair shining with the same golden cast as it flowed down his back. He wore a similar short white tunic, but it was now edged in blood red. Strapped to his long legs from the knees down were heavy gold guards with the same bound to his wrists.

"Oh, my." Euphrosyne's eyes were wide and filled with awe.

"Are you pleased? It is my armor so that all will know I ride with War."

"You are so beautiful." Euphrosyne reached out to run fingers along the etched surface. "Truly."

Dropping her hand to her side, she frowned. "Nevertheless, I do not understand. You cannot go into battle. You are Love's Response. You do not belong to War."

"I do. Now."

"How can that be?"

"Ares demanded a trade. He would go to Aphrodite only in exchange for something I valued. I had nothing to give but myself." He pressed his fingertips to Euphrosyne's lips to stop the flow of protests.

"I know, it is awkward, and I have no doubt Mother will be angry, but it served the purpose. Tell me, sweet Euphrosyne, how goes it with my mother? Did Ares keep his end of the bargain?"

Scarce able to speak, Euphrosyne put her arms about him and laid her cheek against the cool metal. "You are a noble son, Anteros. You have made the ultimate sacrifice, though I can scarce believe it."

She took a deep breath and held it for a moment. "Lord Ares made good upon his promise for Aphrodite is restored to herself. More, she is with child, and that was her purpose."

"Hephaestos fulfilled his duty?"

Euphrosyne blushed. "I cannot tell you who the father of this babe is. Aphrodite has been with both Hephaestos and Ares. It matters not at this point - she is happy and we are relieved."

"Then you will return to Cos and Love's Realm will be whole once more. Better, her attention will be on Eros and the new babe. She will be less concerned with my allegiance to War."

"She will not be pleased with the news of your new loyalties." Euphrosyne wrinkled her nose at the very idea of her adored Anteros riding with bloody War but kept thoughts on that subject to herself. "We now seek our way back to Cos, yet Aphrodite still resists for different reasons."

"What now?"

"It has to do with Lord Hephaestos and his kindness during

these troubled times. It will soon pass, I believe, for Aphrodite grows restless in his home. You have succeeded, Anteros, but at what cost?"

"Do not despair, Euphrosyne." Anteros lifted her chin and kissed each cheek. "I am not opposed to this challenge. In truth, I relish the thought. I have long been curious as to my brother's ways. Now I shall find out for myself."

Breaking away from him, Euphrosyne clenched her dimpled fists. "It is wrong. What will Aphrodite do without you?"

"Once she returns to full power, she will have little need for me. In the end, does it matter one way or the other? If I had not gone to Ares for help, Love would have faded. What then would Response be without Love?"

"But, War's Response?" Euphrosyne lifted both hands, palms upward, toward the heavens. "Everything will change."

"It has already changed." He met her gaze without flinching. "Dear one, do not worry over this."

"I do not know if I fret for Aphrodite, or for us."

"Us. Yes, I also made a promise to you, did I not?"

"Yes." Hope flared in her heart. "I have waited for you."

"Truly, I have not forgotten."

"Then kiss me and let us have our way." Euphrosyne reached for him, her heart fluttering with both joy and fear. All other thought escaped her, for Anteros was too handsome in his finery and her eagerness to be with him drowned out even Thaleia's admonishment to be careful.

"Euphrosyne, we cannot."

"And why not? We are alone." She tugged at his arm.

"No, these are the private quarters of my father. In truth, we should not even be here." He shoved her towards the door, opening it with one hand and pushing her through with the other.

"There are many rooms here, I am certain we can find one with a comfortable place to rest where no one will find us. Come, Anteros, for I have waited so long for this moment." Her breath came in gasps as her breasts rose and fell in rapid succession.

Befuddled, Anteros placed his hand on her heart and felt the pounding beneath his fingers. In the torch-lit corridor he could see her better and the flush that rode high on her cheeks.

"Euphrosyne, what ails you? This is unlike you."

"I am filled with desire for you, Anteros. Can you not see that I need you?" She fair leaped into his arms and began to kiss him with a passion that caused him to fall against the wall.

"Stop, for this is not to happen now." He pried loose her grip and set her on her feet once again as he shook his head. "I must uphold my end of this pledge."

"This does not disturb your pledge to Lord Ares, but keeps your pledge to me as well."

"No." With a firm yet gentle touch, Anteros put her a distance away from himself. "I do not want to anger Ares. I look forward to knowing my father. I do not complain, but my realm at Cos is largely filled with females."

To this, he smiled. "I have noticed the amazing lack of such in War's realm. It is a Brotherhood, something I long to be part of. I did not realize how much I missed Deimos."

"Deimos." Startled, Euphrosyne cupped her hands over her mouth.

"What of Deimos?"

"I am to bring both of you back to Aphrodite."

"Both? What does Aphrodite want with my twin?"

"I do not know," Euphrosyne said. "Is Deimos here?"

"No, he is not. He was called away and has not returned."

"Where did he go? He must visit Aphrodite."

Anteros turned away from her. "I will tell him."

"No! I mean, no. I must talk to him. You avoid looking at me, you know where he is." Grabbing his hand, Euphrosyne forced Anteros to face her. "Please tell me. I have never been sent on a mission before. If I do not do as I am told, Aphrodite will not allow me to go again. I will not tell where I found him, I promise."

Anteros searched her gaze and knew she was sincere. "You will never find it."

"I must try, Anteros. If you have any love for me at all, you will take me to Deimos."

"I am not supposed to leave this fortress, yet I do not think I will be missed if I am away for a very short time."

"Thank you." Relief filled her voice and she threw her arms about him, though she found the golden armor disconcerting and difficult to hug. "Let us go now."

He nodded once and took her hand. "Hurry, then. For I must

return before Ares."

He was uncertain where the cave of Priapos was located but wherever Deimos was, Anteros could follow. It had been such since they were small children. A gift at that young age but, once separated, a curse. No matter where his brother was, Anteros could feel their connection.

Many times he suffered along with Deimos during his trials and, many times, shared the surge of elation at his triumphs. He never spoke of this to anyone and did not know if Deimos held such thoughts of him. Perhaps, soon, he could ask. For the moment, it was sufficient to lead Euphrosyne to the wooded hillside of the Centaur.

And a dismal sight it was that greeted them.

A smoky campfire with the lingering scent of burning meat on its coals cast wavering shadows into the ring of trees. Two hunched near the flames, one the four-legged body of the Centaur and the other much smaller.

Eris glanced up when they appeared but did not greet them. Instead, he stared with an open-mouthed gape. Priapos awkwardly rose to his feet with one hand raised and a questioning look upon his austere features.

"I am Anteros, twin of Deimos. This is Euphrosyne, a Grace of Aphrodite."

Priapos nodded and rumbled, "Welcome, Brother of Deimos and Aphrodite's Grace. What brings you here?"

Once standing, Priapos towered above them. He was a fierce sight to behold with his animal body and broad hairy human torso.

Euphrosyne ducked behind Anteros, hanging on his elbow.

"We seek Deimos. Euphrosyne has a message from our mother."

Eris leaped up and came to them. "Deimos cannot be bothered."

The Sylph was hollow-eyed and menacing as he stared at them. Except for a loincloth, he was naked and streaked in ashy dirt as if he had been burrowing into the ground. One hand lingered on a sharp-looking dagger at his hip, the other hand twitched next to his thigh.

"Eris, why do you speak so harshly to me? I do not come here to cause grief, but to pass a message." Anteros forehead creased with injured feelings.

Euphrosyne crept further behind him and now clung to his waist, fully hidden from their sight. Anteros reached to bring her forward. She resisted as he tugged on her arm, twisting out of his grasp.

"Go away, Anteros. Deimos has nothing to say to you."

"It is no longer such, Eris." Anteros held up his hands and then pointed to the finery on his chest. "We have reconciled."

"What?" Eris circled the two, pausing to give Euphrosyne an appraising stare. She huddled closer to Anteros, pulling long strands of his hair to cover her face. "This one is a Grace? She seems a bit shy for Aphrodite's temple."

"You frighten her," growled Priapos. "After all this time, you still have no manners. Leave the girl alone."

"Manners do not count in battle."

"They count here. Leave her alone."

Eris backed away from Euphrosyne and moved his gaze to the feathered helmet on Anteros' head. "What is this silliness?"

"We do not have time to discuss your opinions. Where is Deimos?"

"He is occupied."

Closing his eyes, Anteros thought a moment before heading toward the mouth of the cave a few steps away. Eris sprang in front of him, dagger drawn.

"And what do you think you will do with that? You cannot harm me."

"We shall see." Eris brandished the blade with serious intent. "You do not enter this cave without permission."

"Priapos?"

"I must agree with Eris." The Centaur moved to stand with the Sylph. "I am sorry, but you must go."

"What is this mystery you guard with such zeal? Where is Phobos? And why is Deimos buried in the depths of the cave and not allowed out?"

"Buried? That is not the case."

Anteros crossed his arms over the golden armor, watching them with suspicion. "More so than ever I feel I must seek out Deimos, for whatever keeps him inside cannot be good."

"No." Eris snatched Euphrosyne by her long curls, dragging her from Anteros and the cave entrance. "You will not go inside."

Euphrosyne began to scream as a dumbfounded Anteros backed away from the entrance. "There is no need for violence. We come only to pass a message from Aphrodite."

"Pass it to me, then, and be on your way."

"I tell no one but Deimos himself," quavered Euphrosyne. She began to shriek his name, "Deimos."

"Quiet, you foolish girl," snapped Priapos. "We do not want the entire world to come to our door."

"Let her go, tree-dweller." Anteros lunged at Eris.

"I will sink my dagger in your heart," howled Eris as he leaped onto Anteros.

When Eris released Euphrosyne, Priapos caught her about her waist and lifted her high into the air. Euphrosyne lashed out and caught him on the nose, which brought an instant roar of pain and a stream of blood.

Inside the cave, Deimos rubbed his bleary eyes and groaned. The commotion echoed eerily off the rock formations and bounced back to him in a distorted array of noise.

"What now?" he muttered. "It is not enough this monolith defies me, but must I listen to that rabble?"

Stiff with weariness, he climbed to his feet and made his way to the cave opening. He could scarce believe his eyes. Amidst the screaming and cursing, it appeared both Priapos and Eris were in hand-to-hand combat with Anteros and Euphrosyne.

"Stop."

Deimos' single word brought the din to an instant halt. Ghastly images danced across their minds and an unnamed dread froze them in their tracks. Euphrosyne began to sob. All turned to stare at Deimos.

"Eris, stand down. Priapos, release the girl. Euphrosyne, be still. Anteros, why are you here? What is that?" He stared at the golden helmet with a waving red feather, now broken in half.

The urge to laugh bubbled up into Deimos' throat, the first hint of humor to strike him since he arrived in the forest. Instead, he coughed, covering his mouth with one grimy fist.

Anteros grimaced, touching the bruise along his jaw. "It is a long story."

Deimos beckoned to him. "I, too, have a long story to share. Let us all sit and sort this out."

It was then Anteros noticed Deimos' haggard filthy face and the slump to his shoulders. "Yes, Brother, let us sit and talk. We are all in need of answers."

TWENTY

The mountaintop was strangely quiet. More than quiet, it was deathly silent. A pall crossed Athos for no apparent reason. Not a creature stirred. Not even one of the many night predators dove across the sky in search of food. Not a twig snapped under the feet of a prowling animal. There was nothing, no noise at all.

Ares leaned against the wooden rail of the walkway and stared down to the sea. It was calm and flat, even the waves did not crash upon the rocky shore. The wind ceased its howling amongst the mountain peaks and did not tweak the surf into a frenzy. There was no more than a gentle slapping sound as the water slipped between the boulders. A ship sat far out on the horizon with limp sails.

There were always periods when the wind died but never to such an extent. Ares could not recall the last time the surf fell so still, or if ever it had. In a slow pace he circled the outside of the fortress, passing from seaside to mountainside. He paused, listening for the sounds of men and their beasts.

Below him was the end of the winding path that led up the mountain to his temple. From his vantage point, he could watch the travelers struggling through the narrow passages with their herds of animals. However, on this night, there were no men. No beasts. No one came up or down or entered into the bowels of the fortress.

There was no bellow of beasts vibrating upward to the top of the mount. No stench saturating the air. Tipping his head back, Ares scanned the clear night sky awash in pinpoints of light. The moon was dressed in a brilliant crescent as it began to wane. It appeared close enough to touch. Clear meant cold on a mountain, except it was not cold. It was balmy, like a spring evening on Cos.

Ares completed the circle around the sprawling keep and returned to the courtyard. He knew before the doors swung inward that Niala was gone. On the threshold, with the silence of the mount behind him, Ares faced the silence of the fortress within.

Though his quarters contained the same things it always had, it now seemed empty. There was no expansion, no expectation. The rooms were devoid of energy, as if they receded into a state of hibernation. Ares closed his eyes and turned, hearing the beat of his own heart and nothing else.

He could not discern even the tiniest speck of Niala's life force. Though he tried, there was no hint of her left for him to absorb. It was if she had been bound to him by the slenderest of threads. Now the connection was broken as if she had never been there at all.

Until that moment, he did not realize how much Niala filled the space. How empty it was without her.

The walls appeared to mock him as he pondered how she escaped. The inert stone knew, but kept her secret. He could not find a trace, an imprint, anything to explain how she suddenly disappeared from Athos.

Once before, Niala ran away, down the mountain into the arms of a woman who adopted her as lover and anointed her as priestess. A woman named Layla brought Niala into the mysteries of Gaea and beat black stain into the shape of a serpent on her body. The serpent represented Kulika, the Night Sky, Protector and Consort of Earth.

Niala had been able to use the magic of the ancient god to shape-shift, allowing Kulika to possess her. What of the winged one on her back - the careful creation of the Corvidae, chariot to Earth. The image was also created with purpose.

Could Niala simply have flown away from him?

He would expect nothing less from her. And yet he sensed no air of enchantment, no disturbance that gave him reason to believe

Niala had done this herself.

Had someone stolen her away? Perhaps Niala did not leave of her own will but by the hand of an enemy, someone who sought to threaten him. Hephaestos leaped to mind.

Had the Forge god discovered the tryst? Did he try to keep Aphrodite by hiding Niala? Hephaestos had not the courage to stand against Ares.

No one did.

He nodded in agreement with his own thoughts.

There was something else wrong on Athos. Ares strode from the bedchamber to the main quarters. He turned once, making a full sweep of the room. His gaze caught and held at Amason. She glittered with her own force, picking up light where there was none.

Amason jiggled with anticipation, calling to him to release her from her rest. Ares reached for her. Amason's spell wrapping about his shoulders like a cloak. Just as his fingers brushed her tip, he noticed the sword hung at a right angle. She was not in the perfect line in which he left her.

Someone had laid a hand on Amason.

His gaze fell to the mantle. It was now one solid piece of marble across the front of the hearth instead of a gaping hole between two shattered halves as he had left it.

Who would dare?

"Anteros." Ares fists clenched into tight hammers, ready to descend upon the head of his son. Not another soul could have caused the swift changes at Athos that he witnessed.

"Anteros, I command you to appear."

There was no response.

No Response.

Ares told him to stay and he did not.

Was Anteros responsible for Niala's disappearance? It would be like Love's Response to feel Niala's anguish and decide to help her. Oh, and yes, it would be like War to exact punishment on he who did not do as he was told.

With a swiftness born of righteous anger, Ares left his quarters and moved down the corridor to the stairwell. Just as his foot hit the first step, he noticed the hallway and staircase were no longer bathed in darkness. Soft comfortable pools of light issued from oil lanterns spaced ever so evenly along the corridor.

Lanterns? Throughout every floor? Each corridor well lit?

The closer he drew to the lower reaches of the fortress, the more he noticed the echoes of his own footsteps. Nothing more. What had been an unearthly quiet in the upper levels was now a deafening silence below.

As he paused, head cocked to one side, he heard naught a breath drawn, or a muffled grunt. There was no metallic clang from either pewter mugs or sparring weapons. No wafting scent of charred meat or spilled ale, no smoke laden with cooking fat, no stink of human sweat, not a trace of the bittersweet scent of blood.

Ares threw open the doors to his temple. He stalked in, only to come to a stunned halt as he stared at the transformation. The once gloomy chamber lit only with a handful of sputtering candles, now shined bright with more of the lanterns he found throughout Athos. He circled the hulking throne and came to a standstill in front of the altar.

The altar to War had stood for a thousand years. A thousand years to a mortal, a blink of an eye to an immortal. Yet, throughout all that time, it had never been touched with the exception of adding more pain. Uncountable layers had turned to dust while others rotted, and still others brought fresh meat.

Never was anything removed.

Bones of the sacrifices of his worshippers marked the stupidity of greed. More came and more was thrown upon the altar. Rivers of blood gushed to the floor, coating the slabs of rock, filling the cracks, thickening and creating patterns, turning all to black until the eye could scarce tell the difference between blood and stone.

Ares left it as it was in homage to the horrors of War. He left it so all would know the god they prayed to cared not that they killed each other. He left it so they would know there was no mercy and no glory, just a pile of stinking flesh waiting to crumble away to nothing.

It was homage to Nothing.

And now it was gone.

All of it, gone.

He stared in utter disbelief at the clean gleaming slabs of black rock, with not a trace of blood, nor its scent in the air. The long low table was covered in virginal white linen and festooned with red blooms. In the center was a large vase filled with more of the red flowers.

Flowers?

Shaking his head, Ares went to the warriors' quarters. The anteroom was silent, empty of all beings. The rough plank tables were scrubbed clean, the flooring scoured, the pewter mugs sparkling and lined up on a new shelf. The once-sickening smell that emanated from the room was gone leaving no sign of animal dung.

Ares passed through the room into the adjoining chambers to find the same. When he threw open the double doors to the stockyards, he blinked, for the sun gilded the mountain peaks. There were no animals, only dry straw strewn atop the mud.

Outraged, Ares stormed back to the altar room, a string of curses following behind.

"Anteros!"

There was no answer.

"Deimos!"

Again, no answer.

"Eris!"

Silence.

"Those who serve War, I command you appear."

All that greeted him was the booming of his own voice echoing back at him. In one wild sweep, Ares knocked the vase of red flowers across the room, taking great pleasure in shattered pottery. The flowers splattered against the wall and slid to the floor in a wet heap.

Snarling like a mad hound, he turned toward his throne to see the arms and back of the chair had been rubbed with gold, the great bull's horns absent. Worse, the black seat was covered with an intricately woven, cheerfully bright material.

His curses bounced from the vaulted ceiling and careened around the room in a ferocious torrent, but brought no one running. As his rage mounted, so did the force with which he sent it out into the world. A great shadow passed over the moon and a rumble of thunder shook the mount.

Anteros hunched before the wrath of Ares and felt the sting of his words as if they were blows. He was certain he would rather be attacked by a thousand jellyfish as Ares' fury poured over him like a giant storm at sea.

It rolled Anteros over, tossed him in the air, and then sucked him under until he thought he would drown. Just before his last breath, he was heaved to shore, battered and bruised, but still alive.

It was then he realized Ares had fallen silent, waiting for him to speak. Anteros could scarce meet his father's glare for fear the rampage would begin all over again. Exhaling, he lifted his head.

Ares stood with fists on his hips and legs wide, his face suffused with heat, his eyes dark and menacing.

"What is this?" Ares slammed his fist into the golden armor just above Anteros' heart.

Anteros staggered as Ares caught the edge of his breastplate, ripping it off. It clanged against the wall as he hurled it across the room, bouncing along the black floor into the shadows. Ares raised his hand and the shin guards flew, followed by the metal sleeves.

With a movement quicker than an eye could follow, Ares grabbed Anteros by his hair and bent him backwards, knocking the helmet from his head.

"Do you want to see what happens to a warrior adorned in gold sporting long pretty curls flapping in the winds?"

A wicked blade appeared in Ares' other hand and at Anteros' exposed throat, biting into his flesh before he could blink.

"They die," Ares hissed.

The knife left Anteros' tender skin and sliced through the twisted knot of hair. When released, Anteros collapsed to the floor onto a pile of golden strands that scattered and caught along the edges of the tiles. The fine soft hair clung to his clothing, his face, and floated into the air like a spider's web. His exposed neck grew cold and a shudder ran his length.

"Get up."

Breathing hard, Anteros stumbled to his feet.

"Restore everything." Ares waved one huge fist at the altar. "Do you understand?"

"Yes." Anteros felt light-headed and dizzy at the prospect. "Yet I do not think I can."

"Oh, but you will."

Anteros glanced over his shoulder at the clean altar. "How?"

"I am certain you will find a way, for if you do not, you will truly wish you had never come to Athos."

"Father, I am sorry. I did not intend to make you angry." One hand crept back to touch the jagged edges of hair lying flattened against his neck. "I tried only to help."

"By sending my warriors away? By destroying my altar?"

"They left by choice. I did not tell them to go. When I went among them, they...." Anteros lifted his shoulders. "They responded to Love, just as everyone does. What could I do to stop them? They took their beasts and left. And then, with everything so filthy, I could not help myself but make it right."

"Did I not tell you to stay in your quarters? I am no fool, Anteros. I know the influence you have on mortals. You disobeyed me, not once, but in a dozen ways."

"I did nothing else."

Ares towered over him, eyes glittering. "You did not take Amason from her resting place?"

"Ahh. Yes." Anteros backed up a step, slipping a bit on the pale strands of hair beneath his feet. "I wanted to know what it felt like to raise a sword in battle. I was just curious. I did no harm."

"Never. Touch. Amason."

Each word was bitten off as Ares' fist punched into his chest. Anteros skidded backwards, stumbling and gasping with each blow. "No, never. I will not, I swear, not even...."

"Not even?"

Anteros swallowed hard. "Never."

"And what of the woman? What did you do with her?"

"What woman?"

"There was a woman in my private quarters."

"There was no one there except me, until...." He stopped, clamping his lips together.

"Until? Until what?"

Shaking, Anteros repeated. "There was no woman. Your chambers were empty."

"Until what?"

"Until I went in. Then, they were no longer empty because I was there."

Eyes half-shut, Ares paused. Though he did not think Anteros helped Niala escape, he knew he hid something. "Where were you when I called?"

"Called?"

"Yes. One thing you must learn, when I bid you come to my side, you do exactly that."

"I did not hear you."

"It is no sound that comes, but a vibration. Like this."

Anteros immediately felt the slap of power and gasped. "I did not understand, I swear. I am sorry."

"Now you know. I will ask you one more time, where were you?"

Hesitating, Anteros thought of Phobos and shook his head. They had told the story, Deimos and Priapos, while Eris crouched in silence by the fire and Euphrosyne wept. After all was said, Deimos led Anteros into the tunnel and showed him the monolith holding their brother captive. The horrid memory overwhelmed him.

Anteros stared at the towering wall of rock in disbelief. How could it be that a timid child such as Phobos could wind up locked into a prison of stone? Anteros laid his hands on the face of the monolith and was hit with a backlash of power that weakened his knees. He now believed it was not the ancient stone that reacted to him, but was Ares' demand that caught him unaware.

Even so, after the wave retreated, there was a sickening blow of fear that brought sweat out on his brow and riveted him to the spot. Behind the fear was a great welling up of sadness. Grief driven by loneliness and nurtured by the desire for love.

Tender love, sweet and innocent, given wisely and without condemnation. There was an aching desire for acceptance and the willingness to sacrifice self to belong. There was integrity compromised, along with the pain of knowing it and of not caring. If only it could become something it was not.

He understood then. Phobos always knew he did not belong to Love's Realm, though in his child's mind, he saw it as rejection. He saw himself cast away like a broken shell, thrown into the world of War because there was no other place for him. Phobos thought he deserved to be shut away.

Anteros knelt before the massive stone wall and wept bitter tears, for Phobos, for Deimos, who surely had lived just such pain when they were torn apart, and for himself, because he loved them both so very much and could do nothing to ease their pain.

For the first time in his life, Anteros felt helpless. Just as he felt at this moment gazing into the hard black eyes staring back at him. He could see no pity, no compassion in those depths. No love. What must it be like for Deimos to go without the vestments of love? And little Phobos, now entered into these hallowed halls, what of him, fresh from his mother's arms?

"You have not answered my question, Anteros. Where were you when I called?"

Ares' stern words cut across his thoughts. Sighing, Anteros said, "It is beyond me to say, Father."

"What is this? Love's Golden One suffers? We cannot have that, can we?" Ares retreated to the massive throne.

As he settled into the chair, it crossed his mind that the improvements made by Anteros were not all bad. Beneath the fabric was a layer of thick padding that would make hours of sitting more comfortable. Still, he frowned fiercely at his second son.

"Pray tell me, what has happened that vexes you so? Does it have anything to do with your selection of clothing?"

Anteros flushed. "I am, indeed, Love's right hand, just as Deimos is yours, which does not relieve me of the sufferings that abound in the world. It is only that I hold hope in my heart and you do not."

"You are wrong to think I hold no hope for the world. I do pray that mortals will come to their senses, yet this 'hope' does not blind me to their ways."

Shifting, Ares balanced one elbow on the carved arm of the throne and touched his fingertips to his beard. "You claim you know what suffering is but, I ask you, has your mother told you of the duality of our realms?"

He gave a sharp bark of laughter. "I can see by your expression, she has not. We are like the cycles of light and dark. You cannot have one without the other. And within each one of us, the opposite side of the cycle plays out."

Anteros stared at Ares with a blankness that served to further irritate him. "What I am saying is you may be golden now but soon you will discover the other half of yourself and it will be shadowed in darkness. And when the shadow falls, I will be waiting."

Closing his eyes, Anteros held himself very still. He did not want Ares to see the stark fear crawling over him like swarms of biting insects. What his father foretold, he knew to be true. He had seen the cycle of light and dark in Aphrodite. He had seen it out of control, careening off into a ruinous pattern. She was near destruction now, brought on by this shadow that lurked deep in her soul.

Ares did not have to tell him about such things.

Albeit, he did not know it, too, could also happen to him. After all, he was light. He was the Golden One, the retriever of lost souls, the one who invoked Response to Love. How could a shadow ever be cast across such a noble cause?

How?

"And still, you have not told me where you were." Ares tapped his fingers against the chair arm in a deliberate drumming sound. "It has occurred to me, with Deimos also missing, that I might have found the pair of you together. And since Deimos, as well as Eris, seem still to be absent, I would suggest you enlighten me before you feel my anger once again."

Paling, Anteros shuffled backwards a bit. "Do not blame Deimos. He merely tries to help Phobos."

"Phobos?" Straightening, Ares leaned forward. "What does Phobos have to do with this?"

"I should not tell."

"But you will, or you will find the darkness in your soul much quicker than you ever believed possible."

At Anteros' further hesitation, Ares came to his feet and barked, "Tell me. Now."

It was beyond Love's Response to lie.

Anteros confessed all.

Ares listened with an impassive expression to Anteros' tale, even when the boy began to weep at the plight of his younger brother. Ares showed no more than a frown at this weakness and wondered if Anteros was oft given to tears, for it was unbecoming to a warrior. Anteros would have to be broken of the habit, to be certain, a fleeting thought to be held for the future.

While Anteros related the story, irritation fought with Ares' restraint. He questioned why Deimos kept this from him. It was yet another disappointment and to be dealt with later, for he would have to see to the child first.

Ares would not have guessed the frightened boy who wet himself would have the ability to join with stone. Phobos should have bounced off the face of the monolith, knocked silly, and woken up with a bruise or two. That he was strong enough to merge came as a surprise. That Phobos could not extract himself did not.

Discovering all believed he would leave the boy locked in a pylon of stone for an eternity - that, too, was not a surprise.

However, Ares knew himself better than they.

When Anteros finished, Ares bid him return Athos to its former state. "This time, do not leave these walls. Phobos' torture will seem inconsequential next to your punishment should you choose to disobey me again."

With this threat hanging over Anteros' head, Ares went to tend to Phobos. Anteros was left with a tedious task and a greater respect for his twin.

The Centaur paced away from the campfire, switching his tail with anxious jerks. He glanced over his shoulder at the pale girl who sat on a log with her hands meekly folded in her lap. "Let us speak away from the mild one."

Euphrosyne would not meet Ares' gaze but kept her eyes focused on her fingers. He could see she was frightened to near illness but made not a peep, even when he demanded to know why she was there.

"Come, Ares," Priapos commanded, ignoring the question.

With a frown, Ares followed Priapos into the woods. There, the Centaur at once launched into a torrent of words before they stopped.

"It is my fault. You entrusted me with your son, and now this horrible thing has occurred. I deserve death." Priapos paused and bowed his head.

The torment in Priapos' voice was more than even Ares could bear. There was no other who held his respect the way the old Centaur did, for it was by his hand Ares learned how to take up the mantle of War thrust upon him at so tender an age.

"If there is any who shall bear this burden, it is I, old friend." Ares held up one palm in peace. "I knew the boy was of a gentle nature, but I compared him to Deimos and thought he would be better for this rigor."

"There is no other like Deimos."

"It is true, there is no other like Deimos. Yet I believe Phobos will overcome his fears and face his destiny."

"Some do not."

"He is of my blood. He will not fail."

"But the child is - forgive me, Ares - the child is hopeless. He is frightened of his own shadow." Exhausted, Priapos leaned against a tree, one hand holding onto a lower branch for support.

"As he should be. He is destined to become Panic and it appears he has discovered this all by himself."

"Yes, Panic. I wish you had seen fit to advise me of this." The words held a tone of rebuke.

"Perhaps," Ares agreed. "If you knew, you would have been overly careful, which would not serve the boy's need to learn."

"Even so, I can do nothing with him." With a heavy sigh, Priapos added, "Could do nothing with him. Now, it seems, no one ever will. The monolith will not release him."

"It is not the monolith, Priapos. It is the boy, himself."

"I do not understand."

"The monolith does not hold him captive."

"But he cannot get free of it. Deimos tries still to reach him and fails. The monolith fights him."

"No, Priapos, it is Phobos who fights."

"Impossible. The boy is too weak and timid to rebuff one such as Deimos." The Centaur began his restless pacing again. "He is imbedded in stone and the stone refuses to give him up."

"Phobos refuses. The monolith is a reflection of all that belongs to Phobos. It has absorbed him therefore, it has become him. What Deimos felt was Phobos in his truest form."

"Sweet mercy," groaned Priapos. "If this is so then is that not the worse?"

"It is worse." Ares stroked his beard and then gave a brief nod. "If he were held against his will, I could free him. This, he must do himself."

"What if he cannot?"

"I trust that any son of mine will triumph. Now let us go inside to end this."

"Yes, let us do so." Priapos' voice held great relief.

"Answer one thing more. Why is Euphrosyne here?"

Hesitating, Priapos wiped the sweat from his face with a red cloth. "She came with Anteros, searching for Deimos. It seems Aphrodite orders his presence. Euphrosyne waits for him. She weeps that she cannot go home without him for fear Aphrodite will punish her."

Ares made a noise somewhere between a chuckle and a growl.

"That is a bit strange, but at least it means Aphrodite has returned to Cos."

"Yes, I…ahh…have heard of your troubles."

"Yes, old friend, it seems our trials never truly end. Now, let us get Phobos released from his prison."

Ares strode into the cave, letting his blood connection to the child guide him to the place where it all began. Here he found Deimos on his knees before the wall, forehead pressed against it, fists bloody from beating against the rough stone. Eris crouched next to him, his face streaked with tears.

"We cannot get him out." Eris wiped his hand across his cheek, mixing dirt and tears into mud.

Ares spoke first to Eris, "Go now, my Son. You have done well to stand beside Deimos."

"I cannot abandon them." Eris' eyes were wide and frightened.

"I bid you go and leave your anguish. I am here now."

"Yes, Father." With one last look at the monolith, Eris disappeared.

With a firm hand, Ares touched Deimos' shoulder, "There is no more you can do."

"I have failed." Deimos' voice shook with an effort to suppress his grief. He would not further shame himself by weeping in front of his father.

"You have not failed. No one can bring Phobos out but himself."

"He cannot find his way."

"That is why I am here. It was the same for you. I was present when you went through your trials."

Deimos shrugged Ares' hand away and turned to sit with his back resting against the stone. His face was filthy and bruised and his eyes bloodshot. "You were not with me during my rites of passage. I was alone in my terror, just as Phobos is alone in his panic."

Bitterness poured from his hot gaze as he challenged Ares. "You left me to survive, or not. You showed no concern for the outcome."

"All this time and still you do not understand." Ares reached down and pulled Deimos to his feet. "I was with you always, waiting to catch you if you failed. All along, I knew you would not."

"Why, because I am your son and could do no less?"

"Because you are Survival, the shadow side of Terror."

"You knew?" Deimos met his father's dark gaze.

"Always." One corner of Ares' mouth lifted. "I have been waiting for you to discover it. And just like Phobos, no one could do it but you. Not even me."

Ares touched a forefinger to Deimos' chin, to a streak of blood and dirt. "But I trusted you would. You have done what you can for your brother, Deimos. You have not given up on him, just as I never gave up on you."

"None of what I have done has helped."

"It has sustained him. Now he must garner his inner strength to push out."

"He does not know how."

"I will show him the way, but then it must be through his own action that he becomes free."

Deimos stared at the monolith. "Do you believe he can?"

Ares thought for a long moment before answering, "Yes, though I do not know how long it will take. You must go to Aphrodite, now. I request you do not inform her of this."

"I do not want to leave Phobos."

"There is no more you can do. If you do not answer your mother's summons, she will grow suspicious. She has had enough grief, let us not give her more worry. Go to her and return when you can."

Deimos bowed his head. "Yes, Father."

"I hope it does not always take a child stuck in stone to get such cooperation." Ares watched as Deimos took his leave.

Now alone, Ares turned his attention to the monolith and his youngest son. Without laying a hand on the rock wall, Ares cast out one word and only one word.

He threw it with all his force, loudly, clearly, his mind pushing the word through layer upon layer of compressed and ancient stone. He could feel Phobos shrink away from him, but Ares' strength far surpassed anything the child could muster. He neither coddled nor coaxed the boy. He said but one word.

"Surrender."

TWENTY-ONE

"Why did it take this long?" Aphrodite tapped her slippered foot on the bronze floor of Hephaestos' living quarters as she stood with arms crossed, a frown marring her perfect beauty. Her gaze traveled back and forth between Euphrosyne and Deimos, one sheepishly apologetic, the other weary and confused.

"He was not at Athos, Princess. I had to search for him."

"Not, I hope, on a battlefield?"

"No, he was elsewhere." Avoiding Aphrodite's penetrating gaze, Euphrosyne stared at a spot of grass stain on her right big toe.

"How did you know where to look?"

"I...."

"She did not, Mother," interrupted Deimos. "That is what took so long, but I am here now, at your bidding. What is it you need from me?"

"Do not be callous, my son, I am merely concerned for Euphrosyne." Aphrodite's tone implied the girl's inexperience with the mortal world may have brought further trouble to the House of Love.

Euphrosyne blushed while Deimos slumped, his shoulders

drooping. His stance had been one of defense, just realized as he searched the depths of his mother's turquoise eyes. So used to Ares' reproach, he did not consider that this could be a blameless encounter.

"Forgive me, I did not intend rudeness, but Euphrosyne has drawn me away from an important task." Deimos tightened his fists to stop the uneasy twitching of his hands. In his palms was the memory of the monolith's scorn and the uncertainty of his brother's future. "One I must return to as soon as possible."

"I see," murmured Aphrodite. "Euphrosyne, you have done well. You may seek your rest."

"Yes, Princess, thank you." Euphrosyne curtsied, then looked past Aphrodite to the rooms that had been opened up to the light by removing heavy draperies. Every bit of Hephaestos' clutter that once decorated the corners had been eliminated.

The walls, once painted with bright hues, were now a stark, sparkling white. No one other than the three of them was about and even the constant humming from the forges below the castle seemed muted.

Hesitating, Euphrosyne asked, "Princess? Where might my sisters be?"

"Aglaia carries a message to Hephaestos in the underground caverns and Thaleia has returned to Cos to care for Eros since Anteros seems to have disappeared. My request was to also locate Anteros, but I do not see him." Aphrodite paused, one eyebrow raised as Euphrosyne was gripped with a spell of coughing. "Did you find Anteros?"

Euphrosyne's coughing grew louder.

"This is not like him. I am concerned."

The more she talked, the worse the choking became. Aphrodite patted Euphrosyne on the back. "Are you all right, Sister?"

"I am fine." Euphrosyne took a deep breath, her face red and hot. "He means no harm."

"Anteros never means anyone harm, but this is unacceptable. Little Eros has been alone with the Dryads and that is never good. They are lovely girls, but have no liking for water and tend to take him into the woods rather than to the sea. He is not yet awakened to his power, yet I fear his time is very near. The Dryads would take advantage of his sexual inexperience if that should occur. I need Anteros to be in attendance at all times."

Aphrodite took in the expression of the red-faced girl. "Never mind. I am certain Eros will be fine for now, but what of Anteros? My last conversation with him was less than what it should have been. He seemed distracted."

Stopping, Aphrodite caught the expression of irritation on Deimos' handsome face. To Euphrosyne, she said, "We will speak of this later. Pray, go and rest." She then waggled a finger at Deimos. "You are so much like your father, it is frightening."

"I am not like him," Deimos growled.

"In many ways, you are. Perhaps in most ways, for I scarce know you anymore. Your separation from my realm is complete and it saddens me."

"What do you speak of?" Pressing his fingertips to his forehead, Deimos rubbed at the stifling ache. "I am what I am, that is all I am supposed to be."

"Oh, my darling Son, I cannot bear that you no longer know love. I once felt your heart stir and thought you found happiness, but it has receded."

"Is that why you dragged me here? To discuss whether I know love?"

"No, of course not. However, you are also of my blood and that should prompt you to have feelings for another."

"Who says I do not?"

"Do you?"

Images of Niala surfaced even as he gritted his teeth to keep a string of curses from spilling out.

"As you have stated, I am like my father. What do you think?" Deimos retreated from Aphrodite's questions. There was little she could say to that and, indeed, she appeared to give up. Inwardly, he felt grim satisfaction.

"Why have you called me here, Mother? I really must return to my work before much more time has passed."

Aphrodite suppressed her mirth at Deimos' struggle to contain his innermost contemplation.

So transparent, my little Deimos, she thought. *Always, since a mere babe, you could not hide your emotions behind a mask the way your father does. You do not even know it is all written there for me to see. Still, it gives me hope that you will someday find a great love to sustain you.*

"Even Ares must admit to that," she murmured aloud.

"What are you speaking of?"

"Nothing to trouble you. Come, you look fatigued." She took him by the hand and led him to a couch with a high, carved back.

Once seated, she was better able to see him, and noticed the dirt and dried blood streaked on his face and the dark shadows beneath his eyes. His black curls were disheveled and dusty, and as she held his hands, she saw ragged fingernails and scratched knuckles, with soiled and blistered palms. "Your father drives you too hard."

"It is not Ares." Deimos could feel his mother's tender influence flowing over him and he feared he would tell her of Phobos' plight.

Nothing would serve her knowing, for she could not help him. It would cause her deep anguish to know her child was caught in so hateful a snare. "What then brings you to such a state?"

"It is my own concern and I do not wish to speak of it." Sighing, Deimos tried to lighten his tone. "What may I do for you, Mother? Please, simply tell me what you want."

"So very like your father." Aphrodite spoke under her breath, but smiled sweetly at her eldest.

"What do you wish to speak of?"

Dropping his hands, Aphrodite stood and began to pace with dainty swaying steps, her blue silk chiton whispering against her legs. "About a mortal woman Ares keeps at Athos."

"Niala." Deimos felt the tenseness creeping back into his shoulders. "You have already heard everything about her."

"Everything? No one can ever know all there is about another and, this one is truly a mystery. Ares claims she is an immortal who has not taken her power. Though I see a spark that could be interpreted as immortal, nothing can be said for certain.

"If she is, who are her parents? Who gave birth to her and then left her in the mortal realm? And why? Was she once Ilya? Ares also lays claim to that possibility, but I think he has deluded himself over these eons. He convinces himself this whole tale is real."

"Mercy. Mother, beat me, banish me, throw me to the hounds, but please, stop."

Aphrodite cocked her head to one side, her lips in a prim line. "I have no hounds, dear, nor does Hephaestos."

"I merely meant I weary of this subject." Deimos raised his hands to the domed ceiling. "She is no longer at Athos."

"She is gone?" Evading Deimos' gaze, Aphrodite walked behind the couch and trailed her fingers along its edges, an amused smile on her lips. "So she has abandoned him once again, just as I knew she would."

"I did not say she left him." Deimos stumbled over his words in haste. "Ares sent her away. He is done with her. You can return to Cos with a light heart."

"Return to Cos? You are, indeed, just like your father. I will return when I am ready."

"Yes, yes, of course."

Aphrodite nodded. "And where is Anteros?"

"Anteros?" Defeated, Deimos shrugged. Why should she not know what Ares had done? "He is at Athos."

"Athos?" Truly surprised, Aphrodite circled the couch. "Why?"

Choosing his words with care, Deimos related the story of Anteros asking a favor of Ares and, in return, sacrificing Love to become part of War.

When Deimos was done, he prepared for the worst. Cringing, he watched Aphrodite's face become suffused with a golden glowing pink. Her eyes squinted shut. Her rosy lips drew up into a becoming grimace and her shoulders began to shake. Deimos withdrew as far as he could in case she would start throwing things.

Aphrodite's mouth fell open and a shriek shook the furniture. Not a scream of anger.

A shriek of laughter.

Aphrodite laughed so hard tears streamed down her cheeks as she clutched her middle. She gasped and fought to catch her breath and fell once more into spasms of giggles, clapping her hands together, and finally shouted her mirth out into the room.

The two Graces appeared, faces drawn with fear for their beloved princess. When they saw her laughter, they, too, began to chuckle, which quickly became the same sort of riotous giggling.

Mystified, Deimos stared at them as if they had gone mad.

"What is it, Princess," gasped Aglaia.

"Oh, it is too rich." Aphrodite's laughter trailed off into faint chuckles. "Ares thinks he has taken Anteros as one of his own."

Sobering, Aglaia grimaced. "Why is that funny? Poor Anteros, that he should have such a hardship."

"Oh, no, my Dearest. Anteros will always belong to me. He is Love's Response and he can be nothing else. Ares has done it to himself this time."

"You are not going to demand his return?"

Aphrodite wiped her face with her sleeve. "And relieve Ares of a long needed lesson? I think not. Imagine this, Love's Response riding into battle."

"Why, Princess, I doubt there would be a fight, for Anteros invokes an open and humble heart." Thaleia bit her thumb, still giggling. "How would the battle begin, with both sides feeling love for one another?"

"Exactly." More chuckles fought past Aphrodite's lips. "Ares will soon discover why Anteros does not make a good warrior. I would enjoy the sight when Ares sees the effect Response has on War."

"He will drive Ares mad." Deimos tried to imagine Anteros in battle and the thought brought a chuckle to his lips as well.

"Yes, he will. Since Anteros has no experience in any other realm, it is time for him to see beyond my walls."

Clapping her hands with sudden inspiration, Aphrodite then pointed at Deimos. "If Anteros must see what it is like to live with War, then you, Deimos, will stay here with Love!"

Aghast, Deimos stared at his mother. "I cannot. I will not. Terror does not belong in Love's Realm. Already, you see, it makes me sweat. I do not belong here."

"Yes." Aphrodite's response was firm. "What better way to appreciate what you are, than to find out what you are not."

"Ares will not stand for it."

"Ares has no choice unless he wants to return Anteros to me."

"Mother, with all due respect, this will be a disaster."

"Perhaps." The warm turquoise gaze turned icy. "I will trade Ares son for son. He will not have both."

"Do I have no say in this?"

"Would you deny your mother?"

"I would not disallow a rational request but this is beyond reason."

"Then it is settled. Let us celebrate this new arrangement."

Groaning, Deimos exchanged a glance with Thaleia. She held up her hands to say she had no power to help as she went along behind Aphrodite into the next chamber. Aglaia and Euphrosyne floated after them.

"Come, Deimos." Aphrodite's voice lilted with excitement, nearly bursting into song.

Would she sing if she knew of Phobos perilous plight? He could not tell her and so Deimos followed them with a fervent prayer that Ares would rescue him as well as Phobos.

TWENTY-TWO

The darkness was thick, thick like layers of soil and just as suffocating. A harsh wheezing noise echoed through the cave as she fought to draw air into her body. Hard labor took every bit of strength left to her. Her body was numb. Clenched as the final round of heaving ripping pain shot through her belly.

Sweat stained the mat she lay upon as blood ran between her legs. Piteously, she begged and cried out to Gaea, but to no avail, for once the babe left her body, it lay dead. She threw her head back, wailing with grief and anger as Gaea betrayed her once again.

But then she heard the whimper of a newborn. It was not dead. Not dead. She scrabbled against the dirt floor, crawling, dragging herself to see her babe, though her mate tried to block her. She fought to see the child, hear its high thin mewling. She wept to hold it, love it.

Then she laid eyes upon the newborn babe.

Aaiee, she shrieked over and over.

Aaiee…not again…not again. He lived, for it was a male, but he had no face.

Why? Why? She screamed. There was a gash where his mouth should be, two holes for his nose, misshapen eyes sloping to the sides of his head. The hairline was low, his jaw sunken, his tiny fingers and toes webbed.

She howled, consumed with madness, grieving for her demon child. She fought her mate to take the babe into her arms. He would not let her touch him. With one last tortured look, her mate carried the child from the cave.

Not again, she wept brokenly. Not again.

Niala came awake with a jerk and threw the sheet from her. Sweating and gasping for breath, she stared out to see nothing. No blood-soaked mat or cave walls, no demon child, no mate. Just darkness.

Every intake of air hurt. She could not unbend her legs: sharp pricks of pain held them where they were, curled up tight to her body. Niala worked her feet free and let them touch the floor. A soft rug met the soles of her feet and steadied her, but she could not stand.

She pulled herself to the edge of the cot and let her head fall back so she could take deep breaths. As the panic receded, she could look out again without seeing the twisted sad little creature lying on the dirt floor.

For a moment, she did not know where she was. Blinking, she rubbed her face and tried to focus on the shaft of pale moonlight streaming through the uncovered window. She was not at Athos. Those were high and shuttered windows.

With effort, she swiveled her head and looked about the tiny room. The dark silhouette of a single three-legged stool and the shelf that held her meager possessions cast shadows in the moonlight.

She was at Najahmara.

Shivering, Niala reached for a wrap before she attempted to stand. The same dream plagued her over and over, repeating the horrific scene as if it had truly occurred. She feared it meant the babe she carried was to be born something other than human.

Niala feared the child would not live, and feared she would. She was to be a child born of War. Who knew what she might become? Could she bring such a creature to fruition with such an awareness?

What if it was a premonition the child would not survive?

Did Gaea warn her?

Nausea rolled up her belly and lingered at her throat.

Coughing, Niala held a hand over her mouth and stumbled across the room to vomit. Naught came up but a bad taste and a bit of water. The effort made her break out in sweat and she could not maintain her balance. The room swirled about her in a broad swath of colors with tiny dots of black cutting holes throughout.

Niala felt herself sliding into the darkness.

When next she opened her eyes, it was to stare with confusion into another's gaze. Zan crouched over her, concern wrinkling his forehead. He held an oil lamp in one hand and with the other he gripped her shoulder.

"Priestess," Zan whispered. "Are you all right?"

He could smell the sourness of vomit and see Niala had fallen to the floor without ceremony. He was certain it was not another strange custom of Najahmara, though he was shy touching her as she was unclothed save for a wrap lying beneath her.

He did not know if he should help her or seek assistance.

"Priestess? Should I get someone?"

With her nakedness, Zan could well see the protruding belly of a waiting child. So this one was also pregnant. He shook his head at the mysteries of the Najahmaran women and how they kept these things to themselves.

Queen Pallin never hinted of her pregnancy until the day she appeared with a thickened middle. Hattusilis was overjoyed, immediately proclaiming the child as his future heir, no questions asked.

Zan frowned but kept his thoughts to himself.

As he stared at Niala's midsection he could not help but wonder who fathered this babe. He shrugged, as if to push away ideas that were none of his concern and turned his attention back to Niala as she stirred.

She struggled to sit up, clutching at his arm for support, not the least bit embarrassed by her unclothed state. As soon as he could, he pulled the robe up over her shoulders and draped it across her front. For this, he was rewarded with a wan smile.

Zan was struck by the smile and wondered for a brief moment if the priestess enjoyed his discomfort until she murmured, "Thank you." Her gaze shifted away to a bare spot on the floor and she swallowed hard.

Her fingers trembled as she lifted them to smooth curls broken free from the long braid. He helped her sit on the low stool, giving her a moment to collect herself before he spoke.

"I am sorry to disturb you, but my king wishes a word with you."

This time the priestess chuckled. "Do not be sorry for I fear I might have lain on the floor the rest of the night."

"What made you fall?" Zan shifted back and forth, a pained expression on his face. He feared she would say it was some female ill that would further mortify him.

Instead, she drew the wrap closer and murmured, "My evening meal did not settle well."

"Are you better, then? Will you speak with King Hattusilis? He cannot sleep. He sits and broods in the round room. He wishes to talk but I am not the company he desires."

"Yes, of course." Niala nodded. "I need to dress and then I will attend to your king."

Zan returned the nod and left her to prepare for an audience with Hattusilis.

Niala washed her face and hands and cleaned her teeth. Her hair would have to wait as it took too much time to undo and comb out her thick locks, let alone plait. She found her advancing pregnancy interfered with the twisting and turning it took to do a proper braid. It was not worth the effort for a midnight meeting with the imposed new king of Najahmara.

As she walked along the dark narrow hall leading to the altar turned throne room, Niala smelled the soot imbedded in the cracks. No matter how much they scrubbed, the grit could not be erased. It was as if the reminder was to forever be with them. She paused at the entryway to see Hattusilis moving uneasily in his chair as he waited for her.

A small fire was lit in the stone circle, projecting shadows of unseen dancers upon the curved walls. The edges of the chamber were locked in deep wells of blackness with the lingering shades of the dead. Chilled, Niala drew her wrap closer as she entered the room. She could not help but agree with Jahmed that this was no longer a suitable place for them to honor Gaea.

Hattusilis quieted his twitching limbs when he saw her. "Priestess, thank you for joining me."

Niala inclined her head. "As you wish."

"Would you like food or wine?"

Hattusilis waved at a table with sliced meat and cheese and a jug of wine laid out. It became clear with his gesture that he had already drunk more than he should. His words were not yet slurred, but they were slow to form as if he had trouble corralling his thoughts.

"No, perhaps water?"

Zan appeared with a cup, handed it to her and receded back to his post without speaking. Niala found both men amusing. The women of Najahmara would never stand silent during someone else's conversation, being unable to resist throwing in advice, requested or not. Likewise, the men of Najahmara took their lead from the females and freely handed out comments on any subject.

Hattusilis was too much like his god, brooding between darkened walls in the middle of the night, though Ares did not dampen his disposition with drink.

"Perhaps he should," Niala murmured, even if a drunken Ares was frightening to consider.

"What did you say?" Hattusilis leaned forward.

"I merely commented to myself that the spirits are restless tonight."

"Indeed. It is that very thing I desire to discuss." He cast a furtive glance side to side and beckoned Niala closer. "Lately, I have felt as if something presses on me."

He passed a hand over his face. "No, not pressing. Not heavy. I do not feel as if a weight is on me but rather a sliding, or slithering. It is difficult to describe."

Hattusilis paused to drink from a full goblet of wine. When he sat it down, the cup was empty.

Wiping his mouth, Hattusilis found the courage to go on. "Something crawls over me. Something touches me, but I do not know what it is."

He stopped abruptly, anxiety embedded in his whistling exhale.

Niala watched his jaw work as he tried to say more but could not before he looked away. With a sudden chill chasing down her spine, Niala crouched before the fire, setting her cup beside her. With care she fed twigs into the flames and warmed her hands while she waited for him to speak again.

"I have told no one of this." Hattusilis spoke in a soft voice. A sheen of sweat stood out on his forehead as he lowered himself beside her with the help of a crutch. The difficulty in getting from his prearranged grand seat to the ground took effort and much of his strength.

Niala could not tell if the shaking of his hands was due to his struggle to walk or the fear oozing from his skin like perfumed oil. The musty smell of the fermented drink was strong on his breath as he bent closer. It gave rise to the nausea lurking just beneath her surface. Coughing, Niala dropped her chin and brought the edge of her skirt to her lips.

"In the cave, something followed me." Hattusilis shuddered. "Something big. I could hear it slithering behind me, hissing."

He made a sound with his tongue. "It was the reason I lost my way in the cave. I stumbled and my torch went out." He paused to dig fingers into his hair, as if to pull out words.

"It cornered me in the stores area. I could not get out, it blocked my path and yet I could not see it. It caused the urn to fall over, crushing me. I lay there for days and thought I would die without being found."

He touched one leg, the pain and terror of those moments giving his face a fiendish expression in the flickering light. Reflected in his eyes, Niala saw all those who had perished in Najahmara from the same pain, the same terror. All from the same source.

She felt Kulika's power the very first day she returned. The Sky god's life force was strongest near the cave, yet she also felt his presence within the temple complex, and now in the very room where they sat.

It was clear the serpent did not retreat as he should but took advantage and fed from the chaos.

"I thought, at first, it was your goddess, unhappy I entered her place of worship without permission, but I have heard stories of a giant serpent." Hattusilis glanced over his shoulder. "I continue to feel this presence. It slides over me, curls around me, like a snake stalking prey."

Eyes wide, voice hoarse, he stared at her. "It hisses into my ear things I scarce understand. You spoke of phantoms. You said they are all around us, and this thing - it is an evil ghoul who torments me. Do you know what it is? Do you know how to banish it?"

Even before he stopped speaking, the dry rattle of a serpent's coils echoed in the domed ceiling. Angry hissing followed. Hattusilis jerked as if stung, his head swiveling with frantic fear to find the creature that hunted him.

The hissing intensified and Niala felt the flare of power. The fire rose and smoke poured from it as the serpent on her leg responded to the call with a writhing twinge. Her babe churned and her skin crawled. Niala gasped at the near-stranglehold Kulika exerted as he tried to force his way into her.

"No." She threw her arms wide as she forced the Sky god away.

Hattusilis sagged. "You were my last hope, for there is no other who can see the phantoms that prey upon me."

"I do not refuse." Niala's voice was calmer. Kulika's energy pulled back and the hissing grew fainter. "His name is Kulika and he is Gaea's mate. He does not seek to harm you."

"I do not believe that." Hattusilis stared down at his crushed leg. "He would see me dead if I weaken enough."

"It is not the dead he wants. It is the living. I do not know what happened in the cave, but he did not wish for your death."

"What, then?"

Niala gave a brief wag of her head. How could she explain to one such as Hattusilis the meaning behind Kulika's presence? Kulika stayed where he should not because he desired a body. His realm was the sky; he was air and fire, unable to hold any shape for more than a few moments. He could manifest as streaks of lightening across a threatening sky or become a wind tunnel tearing over the earth, but he could not hold another to him.

"He wants you." She saw the surprised arch of Hattusilis' brows. "He wants to use you."

"What do you mean?"

"He has no body. He cannot enjoy the pleasures of Earth without one."

In his befuddled state, Hattusilis gaped at her. "But I am crippled."

"Apparently not in the way Kulika likes most, for your wife is with child, is she not?"

"Yes," he mumbled. "She bears my heir, a fine son."

"Or perhaps a daughter." A flash of irritation crossed Niala at his arrogance. "Men are not the only ones capable to rule."

"Then you agree someone must be king - or queen - as you are."

"I am not queen."

"No? Then why do all eyes follow you when you walk through town? Why do they bow to you and bring you gifts? Why do they do as you command?"

"You misunderstand."

"Do I?" Hattusilis leaned toward her, a leer creeping across his sharp features. "I came to Najahmara seeking their queen, and at last, I think I will have her."

His eyes gleamed in the firelight as his voice took on a sibilant tone. Startled, Niala pushed him with one hand splayed against his chest. He pressed back with a sudden burst of strength.

"Do not challenge me." Niala spoke with a fierceness that gave Hattusilis pause. "I am not helpless with hatred as before. Do not make me oust you, Kulika. Go before I force you to leave this man in peace."

"I will go when I am ready," came the hissing reply as Hattusilis reached for her. "Do not refuse me for it is not the first time you have lain with me."

"I take you as your mate, not as myself. You will go, or I will bring forth Gaea."

"Gaea. Yes, let my beloved mate through."

Hattusilis pawed at Niala, his face near hers as if to kiss her.

"Hattu, what are you doing?" Another voice joined them, shrill with distress. Pallin shuffled in from the rear right corridor that brought her from the sleeping quarters.

He blinked once, his gaze unfocused. "Do what?

"You...." Pallin stuttered, unable to speak into what she witnessed.

Hattusilis drew away from Niala with an expression of confusion. He reached to pour more wine from the skin into his cup, oblivious to his mate's displeasure.

Niala greeted Pallin with a bland smile that belied the moment before. Pallin looked between her husband and friend, hand to her lips. A movement in the shadows brought her gaze up. Zan appeared on the other side of the fire. He was the first to break the silence.

"All is well, Queen Pallin. I am watching over King Hattusilis to be certain he does not fall and further injure himself." Zan lifted his hand in a drinking gesture, a pointed look passing between himself and Pallin.

Hattusilis stared at his wife, his jaw sagging open.

"I woke to find him gone. Again." Pallin hunched her shoulders and pulled her wrap tight to her chest. "I was concerned. Of late, he does not seem to rest well. I think he no longer cares for me."

Tears shimmered in her eyes as she placed her palms onto her huge middle. Her gaze rested on Niala's upturned face. "I would not be surprised if he prefers you over this."

Zan was appalled at the blunt declaration. He could do no more than hang his head in silence for what he had seen supported Pallin's inference.

"Pallin, we were speaking of the summer celebration." Niala's focus shifted to Hattusilis. "I was explaining how we will put our phantoms to rest with this ritual. All phantoms that plague us."

Hattusilis blinked. "Phantoms," he repeated. "Ghosts. Those who cannot rest. It would be a good thing to release the poor souls."

Pallin shot her husband a dumbfounded glance but nodded. "Yes, I agree, it will be a good thing to do."

Hattusilis attempted to stand and stumbled, lurching into Pallin. She staggered under his weight but smiled as he placed a sloppy kiss on her cheek.

"You are so beautiful." He stroked her cheek with fumbling and stiff fingers.

"Yes, Hattu, she is." Zan moved to his side. "Very beautiful, as befits your queen. Let me help you to bed. You need to sleep."

"Pallin, my Love, will you come to bed as well?" Hattusilis held out his arms as Zan took a firm hold around his waist, steering him toward the doorway. "I am in the mood for love."

Zan mumbled something into Hattusilis' ear. Hattusilis' puzzled, "Why not?" drifted back to the women as Zan escorted him into the corridor.

"How are you feeling?" Niala rose, hands against her back as she stretched. "Your babe is due any day now, is that right?"

"No." Pallin avoided Niala's gaze. "Not until mid-summer or later."

"You look to be in the last phase."

"It will be a healthy child, a boy, I am certain."

"Certain because that is what your husband requires?"

Pallin flushed, apparent even in the firelight. "Hattu does not require anything other than we survive the birth. He will be happy with son or daughter, as long as he has us both."

"Hmmm." Niala touched the very solid belly beneath Pallin's gown. "The child has dropped. I think you will birth much sooner than mid-summer."

"Then he comes early." Pallin turned away from Niala, hugging herself.

"No, Pallin, the Solstice would not be early." Niala spoke with gentleness. "I have assisted at too many births to be fooled by a babe's arrival. Your body prepares itself even now to deliver."

"Please," Facing Niala, Pallin whispered. "Say no more about this. Let this child belong to Hattusilis."

"If not Hattusilis, who, then?"

Rubbing her face, Pallin answered, "Can you not guess? My first time and I find myself pregnant."

"Deimos."

"Yes. Yes, Deimos." Pallin sank down onto the stool at the foot of the throne.

"Does he know?"

"Know? How would he know? I have not seen him since…since…." Her gaze traveled along the darkened edges of the chamber. "Not that I expected him to return. He is what he is, as he so carefully explained to me. Now it is too late."

"He should be told."

"No, Niala, you do not understand. I am not like you. I could not watch him stay young and handsome while I wither and die. At least Hattu will grow old with me. Together, we can watch our children and grandchildren."

"But you carry the child of an immortal, who is to say what it will be like. How will you explain this to your husband?"

"They are both dark. Any difference will be through me."

"I do not speak only of skin, hair and eyes, I speak of possibilities. A child who belongs to an immortal will not be like others." Niala thought of little Phobos and the trials he had in store. "Deimos should have a hand in his upbringing."

"No, this child belongs to me. His father is Hattusilis. He will be a prince, not a god."

"There are some things that are out of our control."

"Leave this alone, Niala, please. It is none of your concern."

"So the child will be raised as royalty."

"He will become a king." Pallin laced her fingers together in a white-knuckled grip.

"Of what? Najahmara? Is that where you see our future, as subjects under the thumb of one?"

"No." Pallin gave a hesitant shake to her head. "Yes. What choice do we have? So much has changed since you have been gone, Niala. We do what we must to survive."

"And what of your vows to Gaea?"

"I do not abandon my vows. I work beside Jahmed every day, and will, as long as I can, in spite of…." She stopped.

"In spite of your husband, who does not like it."

"He does not, but says little. He tries to understand even though he comes from a tradition unlike ours." Pallin shrugged. "The men take the lead in most matters."

"Women are not permitted a choice. I see he wishes to create such an atmosphere here as well. Your husband does not allow the use of our sacred cave. He changed our Spring rites, and yet, you say you honor your vows."

"I have done what I can." Awkwardly, Pallin rose from her stool and stood panting from the effort. "He wanted the Spring celebration cancelled. We were at least able to hold it even though it evolved."

"Pallin, you delude yourself." Niala spoke in a hushed tone but with a firmness that pinned Pallin in place. "You try to support both causes, but our side is losing. Gaea retreats and Kulika takes hold as these men continue to bring their god into our consciousness."

"Is their god not the same as yours? They worship War though with another name." Pallin was breathing hard. "Jahmed told me you carry his child. How do you strike this balance? Perhaps you can guide me."

"It is not the same. I did not choose to be with Ares."

"He raped you?"

"No." Niala answered not in anger but with a bemused expression. "It was not by force."

"Do you love him, then?"

"In a strange way, yes."

"You see, it is the same for me. I love Hattusilis. I know he does not want any harm to come to us, though his ways are foreign. He and his men will protect us against other invaders. Do not fool yourself, Niala, they are out there. We are isolated and do not know the changing ways of the world. Hattu does."

"Perhaps you are right, Pallin, but we must not let our connection with Earth slip away."

"With you back among us, the balance will be restored."

"While I am here, but what if I am not?"

"Does that mean you will leave again?" There was panic in Pallin's voice. "Please, please do not."

"It would not be by choice, but who is to say? You are right when you talk of change and there is little we can do about it. We must go forward with our summer rites and heal this wound once and for all." Niala touched Pallin's arm. "I need you with me during this ritual."

Pallin pulled away, drawing her wrap closer to her body. "No, Niala, I cannot."

"Why?"

"Because I must walk a thin line if I am to do any good and to participate in the ritual might be perceived as abandoning the king."

"And our people will see it as abandoning Gaea. I need you to do this, Pallin. I need you, Jahmed and Ajah to hold the intention. It is for the greater good of all."

"I do not see how I can do this."

"How can you not? Remember your vows."

"My vows." Pallin laced her fingers together in a grip that left her knuckles white. "To death I am yours and after death I become one with you."

"Stand beside me in life and I will take you after death," Niala gave the response with a smile.

Pallin remained silent for a long time, staring into the fire. With a reluctant nod, she murmured, "I will stand with you though it may dearly cost me."

TWENTY-THREE

Desperation leaked from Phobos like a trail of trickling blood, drop by drop, spreading across the surface of his fear. He could taste the bitter molten scent in his mouth and feel the sweat in his eyes as all hope fled. Panic squatted before him, waiting for the right moment when he was too weak to fight, when his mind would break and all that would be left was to move in for the kill.

He imagined his throat torn out and there, amongst the red gore, a white rasping windpipe trying to feed his body. He saw himself jerk and twist in agony as Panic fed on his flesh, wishing to die, to be put out of his misery. He saw it from wide-open, staring eyes, too frightened to fight back. All he could do was watch himself be eaten alive by this monster, this thing that waited.

"I am patient, Phobos," Panic said. "I can wait you out, for I am far stronger than you. You belong to me now."

"No, no," he screamed wordlessly, for he could not speak.

Panic laughed at him. Great rolling laughs while it fed on his blood and flesh.

Again he screamed. Shrill, long and loud.

Panic did not care. He said, "Go ahead and shriek, Boy. For once I possess you, I will own every last drop." Panic licked its lips. "You will be locked into a mindless feeble place of darkness forever. So, go on, scream. It is all you have left."

From that place of wasting horror, Phobos felt the lash of another's power. He felt it swirl into the darkness, climb over Panic, and whisper in his ear: *Surrender.*

Phobos did not understand. The unidentified power receded and Panic reached for him again, its evil eyes just the tiniest bit uncertain. Phobos saw the gnashing teeth come for him. He howled into the desolate blackness.

"Help me."

Surrender.

The power swept through again and Panic hesitated.

Surrender: to give up, to relinquish the last bit of control. To abandon all hope. To submit. Phobos knew what the word meant, but he would not go quietly. Panic would have to take him, kicking and screaming.

Surrender.

It came again, the surge of authority and the sound of that single word. Phobos did not know where it came from, but he knew it meant something other than his definition.

What? What? He dug through his thoughts, so jumbled, so tarnished with fear, so convoluted and confused, yet he searched in spite of himself. There was something he should know. Something he should remember.

SURRENDER.

Like lightening splitting apart a tree, the power cut through him, rattling against his nightmares as hail is spit from the sky. It tore at his hair and eyes and pulled at his skin until he thought he would disintegrate under the strength bearing down on him.

Panic cowered away from it, mewling that something wanted to steal its victim.

SURRENDER!

One last time, the potent external force crashed over Phobos and his eyes flew open. He gasped and held his breath. Silence fell once more into his dark prison. And then he began to giggle. A few wheezing breaths, and more tentative giggles. Nonsensical giggles.

A deeper breath.

Calm.

Yes.

Yes, he understood now.

Panic consumed his fear, fed on it like bread and cheese, drank it like water. Panic grew stronger, faster, brutal, conniving its way into the deepest recesses of a mind already weakened by terror. Panic could drive one to blind madness, lead one to jump off a cliff in the belief it was safer than to walk into the pain.

Phobos knew what he had to do. He knew he had to step into Panic. It had to flow over him. He could no longer feed it with fears that lay dormant in his soul since the beginning of time.

With a clarity that made him dizzy, Phobos saw his fears belonged to every living creature, mortal and immortal. He had but to claim them all as his own. He had to surrender his fear. He had to surrender his soul and take his power from the thing he hated most.

It was then he knew the real truth.

He *was* Panic.

Soundlessly, Phobos slid out of the monolith and into Ares' waiting arms. Like being birthed again, he was stunned and stared about with unseeing eyes. Clots of clay plastered his curls to his head and streaked a heavy layer of dust over all his body.

After one deeply drawn breath, Phobos began to cry. He threw his arms around his father's neck, wrapped his legs around his waist, and clung to him as if he would never, ever let go.

Ares held him as the wracking sobs shook his thin little body. Phobos pressed closer, his face buried against Ares' neck, the tears wetting his tunic. Ares stroked the boy's hair, unmindful that the stickiness now transferred to his fingers.

"Will he be alright?" Priapos asked, so filled with relief he had to lean against the hard edges of the cave wall to keep from falling.

"He will." Ares splayed one hand across Phobos' back, the long fingers looking huge against the skinny boy. "It is always difficult to discover Self, but he has done it."

Lowering his voice, Ares whispered into his son's ear, "I am proud."

"What now?" Priapos straightened, with the thought it was unbecoming for a warrior such as he to be seen as feeble.

"I think, now, Phobos deserves to rest. He has fought well, but I believe he should return to Cos."

At Priapos' approving nod, Ares tone turned stern. "Just for a while."

"Of course. To get his bearings."

"Yes." Ares patted the boy's shoulder. "Not long, though, for he will need help adjusting to this new self. It is not a journey to be undertaken alone, nor do I think Love can cope with such discoveries."

"Do you fancy their rites of passage are less painful?" Rubbing his chin, Priapos heaved a sigh. "I do not, in truth. I have never found love to be a simple thing."

"Love has never been an easy task for me." Ares carried Phobos from the cave. "But I do not see how it could be as disagreeable as this. What say you, Phobos?"

Though he could not bring himself to speak, the sentiment was not lost as Phobos realized it was the first time his father had ever spoken directly to him. Always, Ares spoke about him to someone else, but never to him.

He now knew he mattered. Phobos was not certain what it all meant, but he was happy. He increased his chokehold around Ares' neck, smiling to himself.

Within moments, he felt the now-familiar surge of Ares' will and realized they had moved from one place to another. The manner in which they transferred had not yet been explained to him - so many mysteries to uncover in his journey.

The relocation created a sensation both hot and cold that went in bursts along his bared skin. Not unpleasant and not quite as scary as the first time when he had been taken from his mother's side.

Now he was going home.

Thaleia greeted them with a startled, "Oh, my!" and as Phobos lifted his head from Ares' shoulder, it turned into a shrieked, "Mercy! What have you done to my baby?"

Ares set the boy on his feet. Phobos staggered a bit before he drew himself up and said with scorn, "I am not a baby."

With one eyebrow arched, Thaleia gave an irritated, "Humph."

"As you can see, the boy has been through a bit of a trial. I thought he should see his mother before he returns to Athos."

Phobos looked past Thaleia with eagerness. "Where is Eros? I want to see my brother."

"First you must bathe, you are disgusting and filthy. Your mother would not approve of this at all."

"Where is Eros? Where is Eros?" Phobos danced around

Thaleia as she tried to grab his hands. "Eros!"

A squeal of delight came from an adjoining room and before Thaleia could stop him, Phobos raced to join his twin. With fists on her hips, Thaleia watched him go and then turned to Ares.

"Wipe that smirk off your face, Master of Misery. What have you done to our sweet little Phobos? I have never seen him so...so...."

"Unafraid? He is growing up, in spite of his mother's reluctance to allow it."

"I sincerely pray the two of you beget no more children together, for my heart cannot withstand more of this."

"A wishful prayer that goes unanswered." Ares tapped his chest with a bark of laughter.

"What?" Paling, Thaleia stared at Ares. "You do not mean what I think you to mean?"

"That Aphrodite bears me another child? Yes."

"But she...." Thaleia passed her hand across her forehead, recalling the bawdy laughter shared between Aglaia and Euphrosyne. Their words now carried new import, and Thaleia bit one nail as she realized the truth. "But I thought...."

"Surely you could tell she is once again pregnant."

"Yes, of course, but I thought it was to be...."

"Hephaestos?"

Thaleia nodded.

"He could not live up to her expectations. She bears my daughter."

"But you refused her. That is what began this entire farce."

"We have made amends, Thaleia, much to your sorrow, I am sure. Aphrodite has returned to me, and Hephaestos can return to his pitiful underground existence and never bother me again."

"Is that so, Lord Ares? Then look about you and tell me if you see Aphrodite anywhere. The answer is no, you do not. Because she is not on Cos, nor any other of her holdings. She remains on Lemnos and in the arms of Hephaestos."

"For how long, dear Grace? I suspect until he finds out the child is not his. His pride will undo this relationship."

"And if she does not tell him?" Thaleia put hands to her hips and raised her eyebrows at Ares. "How will he ever know? He will believe forever that the child is his."

Ares opened his mouth and then closed it, pursing his lips in annoyance. Thaleia could see her sling hit home but she suppressed her grin. Ares was far too smug for her liking and, though he was probably right. Aphrodite would return to him. Yet, Thaleia enjoyed tormenting him as long as she could.

"The child will look like me. That is how Hephaestos will know."

"Or, she will look like her mother and no one will know." Thaleia sent a coy glance through her lashes.

Ares frowned.

Thaleia shot home another bolt of truth. Laughing, she plucked a peach from a nearby bowl and bit into the sweet flesh, grunting with appreciation as juice ran down her hand. She took great care to lick the juice from the fresh bite and then her fingers, one by one.

"And besides," she added as she took another bite, "Do you want to think of Aphrodite lying in Hephaestos' arms, night after night, all the while your babe grows in her belly?

"It takes nine months, you know. If she does not leave him before, who is to say she ever will? And maybe his heart is bigger than yours, and he cares not whose child waits to be born. Maybe it is enough to have Love beside him."

Sucking noisily on the peach, Thaleia added, "Maybe."

Before she could raise a finger to bid him farewell, Ares was gone.

"Too easy," she murmured, dropping the peach pit into a basket. "Too, too easy."

From a nearby hillside, Ares stood ready for the beginning of a spectacular battle. Opposing forces faced off across a deep and muddy field, round shields reflecting sunlight like so many thousands upon thousands of stars. Wickedly sharp spear tips waited with a hunger for flesh in the hands of the first phalanx. As the meadow began to slope upward, rows of archers poised for the signal to release their bolts.

It was a civilized war. Organized, with trained troops under the steady command of generals. Though it would be a fair skirmish, more on one side would be left standing when it was over. It was the kind of battle Ares celebrated, reveled in, sought out to join, for it gave him the greatest pleasure.

He had grown tired of the melees of less defined peoples

where there was nothing more than chopping and slicing with a heavy broadsword. Too many times the combat raged until brother would kill brother along with the enemy.

He waited with relish for this battle. Map were drawn, paths plotted, troops gathered and strategies planned. It would be a stunning dance of technique and skill, the way a war should be.

The violence called to him, a clamoring, seductive call he was ever ready to answer. Fury boiled within him, ready to spill over in a frenzy of bloodletting. Amason felt his eagerness for she quivered in his hand, anxious to begin.

He wanted this fight. He wanted to rip out the heart of any who would get in his way and pretend it was the heart of Hephaestos. He wanted to kill and kill again, to drive away the demons that tormented him before he went to Aphrodite.

She still resided at Lemnos. In spite of her promises, she was still in Hephaestos' arms. Rage threatened to choke Ares as he imagined each and every detail of their lovemaking.

He needed blood.

He needed death.

Why had this battle not begun?

He could not erase Aphrodite from his thoughts without it. The last moments with her replayed again and again and he knew the sting of her lies.

Though Love had momentarily faltered, like a gathering storm on the horizon, she had regained her strength. She was with child and whole again, restored to health and happiness, and it was Ares who brought her back. He had seen how her pale skin appeared against his darkness and smiled. She belonged to him again, bound by the blood of a new life.

Lying there, bathed in her beauty, wounded ego soothed and body satiated, he had let down his guard. They kissed and stroked each other with tenderness, until he whispered into her hair that he would see her next on Cos, for soon he must take his leave.

Fool that he was, when she turned upon her side and smiled at him, he saw nothing but his good fortune reflected in her eyes. Though War was often difficult to carry, to have Love made it bearable. He did not realize until that moment how empty it all seemed without her and he succumbed to her splendor.

He never suspected what she would next say to him.

I cannot yet go. It would not be right.

Aphrodite's tender smile made him grit his teeth.

It was not right for you to be here at all, he responded.

Do not punish me further, for neither of us is without blame, but poor Hephaestos was drawn into this, innocent of our offenses.

To this, Ares shrugged. He conceded the point, though he thought to pick her up and take her back to Cos with force. Aphrodite saw this cross his face and held up one hand.

No, Beloved. I must find a way to break my alliance with Hephaestos, one that will not hurt him.

It has already been broken, Ares corrected.

Not until I say it has, she answered, her glorious hair spilling over her face as she sat up.

I say it has. Ares propped on his elbow, scowling. Gesturing at their nakedness, he added. This says it has.

Not so, my Darling. Sex does not make or break a union, it is the intentions of the two who form the pledge

You know my intention. I will not stand for you to lie with him again.

I have no say in the matter as long as you keep another at Athos. I will leave when I am ready and not a moment before.

This you promise me?

Yes, Beloved. I swear. Soon I will return to Cos and we will be together again. I just do not want to cause more pain for Hephaestos.

Aphrodite remained at Lemnos, in Hephaestos' bed in spite of her promise. Cursing, Ares turned his attention back to the battle. He was ready to fight, to feel bone crumble beneath Amason but there was something decidedly wrong below. The troops intermingled, but without a single clash of shields. It was a strange strategy, or would have been, had they been fighting.

It seemed they were not. Ares scanned across the view, then gazed skyward, thinking another immortal sought to interfere. There were some who would delight in such an act, yet he could find no reason to account for the milling about of soldiers. Warriors dragged shields and spears in the mud, if not altogether dropping their weapons to stare aimlessly at the enemy. Both armies appeared more than bewildered, they were uninspired.

War's minions, too, were missing.

Neither Enyo, nor Eris responded. Deimos was not present. Not a winged blood-sucking Keri in sight, nor the hounds that howled behind him when he charged into battle. This was not a small siege, unworthy of their attention. It was a massive invasion against a strong defense. It should have drawn every blood-monger among the gods, yet he stood alone on the hillside and saw naught but mortal men swarming in confusion.

Ares watched awhile longer, confounded by the feeling of intrusion. When he could no longer tolerate the muddling about, he descended from the hillside and let his presence be felt. Though he did not reveal himself in physical form, he walked among them and let his vigor flow outward over the lingering cloud of doubt that held them captive.

For that was what he sensed.

Doubt.

A cacophony of voices questioned the correctness of killing for the sake of ownership. This war, as any other, was about the control of wealth. Who had the most, who could take the most. Who was stronger, who was weaker. Who would dominate and who would fall.

But these were mortal ponderings. It was no concern of his why they went to war, why they fought or what they fought over. He cared only for the act itself and carried no investment in the cause or the culmination. He did not want to know why they behaved as they did, only that they return to their quest.

As Ares moved between factions, there was a tiny bit of uprising, a seeking of his energy as a source. He reached for the core of greed residing in every mortal and beckoned to it, called it to the surface. Soon, the shields were raised and spears at ready once more.

Commanding generals rubbed grit from their eyes, saw the state of affairs and began to call orders that rippled across the troops like fire. And finally, War won out against Love, for that was the answer.

The armies felt the influence of Anteros, Love's Response.

Aphrodite's son was stronger than he thought, Ares mused. Interesting, but of no consequence. With one final wave of power, Ares brought the men into full-scale warfare. The battle began in earnest, but Ares no longer cared. He could think only of Aphrodite's hollow promise and feel the sting of betrayal once again.

Jealousy rose like a specter.

TWENTY-FOUR

In the distance, Ares could hear Zelos' rattling laughter, and the siren call of Nemesis, she who embodied Revenge. With Amason in his massive grip, Ares would exact payment from Hephaestos for stealing Aphrodite.

For convincing her to stay. Jealousy and Revenge spurred him toward Lemnos, to stare at the shining copper rooftop nestled in the jungle. When he burst into the private quarters of Hephaestos, Aglaia and Euphrosyne shrieked at the site of him.

Both leaped to their feet as if to protect their mistress. Aphrodite did not rise from her cushioned chaise, but watched him through suspicious eyes.

"Leave us." Raw fury billowed out into the room. He swung his arm toward the doorway as if he would strike them dead with Amason. "Now."

Aphrodite stared but did not say a word, nodding only at the Graces to do as Ares bid. The two women scurried from the room in tears, fearful of Aphrodite's safety. Only then, did Aphrodite stand, smoothing her white chiton about her hips with a sensual brush of her fingertips.

"Why do you rant so, Beloved? What has happened?"

"I have had enough of this charade. I will tolerate no more."

Ares advanced and she saw sweat on his brow. Rising to

her feet, her gaze swept up and down, taking in his disheveled state and ugly tone. The scent of Jealousy curled around Aphrodite, tickling her nose and Revenge filled her throat. These two brought a spark to her eyes as they sent a spasm of seething self-righteous resentment throughout her body.

"How dare you come into my chambers in such a manner? You come straight from battle to me? I will not have this crudeness thrown in my face."

"'Your chambers? I thought they belonged to Hephaestos, though I see you have made them more to your liking." His gaze raked the feminine adornments added to a once very masculine quarters. "And here I believed you were to end this simpering display of ridiculous infatuation."

"Ridiculous? What falls into ridicule is no more than yourself and your pandering to any who will spread her legs."

"And what do you call this willingness to bed Hephaestos? It is no less an insult to me."

Aphrodite fair vibrated with venom, her voice pitched low and stinging. "You have no right to accuse me of anything when you take your pleasure with any and all you can."

"While you sleep chastely next to Hephaestos? No, Aphrodite, I know your ways equally as well and your appetite far expands mine.

"I wager Hephaestos has been worn thin by your demands and spends more time away than necessary. Perhaps he tires of you. Perhaps he would be happy to give you back, for you drive the average man to the brink of sanity."

Stung, Aphrodite slapped Ares across the face. She had no more thought in her head than the image of Ares entwined with another. The sudden desire to kill anyone who would take Ares from her filled her with hatred.

"You will not be unfaithful to me again, for I will destroy all who come between us."

Ares stared at her, at the rage-filled twisted features. It gave him pause for this was not Aphrodite's usual state. Slowly, he touched his cheek where her hand left its imprint and felt the heat rise from his skin. She had never struck him before, no matter how angry she was.

Shaking his head from side to side, the buzzing in his mind began to recede. As the numbness cleared away, he saw her weeping into her hands as though her heart would break.

"Sweet mercy, what has come over us?" Ares enfolded her into his arms.

"I do not know. I do not know." Aphrodite's arms went about his broad chest. "Forgive me."

"No, we must forgive each other, for it was Zelos and Nemesis who toyed with us."

"Zelos." Aphrodite rested her cheek against his leather tunic and listened to his heartbeat. "She is not wrong, Ares. I love you more than life, yet I punish you out of jealousy and envy that you do not belong only to me."

"Your punishment is well-placed, for I deserve every bit."

She reached for him and, as he bent to meet her, kissed his lips with a forlorn sigh. "Will it always be like this for us? Inflicting pain whenever we can?"

"It is our nature, Beloved, though we may wish it were not."

"Do you wonder, then, why Hephaestos is attractive to me? He does not argue but is grateful for every moment in my presence. His gentleness soothes the conflict in my soul."

"And though I seek out those who will calm the violence, there is only one to whom I return."

"Then say it," Aphrodite pleaded. "For I need to hear those sweet words from your mouth after this ugliness."

With unusual tenderness, Ares brushed aside a tendril of hair from her forehead and pressed his lips to her fragrant skin. "There is only one I love."

"Who?" Aphrodite pressed, smiling.

"You." Ares laughed. "Always you." He swept her into his arms. "Love and War are powerful burdens. Is it any wonder we lose ourselves in it all? Now, my Love, let us go to bed, for I want only to make amends and pray it is the last time within these four walls."

"Yes, take me here and I swear it shall be the last. I will return to Cos by evening fall."

"And you will tell Hephaestos this was no more than a rude joke to put me in my place?"

Sighing, Aphrodite answered, "I do not promise what my words will be, for I do not want to hurt him."

"It is too late for that, but I bear my share in all this."

"Do I truly hear the great Ares admit he is wrong?"

"You hear what you wish to hear. I say only that I have become a slave to Love and it is time for you to take advantage of my weakness."

"And that I will," promised Aphrodite, biting his earlobe.

When silence fell within the chamber, Aglaia sagged against the double doors. "Thank the gods, they have stopped fighting."

"Should we check on them?" Euphrosyne stared at her sister. "It seems too quiet."

"Absolutely not. There is no doubt they make love now and should have their privacy."

"Hmmm." Euphrosyne twirled a strand of hair around a forefinger. "Ares is quite handsome and I would rather enjoy seeing him in his glory."

Stepping aside, Aglaia waved at the door. "Go in at your own risk for, knowing Ares, he may well draw you into lovemaking with them."

"What?" Euphrosyne took a step backwards. "He would not!"

"And you think he would mind being watched? Not that one. He would take you next." Aglaia leered at her sister, then burst out laughing at the expression of horror on her face.

"Come, Sister. Let us prepare to leave this place, for I think Lord Ares has finally made his point."

When Euphrosyne did not follow her, Aglaia turned back and caught the longing on the girl's face. "Surely, you do not wish for Ares to bed you?"

"No." Euphrosyne's answer was slow. "Not him."

There was no need for her to say whom, for Aglaia had seen her sister's gaze follow Anteros whenever he was near.

"It is not your time, yet. Do not try to trick the Fates into allowing that which is not yet written to take place."

"But, why not? I love Anteros."

"Does he love you?"

"Yes, I think." Euphrosyne lifted her shoulders. "I hope."

Aglaia shook her head, "Maybe he does and maybe he does not. Still, you must remain virgin until Aphrodite gives you permission."

"Aphrodite must give permission to make love?"

"Well, of course." Aglaia bit her lips and avoided Euphrosyne's gaze. "She is Love and it must be agreeable with her, for you and Anteros. He is her son and perhaps she has other plans for him."

"You babble. I do not wish to hear more." Euphrosyne turned on her heel, her long hair swishing behind her. "I will decide when I will have a mate."

"Aphrodite will decide who and when."

"Did she pick a lover for you?"

"Why of course." Aglaia stifled a laugh.

"When was that?"

"Oh, long, long ago, before you were with us."

"Who was it?" Pausing, Euphrosyne put her hands on her hips. "Who was your first?"

"Ahh…it was…ahh…." Turning a deep wine color, Aglaia blurted, "No one you know."

"You lie! Look at you blush. Tell me who." Euphrosyne dove at her sister, digging her fingers into her ribs.

"No." Scooting backwards, giggling until breathless, Aglaia held her arms across her chest to block her sister's jabs. "Stop."

"Tell me. Tell me, or I shall…."

Their banter was cut off by a ghastly shriek. Both women froze.

"Now, that," Aglaia pointed, "We should check."

They threw open the heavy wooden doors and raced toward the inner chamber only to see Cedalion standing by with a dagger in his hand. The blade dripped a bloody trail from the bedstead to his feet. He stood like a small carven statue staring at the bed.

Aphrodite thrashed and screamed, while Ares lay unmoving and silent beside her. The thin netting of gold that had draped like sails over the bedstead now wrapped around them and bound them in place. Though Aphrodite struggled, she could not get free, for each time she kicked, the web-like links grew tighter to her form.

"Princess! My lady," cried Aglaia, running toward her, with Euphrosyne on her heels.

Before they could reach Aphrodite, Cedalion darted in front of them, the bloody dagger swishing through the air in a warning to stand down.

"Cedalion." Euphrosyne looked upon Aphrodite and Ares with dread. "What have you done?"

"Let us pass, Dwarf," shouted Aglaia. "We must see to our

mistress."

Cedalion shook his head, his black eyes bright with vengeance. He waved the blade at them again.

"Cedalion, please." Euphrosyne held out her hands. "Our mistress needs us. What have you done?"

"He has done my bidding." A pitiless voice spoke behind them and they all turned. Hephaestos stood bold with righteous wrath, his freckled countenance flushed, his body tightly held, but his eyes - those amber mirrors were raw with pain. His voice rumbled out into the room with an awful proclamation, silencing even the shrieks of his wife.

"He has slain the war-monger and imprisoned the adulterer."

Horrified, Aglaia and Euphrosyne stood frozen within a few feet of Aphrodite, unable to assist her as she wept with broken sobs.

"Beloved, speak to me. Say you live. Speak so I may know you breathe still." Aphrodite begged through her tears. Her voice quavered, desolate and fearful, on the edge of an abyss. One misstep and she would tumble into the black void of sorrow, never to emerge.

She did not believe he was gone. He could not be dead. None could touch him, for he was War, destined to live forever. Yet Aphrodite was reminded there had been one destroyer of the immortals named Amason from the anvil of Hephaestos.

There was no reason another could not exist.

"Ares, Ares, my eternal love. Do not leave me," Aphrodite wailed, still fighting against the golden web that shackled them to the bed.

She could not even reach out to touch him, to see that he was warm beneath her fingers, or that he grew cold in true death.

"Beloved. Be nah zeer." She fell into an ancient pelagic tongue, babbling her lament over and over to no avail, for Ares did not respond.

"You see how she weeps over this butcher," Hephaestos raged. "You see how she has defiled our marriage bed, how shamelessly she flaunts her deed."

Aglaia and Euphrosyne clung to each other, sobbing. Their fright knew no bounds as Hephaestos lumbered back and forth, baying his outrage. His face was bloated and purple, his eyes bulged and his great hard fists flung outwards in wide circles as if he fought off demons.

"Adulterer. Whore. I should dispatch you into Hades' arms."

Hephaestos stood over Aphrodite, his legs bumping the bedstead.

The loyal Cedalion jumped to his side, the wicked dagger poised above Aphrodite's heart. He looked up into his master's eyes, waiting, waiting for the moment when he could plunge it into her flesh.

"No," shrieked Euphrosyne. "No, Cedalion, do not, I pray, do not hurt her."

For one second, Cedalion's black eyes slid to the corners as if he weighed her anguish with that of his master, then he returned to his duty, the sharp edge pressed to Aphrodite's bosom, separated only by the cobweb of links.

"Slay me, yes, slay me, for I cannot endure this. Ares, Beloved, be nah zeer. Awaken, Beloved, please."

"Stop," wept Aglaia. "Stop. She does not deserve this horror."

"Yes, stop." Hephaestos held up his hand, palm out toward Aphrodite. "I choose to keep you here. I will not release you to any semblance of peace, for I would rather see your endless suffering."

Cedalion, ever obedient, stepped back. The dagger slid out of sight into a sheath at his side. Hephaestos, fingers trembling, caressed Aphrodite through her bonds. "You were mine. Mine. Mine in solemn trust. I gave you everything and all I asked in return was faithfulness, that you forsake this warmonger, this murderer.

"That is all I asked. Why could you not do it? Am I so pitiful you could not love me enough to turn away from one so despicable as he?"

There came no response from Aphrodite. She had dissolved into sorrow beyond his reach. Hephaestos was fully enraged again, for there was not even an apology forthcoming from his bride, no words of repentance, no regret.

He threw back his head and howled, "Father Zeus and all the Ages, I call you here, so you may see this cruel and hateful whore caught in my snare. I call you to see what Love has done.

"Your beauteous Aphrodite is well and truly ugly to look upon in her lust for the bloodthirsty Ares. Come one and all and view my righteous punishment."

Hephaestos appeal went out and was heard by all the Ages.

They came from every corner of the universe, compelled out of curiosity to see one such as Ares made into a buffoon for their enjoyment. There was little affection lost between War and the Council. Not one among them would mind seeing him caught in the trap of his own deceit.

They gathered in the palace of the Forge god with ribald jokes and unquenchable laughter as, even yet, Hephaestos complained of his ill fortune.

"Because I am crippled and slow, though a loyal and loving husband, this traitorous wench would rather lie in the arms of a butcher like Ares because he is handsome and swift. I beg you all to understand their deed is the worst of the worst and their punishment is well deserved."

On first glance, they saw the golden web holding a very naked Aphrodite and Ares fast to the bed and this brought great laughter from all but Hera, who frowned at Hephaestos.

"Do not look so at me, my mother, for I have been betrayed and what I have done is justifiable."

Hermes spoke up and said, "Would there be three times the shackles and every creature in Olympus looking on, and I would still lie beside the beauteous Aphrodite, if I could."

This brought a cadre of agreement from the males, while the females shook their heads at this sentiment.

"Poor Aphrodite." Athena shifted from one foot to the other. "This is a matter of great embarrassment and I have no further need to watch. I will take my leave now and let this matter settle itself."

Even those whose jealousy extended far beyond Hephaestos' palace had to agree and every female in the gathering left in protest, all but Hera and Iris, her loyal servant. Iris glared at Hermes but did not speak, just stood in mute support of her mistress.

Ares and Hephaestos were both Hera's children. She did not approve of such a display between them. She gave the men in attendance a cold eye and the laughter died down. It was then, upon a second and closer inspection, they saw Ares' lifeless body next to a weeping Aphrodite.

Hera shrieked and then fainted. A collective gasp rose up amongst the men. Iris held a cloth to Hera's forehead and whispered encouragement.

"What is this?" Zeus pointed at the inert Ares. "How could you do such a thing? It is forbidden for one immortal to slay another under any circumstance."

Hephaestos did not cower, but met his father's gaze. "What they have done is unforgivable. Ares made forfeit his life for his sin."

"It is not your judgment to make. Remove the net at once and release them from this prison."

Zeus' enormous thundering power rolled over Hephaestos and still, the Forge god stood his ground.

"I refuse. Ares no longer cares where he lies, but Aphrodite, I wish for her to stay where she is, so she may look upon the face of her dead lover day after day for an eternity. That is her punishment for betraying me."

"I will not allow this." Zeus advanced upon Hephaestos.

"You cannot prevent it. There is no one save myself who can lift this snare from them. They are trapped forever."

"Mercy, Hephaestos." Poseidon placed a hand over his heart. "There is no one who deserves such a cruel fate. Release them both, I beg you."

"This is no way to treat Eternal Love." Apollo's face shone with the brightness of the sun. "No matter what the affront, Love, by virtue of all our hearts, deserves another chance."

"I will not have her as my wife. I leave her bound to the one she has chosen that they may both rot."

"Please, Hephaestos." Poseidon raised a placating hand. "Do not do this. It is an affront to nature. I swear any demand you wish will be yours, if you would but release my daughter."

Hephaestos turned his back and listened no more to the immortal males, but when his mother, Hera, awoke and railed at him, he glared at her. "You have always loved Ares more, for he is beautiful and whole, while I am lame and ugly.

"Tell me, Mother, where in all my life, has love ever served me? Why should I now favor Love, for any reason?"

"Because, beyond all, she rules our hearts and Ares is your brother. How can you be so cruel?"

"Does no one care for me? Does no one see what this has done to me?" Hephaestos anguished. "I am outcast, even in my betrayal."

"Remove this bondage, I command you." Zeus' voice boomed throughout the chamber. "Or your punishment will be far worse than what you conjure up for Aphrodite."

Lifting his hand for quiet, Poseidon once again brought Hephaestos attention to himself. His voice as soft and calming as the ocean itself. "Nephew, I swear to you once more, should you release Aphrodite, I will make amends in whatever way you request. Be it another wife, or a fortune, I will see you have all you desire."

"Can you assure me of good legs and straightforward feet?" Hephaestos' lips twisted with bitterness. "Can you give me a graceful stride and a strong stance? No, Uncle, you cannot, therefore, do not taunt me with tarnished promises."

"It is true, I cannot grant you the physical prowess you so badly want, but I can assure you and all who stand before us, you will never hear another word of ridicule and all your talents will be lauded as the riches they are.

"Life is not all about our looks, but more about our character. Who here has respect for Ares, though he is beautiful to set sight upon? Inside, he is brutal, twisted and ugly and can scarce be tolerated. Is that your request? To be turned inside out?"

To this, Hephaestos had no answer.

Hera went to her son and laid a kiss upon his cheek. "You have always been loved, no more and no less than Ares. It is only in your own eyes you have not been equal in my heart."

"Good Hephaestos, free Aphrodite so she may return to Cos. Let us bear away the body of Ares to his native land, so you may be done with this disgrace and let your life once again resume." Poseidon bounced his staff upon the bronze floor, making the sound of a hollow drum.

After a lengthy wait and much pacing, Hephaestos answered, "Uncle, I cannot deny your request. Cedalion."

Together, they removed the web of golden links, folding it back until Aphrodite was able to spring up from the hateful bed. Aglaia and Euphrosyne waited with robe in hand to slip over her nakedness. She fell into their arms and looked up only as Zeus and Poseidon lifted the body of Ares to bear it away.

"No, no, my Beloved, you must not be dead," Aphrodite wailed as if the mortal world ended. The Graces restrained her from throwing herself across his inert form. "It cannot be. It cannot be."

"It is not, Princess of the Oceans." Poseidon also placed an inhibiting hand upon Aphrodite. "For I have seen the slightest of breaths give rise to his chest and, see there, his fingers twitch. Ares is not dead, but gravely wounded."

Aphrodite crumpled to the floor in a swoon.

As the Council moved to disband and Ares to be carried away, Zeus turned to Hephaestos. "As for you, consider yourself fortunate, for to kill another immortal is death unto yourself. However you did it, it would be wise to destroy such a weapon before another falls."

Hephaestos bowed his head and spoke no more to any of them.

TWENTY-FIVE

Aphrodite wiped away a tear as she spoke to Deimos. "The fault lies with me, all of it." The expression on her face was one of defeat and loss. "Had I not been selfish in my pursuits, this dreadful thing would not have happened."

"Who is to know what would be, Mother." Deimos sat next to her on a brocade chaise, his arm around her drooping shoulders. "For even we have no designs on the future. We live out destiny just as all others."

"This, my Son, this I should have foreseen. When Love plays the fool, there is no end to the grief at hand."

"Ares and Hephaestos have long hated each other. Sooner or later, something of this magnitude would have occurred."

"Yet it was by my actions. That is what so thoroughly pains me." Aphrodite appeared more fragile than ever in a gown that matched the ever-changing sea shades of blue and green in her eyes. The color enhanced the foamy whiteness of her skin and pale hair, but brought out the pinched lines of distress on her face.

She shrugged off his arm and rose to pace before the open veranda that framed her beloved ocean. Wringing her hands, she moaned every now and then as a new transgression occurred to her.

"Mother, you blame yourself needlessly." Deimos followed her to the serene view of Cos. "You could not have known what was to happen. Perhaps, it was fated for some reason beyond that which we can see."

"You do not understand, Deimos." Aphrodite paused to meet his gaze. "I knew being with Hephaestos no longer served a purpose. Whatever was to come of our alliance was not the reason I stayed. It was not even born out of a desire to torment Ares. It was because I truly care for Hephaestos.

"There is something about him. My heart aches when I look at him and I am filled with compassion. He is a lost soul set adrift in a body that defies him. And he so longs to be included. She paused and moistened her lips. "Yet he is always apart. I cannot help but love him."

Her confession startled Deimos. There was nothing she could have said that was more perplexing than declaring love for the Forge god. He searched her face, hoping it was no more than guilt that made her want to believe there was more to her union with Hephaestos than what it truly was.

"That is not the way I understood it."

"No, of course not. You heard from those around me and not from my own lips." Aphrodite rolled her head from side to side, her long curls caressing her body as she moved.

"And how could any of them know differently when I, myself, did not?" She stared down at her unadorned fingers as if they were stained with filth. "I thought it no more than a game, albeit a dangerous one. I believed Hephaestos accepted my offer for what it was.

"I was honest when I went to him. I sought a child and no more. It was he who insisted upon the alliance. I thought, why not? Ares had given me a bitter pill to swallow and I believed he deserved such an insult.

"I should have said no. Hephaestos would still have bedded with me, for he could not turn away under any circumstances. He desired me too much."

Lifting her chin, she met her son's gaze without pretense. All manner of shields and mask were stripped away. What he saw was the brutal exposure of her emotional tides as they beat upon the shores of her conscience.

"And though I wanted a child, I wanted more to cause Ares pain. I acted rashly and without thought of any but myself. It is why Victory would not come to me. There is no victory in deception."

"You could not have foreseen this tragedy," Deimos insisted. "Though your power is beyond most, even Love cannot see other than what the Fates will allow."

"You are a noble and loyal son. Perhaps your father has done better by you than I ever expected." Her smile was wan. "Or perhaps it is just you and your goodness, in spite of your parents."

"I am made of many lessons, the best being that once something is done, it cannot be undone. We can only go forward."

"A worthy sentiment, but how can I go forward knowing Hephaestos' greatest fear is humiliation under the eyes of those whom he considers to better him. Humiliation by my hand.

"And, as if he has not suffered enough, I do not even yet know what punishment will come his way for this act. Whatever it is, it is certain to worsen his pain."

She looked away from Deimos then, towards the great expanse of ocean beyond her window. The surf rolling against the white sand with its ever-present noise seemed insignificant next to the low moan that came from Aphrodite's throat. "And Ares. I fear he will not survive. I cannot live without him."

"He could he be mortally wounded?" Deimos reeled with this news, unable to comprehend such a thing. "It is not possible."

"It should not be possible, but it is," mourned Aphrodite. "Even now, he lies in a stupor at Olympus with only the barest breath left in him."

"Why are you not at his side?"

"Shame chains me to Cos, for I cannot face any of the Ages now. Further, Hera forbids my presence and I have no fight left to argue."

"Not even for Ares' sake?"

"He does not know who sits beside him."

"He is truly that far gone?"

Aphrodite took her son's hand between her own, grateful for the warmth and solidity of his flesh. She clung to him for a moment with eyes closed and then spoke in a choked voice. "You must go now to your grandmother. Hera has bidden you to come at once and I fear the worst."

She kissed his fingers. "You no longer owe me allegiance but must follow your own destiny."

"What do you mean?"

"You were mine to keep in exchange for Anteros."

"Yes, that." Deimos shrugged, for he had never taken her whim with any seriousness. "But what else do you speak of?"

"Fate," she whispered. "Go now, Beloved Son, and see to your father's house. And when you can, send Anteros back to me."

There was no joy at Olympus, for though Ares was not well liked, there was no one who wished him dead. There was no one who thought War could be destroyed, and therein lay the biggest fear of the immortals.

If the brutal and bloodthirsty Ares could be slain, then all were at risk. Somber faces greeted Deimos upon his arrival and the whispers followed him through the halls of his grandparent's palace.

"So much like his father, with blood on his hands."

"He strides with his father's wicked purpose."

"There, that cruelly beautiful face, just like Ares."

"I would think it was the Warmonger, if I did not know."

"He follows in his father's evil footsteps."

To them, Deimos wanted to rage, "You judge but you do not know."

He wanted to release all the power behind Terror and let them shrink back, weak and wilting beneath the full impact of that which was not War, but War's son.

When he reached the chambers that held Ares, he found himself trembling. The vicious thoughts, along with the desire to strike out, left him feeling oppressed and sickened, as if he carried the weight of a mountain upon his shoulders. The knot in his gut grew harder as he approached Hera and his breath grew strained.

His grandmother met him at the entrance with a quick embrace and a touch of her cool lips to his cheek. Tall and imposing, full-bodied and gifted as the staunch guardian of hearth and home, Hera was not easily given to emotions, but there, within the depths of her golden eyes, Deimos saw raw grief.

"Come, Child, view your father."

Deimos hung back, panicked. "I cannot."

"You have seen Death countless times, why now do you fear him?"

"He is not...?"

"Hades' son, Thanatos, hovers near, yet has not been able to claim Ares. I keep Bitter Death at bay with my threats, but how long before Thanatos defies even me?"

Hera bowed her head and the coronet of brown braids caught the lamplight, setting off golden strands as if the sun was laced into her hair. She wore no circlet other than that, and was dressed in a simple chiton made of dark blue linen that hung straight to the floor. Her waist was corded with a string of pearls, her feet encased in delicate slippers.

Her beauty was impeccable even in her pain.

The only thing out of place was the haunted expression in her eyes, though her firm grip belied it. Hera took him by the elbow and led him to an inner room, throwing open the door with a forceful thud.

Anyone asleep would have jumped at the sudden noise, but the body upon the bier did not move. Ares lay silent and gray, naked save for the white sheet covering him to the waist. There was only the shallowest rise and fall of his chest to show any life remained.

Deimos stared at his father. He was shorn of his beard and long hair, leaving him exposed, as if being hairless him stripped of his defenses and all his secrets were laid bare. He appeared now as no more than a youth, innocent in his sleep, unencumbered by the burdens of war and the mortal world that worshipped him.

"Why?" He touched his own clean-shaven jaw and turned a stricken gaze to his grandmother. "He would not be pleased."

"No, but for once, he cannot argue with me." Her lips turned up at the corners in a grimace meant to be a smile.

"Whatever Ares is to the world, he is still my son. I could not bear to look at him in the guise of a warrior." She waved a graceful hand toward three women in white hovering near the raised dais. "I bid them shear it off and be damned later."

"He will be angry."

"Good. I will gladly listen to him rant." Hera bent over Ares and stroked his hair. He did not even twitch at her touch. "He was not always angry, you know. When he was a child, he was very different."

"It is hard to imagine him as a child, let alone different than I have known him."

"As hard as it was for him to imagine me as a new bride, bedazzled by his father and forgiving of every indiscretion."

Bitterness edged in before she swallowed and went on. "It is difficult for children to see their parents in any way other than what we are now. Remember that, Deimos, when your offspring proclaim their hatred for you."

"He does not hate you." Biting down on his lip, Deimos went silent.

"No, he does not, but he hates his father and declines to make peace."

"Grandfather's disapproval is well known, complicated by his demands upon Ares to be something he is not."

To this, Hera chuckled. "I see Ares has schooled you well in his ways. You perfectly mimic him."

In a rush, Deimos saw the very thing everyone commented upon. He saw how much he resembled his father, both in word and appearance. He could not tear his gaze from that visage of himself, etched in the pallor of death. And even yet he could not believe he looked upon Ares, the mighty warrior, fallen to one such as Hephaestos.

A sob rose up and Deimos clamped his lips together to stifle it. With a quiet word from Hera, those who attended Ares retreated to a far corner of the room, nearest the fire burning in the hearth. The Moerae, those old women who were also called the Fates, huddled with their backs to the bier, muttering amongst themselves.

"What do they say?"

"They say there is no change."

Blinking rapidly, Deimos stared at Hera.

"There is no change," she repeated.

"Yet, he lives."

"He breathes. We do not know if he will ever truly live again, though he may never fade into the Shadowland either."

"Neither dead nor alive?" Revulsion colored Deimos' words. "How could this have happened?"

"Aphrodite did not tell you?" There was scarce concealed contempt in Hera's tone. "Hephaestos took his revenge through Cedalion and a poisoned dagger. Had Cedalion's aim been truer, Ares would now reside with Hades.

"But Cedalion missed his heart by a slim measure. A mere slash he could recover from, but the poison." Hera inhaled with deliberate slowness then expelled the air before going on. "The poison's intent was to cause paralysis. Had it entered his heart, it would no longer beat. As it was, in Cedalion's haste, the blade slid between Ares' ribs and hit lung, causing suffocation."

She gestured at the wound in Ares' side. It was covered with a bandage but was stained with nearly black blood.

"The wound continues to ooze. It refuses to heal even the smallest amount, no matter what healing measures are applied."

Hera raised a fist to her forehead, grinding her knuckles into the unlined skin. Her grief was thick in the room. For a moment she was silent and then went on without wavering.

"But Ares is strong, stronger than any knew. In spite of the poison, he draws breath still, though very little, it is enough to keep him between worlds."

"If he dies, I will kill them both," gritted Deimos between his teeth. "I swear it. Father, do you hear me?"

He gripped Ares' fingers scarce noticing how cold the hand was as it lay in his. "Hear me, Father, you will not go unavenged. I will bury Amason in Hephaestos if you leave."

"Do not say such a thing, I beg you." Hera turned away from the bier to wipe away a tear. "Hephaestos is also my son."

"I do not care. They will both die if Ares passes from this world."

"No, Deimos. For now, revenge is not to be yours. You must carry on." Clamping a strong hand around his arm, Hera drew Deimos away from Ares.

"What do you mean?"

"The Mantle of War now belongs to you."

"I do not understand."

"You assume the House of War until Ares is recovered." She lifted her shoulders. "If he dies, you become War."

"I cannot," Deimos gasped. "I will not."

"You have no choice. It is already decided."

"By whom?" Casting a desperate glance back at Ares, Deimos shook his head. "Do they give up so easily on him? Am I not even allowed to speak? They cannot force me to this."

But he knew they could, for the Council of Ages combined together was a formidable power and he had not the strength to resist.

"I do not want the Mantle. If Ares fades, then let War go with him."

Hera watched him with sad eyes. "The mortal world will not allow War to recede."

"Then Ares must recover."

"Deimos, hear me out. We are not born wearing the mantles of our power. You know this well. We come into this life willingly, knowing what will be asked of us. Until now we assumed that if one of us should pass through the portal of true death, we would take our power with us. No one has gone before, save for the giants, so we did not know this could happen."

She paused to press a square of linen to her nose. "We did not understand that the power remains regardless of our passing. Without Ares to control it, War will become a monstrous thing, devouring all in its path. The mortals fight now without conscience, what will happen if there is no one to call them into account? You are our best hope."

"I will not agree to this." Deimos began to pace. When he realized it was the same pattern Ares always walked, he forced himself to stand still. "I will not do this."

"It has already been done. Do you not feel it?"

Deimos closed his eyes and gathered himself into the darkness within. Yes, there was a difference. He felt it before arriving at Olympus. He felt it now, bearing down on him, growing bigger, the aggression, the anger, the resentment. The desire to kill.

"No. No, I am Terror, and those things are also part of me. This coercion will not work."

"There is nothing else to be done here. Ares rests in the hands of the Moerae. The Fates will decide if he lives or dies." Hera gave her grandson a gentle shake. "Return to Athos, Deimos, take up the reins of War and when the Council calls, do not ignore them."

Deimos sat upon the throne of War in the altar room at Athos and wept. He held his hands over his face, not to muffle his desolate moans, but to shut out the sights around him. He sought the familiarity of this room because it was where Ares spent much of his time, only to discover it, too, was changed.

Everything Ares had been was gone, wiped away as if someone knew Ares himself would be destroyed.

All his life, Deimos both dreaded and embraced that which was his father. He fought Ares, but also accepted him as law. He gave him grudging respect, but silently mocked him. He hated what Ares was and also knew that he, Deimos, was born from the same cast. He was the right hand of War.

And now, Ares was neither dead nor alive and the throne waited for him.

"Deimos?"

Anteros emerged from the side doorway, surprising him. Deimos scrambled from the throne as if he had been caught in a traitorous act.

"Deimos, what is wrong? I heard an odd noise in here. "

"Nothing. You heard nothing." Deimos wiped his eyes with his sleeve, and then coughed. "It is nothing."

"You look distraught, Brother, and I think here." Anteros placed his hand over his breast. "Something is wrong."

"What is wrong is this." He gestured toward the pristine clean chamber. "What have you done? Ares will be very angry."

Anteros touched the ragged edges of what was left of his hair. "I have already discovered how attached he was to the disgusting things that once lay upon that shrine."

Deimos' gaze followed Anteros fingers. "What has been done to you? You appear as sheep that has been sheared by a one-handed herder."

"It will be restored soon enough." Biting his bottom lip, Anteros reflected upon the altar. "Not so with that. I have been commanded to return it to its prior state. I have spent days trying to put this chamber right and still cannot."

"Do not worry yourself with it." Head tilted to one side, Deimos stared at the transformation. "I believe it looks better. It certainly smells better."

"Indeed, but the demand has been made to restore it to its former splendor."

Raising his palm in the air, Deimos shook his head. "It is not necessary."

"But I must."

"No. Leave it as it is. I have come to tell you that you are released from your bondage to War and may return home."

"That is Ares' command?"

"Yes." Sinking to one of the steps leading to the throne, Deimos turned his gaze to his twin. "No. It is my command. My request." Weary to the bone, he supported his head with his hands and told Anteros what had taken place.

"Mercy." Anteros sat next to him.

"Yes, and it would be well for you to go to our mother's side, for she needs you."

"But what of you? I do not wish to leave you alone with this burden."

Bleary-eyed, Deimos lifted his chin. "There is naught to be done about it. Go where you can do some good."

"I will do as you bid." Anteros repeatedly laced and unlaced his fingers. "Do not make jest of what I now tell you. I regret that I must leave, however, when Ares awakens and demands my presence, I will return."

"Why? I seek to escape and know I never can, yet you want to return."

"I tire of my simple life. It is too easy."

"So you would join the ranks of War for the challenge?"

"I am Response. I reply, I react, but I do not initiate. Terror - you cause the uproar. I elicit an answer to the uproar. My role in Love's Realm is to echo sentiment, to invoke an answer when confronted with emotion.

"In the wake of Love, there are many who are devastated, left without a way to respond to the pain in their hearts." Anteros touched his chin with his forefinger. "And then there are the ones who are so deeply smitten they cannot find words to describe the swelling up inside or outside. It is Response they look to for help."

"It is a noble path, Brother, and does not sound either simple or easy to me."

"Perhaps it is not but, still, I would relish the change. I want to ride into battle. I want to know what it feels like to have blood on my hands."

"You have been here too long, Anteros, when Love's Response wishes to invoke violence."

The two brothers stared at each other, one pale and one dark, both stricken.

"Violence and love." Anteros was scarce able to speak.

"Perhaps you are right. I will go now to Cos."

Deimos nodded. "We will speak again, soon, but do not tell our mother what has become of me, only that Ares still lives."

"She will hear of it, Deimos. Would it not be better if I told her?"

"I can no longer judge what is best and what is not. Do what you will."

"And you? Will you stay here all alone, waiting?"

"There is nowhere else for me but here." Deimos shuddered at the thought of Olympus. "There is one happy thought amongst all this desolation. Phobos has been freed from the monolith and he is at Cos, where he belongs."

"Truth?" A grin split Anteros' face. "You pulled Phobos from that beast?"

"Not I. The boy did it himself. Go to him and to Aphrodite and any other that calls to you."

"You speak now of Euphrosyne." Sighing, Anteros stood. "That is another tale and I do not yet know the end to it. I bid you farewell, Deimos, with hope all will be well when next we meet."

Would all be well? Deimos pondered this as he walked the empty corridors of Athos, wondering when that might be. Never, if he truly was to be War. He had watched Ares' torment too long to fool himself into believing there would ever be calm. When was the last time he felt at peace?

He stood in the doorway to Ares' private quarters, reluctant to enter. Sunlight tried to creep between the bolted outer doors with little luck, leaving the room dark and cool. Even without light, he was aware that Amason hung above the yawning hearth, calling to him, but he would not go to it.

"Not yet," he mumbled. "I am not yet ready to accept this talisman of War. "Wait, Amason, for your true master. I believe he will return."

The sword glinted even in the darkness, eager to be taken from its place upon the wall. Turning his back to the blade, Deimos sought to retreat. He was not comfortable in those chambers and would never take them as his own, regardless of Ares' fate.

A swatch of cloth caught his eye. A cloak hung over the back of a chair. He reached for it and when his fingers brushed the soft wool, he knew it belonged to Niala.

The only one he had ever felt love for and she, too, was out of his reach. On quiet feet, he closed the door to his father's quarters and left his thoughts of Niala behind.

How did it come to be that all things known to him were chaos? Too weary to think any longer, Deimos fell into his own bed and was instantly asleep.

TWENTY-SIX

From his seat in the gardens, Hattusilis listened to the merriment echo into the valley from the plateau. He sat alone with a single guard left to watch over him. And that one also listened, with intense longing to join the celebration. Hattusilis could feel the man's eagerness and see the way he leaned forward as if he would project himself into the midst of the people on the ridge.

Hattusilis felt the draw. It reached down like a giant hand urging him to be part of the celebration, but he would not allow himself to be carried up the steep path. Walking on his own was out of the question, for he could scarce get from his quarters to the gardens without help.

Pallin was disappointed. She wanted him there. He was touched by her desire, yet not even for her would he degrade himself and be carried. Zan said they could make a mobile chair, born by four soldiers, and he could ascend to the mount as a king should, on the shoulders of his men. Hattusilis refused. There was another reason he would not voice, one for which he was ashamed.

He was afraid. Since Niala's return, there were too many strange happenings. Before, he managed to put aside most of his worries and focus on regaining his health. On the heels of her arrival, it seemed all those terrors came rushing back. She called them phantoms, ghosts of the restless dead, those killed during the invasion.

Those specters did not explain the serpentine sensations that continually crawled over him..

At this longest day of the year ritual, the priestess pledged she would release that one as well, the one named Kulika. Hattusilis prayed it was true for he could scarce stand any more of it.

The serpent haunted him day and night, making sleep impossible. Its demands were beyond him, beyond anything he could offer to satiate the spirit riding him. He prayed she could put an end to this thing that plagued him. Hattusilis was afraid of it and could not control his inner turmoil long enough to attend the ceremony.

Not that he really wanted to. It was foreign, just like the first one in the cave, hidden away, bowing before a goddess who offered words. Just words. His god gave them more than that. His god gave them strength and courage. His god gave them victory. No words to mince, no ideas to propose. It was blood and bone, winner takes all.

That was Teshub. Hattusilis did not understand the goddess of these people. She did nothing to help them, nothing to stop the destruction, nothing to ease their pain, and still they worshiped her. Still they honored her.

Shaking his head, Hattusilis glanced upward. The sounds of gaiety continued as they had all evening. Feasting, dancing, shouts of laughter and music, many drums and high-pitched flutes joined with the stringed instruments from the Steppelands. His men celebrated with the townspeople, all save for the guards on duty and his lone companion who watched with lips parted and eyes alight with vicarious enjoyment.

Hattusilis sat and listened until the sun sank below the backside of the plateau. Dusk settled and the noise dimmed. As nightfall wrapped over Najahmara, the people fell silent along with the music. All that could be heard were the insects buzzing and chirping. Not even the wind stirred in the trees.

"What are they doing?" The guard, whose name escaped Hattusilis, spoke in a whisper as if he would disturb the celebration.

"I do not know." Hattusilis kept his tone bored but, in truth, he was anxious. What manner of mischief was this priestess up to now with his gentle Pallin beside her?

He disapproved of Pallin's involvement. She was far too pregnant to ascend to the top, far too close to birthing to risk injury, but she would not listen. She insisted on doing as she pleased.

When full darkness cloaked the valley, a great column of orange fire shot toward the sky. Hattusilis jerked with frantic fear and lurched to his feet. She had set fire to the entire plateau and all would perish. He clutched at the man beside him, shouting incoherent orders to get help, but all help was above them, trapped by the evil hand of this priestess.

"My King. Sire, it is alright. They light the bonfire, that is all." The soldier pressed Hattusilis back into his seat. "It is no more than the dry wood taking hold."

Shaking, Hattusilis dropped back into his chair. "Are you certain? I have heard the fire that destroyed our men described the same."

"I saw it myself this morning, the way it was stacked high to create such flames. There, you see, it has died down and all that is left is the glow of a normal fire."

"Yes. Yes, I see now." Sweating, Hattusilis shifted his weight. "Everyone is alright?"

"They are fine."

"Yes." Hattusilis nodded, cursing himself for his cowardice. His fear for Pallin magnified tenfold as he waited for her to return from the celebration.

Niala watched the faces of the people as flames streaked upward to meet the stars. They stood at solemn attention, ten deep around the wide circle, soldiers and followers mingling with natives of Najahmara, with scarce a difference in their sad expressions. Many were wet with tears, others stood dry-eyed, but all had offered their sacred wounds as kindling for the fire.

All but her. She was not ready to relinquish her pain.

Those who assembled this night deserved solace and healing, for none of it was of their making. Even the soldiers who did the bidding of their king. It was the only life they knew, the way they were taught. None of them created the tragedy, but all were caught up in the losses. Grief was thick in the air as people watched their pain go up in flames.

The day had begun with a gathering below, with a prayer and a blessing to find something that would represent release. They were to find and hold this symbol close to them, pass to it the suffering and anguish within, and then place it on the unlit fire sometime during the evening feast.

Niala held sacred vigil upon the plateau the entire day. She watched as familiar faces laid belongings upon the woodpile. She watched as those she did not know hesitated and then added to the pyre. She watched the healing begin and saw a community coalesce. That which had been torn apart was now coming together in a dance for both living and dead.

After this night, they would be bound to each other in a shared vision of Najahmara. After this night, there would be no outsiders, for they would all become a part of the next in an endless chain of humankind.

The pyre held a curious assortment of offerings. Ornate wooden shields and plain sticks laid side by side. Remnants of carved toys and statues were next to simple packets of herbs. Torn clothing and partially burned belongings next to dried flowers. Fresh flowers and boughs of tender green leaves lay atop bits of charred pottery and broken beads in ever growing layers. There were things that held no meaning other than represented to the one who placed it. The simplest things spoke louder than any words ever could.

Niala was overwhelmed by it all for their grief mirrored her own. Their guilt was written upon her soul, their desire to put it in the past and release the restless spirits was her balm. The ever-growing tide of mortal strength gave her some small sense of peace and the possibility that victory could be had over this unseen enemy.

There was no room for regret, no place for remorse. This was a time of healing. Those were Niala's words as she spoke to the grave faces before her.

"As the fire burns away our losses and returns to Beloved Earth the remains of those we treasured most in life, let us say goodbye and wish them safe journeys."

Eyes shiny with unshed tears, Jahmed spoke next. "Be they friend or foe, I offer Gaea's blessing that they find peace, and those of us who stay behind find fellowship."

"Push beyond our pain, for rebirth awaits us." Pallin stepped forward and held out her hands. "Let us create a new life together, celebrate our differences, and bring forth unity."

Niala nodded, swallowing past the ache in her throat. "Our loved ones, our friends and family, our comrades and companions, they hover nearby and wish us well. It is time for us to release their spirits so they may go forward. Speak out and tell them good-bye. Give them joy with your parting words."

A deep well of silence lasted for long moments before a murmur began. Lips moved with prayers of comfort, offerings of wit and wisdom laced with sorrow. It started low and grew in volume as more joined. It became a roar of whoops and shouts, of screams, of wails and weeping, of laughter and tears. Words poured out in a continuous stream of emotion, rolling wave upon wave through the crowd.

Niala stood in stoic silence, having spoken only two words, "Farewell Seire."

She could do no more for guilt ripped at her heart and the release of souls worsened the hurt. The voices around her joined together to make one, ascending into a chant of magnificent proportions that reached up to stroke the heavens.

In wrenching response, Niala felt a gentle kiss upon her cheek. A feather-light brush of lips and a sighing whisper. *There is no end to the circle, Niala. No end.*

A dry bony hand slipped into hers and squeezed.

Affectionate, cackling laughter followed. Other hands caressed her face, her arms, her fingers and Niala knew each touch. She wept as each one said goodbye, each offering assurance and forgiveness.

And last, an old soul, an old friend, an old love kissed her lips and said, "Forgive yourself."

"Layla." Niala smiled. "My sweet Layla."

And then they were gone, each to a different destiny. Niala shuddered in abject and open grief, the pain of knowing she lived and they did not. She felt as if she would collapse and never recover until a familiar surge of energy wrapped around her ankles.

It flowed up her legs to her thighs, passed through her base and into the trunk of her body. It burst over her head in a shimmering fall, blurring her vision, as if she looked out from behind a curtain of water. The torchlight became bright specks doubled, tripled by the power flowing around her and the earth spun madly.

The babe inside her began a frantic churning as the energy pulsed through its tiny body, fed to it from her own. Somewhere in her mind, pain registered, but was fast dismissed, as the force grew stronger, lifting her upwards. She had no time to suppress her own consciousness for her spark was caught up into the whirling light, expanding and intermingling with that of the Great Mother.

Gaea took her.

There was naught for Niala to do but give herself and the child over and let Gaea have her way. She bore no fright from it, but was filled with ecstatic joy as relief flooded through her. The world was no longer contained within her physical body, but reached out to the stars and the moon, to wind and fire and water, and finally, to those who stood before her.

Gaea fully rose into Niala and looked through her eyes and heard the night through her ears. She threw her head back and sucked in the fresh cool air. She felt the tingling of flesh over bone, felt blood pounding within her heart. She felt alive.

Niala's robe slid to the ground and she stepped over it as she began to sway. Her breasts felt heavy, her belly hugely expanded, her body ready to give birth. Gaea rejoiced and thanked Niala for bringing forth this child into her, for Gaea had missed the fullness, the satiation, the expectation of pregnancy.

Gaea began to dance. Oh, how she delighted in moving!

Fingers swirled through the air, touching the breezes and reaching for the tiny sparks that shot from the fires around her. Gaea's feet traced the patterns of the earth beneath them, toes digging into dirt and dust and the cool damp grasses. She danced in slow sensuous circles, dipping, twirling around and around as the earth moves through the sky.

She stretched her arms up with invitation to her mate, Kulika, the Blue Serpent who surrounds the Earth, who was now shrouded by Nut, the Night Sky, in her sparkling dark glory.

Gaea began to sing of her love in high, piercing notes that brought many to tears. She sang of missing him, of her loneliness, of their creation and how they were parted.

She sang on and on, twirled on and on, searching for him in the faces before her. Who would hold the spirit of Kulika? Who would come dance with her while she was released from her crushing form to play upon the surface?

All men were mesmerized by what they saw. Every man stepped forward with an expectation they did not understand, breathless, waiting for one to be chosen.

Through the eyes of the priestess, Gaea searched for the One, and when she did not see him, she was giddy with anger, for it seemed Kulika scorned her in her moment of glory. She stamped her foot and tossed her hair. He would come to her, Kulika would come to her. She would make him come to her.

There was only one strong enough for her demands. "Deimos," Gaea called. "Deeeiiimmmosss! Come to me."

Jahmed stared at Niala in stunned surprise as the gown slipped from her shoulders and she began to sway back and forth. "It is Gaea," she said to Pallin in an undertone. "Mercy on us, look at the faces of those foreign ones, they cannot believe their eyes."

Pallin stared, too, in transfixed. "Stop her, Jahmed, stop her. We cannot let this go on, you know what will happen next."

"I cannot stop Gaea, nor can you."

"Oh, no, she calls to Deimos. Not Deimos," Pallin moaned and clutched her belly. "Is he here? I have not seen him. Is he here?"

"I do not think so," Jahmed murmured. "But I wager he will be soon enough."

"He will not answer the call of Earth, will he?" Pallin turned around scanning the crowd. In the dim torchlight she could not distinguish one from another. "He does not respond to Earth, only to War, not to Gaea."

"He does not, does he?" Jahmed gripped Pallin's arm and pointed toward the fire. Deimos had appeared on the opposite side of the flames, a confused scowl on his handsome face.

Pallin saw him and felt an instant stab of pain in her lower belly. The dull cramps had been with her all day though she chose to ignore them. As the evening wore on, the pains had worsened. Now, upon sight of Deimos, she was gripped with an excruciating spasm that doubled her over.

"What is it?" Ajah bounced on her toes, anxiety creasing her forehead. "What is happening? What should we do?"

"Look." Jahmed felt a tingle of fear slide down her back as the men of Hattusilis' legion recognized Deimos. There was an immediate surge of interest as men slapped each other on the back in congratulations as one of their own was selected. A few bawdy words were exchanged.

"Kulika cannot have him," Pallin cried. "He cannot be with

Niala." Another pain brought a gasp from her lips as she watched the struggle come over Deimos.

They all could feel the swell of energy as Deimos fought Kulika for control and it appeared Deimos would win. Pallin exhaled in relief only to see a strange expression cross Deimos' face and an air of acceptance settle over him.

"No," she moaned, the pain twisting in her belly again. "Not Deimos."

A gush of water slid down Pallin's legs and wet the front of her gown. Inside, it felt as if a hot coal was applied to her womb.

"Jahmed." Her voice was pinched with pain. "Jahmed, something is wrong."

"Ahh," Jahmed grimaced. "Your babe wants to see the morning light." She placed her hand on Pallin's belly, feeling the hardened ball of a child preparing for birth. "Ajah, call Zan over. He must take Pallin back to the temple right away."

"Oh, it hurts, it hurts so much." Pallin staggered as Zan rushed to her side and lifted her into his arms.

"Be strong, Sister. The first is always the hardest. Ajah, you stay here."

The girl froze in her tracks. She had been about to follow the big man down the pathway. "But she needs one of us to assist."

"Send one of the younger girls. You must stay here and help get everyone off the plateau."

"But why? They seem to enjoy this display."

Jahmed glanced over her shoulder to see Gaea and Kulika squaring off. "It will not be pretty for it appears they argue."

Kulika sprang forth from his hiding place in the mortal world the moment Deimos gave in. He exulted in the fine body, with arms to hold his beloved Earth and legs to stand upon. He felt the stirrings of sex, the rising of desire. He was overjoyed as he writhed with the passion of one who protects Earth.

Consumed with ecstasy, Kulika went to Gaea with the clear intent to mate.

With hands on her hips, Gaea tossed her hair and began to walk in measured steps. When Kulika advanced, she held out one hand to stop him, glaring with contemptuous wrath. "You denied me."

"I am here, now." Kulika began to shed the clothing that bound him. He did not like the feel of cloth against skin, of leather tightly binding feet and legs. He wanted the wind to caress him, to cool the sweat gathered beneath his garments. He wanted his sex to be released, for Gaea to be reminded of the pleasures he could bring her with this body.

An outstanding body, one fit for Sky to inhabit. It was strong and well built, different from any other he had taken. This one belonged to an immortal, one who could carry his purpose, who could bear the strain and last a very long time. Kulika approved of Gaea's choice as the last piece of clothing fell away. Highlighted by the shooting flames, he stood naked and erect.

Gaea paused to stare at him, her tongue flicking out to wet her lips. Kulika's thick shaft strained forward, instinctively seeking her cave, as if their two parts would have their way in spite of her anger.

No. She braced herself, refusing to yield. "You did not call me to join you."

"I have never been brought forth without you." Kulika advanced toward her, his hips rocking with a hint of his prowess.

"You did not invoke me to lie with you." Gaea's voice was cold, an ice-drenched forest of danger as she held him at bay.

"I was caught up in the moment."

"You chose another."

"I have never had choice."

"And when you did, you took a mortal without me." The plateau shuddered with Gaea's wrath. "You brought terror and death to my worshippers and failed to invoke me to heal their wounds. You did not return to your realm but stayed on to toy with them. How dare you do this?"

"They are mine as well," Kulika answered with heat. The starlit sky darkened with a gathering storm. "Though you always claim them as yours alone."

"I gave birth to them. They live upon my body, harvest my bounty. They belong to me."

The ground shook and the single white stone swayed.

"I am their father, I watch over them and keep them safe. They, too, belong to me."

The heavens rumbled and lightening streaked across the sky. Screams of fright rose from the crowd as they stared at Gaea and Kulika in fascinated uncertainty.

"Quickly, quickly, we must get the crowd down the path," Jahmed called to Ajah. "Now, before things become worse."

"The folk do not listen," Ajah cried. "They are enthralled and will not go. Can you not intervene?"

"With Gaea and Kulika?" Jahmed shook her head, throwing her braids all about her face. "Never. They must sort this out between them."

"But what of Niala?"

"We must trust she will be alright. Let us get all these others away before for they are injured."

Huge drops of rain began to splatter across the plateau as the winds howled around them. Gaea and Kulika continued to rail at each other, first accusing and then demanding. Jahmed pushed people toward the closest path. Ajah followed suit from the other end, propelling even the biggest men to set their feet downward.

"You betrayed me." Gaea shrieked and the soil cracked beneath her feet.

"I worship you." Kulika was close enough to catch her flailing hands. "I reacted with human emotion. I am not used to such things."

"You did not call me." The hurt reflected in her eyes cut across the brown depths like a great canyon. "You did not call me."

"Forgive me." Kulika held Gaea with tenderness, his hands following the abundance of her breasts and belly to her rounded hips, pressing her as close as he could. As close as she would let him. "I lingered too long in the mortal world and forgot what was important."

Gaea sighed as she looked into the eyes of her love. "You must return to your realm."

"I will, Beloved, for I am your protector. I should not have abandoned my place over you. Forgive me." His lips touched hers in a sweet caress.

Gaea sighed again and the grasses sighed in compliment. The earth ceased trembling as she leaned into him. "I forgive you."

The sky cleared and the stars shone with more brilliance than before. Kulika and Gaea began to dance around the fire, moving as one, locked together in the eternal exchange of love between Earth and Sky.

As if in a dream, they wove between the torches, around and around the fire, with lingering touches and languid motions. There was no need to rush, for they were once again in each other's arms.

Deimos had no idea when he and Niala drifted into the shadow of the stone marker. He remembered little as it was. He felt the impact of Kulika's spirit as it descended into him. He recalled how the world became slanted and his focus sharpened.

He knew how he caught every tiny movement, even the slightest of breaths and how his body burned as if on fire. He was aware his clothes were too confining and he tore them off to dance naked around the fire, his body lithe and sweating as the red and gold flames danced with them.

The rest was dim in his mind. He knew not how long they spent before the fire, only that he awoke to himself as they were in the throes of love behind the tall white stone. They fell upon each other as if starved, driven by Gaea and Kulika, the two that held them in thrall.

Their hunger rose above mortal desires into the patterns of universal creation. Deimos, who longed madly for Niala, allowed his lust to be wrapped within that of Kulika's. Their lovemaking was not gentle.

Two spirits brought together in flesh. The same who brought forth the rivers and mountains, the great deserts and grasslands, two who created all that any knew. Their lovemaking was cataclysmic. Deimos could do nothing to lessen their passion.

On his knees, he thrust into Niala one last time and awoke to her scream. It was a wrenching cry, not one of pleasure. Kulika's spirit fled as Deimos fell back, gasping for air. He passed a shaking hand across his wet brow, and called to her. "Niala, I am sorry."

She could not respond, for she fought nausea. Her gut heaved as the pain intensified. Something had torn inside her and she could scarce draw breath. Holding her belly, she knelt forward.

Deimos crawled to her and gripped her shoulder. "I am sorry, I am sorry. I could not stop."

Trembling, biting back the searing pain, Niala said, "It is not your fault."

"But I have hurt you."

"Not you, Kulika."

"How could this happen? I would never harm you."

"Do not blame yourself, it is their way," Niala panted. She tried to stand but her legs wobbled with weakness.

"Gaea, help her," Deimos begged.

"Gaea is no longer here."

Deimos held Niala up, looking about with panic in his eyes. When her knees buckled and she cried out again, he saw the dark fluid running down her legs and smearing across her feet. A puddle was fast growing in the grass. He did not have to be told it was blood, for he well knew what blood looked like, even in the dark. He knew what it smelled like.

"Mercy. You bleed."

"It is the babe. She forces herself out." Niala's voice was constricted and she gripped him with her nails as another twist of pain flailed her.

"Now?"

"Now. Let me down." She sank back to her knees, legs apart and squeezed his fingers as if she would rip them from his hands.

"Should there be so much blood?" Deimos knelt with her, slipping in the dark pool in front of her. Her eyes were wide, the whites reflecting starlight. She could barely speak.

"No, it is too much."

"Let me get Jahmed."

"Do not leave me alone." Another pain ripped through her and she vomited. Deimos dragged her away from the mess to a clean place on the grass, holding her up, feeling her swollen and straining belly against his. "I do not know what to do for you. Let me get your women."

Niala shrieked and the baby crowned between her legs. "Catch her."

Deimos reached out and the babe slid from her mother's body into his hands. She was so small, smaller than the width of his outspread fingers. He had never seen anything that tiny, that helpless, a diminutive wrinkled being covered in white slime and blood with open mouth and silent cry.

He stared in wonder at the child, captivated by the dark eyes that now opened and stared back at him, all the while reflecting what little light encroached on the shadows. Did she see him, truly, or was she blind as all newborn things? He wanted to believe she knew him for he felt there was a connection, something he could not explain. The babe made his heart beat faster.

"Deimos." Niala's voice was faint. She spoke just that, his name, before she collapsed onto her side. Tearing his gaze from the little one, Deimos saw Niala fall, saw the thick black stream as it poured from her body, saw the cord in his hands still tying the babe to her mother.

Niala faded before his eyes. "Niala, no, do not pass away from me, I beg you."

Niala's eyelids fluttered.

"The babe," she whispered.

Deimos held Niala's daughter, giving her sight of the infant. Weak tears rolled from her eyes. She could not even lift her hand to stroke the babe. The little one stared at her mother through the same dark gaze she had given Deimos and her tiny mouth opened in a cry.

"She is good?"

"Yes, she is well and good." Deimos laid the babe on the ground cradled against Niala's breast. "I must stop this blood or you will die."

Her breath came in short gasps. "You can do nothing to stop it."

"I will not let you die."

"Even you cannot stop what is fated." She pressed her lips to the wet wisps of hair on top of her daughter's head. "Take care of her."

"Always." Tears ran from his eyes. "Always."

Deimos tried with all his immortal soul to staunch the blood flowing from her body. He did his best to pin Niala to the earth, but she slipped away from him without another word. He knelt in her blood, next to her body, rocking back and forth in silence, cheeks wet with his grief.

The last of the folk finally descended from the plateau though it had taken much urging. The younger girls joined Ajah and Jahmed in herding people towards the valley, following along behind so no one remained. Jahmed and Ajah slumped on the ground, exhausted, looking toward the tall white stone at the opposite end of the clearing.

"How long should we wait," Ajah whispered.

"You do not need to speak softly, they cannot hear us." Jahmed wiped sweat from her brow with her sleeve. "They have no interest in us."

"But how long should we wait?"

Jahmed rolled her eyes. "Until they are finished."

"Should we just leave them?"

"Absolutely not. You must never leave Niala, or whoever is in aspect with the goddess, alone. She will need tending, for Gaea saps her strength, as well as other strange things that can happen afterward. No, we will wait as long as it takes."

Ajah sat in silence, listening to the insects chirp. Jahmed rested her chin in her palms, her elbows propped on her knees. After a few moments, she raised her head, cocking it to one side. "It is too quiet. I do not like this."

"Perhaps they have fallen asleep."

Nodding, Jahmed climbed to her feet. "Perhaps. If Gaea and Kulika left them, they might well fall asleep. I will check." She lifted her forefinger to her lips. "Shhh."

On tiptoe, Jahmed crept across the grass, skirted the fire circle, and approached the marker with caution. When she was just on the other side of it, straining to listen, she heard muffled sobs. In the same moment, a breeze brought the unmistakable bitter scent of blood wafting her way. Fear ignited like a torch and she flew around the corner, screaming for Ajah.

"Oh, mercy." Jahmed, eyes blinking rapidly, tried to take in what was before her. Blood, pools of blood, afterbirth, and the acrid scent of human waste. Niala lay crumpled on her side, unmoving. Deimos hunched over, rocking to and fro. It was his sobs she heard but he did not answer her frantic questions.

"What happened? Niala! Oh, my goddess, Niala." Jahmed could scarce speak as she dropped to her knees beside her. "Ajah, a torch. Hurry."

With great care, Jahmed rolled Niala onto her back. The blank, staring eyes reflected the flickering yellow torch as Ajah rounded the corner. With the light cast upon the ground, the sight was more gruesome. Niala looked toward Deimos and her child, as if even in death she watched over her newborn daughter. Between her legs was torn and bloody flesh, oozing still with slick dark clots. The cord was a knotted brown slash still attached to the birth pouch.

Ajah shrieked and began to weep, the light vibrating in her hands.

"The babe?" Jahmed scrabbled through the bloody grass on her hands and knees searching for the child. As she grabbed the cord and tugged, Deimos lifted his head.

His gaze was vacant, his mouth slack. When his lips moved, no words emitted. The babe was cupped in his hands, lying so silently Jahmed feared the child was dead.

"Does she live?" Tears fell from Jahmed's eyes so hard she could scarce see. "Dear Gaea, please say the babe lives."

Deimos gave a slight nod and closed his eyes. He brought the babe to his chest, one bloody hand covering the other.

Jahmed pulled a lace from the neck of her gown and tied off the cord with shaking fingers. From the belt at her hip, she drew the sharp knife she always carried and cut through the last connection the little one had with her lifeless mother.

Ajah sobbed as she cradled Niala's head in her lap, stroking her hair, oblivious to the damp smear of red she left behind. "He killed Niala. What are we to do?"

"The babe delivered too soon." Jahmed's voice was toneless. "It was the mating of Gaea and Kulika."

TWENTY-SEVEN

From the moment the child dropped into his hands, Deimos heard a buzzing in his head. It grew in volume, whirling about like a windstorm gathering force, carrying with it the demon voices of Aggression.

The noise roared down upon him, a raging, sucking current of all those who committed acts of violence in the name of War. Too late, he realized it was his father's mantle falling across his shoulders. The Mantle of War brought with it every horror that had ever tormented Ares.

Was Ares dead?

Deimos had a fleeting moment to wonder about his father's fate before the clamor consumed him. The voices grew to a numbing drone so that Deimos could no longer think for himself. He became Mortal Aggression's puppet, for he had not the strength to push it away.

The babe was silent as he clutched her to his chest in a grip so tight she could scarce breath. The women screamed at him to put the child down. Deimos could not hear their words. He heard only the raging pitch that joined with the rest in his head. He backed away from them, his right hand outstretched to keep them away.

"Give us the babe, Deimos. Please, give us the child. Do not hurt her, I beg you." Jahmed started forward only to be rebuffed with a hard shove. Stumbling, she fell to the ground, slipping in the wet grass.

"Please listen, Deimos. There is no more you can do. Let us care for Niala's child. Oh, please let me have her." Ajah held out her arms and took a step forward.

The voices battered at him without relief: 'Do not trust. Do not believe. Do not surrender. Fight. Fight. Do not trust. Do not believe. Do not surrender.'

"Please, Deimos, we are her people. Give her to us," Ajah begged, while Jahmed wept, "Do not hurt her, please, do not hurt her."

Deimos bumped into solid rock, felt it grind into his naked back, felt the pain, felt it tear his flesh. The burn felt good. For a moment, his head cleared and he could see the babe's tiny face with dark eyes so like his own. She gazed at him, calm and trusting. Yet the women cried for the child, they wanted to take her away from him.

No. He promised to always watch over Niala's daughter. He swore an oath to Niala.

A howl rose in his throat. He released it with a fierceness that stopped the women in their tracks. They cowered before him as the spirit of War truly descended into him.

The raging in his head hit a volcanic pitch and the bloodshed of an entire world streamed down upon him. Before he could do more harm, Deimos fled Najahmara, taking Niala's babe with him.

The silence of Athos was punctuated by the little one's shrill cries, yet they fell on deaf ears as Deimos paced around and around the altar to War. He had returned to his only sanctuary, to the throne that now belonged to him.

The child lay on the altar, upon the pristine white cloth, shivering from the cold. Her skin was taking on a faint bluish hue and her chin quivered as her wails grew strident. Deimos scarce noticed for the demon voices clamoring in his own head were deafening.

They were the shrieks and moans of countless acts of violence from stray curses to slit throats, from violation to disembowelment. He saw visions of death in ways he never imagined, cruelty that surpassed belief, and made even the heavens shudder.

Deimos could not breathe, he could not even weep, for it gripped him in a paralyzing hold. He raged at the four walls with kicks and guttural grunts, slamming his fists into the black stone. He tore down the red draperies. He hurled heavy urns to the far end, gaining a grim satisfaction as they shattered into pieces.

Amidst this came Strife, who should have relished the chaos, for it was in his realm that Deimos flailed, yet Eris stood to one side, staring in doubt. He had been called by War, but Ares was not present. The essence of War, the dominant overpowering spirit of War permeated the room, but Ares was not there.

"What madness is this?" Eris' gaze was drawn to the babe upon the altar. His pointed ears twitched at the thin cries as he leaned forward to better see the tiny wrinkled being laid out upon War's altar.

Her skin was translucent, marred only by the ugly brown cord that came from her belly. Her head was covered with matted reddish wisps of hair that curled around perfect shell-like ears. Her chin quivered as she screamed her unhappiness, wrinkling a tiny nose and forehead and pulling down the corners of her small mouth.

Eris was fascinated by the creature, having never been so close to such a thing before. Her howls were loud for one so small, and she threw her teeny curled fists and feet in the air as if to conjure up a cyclone.

"Deimos, what is this?" Eris crept closer, keeping an eye upon his brother, for Deimos paced wildly about the room, swinging his fists as if he fought off a thousand legions.

"Deimos, what do you do? Why has Ares called us?"

"He has not called you," Deimos panted, eyes wild. "Why do you come here?"

"War has sent out a command to appear and I answer." Eris was nigh to the altar. He reached one tentative finger towards the child. He touched her waving fist and her tiny cold fingers wrapped around his. His mouth rounded in surprise and swift pleasure.

"Who is this and why does she lie upon War's altar? What are you going to do with her?" Eris' eyes grew big as he pondered this for a moment. For what happened on this altar, but sacrifice?

"Arrgh." Deimos lashed out at his brother. "Go away, Eris, for Ares has no need of you."

"What is wrong with you? Where is Ares?"

"Ares is no more. War has descended upon me, and I am gripped with its madness."

Eris blinked, withdrawing his finger from the babe's grip. "This cannot be true."

"It is true. So true, though I wish it were not." Deimos' face twisted in torment. "Poisoned by Hephaestos and the dwarf Cedalion. Now I have received his mantle, though not by my choice."

"You have become War?" Eris stared, eyes huge. "But how? Does this mean Ares is dead?"

"I do not know what it means, only that his torture is now mine. I walk in his footsteps and bear his burdens. But lo, Brother, I am not as strong as Ares and I cannot take this lunacy." Deimos covered his head with his arms and stumbled from the altar.

"I do not understand what has happened here." Holding out both hands, Eris waved at Deimos. "But you must gird yourself, for soon the hordes arrive. I am not the only one who has been summoned."

"No, I do not want the minions of War snapping at my heels. Turn them away."

"I cannot, for you know I have no such power. You have called them. You who must direct them."

"I cannot."

"You must, for they will scatter out of control if you do not. Once word of Ares - once word that he is no longer in power is spread, his realm will shatter and all will do as they please."

As Eris considered the possibilities, he grew agitated. "Brother, you must take control."

"I do not know how." Deimos' eyes dilated with fear.

"Where is Amason? The sword will give you some sense of what you must do. And also…." Eris eyed his brother's nakedness. "You must clothe yourself in battle arraignment. Hurry, for they fast approach."

"Yes. Yes. And Amason." Deimos spoke more to himself than knew Eris. He knew his brother was right, for the air was beginning to roil with immortal energy. "Amason!"

None was more surprised than he when the sword came to him

with swift speed. It appeared in his hand, its leather grip fit perfectly to his hand. As his fingers wrapped around it, confidence built. He could feel its cold light filtering into him, cold feminine light. He had but a moment to savor this revelation before the fire that had forged the great blade flowed through his fingertips.

With Amason's glory, she brought the siren song of bloodshed and gory battle. Deimos sagged at the knees with dread. He had witnessed much during his life but none as cruel as Amason's story.

"Brother, they come," cried Eris. "What of this babe? What has she done that she lies upon the altar of War? What is your intention with her?"

"None." Deimos could not take his gaze from the cold fire of Amason's blade. "She is the daughter of Ares and must be kept safe. Take her away. Hide her."

Rushing winds swirled through the room and from the cosmos came the minions of War. They spilled into the room, a great horde of creatures, every last thing that served within the realm of War.

Enyo, that horror of horrors, she who swallows the souls of the dying, arrived with a jubilant ululation. She led the multitude of beasts as they converged upon Deimos in a howling screeching mass demanding their master.

With the last bit of self-possession, before the masses could consume him, Deimos shouted, "Take her, take the babe."

Eris could scarce hear him, let alone follow direction, for he, too, was a minion of War. This call was as overwhelming to him as it was to all others who answered. He watched through glassy eyes as they converged upon Deimos and felt the pull of their wretched glee as War's power glided over them.

He was one step from leaving the child's side when he heard her scream, a piercing wail that brought his attention once again to her tiny shivering body. When Enyo turned her skeletal head towards the same cry and her terrible gaze fell upon the babe, Eris was compelled to action.

Enyo's tongue wet her skinny lips and snaggled teeth bared in a grin as she reached out toward the altar. So frightened was Eris that his breath stopped. He did not hear what hollow words might come from that wretched mouth.

In haste, Eris scooped up the babe, cloth and all, from the altar and leaped away just as Enyo's bony fingers brushed his hand. All he left behind was his own screech at the terror she caused within his own heart.

Eris feared for his brother yet could do naught but escape with the child. It seemed those creatures would tear her apart with their wanton vile ways. The last wild look Deimos cast his way was one of gratitude. Eris had done the right thing by taking the child, but what now was he supposed to do with her?

Eris paused within the forests at the base of Athos, astride a thick limb in the canopy of leaves and wrapped the white cloth around the babe. Tucked tight within its folds, the child quieted to a whimper and Eris held her close to his heart so she might be comforted by its solid rhythm.

This much he remembered from his own mother. How she had held him to her breast, and how she contented him with the steady beat in his ear. He could give the babe that, but he had no milk, no way to feed this little one who trusted him, and he knew not where to find such things.

"What has happened to your mother?" Eris spoke in the lilting tongue of the Sylph. "Daughter of Ares, how did you come to be in such a cold place as Athos without her?"

For Eris now realized who had birthed the babe for Ares, but what had become of the female remained a mystery.

Daughter of Ares. Eris smiled. That made this girl-child his sister. "Sister," he whispered. "I like that. Sister to Eris. You seem more like me than any other. Deimos far more resembles our father, and the rest - well, my pretty one, you have seen them, have you not? They crawl upon the ground like snarling beasts."

Eris shuddered and brought the babe closer. She could not return to Athos, that much was certain. Since he did not know where her mother was, he must find another to watch over her.

If not her mother, then perhaps, his mother? He had not seen Aglauros since Ares took him to serve under War. It was forbidden for him to return to the Sacred Grove where he was born and raised. His only consolation was that Ares protected the Sylph and their home against intruders.

Never, Ares had sworn, would the Sacred Grove of the Sylph people be destroyed. The Grove was safe and would remain safe for all time.

Eris grinned. What better place for the daughter of Ares, his sister, to be than Ellopia, the Sacred Grove of his people?

So there it was he deposited the child into the arms of his own mother, Aglauros, whose tears at his arrival were honest and true. She could do naught but agree with his request after the kiss he left upon her cheek. Then, one look into the dark eyes of the little one, and her heart was lost again.

"What is her name?" Aglauros sat cross-legged, nestled in the twisting limbs of a huge oak, holding the babe to her breast. With a bit of encouragement, the child began to suckle, making small sounds of contentment. Soon, her shivering ceased and the bluish white tinge of her skin was replaced with a pale green that reflected the darker hue of the Sylph.

"She has no name." Eris touched his own chest. "But she is daughter to Ares, himself, and I have been given her for safekeeping."

"Here, she will remain safe." Aglauros smiled, a smile much like Eris, with sharp pointed teeth against her full bottom lip. "There are those, I think, who will believe I birthed this little one for Ares."

Eris shrugged. "Let them accept it as truth, for what does it matter? She has no mother of her own."

"Then to please you, my Son, I will take her to foster, but I want no interference from Ares. He has taken one child from me, and he will not do so again. This one, I will keep. Make certain he understands or I will not have her."

Without hesitation, Eris said, "Have no fear, Ni'madra, Ares will leave you in peace. And further, he has given me leave to visit when I wish."

"Is this true?" Aglauros cried, for losing her only child to the legions of War had long pained her.

"I promise. I will visit you, and my sister, often. For now, though, I must take my leave."

"Go, then, without fear. I shall care for her." Aglauros stared down at the peaceful face of the sleeping babe in her arms. "But to have no name." Aglauros thought for a moment and then said, " I shall call her Alcippe."

"Call her what you will, Ni'madra, just keep her safe."

"Ahh," murmured Aglauros, happy once again. "A

daughter. Yes, I will keep Alcippe safe. Be well, my Son. Visit soon."

Eris cast one last glance at the child and returned to Athos to answer the call of War.

Epilogue

The laid Niala Aaminah to rest inside the sacred cave, to be forever in the arms of the Great Mother, Gaea. The priestesses did so but not without battle, for King Hattusilis was against such barbaric practices. He would rather they set her body atop a pyramid of wood and set fire to her, for he found burial to be abhorrent.

"Unclean," Hattusilis proclaimed. "Unwise. Bones lying just beneath the earth gives rise to ghosts and allows them to walk amongst the living. Let her rest in peace through the winds."

His greatest fear was that the spirit of Niala Aaminah would haunt him, yet he relented because Pallin, begged as she lay with their newborn son cradled in her arms. His love for his wife was strong and he wanted to please her.

Hattusilis allowed Niala to be placed on a bier within the confines of the mountain on one condition: the sacred cave of Gaea must be sealed and never opened again.

One last time, the folk of Najahmara wound their way through the cavern to say goodbye to their beloved leader. Jahmed and Ajah were the last to see her, to kiss her still face and to pray to Gaea to comfort Niala well into the next life.

The women were dragged out, their sobs echoing in the high chamber as Hattusilis watched without pity. The valley belonged to him, now, and his word was final. It was with great satisfaction he saw the interment of Niala Aaminah Zahava and the careful alignment of stones and mortar that closed up the entrances forever.

IMMORTAL CHARACTERS

NAME:	ROLE:
Aglaia	Love's Brilliance/Dismay, Middle Grace,
Aglauros	Mother of Eris, Wood Nymph
Alcippe	Sylph name for Niala's babe
Amason	Ares' broad sword
Amphitrite	Queen of the Ocean, Aphrodite's adoptive mother
Anteros	Love's Response/Manipulation, Deimos' twin
Aphrodite	Eternal Love/Hatred, Wife to Ares, and briefly to Hephaestos,
Ares	Endless War/Creator, Husband to Aphrodite, lover to Niala,
Cedalion	Mountain Dwarf, loyal servant to Hephaestos
Corvidae	Raven Spirit Guide
Chronos	Titan, father of Zeus
Council of Ages	Ruling body of the Immortal Realm
Deimos	War's Terror/Survival, Son of Ares & Aphrodite, Anteros' twin
Delphinus	Dolphin Spirit Guide
Dyad	Tree nymph, particularly Oak trees
Enyo	War's Disgrace/Pride, Eater of souls (female)
Eos	Titan goddess of the Dawn – Ares' lover
Eris	War's Strife/Peace, Son of Ares & Aglauros
Erinnyes	War's Punishment/Reward, Ares' minions (also known as the Furies)
Eros	Love's Passion/Fury, Son of Ares & Aphrodite, twin to Phobos
Euphrosyne	Love's Rejoice/Grief, Youngest Grace
Fates	Three immortal females who weave destiny (also known as Moerae)
Furies	The Erinnyes – War's minions
Gaea	Immortal Earth/Abundance, Mother of All, mate to Kulika
Graces	Aglaia, Thaleia, Euphrosyne – servants to Aphrodite
Hephaestos	Alchemy/Separation, Second Husband to Aphrodite
Hera	Queen of the Immortals, Ares' mother
Hermes	Communication/Silence, Zeus' messenger
Keres	War's Penalty/Return, Female Death Spirits – Ares' minions
Kulika	Immortal Sky/Proliferation, Blue serpent, mate to Gaea
Lyda	Nursemaid to children on Isle of Cos
Moerae	The Fates – three immoral women who weave destiny

Nemesis	Love's Revenge/Forgiveness
Nut	The Night Sky
Odyne	Love's Pain/Balm
Oizus	Love's Misery/Joy
Panic	Phobos - son of Ares & Aphrodite
Passion	Eros - son of Aphrodite & Ares
Phobos	War's Panic/Surrender, Son of Ares & Aphrodite, twin to Eros
Poseidon	King of the Ocean, Aphrodite's adoptive father.
Priapos	Centaur who trains warriors
Rebellion	Immortal Spirit drawn into Niala Aaminah
Response	Anteros – son of Aphrodite & Ares
Rhea	Titan, Mother of Zeus
Selene	Moon goddess
Strife	Eris - son of Ares & Aglauros
Sylph	Fey folk of the Sacred Forest – Eris' people
Synod	Winged horse in service to the Immortals
Terror	Deimos – son of Ares & Aphrodite
Thaleia	Love's Bloom/Decay, Middle Grace, (female)
Thanatos	Bitter Death - son of Hades
Zelos	Love's Jealousy/Truth (female)
Zelus	Love's Rivalry/Friend
Zeus	King of the Immortals, Ares' father.

MORTAL CHARACTERS

NAME:	ROLE:
Ajah	Sixteen year old girl, Priestess in training
Anyal	First Man in ancient story of creation
Azhar	Hattusilis' first wife, now deceased
Benor	Trader from the Steppelands
Connal	Zan's brother, soldier in arms
Deniz	Twelve year old girl, Priestess in training
Edibe	Helped rescue Niala from Athos, founded Najahmara
Elche	Second Woman in ancient story of creation,
Hattusilis	King of the Steppelands invaders
Ilya	First Woman in ancient story of creation
Inni	Third Priestess of Gaea
Jahmed	Second Priestess of Gaea
Layla	Rescued Niala from Athos, founded Najahmara
Mahin	Rescued Niala from Athos, founded Najahmara
Niala Aaminah	First Priestess of Gaea – Ares' obsession
Pallin	Fourth Priestess of Gaea
Seire	Fifth Priestess of Gaea, Niala's daughter
Seyyal	Helped rescue Niala from Athos, founded Najahmara
Telio	Nephew of Hattusilis, invader from Steppelands
Tulane	Fourteen year old girl, Priestess in training
Warsus	Slayer of Niala's original tribe
Zahava	Teacher/healer, term of respect
Zan	Second in command, invader from Steppelands

LOCATIONS

ANKIRA: City in the Steppelands from which Hattusilis and legions began their journey. (Mortal Realm)

ATHOS: Home of Ares the Destroyer, a gray fortress located on a mountain in Thrace. (Mortal Realm)

COS: Home of Aphrodite, a beautiful, sunny island located in the South Aegean Sea. (Mortal Realm)

ELLOPIA: Homeland of Eris, the Sacred Forest of the Sylphs (Mortal Realm)

LEMNOS: Home of Hephaestos, a green, verdant island located in the North Aegean Sea. (Mortal Realm)

NAJAHMARA: A village nestled between the Bayuk and Maendre rivers located in south Cappadocia. Founded by Niala Aaminah and her four companions. (Mortal Realm)

OLYMPUS: Home of the Council, a golden city with Zeus and Hera reigning as king and queen. (Immortal Realm)

PRIAPOS' CAVE: Home of the warrior centaur, the remote and heavily forested island of Kerkyra

SHADOWLAND: Resting place for spirits of the dead. (Hades Immortal Realm)

STEPPELANDS: Far northern reaches of Cappadocia. (Mortal Realm.)

MAP OF THE KNOWN WORLD

ABOUT THE AUTHOR

Ruth Souther has written three Mythic Fantasy novels *(Immortal Journey series*) and an intuitive instructional book on Tarot (*The Heart of Tarot*) all available through Amazon. She lives in Illinois and is happily married to a wonderful man. They have four amazing children, along with their spouses, grandchildren and great-grandchildren. Life is good.

Facebook: Immortal Journey Book Series

www.ruthsouther.com

www.astarsjourney.com

AND NOW,
A SNEAK PEEK
AT

RISE
OF
REBELLION

VOLUME 3
OF THE
IMMORTAL JOURNEY
SERIES

ONE

Deimos propped his elbow on one arm of the massive throne and closed his eyes. He was weary to the bone, too tired to strip away the remnants of battle or wash the blood and grime from his skin. Slack-jawed, he slumped further into the monument to War desiring only sleep. His body was pushed beyond limit, his mind was numbed by the staggering weight of his father's mantle, his voice was hoarse from the roar of War, and yet, rest was impossible.

He who held bitter fault with Ares now found himself ensconced in the same treacherous circle. Sleep would not visit. The god of Good Rest, Hypnos, shunned Deimos, unwilling or unable to reach him since the hordes of War began to feed upon him.

This was the first silence he had been allowed since Ares had fallen to the poisoned dagger of Cedalion.

Deafening silence.

Quiet torment.

A moment alone but without peace. His thoughts would not

cease long enough for oblivion to take hold. Deimos' mind endlessly churned, returning to his last moments at Najahmara, a small village nestled in a fertile valley. A village bordering on near destruction from the invasion of an army assisted by Deimos before he understood that Gaea, Mother of All, watched over the land.

Over half of Najahmara's inhabitants, along with much of the invading army, died in the battle for control of the valley. Upon the night of the Summer Solstice, Deimos returned to the village, called by Gaea herself for a night of celebration.

It was meant to ease the pain of the invasion by the Steppelands soldiers and their king, Hattusilis - to be a festival of healing to unite the people in peace. Gentle Niala Aaminah, she who served as a priestess to the Great Mother, Gaea, led the festivities. Niala Aaminah held the power to invoke Earth and allow the spirit of the goddess to have a physical presence in the world she created. As Niala brought forth Gaea, Gaea summoned Deimos.

He had no choice but to respond.

The call was too strong to ignore and Deimos did not struggle against Gaea's command. He was overjoyed to go to Niala Aaminah under whatever guise, for he had fallen in love with her, knowing she was destined to become consort to Ares the Destroyer. Deimos had already crossed a forbidden line by stealing Niala from Athos and returning her to her people.

In doing so, Deimos caused Niala's death.

That moment of agony returned to him and once again brought the assault of images into his presence. Niala called Gaea into her so that Gaea could dance amongst her people, but Gaea was not content. She longed to settle an argument between herself and her mate, Kulika. To do so, Gaea needed a strong viable male to hold the spirit of the Sky God and who better than the son of War?

Deimos still vibrated to the depths of his soul. He still felt the fierce joy as Kulika's immortal soul flooded into his body, pushing Deimos' own essence down until Kulika had control. Once they settled their argument, Gaea and Kulika came together in a furious coupling, one that Deimos felt in his body but could not touch with his mind.

Their riotous sex caused a pregnant Niala to birth early. As the blood streamed from her body, the essence of the Sky God abandoned Deimos. At the same moment, Gaea receded from Niala, leaving her to die.

For this, Deimos would not forgive either of them.

Sweating, Deimos could not help but bring his hands in front of him as if he once again held the tiny babe. He felt again the sting of jealousy that this child was fathered by Ares and not himself. The overwhelming grief enveloped Deimos as he relived the moment Niala lay bleeding to death while he could do nothing to stop her life seeping from her.

And the final, all-consuming rage followed by madness that descended without warning.

Deimos could not decipher the exact moment when the Mantle of War became his, but it had indeed crashed down upon him that same night. He remembered the tension as it coiled inside his body when Jahmed tried to take Niala's child from his hands. He had dim recollection of backing away, holding the babe so tight she cried, and then taking her without thought of what he would do with this fragile female. He was aware only that the babe was that of Niala and a daughter of War.

The child was special. She belonged to the immortals. Still, he had no plan in mind when he stole the child. By instinct, he returned to the place that had been his home for eons. He returned to the very room in which he sat, the altar chamber of War.

When the whirling shrieking hordes that claimed War as their master descended upon him, all was lost. There was a faint memory of commanding Eris to take the child from Niala' to hide her, to keep her safe. Then everything went black.

Deimos remained in that darkness for months, caught up in the brutality that consumed the mortal world. He now had a far better understanding of his father. Oh, how much more compassionate, more understanding was Deimos of Ares' life, for all the good it did. Deimos regretted that he did not pay more attention to Ares' woes, and more, how Ares handled the pain of his existence.

Deimos could only wonder at the righteous disgust he had voiced at Ares' display of raw sexuality, of the hours spent seducing mortal and immortal alike. Deimos shook his head at his own self-involved pity, and his escape into the earthly world.

He did not journey into the Mortal Realm as a seducer, but as one who was seduced by the many mysteries of being human. He was fascinated by those folk whose lives were so very short, whose deaths were often violent and without grace. Yet they lived with great passion and pleasure.

His meandering thoughts brought him back to Niala's child. In the rare lucid moments he questioned Eris on the whereabouts of the babe.

"Where have you hidden her?"

The young man's reply was always the same.

"I will tell you later, when you are less preoccupied, when you are able to shield yourself from this onslaught of blood and bone. Trust me, she is safe."

Deimos recognized the truth as he looked into the hard gaze of his half-brother. He could fully trust Eris to have his back. This was a new revelation, one that took time to sink into Deimos' fevered brain.

Eris had been so long locked into youthful misbehavior - and perhaps even encouraged by Ares to keep his childlike delight in the vicious bloodletting of battle - it was difficult for Deimos to view him any other way. Mischievous Eris, unfit to lead, unfit to stand close to the throne of War, rather, left in the background with the rest of the minions.

Eris, son of Ares. Eris, he of fierce and brutal loyalty - he who ran forward during crisis. That Eris feared only his father while he found delicious delight in tormenting his brother, Deimos.

A very different Eris charged forth during the chaotic bleak moment when Deimos was engulfed by the hounds and hordes of

War. A responsible Eris had taken the child away.

This Eris was now the right hand of War. Eris kept Deimos sane during the worst of it, and the mysterious whereabouts of the babe was left for another day.

There were small opportunities that allowed Deimos to barricade himself against the assault of War. These times lasted no more than a flick of an eyelash, and then the hordes were on him again and again and again.

But with each surge, Deimos discovered new strength to push back. Minutes became hours, hours became days. When he finally found the ability to banish War's minions from his sight, triumph belonged to him - until the time came that he was forced to call the hordes back. With each act of violence in the mortal realm, his unshakeable connection to human bloodlust resurfaced and Deimos lost control all over again, and the vicious cycle resumed.

Exhaustion brought Deimos' thoughts back to the present moment. He rubbed a roughened palm across his bearded face and squeezed shut bleary eyes. He should go to his quarters, bathe and rest while he had the chance, for soon War's blitz would return.

Instead, he stared at the barren dais before him. Stripped of its grotesque garnishment of blood and bone - the sacrifices of both animal and human a thousand years gone – the altar stood in mute testimony to the absence of Ares, the Destroyer.

The black marble was draped in a pristine white cloth with gilt thread woven around the edges. A vase of fresh flowers stood in the center, flowers that most certainly did not come from Athos. There was only one who would dare and that was Deimos' twin brother, Anteros.

He who represented Love's Response, belonging to the House of Love, to their mother, Aphrodite. Anteros thought to sacrifice himself on the altar of War to save Aphrodite from making a huge mistake. Upon his arrival, he could not abide the horror of rotted carcasses.

Anteros did not think it was appropriate in a place of worship. He could not help his response to violence for his nature dictated that beauty and harmony were the solutions to all matters. Therefore, he cleansed the entire area and transformed the ugliness into splendor.

At the thought of Ares seeing his precious altar with an embroidered cloth and flowers bedecking the marble, Deimos chuckled. The sound echoed into the length of the great chamber, which startled himself, for Deimos had not laughed since Ares passed into the Realm of Sleep.

There was not a single offering made during Deimos' reign as War. The adjoining hall was once filled with warriors waiting to honor their god; the stockyard was filled with animals waiting to be sacrificed. But no more. Those who sought Ares abandoned Athos, sent away by Love's Response. Not intentionally, but again, because Anteros was who he was, and there were none who could refuse to honor Love when he was near.

All save for Ares, who would destroy Anteros precisely because of his innate nature.

Deimos could find humor in it all now. His twin invoked the gentler side of the hardened soldiers with his fine touch. They all filed down the mountain, taking their beasts with them, never to return. This action, this response spread as a single drop upon a pond, and Athos receded into the mist.

The face of War was forever changed. No longer was this god sought out upon a distant mountaintop and extolled fortune in battle begged. The fires still burned across the countryside, stretching into faraway lands, but the stench did not cover Athos.

Deimos detested the thought that the responsibility was now his and would always be so. He held hope that Ares would awaken someday, yet in the same breath thought of the burden if he did not. If Ares did awaken, he would despise it all.

And when Ares realized Niala was dead, there would be no end to his fury.

Niala.

Dead.

Deimos witnessed the life fade from her eyes. Her blood had covered him. Grief fought for a hold, tried to overcome him, but he would not allow such emotion to bubble up and boil over. Deimos could not face his loss. He could not afford a moment of weakness.

War's minions were slaves only to the one who held the power. They had already attempted to destroy him, and would try again. All but Eris and Phobos.

Phobos, the latest addition to War's entourage. Phobos, the sweet lad who was wrenched from his mother and thrown into horrors he could never have imagined. Instead of grieving for the soft life at Aphrodite's knee, Phobos embraced his strength. He stepped into the role meant for him from birth: the God of Panic.

Eris and Phobos were inseparable now. Where Eris went, Phobos followed. The two youths most likely were settled in somewhere for the night. Whether forest or seaside, or one of the many chambers within the fortress, Deimos was unsure as he did not lie claim upon their every breath. He allowed them certain freedoms, unlike Ares, who maintained control of all aspects of their existence.

Deimos, too, should seek his bed, a useless gesture, for he could not sleep. The moment he closed his eyes, he was devoured by the mortal world's aggression. He refused to sink into the mire that eased and abated Ares, that of sexual indulgence. Bodily gratification that drove away all else and eventually led to blessed rest.

Deimos now understood how movement could overtake the mind. It was the rush that swept him forward during battle, the force of his body moving toward its destiny, with the blood-thirsty sword Amason held high, slashing bone and flesh, crushing everyone without regard to which side they hailed. Another discovery Deimos made about the Mantle of War - there was no discernment during battle.

How he wished he had listened to his father, the little Ares spoke of his trials. Deimos regretted that he did not ask his father what transpired when War descended, and his age when the mantle was bestowed.

What rites of passage ushered Ares' into his power?

Deimos was never told; he had never asked. He had been too bitter about the pain of his own passage and cared not what had befallen his father. At times he imagined Ares' ritual worse than death and was glad for it. Now Deimos sat on the throne of War with no guidance, save his own experience in the Mortal World.

This was the state of his thoughts these days. Constantly turning, constantly questioning, constantly finding no answer, no rest. Not even in the silence. His thoughts thundered and rattled as if a thousand hooves struck against the stone floors. Alone but not alone. Never to be truly alone again was almost too much to bear.

Ares must recover.

He must.

Deimos could not carry this burden into eternity.

But what if there was no choice?

Cursing, Deimos rose from the throne, driven now to action. He loathed the thought of seeking yet another skirmish, another hate-filled battle that was not his own. He refused to find gratification based only on the driving need to give himself over to the corporal.

There was not a soul about upon which to release his anger, no one to hear his rant but himself. Restless, Deimos circled the room, with a mere glance at the hulking chair that served War. Deimos saw his brother's touch in the embroidered cloth that draped the throne, the brother who had been so long absent from Deimos' life, and now thrust violently back into it during the storm surrounding their parents.

Aphrodite, their mother, held the Mantle of Love just as Ares had once held the Mantle of War. Aphrodite, who, in a fit of madness, destroyed the bonds of her marriage to Ares, took a new consort in the form of Hephaestos, God of the Forge. Aphrodite, who bore a daughter named Harmonia, now refused to speak of her father.

Was it Ares or was it Hephaestos?

One could not tell by looking at the child. Harmonia was a pretty pink-cheeked babe with golden curls that lay against her round head and a sweet forgiving smile. The little girl, content to be in the arms of one of the Graces, did not seem to mind that her mother ignored her. Like all immortal beings, though she was so very young, she was already cognizant of her surroundings. Harmonia was like a tiny shining shadow, her wide blue gaze always steady in what appeared to be deep contemplation of Love's Realm.

As the months passed, and Ares remained locked within his slumber, Aphrodite receded. After Ares fell, Aphrodite shunned her duties and withdrew into a morbid silence, leaving Anteros to hold Love in check. Anteros became parent to both Harmonia and Eros.

The Realm of Love became Anteros' burden. Though not entirely, as Aphrodite was aware, unlike Ares who lay between the worlds. Yet both brothers faced the same dilemmas - the struggle crushing to keep balance between mortal and immortal. Though the brothers served different purposes, they lived parallel challenges.

Deimos turned to stare at the dark recesses of the chamber. A place that once echoed with the ribaldry of battle-hardened warriors waiting to plead for good fortune with sacrifices to their god. It no longer reflected Ares, nor did it match the violence of their existence.

How long could Deimos sustain this change? Was he doomed to repeat the patterns of his father? Yet Ares did not create the chaos, he merely represented it. Was it possible War could evolve?

There were no answers. Deimos could not find stable footing though he knew it could be done. Ares had achieved the balance. But Ares was wedded with Aphrodite which brought the counterweight necessary to maintain both realms.

Deimos had no one.

Aphrodite told him to find love. Until he did, he would be

a restless soul without an anchor.

Love brings purpose into disorder and without it, madness ensues.

"And yet, I have seen as much madness on the side of Love as I have War. Is one worse than the other?" Deimos' voice echoed throughout the vast and lonely hall. "I loved someone and now she is dead. How does that balance my soul, Mother?"

The reply was swift yet quiet, a voice within Deimos or was it Love's Response who hears all devotional yearnings?

Are you better for having had this love within your reach?

"Yes, but she is gone and I am alone."

You will know love again if you remain open to the possibility. If you refuse, you will continue to struggle. War needs Love.

"I am not my father." Deimos strode into the center of chamber as he made his declaration. "I am not Ares, and I refuse to walk in his footsteps. I will not resort to raw passion to keep the House of War in order."

Even if it is someone who can alter the course of War? Someone who can help hold the balance and bring forth a new alliance that will awaken Peace?

"And what would Peace do for War?" Deimos gave a harsh bark of laughter. "No one truly wins. Defeat and death repeat over and over again. There is no honor in Peace."

With this truth spoken aloud, Deimos felt different, as if those words somehow changed the fabric of War's Mantle. Indeed, the power shifted, lost some of the awkwardness and settled upon Deimos with intimate faith in his control.

Deimos twitched and a shudder ran down his spine as he accepted that which he could not change: the Mantle of War was his and he must wear it well. No longer would the energies of War suckle at him. He was their master.

So be it.

IMMORTAL JOURNEY SERIES:

VOL. 1　DEATH OF INNOCENCE
VOL. 2　SURRENDER OF EGO
VOL. 3　RISE OF REBELLION

AVAILABLE 2016:

VOL. 4　OBESSION OF LOVE

Made in the USA
San Bernardino, CA
23 September 2015